Dakota Peace

by
Megan Kinney

GUIDING LIGHT
WOMEN'S FICTION
COMPELLING STORIES, BEAUTIFULLY WRITTEN

DAKOTA PEACE BY MEGAN KINNEY
Guiding Light Women's Fiction is an imprint of LPCBooks
a division of Iron Stream Media
100 Missionary Ridge, Birmingham, AL 35242

ISBN: 978-1-64526-255-8
Copyright © 2020 by Megan Kinney
Cover design by Hannah Linder
Interior design by Karthick Srinivasan

Available in print from your local bookstore, online, or from the publisher at:
ShopLPC.com

For more information on this book and the author visit: https://megankinney.net/

Brought to you by the creative team at LPCBooks:
Eddie Jones, Karin Beery, Shonda Savage, Brenda Kay Coulter, Lucie Windborne.

Library of Congress Cataloging-in-Publication Data
Kinney, Megan.
Dakota Peace / Megan Kinney 1st ed.

Printed in the United States of America

PRAISE FOR *DAKOTA PEACE*

The author's voice in this is incredible. You can tell she threw all of herself into the story, the research, and the characters. She wastes no time on one-dimensional descriptions or cookie-cutter plots. Everything is raw, real, and riveting to the very end. A story stocked full of trauma, romance, familial love, and suspenseful twists will keep you turning pages. You won't put this book down. I guarantee it.

~Hope Bolinger
Author of the *Blaze* trilogy

Dakota Peace introduced me to Natalie and Travis, then I followed them to the last page. These characters have realistic and relatable struggles. The author dug deep, and all those little details that make a novel resonate with the reader hours—no days—after you've left their story world. The quality of Meghan Kinney's debut novel gets me excited to read her future work.

~Cindy Ervin Huff
Award-winning author of *New Duet*

Readers will enjoy Megan Kinney's knowledge of law enforcement—which adds an intriguing element to her story—and her skillful phrasing. The small-town setting in *Dakota Peace* creates a sense of community many will find endearing.

~Jennifer Slattery
Multi-published author and ministry leader
Author of *Hometown Healthy* and *Building a Family*

Acknowledgments

They say it takes a village to raise a child. If that's the case, it takes a metropolis to publish a book. I'd like to thank my husband Kevin and our daughters, Emma, Angel, Alicia, and Kylee, for being my biggest fans and understanding why Mommy had to take her computer almost everywhere, including the lake. I'm grateful for my parents, Gale and Janet, who have always encouraged my dreams, and to all my family and friends who have encouraged and celebrated with me.

I did a lot of research for this book, but I also relied my own experiences. My husband has been a state trooper for most of our marriage; he's passionate about improving officer wellness. We became foster parents over a decade ago and were able to adopt three Native American sisters with the blessing of their tribe and their biological mother. Our family enjoys learning about the Lakota's rich culture so my daughters always feel proud of their heritage.

A huge thank you goes to my editor Karin Beery, who took a chance on a first-time author, spending hours and hours teaching me with her edits. Her valuable insight challenged me to grow as a writer. I feel blessed to have her support along this journey. You're amazing!

I couldn't have written this story without the expert knowledge of emergency dispatcher PJ Bahr, who read and re-read my manuscript, pointing out the errors and answering my many questions. My thanks to nurses Carrie Ham and Carol Ritter, who helped this nursing school dropout get all the medical facts correct, and to victim specialist and police officer Cora Olson for reading through the manuscript and offering her expert advice. To Sergeant Todd Albertson, a Native American trooper with the SD

Highway Patrol, thanks for reading my manuscript on short notice and making sure I've portrayed the Lakota culture accurately. I'd also like to thank Tifani for answering my foster care questions and Joyce and your beautiful daughters for sharing your Lakota culture with my family. Any mistakes are purely my own. I'm grateful to Heather, Hayley, and Jeanie in my critique group and to Kristi and Melody for helping to start our writers' group. Their advice and prayers have encouraged me. Thanks go to Amy Oyler with Legacy Photo and Design for taking my headshot.

I'd like to thank everyone behind the scenes at Lighthouse Publishing of the Carolinas and Iron Stream Media, from cover designers to proofreaders to the marketing team and everyone in between. Their talent amazes me. And to Eddie Jones, who challenged a want-to-be author to dream big. We have him to thank for the opening scene.

To the South Dakota Highway Patrol, I thank you for your support. All the characters and events in this book are completely fictional. To the dispatchers, police officers, and emergency responders, I thank you for your service, and I'm proud to be a part of the blue family. You are not alone in your struggles, and I pray you'll reach out if you need help. To the many foster parents out there, I'm grateful for the sacrifices you've made to care for children in need of a safe, loving home.

And, most of all, I'd like to thank God for blessing me and allowing me to serve Him in this way. May He be glorified.

Dedication

To Kevin:
My favorite state trooper, best friend, and greatest love.
You inspire me.

CHAPTER 1

Be brave. Natalia Brynner took a deep breath and leveled her gaze at the monitor. The clicking of computer keys and monotone voices floated over to her. Stomach acid burned her throat.

A heavy hand rested on her shoulder. She didn't need to look up to know it belonged to her boss, Hayden Boyd. A bottle of water fogged over with condensation appeared in front of her. She opened it and drank. The cool liquid soothed her aching tissue.

"The captain sent a text," Hayden said. "It's time. There's an arena full of people as well as on-duty first responders listening. Don't choke up."

Natalia sat straighter and secured the headset over her blonde curls. With shaking hands, she picked up the paper in front of her.

Hayden cleared his throat.

After the blaring, six-beep emergency tone quieted all radio traffic, Natalia adjusted the mouthpiece. "Attention all units. Stand by for last call. PD 277, 1-2." Silence. "PD 277, 1-2. Officer Mason, do you copy?"

She took a deep breath and mentally counted five seconds. No one responded. Tears welled up in her eyes, but she blinked them away.

"Negative contact with PD 277. You're clear to end your tour. Thank you for your dedication, loyalty, and exemplary service to the citizens of Sioux Falls, South Dakota. Together we form the thin blue line, protecting the good from the bad. May you rest in peace. We'll take it from here."

* * * * * * *

Trooper Travis Wilkins sat on the white-and-blue quilt that covered his bed and tightened his fingers around the handheld service radio. The female's voice strained as she finished reciting the last call for the fallen Sioux Falls police officer. Another death in the line of duty engraved in the hearts of his brothers and sisters in blue. It didn't matter that Travis had never met Officer Mason. He felt the loss just the same.

He tightened his Kevlar vest, then slipped on his shirt. With a heavy heart, he pulled the black, elastic band around his badge and strapped his duty belt around his waist.

His boots echoed against the wood floor as he walked through the living room. The pottery on the maple table and the painted buffalo skull hanging above the river-rock fireplace featured his Lakota roots. In the kitchen, he filled a travel mug with coffee, grabbed his laptop, and stepped onto the deck, like any other day. His blue heeler lifted his head but didn't move from his spot next to the door. "I see you're at your post, Jeeves. Good boy." Travis scratched the hound's ears.

The rising sun heated his face. Under the canopy of a large oak tree, he strode to his black patrol car, the grass crunching under his feet. Among the knee-high grass, yucca plants dotted patches of yellow sweet clover, covering the rolling plains that surrounded his cabin. A trickle of sweat ran down his neck even though it wasn't yet ten o'clock, but that was normal for an August day in western South Dakota. He scooted into the driver's seat and turned on his laptop, then he pushed the radio mic. "Northern Hills HP 352."

"Go ahead, HP 352," the female dispatcher responded.

"Good morning. I'll be 10-8."

"Good morning, HP 352, 10-8 at 1002."

His cell phone rang. "Wilkins."

"It's Sergeant Black. You know that Amber Alert that went out last week?"

"The boy kidnapped by his foster parents in Rapid City?"

"That's the one. A black pickup matching the description of the suspects was spotted traveling east from Sturgis a few minutes ago. I want you to search the roads northwest of Alkaline. I've got other units headed that way too."

Travis's heartbeat increased. "You got it, Sarge." So much for a normal day. If he was lucky, he'd have the boy safe and his kidnappers behind bars by the end of his shift. He dropped his phone into the cup holder and sped off.

* * * * * * *

Almost six in the evening and the end of Travis's shift loomed, but there was no sign of the pickup or the kidnapped boy. With nowhere left to search, he parked his patrol car at the intersection of Highway 34 and Hope Road to plan his next move.

Until that morning, he hadn't spent much time thinking about the abduction. It had occurred in a town seventy miles south. The likelihood of the kidnappers coming this far north had been slim, but now they were in his territory, and none of the troopers knew this area as well as he did.

Cool air blasted from the vents as he grabbed the map from the passenger's seat and draped it over the steering wheel. He grabbed a red Sharpie. The stinky marker screeched as he circled the area he'd searched, drawing over Highway 34 heading west, then up Juniper Place and circling back to the intersection at Hope Road.

Hope. He could sure use some of that. The search was nowhere near as simple as he'd thought it would be.

Maybe he'd drive south. Other troopers had been in that area, but the hidden driveways and unmarked dirt roads could be confusing.

He rubbed the edge of his itchy eyes, blurring the lines of the map. With so many places to look, how would they ever find the boy?

Travis crumpled the map into a ball. Sarge had called off the search hours ago, but Travis refused to comply with the hasty decision. He needed to keep looking, to find the boy and calm the restless anxiety this search had stirred in him.

Memories of his time in the system flashed through his mind. The foster dad who woke him at six every morning for a five-mile run. The older son of a foster family who slapped and pinched him when his parents weren't looking, then smirked when Travis was punished for defending himself. The endless days of wishing his mom would come for him and crying himself to sleep when she didn't. Of course, it beat the alternative—shivering in a cold room, his stomach rumbling from lack of food, his mother passed out on the worn, green couch. He couldn't change the past, but he could find this boy and get him into a better home. If only Sarge hadn't called off the search.

Travis stared through the bug-splattered windshield. In the distance, a herd of quarter horses galloped across the hayfield, disturbing a flock of sparrows. The birds launched from the barbed-wire perch into the darkening, western sky. Storm clouds. Great. Though they needed the rain, a storm wouldn't help find the boy.

The prairie's valleys, peaks, and draws bubbled into a maze that could hide the family for a long time, if the reported pickup even belonged to the kidnappers. Black trucks weren't exactly rare in western South Dakota.

Red flashed in Travis's peripheral vision. A car sped past the stop sign. He pushed the map aside and took off after the speeder. Adrenaline rushed through him. The hum of his radar morphed into a high-pitched squeal. He locked in the speed at sixty-five, then flipped on his lights and sirens before grabbing the radio. "Northern Hills. HP 352."

"Go ahead, HP 352."

"I'll be 10-44 with South Dakota plate one, Edward, king, nine, four, three on Highway 34 at Hope Road."

"10-4 HP 352, 1754 hours."

The car pulled over and stopped. Travis parked behind it. He secured his wide-rimmed hat to his head, walked toward the car, and touched the metal above the taillight, watching the occupant's movements for anything suspicious. What seemed routine could turn deadly in an instant. When he reached the driver's side, a young woman handed him her license, registration, and proof of insurance. Blonde curls framed her red and blotchy skin, though oversized sunglasses covered a good portion of her face.

He glanced at her license—Natalia Brynner—then back at her. "The reason I stopped you today, Ms. Brynner, is because you were going sixty-five in a forty-five, and you sped past that stop sign back there." He leaned in closer and smelled vanilla, not alcohol.

"I'm sorry, Trooper." Her voice cracked. "I didn't see the sign, and I thought the speed limit was sixty-five." Tears slid down her face.

Great. A crier. He rolled his eyes. He had no patience for manipulation today, not when a child needed to be found. "It was sixty-five but changed to forty-five since Alkaline is only a mile down the road. The signs are clearly visible. We had a major crash at that intersection last Friday night. Kid's lucky to be alive." More tears. Travis pinched the bridge of his nose.

"I truly am sorry. If you'll just give me my citations, I promise to pay more attention."

"It's highway patrol policy to ask you to come back to my car."

Her shoulders drooped, but she opened the door and stepped out of the vehicle, smoothing her black skirt. Her heels crunched on the pavement as she walked to his car.

"Go ahead and have a seat on the passenger's side." Travis fell into the driver's seat while she slid in beside him. "Would you please remove your glasses?"

Her long fingers snatched them from her face. "Sorry." Her blue eyes focused on his. Good. She didn't seem to be under the influence. He didn't want to make the forty-minute trip to the county jail today.

Travis typed her information into his computer. "Where you headed?"

Natalia took a shaky breath. "Back to Sioux Falls."

"What brought you to the western part of the state?"

"I got in the car and drove. Ended up here."

He looked at her. Who drove five hours across the state for no reason? "Where did you begin this drive?"

"My office."

"In Sioux Falls?"

She nodded.

"What time did you leave?"

She shrugged. "Sometime midmorning."

He couldn't tell if she was purposefully giving vague answers or was just an odd person. He glanced at his computer. The nearest K-9 officer was in Rapid City and wouldn't appreciate being asked to bring his dog to Alkaline if Travis didn't have a concrete reason to suspect drugs. But something didn't feel right.

****

Natalia took a deep breath. She'd driven for six hours and all she wanted was to go home. The trooper typed her information into the database, but she knew what he'd find. Nothing. Before that evening, she'd never been pulled over, not even a parking ticket to her name.

She had no idea how much her fines were going to cost, but they'd be hefty. When would she learn that she couldn't outrun her pain? It always came with her and usually found trouble along the way. A fresh wave of tears pooled in her eyes.

His fingers froze on the keyboard. "Why are you crying?"

"I'd rather not talk about it."

He filled out her citation, then handed her the ticket book.

"I know. Press hard, three copies." She grabbed his pen with shaking fingers and carefully signed her name.

"Are you in law enforcement?"

She shook her head.

He took the ticket book back, his forehead puckering. "Why are you upset?"

She glanced at the black, elastic band surrounding the badge pinned to his taupe, polyester shirt. "I knew the Sioux Falls PD officer who was killed. I dispatched the initial call when Officer Mason was shot, so today I recited last call."

His face relaxed as he handed her a tissue from his center console. "I heard you. It was a powerful moment. You did a good job."

"Thanks." She sighed. "I know it was crazy to drive this far, but I needed to put some space between me and my office."

He handed her the citation. "The court date is at the bottom, if you'd like to refute the ticket. Maybe the judge will have more compassion than me and throw it out."

"I won't fight it. I deserve this." She scanned the document, but it only mentioned the stop sign violation. She looked at the trooper. "What about the speeding?"

He shrugged. "I think I can extend some grace today."

"Thanks." She tried to smile, but the stress of everything had caught up to her and it turned into a yawn. "Where's the nearest place to get coffee? I'd better get some caffeine in my system if I'm going to make it home."

"Alkaline is east about a mile. The Prickly Pear Bistro has the best coffee, but you can also get some at the gas station a bit further down the road. You can't miss either one, but are you sure you're okay to drive back?"

"I'll be fine. Thanks again." Natalia stepped out of the patrol car and rolled her foot. Stupid heels. If she hadn't been planning on going to the funeral, she would be in her sneakers.

"Are you okay?" the trooper yelled through the window.

She turned and gave him a small wave. Her ankle ached as she walked back to her car. She pulled away from the shoulder, careful not to exceed the speed limit and keeping her hands at ten and two.

A loud bang sounded and her car shook. It pulled to the side, thumping, so she tightened her grip on the wheel. The tire sensor on her dashboard lit up. Gritting her teeth, she pulled back onto the shoulder. Amber lights reflected in her rearview mirror. Could the day get any worse?

She stepped back into the August heat and walked around to the passenger side. The front tire lay flat against the road.

The trooper strode up beside her and kicked a piece of shiny metal off the road. "Leftover debris from that wreck last Friday. It's probably what punctured your tire. I'll help you change it."

"I have towing insurance. I'm sure you've got better things to do."

"I do it all the time for stranded motorists. Pop the trunk, and I'll get the tire out."

Natalia hurried to the driver's side and pulled the lever, then walked to the back of her car as the trooper pulled out the spare and jack. "What can I do to help?"

"Grab the lug wrench." He left her to wonder what a lug wrench was. The only thing left in the small compartment was a metal, X-shaped tool. She grabbed it and followed him to her flat tire.

He positioned the jack under the car before grabbing the wrench from her. "Thanks."

"I'm the one who's thankful. I'm sure changing a flat tire in ninety-degree weather wasn't on your agenda."

His tanned bicep bulged as he loosened the bolts. "Glad I can help someone today." He put the wrench on the ground and pumped the jack up.

While she waited, Natalia watched some horses run through a field of tan grasses. They looked peaceful. She envied them.

The trooper grunted. He was on his knees pulling the flat tire off the car while she was sightseeing.

"Here, I can take that." She grabbed the tire as it landed on the road, then rolled it to the back of her car. When she hefted it into the trunk, it left dirt streaks on her black dress. While she brushed them off, the trooper set the wrench and jack beside the tire. She peeked at his name tag, then held out her hand. "Thanks, Trooper

Wilkins. I'll be sure to let your supervisor know how helpful you've been."

He shook her hand. "Just doin' my job. If you want, you can follow me into town and I'll show you where the mechanic's shop is. If he's not open, I'll show you were you can get that coffee."

"I'll take you up on that." She shut the trunk and got back into her car. All she needed was a tire, but with the way her day was going, she doubted it would be that easy.

CHAPTER 2

Travis opened the door to the Prickly Pear Bistro and followed Natalia in. The scent of roasted meat welcomed him back. It had been only a few hours since he'd had lunch there, but he could eat at the bistro for every meal and never grow tired of it.

Dirty dishes covered the booths that ran along both sides of the dining room. A teenage waitress wiped down a white tabletop, then looked over at them. "Hi, Trooper Wilkins. Your usual table's still dirty. If you'll give me a second, I'll clean it up for you."

He glanced at his favorite booth in the corner beside the front windows and the red brick wall at the back. Besides the dirty plates still covering it, someone had spilled liquid on the dark-blue vinyl. "No need, but thanks."

She nodded, then continued stacking dirty dishes into a large tub.

Travis escorted Natalia across the black-and-white tiled floor to the round, vinyl stools at the butcher-block counter. "I'll introduce you to Rosemary. She owns the bistro, and she'll take good care of you until the mechanic can get your tire fixed." He pulled a business card from his shirt pocket and handed it to her. "Call me if you need anything else."

Her smile wobbled as she took his card. "Maybe you could join me? I know it's against policy, but this place is deserted. I hate eating alone."

He'd eaten a club sandwich, potato salad, and apple pie à la mode barely three hours ago, but maybe a snack would inspire his search for the lost boy. And who would know? His nearest supervisor worked an hour away. "Just a quick bite."

Natalia's smile steadied.

The waitress walked by with a full tub. "I'll send Rosemary out."

Natalia unwrapped her silverware and sat, placing the napkin on her lap. "Thanks for joining me."

Travis sat beside her and set his hat on the stool next to him, then swiveled to face her. "How long have you been a dispatcher?"

"Two years."

"Was this your first time dispatching a police fatality?"

She nodded. "I keep replaying everything in my mind. Officer Mason's last words to me were *shots fired*. I dispatched all available units, and they ran hot, but by the time they got there the gunman had fled and Mason was bleeding to death. The Department of Criminal Investigations examined the incident and I was cleared of negligence, but I still wonder if I could have done something different. It was supposed to be a routine traffic stop."

Travis's chest tightened. "Nothing is routine in this job. Dispatchers are the first, first responders. Taking calls from hysterical or angry people while being our lifeline on the radio. You—"

Natalia's phone rang. The song continued to play as she searched in her purse. When she pulled it out, she silenced the call. "Sorry about that." The phone buzzed, but she dropped it back into her purse.

"You can return that. I don't mind."

Red tinged her cheeks. "He can wait."

Rosemary walked through the swinging doors from the kitchen. A navy apron wrapped around her petite frame, and short red hair framed her wrinkled cheeks. The doors smacked behind her as she placed a large glass of water in front of Natalia and a cup of black coffee by Travis. "You caught us at the end of our supper rush. Thanks for your patience."

"Rosemary, this is Natalia. She ran over some debris and punctured her tire. Hopefully, it can be fixed, but she's stranded here until then. Thought I'd show her a bit of our small-town hospitality while she waited." He grinned at Natalia. "Rosemary owns the Prickly Pear Bistro." He leaned closer to her and lowered his voice. "Formerly the Prickly Pear Café before she got all fancy."

Natalia chuckled.

Rosemary smacked his arm. "Oh, you quit. I think the new name and atmosphere lends a classier ambiance. If only I could get classier clientele." She winked at Natalia and plopped down two menus. "Our dinner special is oven-roasted brisket, mashed potatoes and gravy, plus a side salad."

Travis couldn't resist. Rosemary's brisket fell apart with each juicy bite. "I want the special with Ranch dressing." He pushed the menu back at her.

Natalia scanned the options. "I'll just have a bowl of your creamy potato chowder."

Another favorite. "That sounds good. I'll have some too."

"A bowl or cup?" Rosemary wrote their orders on a green pad.

"Bowl, of course."

She clicked her tongue. "Where do you put all that food?"

He rubbed his stomach. "Storing up for winter. Rosemary leaves us for sunny Arizona before the first snowflake hits the ground. Closes up the place and makes me drive to Sturgis for a decent meal, since no one else will take pity on me."

"The way I see it, you've got two options. Learn how to cook or marry someone who does."

"I've already asked, but you turned me down."

She patted his face. "Not even your handsome mug could get me to stay through another South Dakota winter." She turned to Natalia. "Can I get you anything else to drink?"

"I'd love a cup of coffee with plenty of creamer."

Rosemary's hazel eyes lit up. "We've got all kinds of gourmet creamers. I'll bring you an assortment to pick from. Most of my customers are farmers who drink their joe as black as a starless night, but here at the bistro you can get coffee as good as those fancy shops for half the price." She practically skipped off to fetch the fancy options.

Travis chuckled. "She's trying to make her café special. Last winter she hired a contractor to gut the place and replace all the booths, tables, and chairs. I'm not quite sure why since it's only open April through September."

Natalia's phone vibrated.

"I'm going to use the restroom." She grabbed her purse and hurried away.

****

Natalia splashed cold water on her face. As she blotted it with a paper towel, she examined the blotchy skin around her slightly swollen eyelids. Her emotions teetered on the edge of stable, and if she didn't rein them in, she'd start crying again.

She reapplied her mascara and lip gloss, then finger-combed her hair. Satisfied that she didn't look like the living dead anymore, she took a deep breath.

Her phone rang. She glanced at the screen and sighed. "Hi, Dad."

"Nattie! What happened to you? You just took off from the funeral without a word. Your mom wanted to call the police."

Of course she did, because Mom thought she was incapable of making rational decisions. A dull pain radiated through her head. "I'm sorry. I don't answer calls when I'm driving."

"You've been driving all day? Where are you?"

"A little town about an hour east of Sturgis."

"You drove to the other side of the state? What's gotten into you?"

"I don't know. It's been a while since I've seen Mount Rushmore."

"Not funny."

"Sorry."

"I know you're hurting, baby girl." Her dad's voice warmed.

"You need time to process everything, but we've been worried about you."

"I wouldn't do anything stupid."

"I know, but you never know what could happen."

"I'm sorry. I didn't mean to come this far. You shouldn't have talked me into the fuel-efficient vehicle."

He groaned.

"I was actually on my way back when I got a flat tire. I can't travel that far with the donut, so I'm waiting for the mechanic to fix it. As soon as it's ready, I'll leave. I'll call before I head out."

"If you're sure you're all right, then I'll talk to you later. Do you want to speak to your mom?"

And have to justify her actions as the always-disappointing average child? Not a chance. "I don't have the energy for that conversation."

"Okay. You get some rest, but please pick up when we call next time."

"I will. Love you."

"Love you too."

When the line went dead, Natalia scrolled through her text messages. Among the ones from her mom was one from Hayden. *Call me. H.* He'd already waited hours for a response. One more wouldn't hurt him.

She made her way back to the counter. Travis was on the phone when Natalia reached him. A faint hat ring circled his black hair, which was short along the back and longer on top. Black stubble covered his tanned jaw. His dark eyes stared straight ahead. Even sitting he was a bit taller than she, and—at five nine—most people considered her tall.

"I drove down as many side roads as I could with no luck," he said. "Do you want me to extend my shift and keep looking? Tomorrow's my day off, but I can head back out."

She slipped onto the stool, plopped her elbows on the counter, and rested her head in her hands. The aroma of coffee floated toward her as Rosemary slid a white mug and basket of creamers in front of her.

Natalia inspected the basket. Hazelnut, Irish Cream, Chocolate Delight, Caramel Nut. They all sounded delicious, but her emotional level needed chocolate. She poured two small cups into her mug and stirred, watching the dark and light brown blend together. It was oddly comforting. And encouraging. While Travis talked, she pulled out her phone and typed out a quick text.

Hey, Hayden. Sorry I missed your text. I'm not able to talk. Also, I'd like to take a personal day tomorrow.

She pushed SEND before she lost her nerve.

"Everything all right?" Travis dropped his phone into his front pocket.

Normally she'd keep quiet, not wanting anyone to know her business, but she doubted she'd ever visit Alkaline again and Trooper Wilkins seemed trustworthy. "I have a slight headache, my parents are about to send out search and rescue to find me, and my boss wants me to call him." Natalia sipped her coffee. Barely tasting the chocolate, she added more creamer.

"You're self-medicating with chocolate creamer?"

"Only the best for a day like today." She offered the basket to him.

He shook his head. "Only drink it black. Why are your parents looking for you?"

Natalia shrugged. "They worry. It always starts with my mom. Usually my dad's the reasonable one, but sometimes she gets him all worked up until they both drive me crazy. I feel like she thinks I'm too stupid to make my own decisions."

"Why would she think that?"

"My brother's the high school valedictorian, graduated with honors from Georgetown Medical School, then moved to Sioux Falls to open a pediatric clinic after he got married. He became a foster dad and adopted two sweet girls. I struggled all through high school, dropped out of college to become a dispatcher, and am still single."

"As a dispatcher, you've learned all the 10-codes and signals, you calm people down in their worst moments, give CPR and first aid instructions, all while answering and monitoring radios. I think you're too smart for college."

"Thanks."

"Is that why they're harassing you today? Because of your job?"

She cringed. "I didn't exactly tell anyone where I was going when I left home this morning. I left right after Officer Mason's funeral to try to escape all the emotions for a while. I haven't talked to my mom yet, but I expect she'll use my reaction to prove to me that I never should have become a dispatcher in the first place."

"I'm sure she's just concerned about you."

"Maybe, but do you have any idea how frustrating it is to have people fuss over you all the time?"

"No, I don't."

"Your mom doesn't worry?"

"My mom's dead, but I don't think she ever cared much when she was alive. I practically raised myself until I turned nine."

Natalia looked at the steam rising from her coffee. How thoughtless. Her family loved her. She should be grateful. "I'm sorry."

"Don't be. My life wasn't easy at the beginning, but I didn't know any different."

"What happened when you were nine?"

"I went to my first foster home."

* * * * * * *

Natalia handed Rosemary a ten-dollar bill as her phone rang. She didn't recognize the number so she motioned for Travis to go outside while she answered. "Hello?"

"Is this Natalia Brynner?"

"It is."

"You ripped a hole in the whitewall. I don't think a patch is goin' ta hold. You're goin' to be needin' a new tire."

Why couldn't she catch a break? "Okay. How much is that going to cost?"

"Well, here's the deal. If you replace the front right tire with a new one, you'll need to replace the left one too."

"Why would I need to replace a perfectly fine tire?"

"You've got some choices, miss. I can try to find a used one with similar wear as the other front tire. That'll run you about a hundred. You can buy two new tires, which will set you back four hundred. Or you can drive on uneven tire treads and die in a crash. That one's free."

She sighed. "If you could get me a used tire, I'd appreciate it."

"The thing is, I won't be able to get the tire 'til mornin'."

"I don't have another option, do I?"

"Sure. I gave you two."

She hated to spend money on new tires, but death wasn't really an option. "Look for a used tire, please."

"Good choice. I'll call ya when it's done." He hung up.

Her phone buzzed. *Found a sub for you tomorrow. Still need to speak with you. H.*

Call you tomorrow. Thanks. Natalia put her phone in her purse before heading outside. A breeze kissed her skin. Dark clouds filled the sky.

"I think we're in for a storm." Travis glanced down at her.

On cue, the wind picked up as the clouds let loose large drops of rain. They ran back into the bistro as the rain drenched them. Once they were inside, hail beat against the windows.

"I guess we aren't going anywhere soon." Natalia wiped a drop of water from her cheek. "It doesn't matter though. That was the mechanic. My tire is ruined. He's looking for a used one, but my car won't be ready until the morning. Is there a hotel around here?"

"Not in Alkaline."

Rosemary hurried over and handed them each a towel. "Oh dear, that storm came up quick."

Natalia nodded as she dried herself off, rubbing her skin until it hurt. What else could go wrong? Without a hotel in town, she needed to call the mechanic before he left his shop so she could get those new tires.

"I overheard you talking," Rosemary said. "Do you need a place to stay? I live around the block if you'd like to spend the night. It'll be just like the Holiday Inn Express, with a continental breakfast included."

Natalia didn't know what to say. While she relished the chance to delay her return and save on the price of new tires, she didn't know Rosemary at all. She glanced at Travis. Surely a cop wouldn't steer her wrong. "What do you think?"

"It's a great idea." He placed his towel on the counter. "I bet Rosemary's guest room is as fancy as her bistro."

Natalia faced the grandmotherly café owner. "If you're sure I won't be a burden, I'll stay."

Rosemary gathered their wet towels. "Not at all. I love having guests."

Travis's radio squawked. "One-two to any available unit. Signal one at the intersection of Highway 34 and Hope Road."

"I have to respond to this." Travis put on his hat. "I'll try to stop by in the morning, but if you need anything you have my card."

Natalia smiled. "Thanks for your help and company."

He nodded, then ran outside through pea-sized hail to his patrol car.

"How about some more coffee?" Rosemary guided her back to a stool.

Natalia scanned the nearly empty but messy dining room. "Actually, I'd like to keep busy. Can I lend a hand? Too much time to think may not be the best option for me right now."

"Sure. Grab an apron from the kitchen so you don't get that pretty dress of yours dirty."

Blue and red lights flew past the windows as Natalia tied the apron around her waist. What if she stayed in Alkaline for a while? She could spend some time not trying to please anyone else or having to deal with other people's emergencies. Maybe her flat tire was a blessing in disguise.

As she helped clean tables, Rosemary told Natalia about Alkaline High School's football team, the 4-H rodeo club, and the upcoming volunteer fire department auction. The more Natalia heard, the more she wanted to stay.

CHAPTER 3

Natalia flopped onto the lace comforter on Rosemary's guest bed and slipped off her shoes, stretching her toes in the cool air. Matching lace curtains framed the window and prints of cafés hung on the walls. She yawned and closed her eyes as she waited for her host to return with pajamas.

A knock jolted her awake. Light blazed overhead. Another knock. "Come in." Natalia blinked against the light as she sat up.

Rosemary poked her head into the room. "I borrowed a t-shirt from my neighbor. I thought it could be a nightgown."

Natalia took the shirt. "Thanks." She held up the faded green fabric. It unfolded to her knees.

Rosemary pointed down the hallway. "My room is next door if you need anything else. Good night, dear."

* * * * * * *

"Shots fired!" Natalia yelled, sitting up and struggling for air. Her heart raced as she looked around, searching for Officer Mason. As reality set in, her stomach heaved with every shallow breath. She clawed at her neck and chest, desperate for air but only managing to scrape her skin. She was going to suffocate!

The door opened, and Rosemary hurried to her side. "What's wrong?"

"Can't … breathe. Call … help."

Rosemary ran out of the room.

Natalia gripped the blanket as she tried to open her lungs.

Rosemary returned and covered Natalia's mouth with a bag. The paper crinkled as she inhaled and exhaled. Rosemary rubbed her back until her breathing slowed. When her lungs finally relaxed, Natalia lowered the bag. Exhausted, she rested her head on Rosemary's shoulder. "How did you know what do to?"

"My stories."

"Your what?"

"Soap operas. There's always someone hyperventilating. I never thought those silly shows would come in handy." She laid her hand on Natalia's trembling fingers. "What happened?"

"It was just a nightmare."

"Do you want to talk about it?"

She crumpled the sack. Images of Officer Mason's bleeding body flashed through her mind. "Not really."

"Do you think you can settle yourself back to sleep now?"

"I think so, if I can get my brain to slow down and stop imagining the worst."

"The worst what?"

She took a deep, calming breath. She could at least be honest with her host. "Calls. I'm a dispatcher. I took a bad call. I keep imaging how bad tomorrow's calls might be."

"Tell that brain of yours to stop worrying about tomorrow. Today has enough worries of its own." Rosemary patted Natalia's hand before she straightened the bedspread. "Try to get some rest." She turned off the light as she stepped into the hallway.

Natalia lay down and closed her eyes. If only Rosemary's commands were that easy.

****

At noon, Travis pulled his pickup into the only available parking spot outside the Prickly Pear. After working at a crash scene until two that morning, he slept through breakfast. His stomach rumbled as he walked into the bistro. The lunch crowd filled the tables. He scanned the room for Rosemary, anxious to find out if Natalia had made it home okay.

But it wasn't Rosemary carrying a carafe from table to table.

With a smudged apron wrapped around her black dress, Natalia poured coffee for the locals. Why was she still there? Had something else happened? Yesterday had been hard enough on her. She could use a break.

Travis slipped into his favorite booth and watched her work. Her face glowed as she talked with the customers, her braid swinging along her shoulders as she moved.

When she spotted him, she picked up an empty coffee mug and headed toward his table. "Hello, Trooper Wilkins." She filled the mug with black coffee.

"Call me Travis. You're still here. Was there an issue getting a tire?"

"Thankfully, no. But after yesterday's troubles, I wouldn't have been surprised if there was. One of Rosemary's servers called in sick, so I offered to fill in for her before I head home."

Rosemary stepped up behind Natalia and untied her apron. "Break time. Enjoy some lunch on the house. You've earned it." She motioned to the seat opposite him.

Natalia took off her apron. "I guess I have a little free time if you'd like to have lunch with me."

"Of course. Sit down."

Natalia sank onto the bench.

Rosemary pulled a green pad from her apron. "What'll you have? I'd better get the order in before my cook leaves for the day."

"The special." Travis and Natalia answered simultaneously.

"Good choice." Rosemary headed to the kitchen.

"Is your car ready yet?"

Natalia nodded. "I'm picking it up this afternoon, but I'm not in a hurry. I'm actually trying to think up a reason to stay another night."

"Why's that?"

"If I stay, I'll get another caramel roll in the morning."

"That sounds like a good enough reason to me." Travis scanned the busy restaurant, not only impressed that she was willing to fill in for a complete stranger, but also that the diners all seemed to be well taken care of. "How was your morning?"

"I've had a blast. Waiting tables is a lot like dispatching. You have to assess the situation, take charge of the scene, listen to multiple voices at the same time, then make sure everyone gets what they need. Except this is a lot less stressful and much more entertaining. These patrons are a hoot, especially that table over there."

Travis glanced at the back table full of gray-haired men. "I'm sure they loved having someone new to listen to their stories. We've all heard them at least a dozen times. Most of them are retired ranchers and a couple were truck drivers, but the one with the black hat is Carl Jackson. He's a retired sheriff's deputy who's always giving me advice. When I was a trouble-making kid, he and I played cat and mouse 'bout every chance we got."

"You were a troublemaker?" She tilted her head.

Travis shrugged. "I might have started a small barn fire one night. Stolen Rosemary's car when I was twelve. Done a lot of underage drinking. Your typical teenage rebellion."

Natalia covered her mouth with her hand. "Why did you steal Rosemary's car?"

"It was right after my foster dad announced he wanted to adopt me. Figured he would keep me from my mom, so I went looking for her."

Natalia lowered her hand, her eyes wide. "Was your foster dad cruel?"

"Not at all. Hank was a quiet rancher who worked me hard, especially when I got into trouble, but he was kind."

"Did he adopt you then?"

"Yep. A few months later. He's why I'm a state trooper. He taught me to work hard and respect people, including myself." His chest tightened. No one had a heart as big as Hank, and no one had ever loved Travis so unselfishly.

"Does he still live in the area?"

"He passed away a few years ago. Pancreatic cancer." He braced himself for the two words he knew would come next.

"I'm sorry."

There they were. Travis bent his head, trying to think of a different topic.

Rosemary set two plates in front of them, each piled high with mouth-watering chicken and mashed potatoes. She couldn't have dished up a better distraction.

"You sure you won't marry me, Rosie?" Travis pushed out his lower lip.

"If only you were my type, and don't call me Rosie." She scowled, then moved to the next table.

He attacked his food with gusto.

Natalia bit into her lunch and groaned. "These are the best potatoes I've ever eaten. I can see why you keep proposing."

Travis chuckled. He'd enjoyed his time with the pretty out-of-towner. He wouldn't mind if she invented a reason to stay to enjoy a few more sweet rolls.

****

Natalia used her bread to mop up the last of the gravy. "I ate too much. I think I'm going to have to go jogging when I get home." Jogging! "My gym bag is in my car! My sneakers are in there. These heels are killing me."

Travis looked under the table. "You've been waiting tables in stilettos?"

"They're hardly stilettos." Natalia tapped her three-inch, chunky heels on the floor a few times.

"How's your ankle?"

She blushed. "I was hoping you'd forgotten about that. It's fine."

Rosemary hurried back to their table and faced Natalia. "I've got a problem. My day waitress who called in sick today went to the doctor. She's on her way to Rapid City for an appendectomy, and she's going to be out of commission for four weeks. When are you expected back home?"

"I can probably take a few days off, if you don't mind me crashing with you again."

Rosemary smiled. "Thank you. That will give me some time to find a replacement. I'll print out her schedule and, of course, you're welcome to stay with me."

"It's my pleasure." An unexpected lightness lifted Natalia's spirit. Hayden and her mother wouldn't like the delay, but at least she had a few days to prepare herself before she had to face them.

"Empty plates, full bellies, and happy customers is what I like to see." Rosemary took their dishes. "Leave room for dessert?"

"Always." Travis said as Natalia shook her head.

"I've got lemon meringue pie."

"In that case, make it two slices."

Rosemary laughed. "I'll be back in a few minutes."

"That was nice of you to offer to help," Travis said.

"Rosemary has been an unexpected blessing. I'm happy to pay back her kindness."

"Good. I was a little scared she'd ask me to fill in. I can't say no to her."

"Since I'll be staying a little longer, I need to get a few things. I don't suppose there's a department store in Alkaline?"

"There's a convenience store further down Golden Street next to the hardware store. You might find what you need there. And one of the local churches has a charity clothes closet. They might have some clothes in your size."

"I'd hate to take clothes from the needy."

"I'd say you're pretty needy at the moment. If you're that worried about it, leave a donation. Or you could head into Sturgis. It's only an hour away."

The retired deputy approached and stopped next to their table. "I see how it is. I thought I was your favorite customer."

"Oh, you definitely are." Natalia smiled at the older gentleman. "It's just that I took pity on Trooper Wilkins sitting here all alone."

Travis laughed.

Carl squeezed Travis's shoulder. "Any updates on the missing boy? I heard their vehicle was spotted in the area."

His grin disappeared. "We weren't able to locate it, so we have no clue if it's them. Sarge called off the search for now. Doesn't want to waste manpower on so little information."

"What do you hear from the tribal officers?"

"They haven't seen him. The foster parents aren't Native American, so it's doubtful they'd head that way."

Carl nodded as the other retirees left the restaurant. "I've gathered a posse. We aim to check some of the trails south of town."

"Make sure you call the police if you find anything. You're retired, remember? No hotshot moves."

"Don't worry about me. My hotshot days are behind me. I've had both knees replaced and my hip's giving me trouble. Probably from all those years I had to chase you down." He chuckled.

"Just be careful."

"And you"—Carl looked at Natalia—"watch yourself around this one. I could tell you stories."

Travis pointed to the men outside mounting their four-wheelers. "I think your ride is leaving."

"Eh. I can outrun those farmers any day." He covered his white hair with a black ball cap and headed outside.

Natalia watched them drive away. Each of them wrinkled and slow moving, but heading out to help when needed. Another thing to love about the people of Alkaline. "When was the child taken?"

"The lead detective thinks they took off early last week. When the family didn't show up for their monthly home visit, the social worker got worried. It took two days before they issued the Amber Alert. With that much time passed, all the clues were old."

"Home visit?"

Travis nodded. "He's in foster care."

"Why would the foster parents kidnap him?"

"They wanted to adopt him, but the boy is Native American and the parents aren't, so they can't. Apparently they got desperate."

Natalia's gut twisted. "The Indian Child Welfare Act. I learned about it in foster care classes."

His head tilted. "You're a foster parent?"

"Yes, but I've only done respites for my brother and sister-in-law. With my crazy work schedule, I can't foster full-time, but I like to help when I can."

Travis's phone rang. He pulled it out of his pocket and answered it. "Trooper Wilkins." His face scrunched as he listened, nodding occasionally. "You got it, Sarge. I'll grab my gear, then head that way." He ended the call, pulled out his wallet, and threw a twenty on the table. "Duty calls. Make sure Rosemary saves me some pie." He dashed out the door before she could respond.

As Natalia watched him drive away, Rosemary appeared with dessert. "Where did Travis run off to?"

"He got called into work." She stood and handed Rosemary the twenty. "How long will you need me to help today?"

"My evening server is scheduled to arrive in a couple of hours if you can stay that long."

"Sure. After that, what's there to do around here? I'd like to keep myself busy. My mind wanders if I have too much free time."

"There's not a lot to do in Alkaline." Rosemary pressed her lips together as she looked around the diner. When she looked out the front window, her eyes and mouth rounded into matching O's. "I own the apartment upstairs. It's a bit of a disaster—I've got stuff everywhere and the kitchen faucet leaks—but if you want to clean it up a bit, you're welcome to stay there. Then you won't have to share a bathroom with an old lady."

"You're hardly old. You have the energy of a twenty-year-old."

Rosemary fluffed her bangs. "I don't know about that, but I know I don't look sixty since I colored my hair. I used to have long light-orange locks, but this red is as close as my stylist can get. They say blondes have more fun, but that's only because they follow the schemes of a redhead."

Natalia laughed. "I don't doubt that. And I'd love to help with your apartment."

* * * * * * *

After her shift ended and she'd picked up some clothes at the church, Natalia explored the convenience store. She threw a toothbrush, toothpaste, and hairbrush into her basket. The prices were outrageous, but she still didn't have her car and couldn't wait another day to brush her teeth.

Wanting her own shirt to sleep in, she sorted through a rack of Sturgis Motorcycle Rally t-shirts. The hangers squeaked across the bar. Then someone giggled. She pushed aside the shirts. A little boy with shiny black hair and dark eyes smiled at her.

Her heart skipped, but she knelt to his eye level. "Hey. What are you doing in there?"

"Hiding," he whispered.

"Gotcha!" A woman with reddish-brown curls parted the shirts, then scooped him into her arms and tickled his tummy.

He giggled.

"My silly Marcus. Daddy will be here soon, and you haven't picked out a coloring book yet."

"Then we go swimming?" He wiggled in her arms.

"If Daddy says it's okay." She set the boy down, and he ran toward the magazine rack.

Natalia stepped beside the woman. "He's cute."

She jumped. When she faced Natalia, she pressed a hand to her chest. Without a word, she ran after the boy.

So, not everyone in Alkaline was as friendly as Rosemary. Natalia picked out a shirt, then headed toward the checkout counter as the young mother and toddler hurried outside. A middle-aged woman with a butterfly barrette in her tightly curled hair rang up the items.

"That was a cute boy. Do you know the family?"

"Know them as well as I know you." She peered at Natalia through sapphire, wing-tipped glasses.

Point taken.

CHAPTER 4

Northeast of Alkaline, Travis drummed his fingers on the steering wheel of his patrol car. In front of him a pure blue sky met the tan, grass-covered field, and at the edge of that field sat a black Chevy pickup covered in mud. No one was in sight. Backup was taking forever. There was no reason for him to wait to search the truck.

Exiting his car, he drew his gun and crept toward the vehicle, hoping no one waited to ambush him. When he was close enough, he peeked inside the cab. Toys and fast-food trash littered the backseat, but no occupants.

He holstered his gun and moved to the back of the truck to wipe the plate clean. "Northern Hills. HP 352, 10-28."

"Go ahead, HP 352."

"South Dakota, two, Henry, Paul, zero, three, nine."

"HP 352, SD 28. Two, Henry, Paul, zero, three, nine returns on a 2016, black Chevy Silverado registered to Caleb Russell. 10-16 hit out of Rapid City on registered owner for possible kidnapping."

Travis smiled. Finally, a solid lead. "Copy. Confirm sixteen hit and send a wrecker to the end of Omega Place, two miles north of Highway 34."

"10-4. HP 352, 1312 hours."

His stomach fluttered. The Russells had to be around there somewhere, but where? He scanned the rolling pasture. A prairie dog popped his head up from the ground. To his left, something rustled and grunted. He pulled his weapon, his heart racing. A large man dressed in dirty overalls lumbered into view with fishing gear in one hand and a case of beer in the other. Travis couldn't remember his name, but he recognized him from their school days so he holstered his gun.

The fisherman spotted him and narrowed his eyes. "Hey, what you doing sneaking around my truck, Wilkins?"

"This isn't your pickup. It's registered to Caleb Russell."

"Bought it yesterday. Title's in the glove box." Metal clanked when he threw his tackle box into the bed. "Want to see it?"

"No." Disappointment filled Travis's stomach. "How did you end up buying it?"

"My cousin saw a for-sale-by-owner sign in the windshield at the Pamida in Sturgis. Guy only wanted ten grand for it, but it had to be cash."

Travis pulled out his phone and pulled up the picture of Caleb from the Amber Alert. "Was this the guy?"

"Sure as shootin', that's him. It ain't stolen, is it?"

"No, it's not. Was anyone with him?"

"He was by himself. I didn't get swindled, did I?"

Travis shook his head. "Did he say where he lived or where he was going?"

"Why all the questions? Geez, who'd he kill?"

"No one." Travis tucked his phone back in his pocket and pulled out a pen and pad. "Write down your phone number. A tow truck is coming, and your pickup will be impounded until the investigators are done searching through it."

"That ain't fair. I paid good money for it. I have the title!" He reached for the door handle.

"There could be evidence inside." Travis pulled him away, but the man swung, striking his jaw. Travis's eyes watered, but he tackled the fisherman to the ground and pushed his knee onto the middle of his attacker's denim-covered back. "Now, why did you go and do that?"

Dirt flew around them as the man squirmed under Travis's weight. Travis grabbed the man's arms and handcuffed him. When the metal clicked tight, the prisoner cursed but lay still.

Travis stood. Sweat and dirt covered his neck. He finally had a fresh lead, but instead of chasing it, he had to haul an angry local to jail. Great.

* * * * * * *

Natalia set her shopping bags on the mechanic shop's chipped, yellow counter as she hit the bell for the third time. A coffee pot surrounded by mugs sat on a metal cart to her left and three brown folding chairs sat along the wall under a dirty picture window. The *Ring for Service* sign behind the counter mocked her.

"Hello? Anyone here?" She leaned across the counter and peered into the room to her right. Nothing but a metal desk covered with papers. She took out her phone and dialed the mechanic's number. The brown corded phone in front of her rang. "Well, that's helpful."

She tossed her phone into her purse, snatched her bags, and stormed out of the shop. The bell above the door clanged. Maybe someone was around back. She walked past two overhead garage doors to a regular-sized door and tried the knob. Locked. She peered through the window and saw her little red car but no one else.

"Do I need to haul you in for unlawful entry?"

Natalia spun around.

Travis sat in a silver truck idling near the curb.

"I'm trying to get my car but no one's here."

"That's my fault. Had to call him away to tow a vehicle to the impound lot."

Great. She'd have to work another shift in heels, but before that she'd need to check out her new place. And it sure would be more fun with help. She stepped closer to the truck and smiled. "Rosemary's letting me stay in the apartment above the bistro. She said there's a lot of cleaning to do, and a leaky faucet to fix. You wouldn't moonlight as a handyman in your spare time, would you?"

"I can take a look. Hop in." He motioned his head to the

passenger side.

"Thanks." She climbed into the truck and set her bags on the floor, then slipped her sore feet from her heels. Sweet relief!

Travis turned onto the main street. "Been shopping?"

"I stopped by the church and the convenience store."

"Did you find what you needed?"

"There were two pairs of jeans and a few shirts that will work, but no shoes that fit. I wanted my sneakers more than I wanted my car." She sighed. "There are blisters on both my heels. These things give new meaning to the term killer shoes."

"Ouch."

They passed the Red Barn Bar, the post office, Alkaline Vet Clinic, and the front of the bistro before Travis parked along the back, brick wall of Rosemary's building. Natalia grabbed her things and stepped down from the truck. A rock dug into her foot, but the sharp pain was worth keeping her shoes off. Travis climbed out and rummaged through a metal box that ran the length of the truck's bed. He pulled out a green canvas bag.

Natalia led the way to the back door. "Rosemary gave me the key earlier, so let's go see my new place." They climbed the creaky wooden steps. At the top, she unlocked the apartment and pushed the door open. Hot, musty air escaped into the hallway as she stepped inside. A large picture window filled the wall to her left. Natural light filtered through it onto boxes, a recliner, a couch, three lamps, golf clubs, and a china cabinet. A table and chairs covered in dust filled the dining room. An L-shaped kitchen ran along the far wall and corner.

Travis walked to a window and pried it open. "I think we're going to need some fresh air."

The breeze cooled the room, but it also stirred up dust, tickling Natalia's nose. "We'd better get this cleaned before—" She sneezed.

Travis held his phone to his ear. "I think I just got called into work." He winked.

Natalia threw a shoe at him. "It's not that bad." She hoped.

She walked to the first of three doors on her right and opened it. She cringed at the mustard-yellow toilet between a baby-blue pedestal sink with a brass framed mirror above it. A claw-foot tub sat on white octagon tiles. She enjoyed color, but the bathroom was a bit much even for her simple tastes.

Next, she peeked into the room next to it. More boxes and a queen size bed. A smaller room to the right held even more boxes, a twin bed, two dressers, and a rocking chair. Back in the kitchen, Travis was already peeking under the sink.

"I appreciate the help," she said. "I think I was sick the day they taught plumbing for dispatchers."

"No problem." He stood and turned the faucet on and off.

"How long did you work today?"

"Not long. The lead on the kidnapper's vehicle led me straight to it."

"That's great. Did you find the boy then?"

"Unfortunately, the foster dad sold the truck to a local rancher yesterday. The guy didn't want us taking his truck, so he hit me. He'll be cooling his temper in a cell tonight."

It wasn't until he mentioned the hit that Natalia noticed the pink mark on Travis's tanned jaw. "Were you hurt?"

"Sore jaw, but nothing worse than I've had before." He shrugged. "I'll be okay. Fun way to spend my day off. I wish we could've found the boy though. Tomorrow I start night shifts, so I'll only get a few hours of daylight to search."

"Knock, knock." Rosemary poked her head into the apartment before carrying in a box. "Oh, my. This place is worse than I remembered. Are you sure you want to stay here? You're welcome to my guest room."

Natalia swatted at a fly. "I think it's charming, and it will keep me busy."

"I like your optimism." Rosemary set the box on the counter. "I brought some things you might need. Cleaning products, bedding, and light bulbs. Oh, and there might be some freshly baked peanut butter cookies in there."

Travis rummaged through the box and pulled out a plastic food container. "I know where I'm starting."

"Good plan, trooper." Natalia grabbed a cookie. The tightness in her chest, the weight of her job, and the anxiety of her future lessened as she unloaded the cleaning supplies. She was probably crazy to take on such a big project for only a few days, but she welcomed the challenge of it. And the distraction.

****

Red and blue lights flashed behind Natalia, so she pulled onto the shoulder of the road. What had she done this time?

She looked in the rearview mirror to reapply her lipstick, then caught a glimpse of the officer's reflection and smiled. Travis. She stepped out of the car.

He stopped a few yards away and drew his gun. "Stop right there!"

She raised her hands as a tremor ran through her body. "Travis, it's me. Natalia."

BANG! BANG! BANG!

He crumpled to the ground.

Natalia screamed. She ran to him. Blood flowed from his neck. "Put pressure on the wound!" She tried to help, but her arms were frozen. Why couldn't she help him? "Shots fired! Officer down! Send more units!"

Natalia sat up. Her chest heaved with painful breaths. Falling back onto her pillow, she tried to slow her breathing by focusing on the moonlight streaming in through the broken blinds. Slowly, painfully, her lungs relaxed.

Maybe she should have stayed one more night with Rosemary. Then, at least, she'd have someone to talk to. She glanced at the clock. Two thirty was too late to call her.

Travis. He'd told her to call if she needed anything, but did that mean at all hours of the night? Before she could talk herself out of it, she grabbed her cell phone. Shuffling out to the living room, she dug through her purse to find his business card, then dialed his number.

CHAPTER 5

The patrol car's headlights illuminated the road and the bugs that flew at Travis's face as he gripped the leg of the dead deer and pulled it into the ditch. Animal removal could pick it up in the morning.

Wiping the sweat from his face, he slipped into the car and turned up the air conditioner. He glanced at his phone. Natalia had called twice about five minutes ago. He tapped the screen to call her back. Late night calls worried him.

"Hi, Travis."

"Hey, I see I missed your calls. Is everything okay?"

She sighed. "It's fine. Thanks for your help today."

"You called me at two thirty in the morning to thank me? Are you sure you're okay? I can swing by if you need anything."

"No, it's all right. I had a bad dream, and I needed to talk to someone. Just hearing your voice helps."

Travis sat straighter. "Do you want to talk about your dream?"

"No. Did I wake you up?"

"I wish. I'm working. I got called to a car-deer crash."

"You started your night shift early?"

"Not by choice. Some day off, getting called into work twice. Good overtime, though."

"Any word yet on the missing boy?"

"Not yet. I was planning on looking for Marcus this morning, but now I'll be sleeping." He pinched his nose as his disappointment rose.

"Did you say his name was Marcus?"

"Yeah, Marcus Elkhorn. His foster parents are Caleb and Mary Russell."

"How old is he?"

"Three. I'll send you the Amber Alert." He scrolled through his phone, then texted the picture. "I just sent it."

She gasped. "That's the boy and the woman I saw at the convenience store."

"You saw him? When?" Travis tightened his grip on the phone. Frustration and excitement battled within.

"This afternoon, before you picked me up at the garage. He was with this woman in the picture. I didn't know it was him."

His pulse sped up. "Was he okay?"

"He seemed happy."

"Did you see where they went? Can you think of any other details?"

"This woman, Mary, told Marcus that his daddy would be picking them up, but I didn't see where they went."

"I need to call the lead investigator. He'll want to talk to you."

"Can't you give him the information?"

"I can, but you're an eyewitness. He'll want to get your statement." Something rustled on the other end of the line. "You okay?"

She sighed. "I've been on edge for days and I was finally starting to relax. Now a little boy's life might depend on what I can remember."

"His life doesn't depend on you. It depends on our ability to use your information to find him. Anything you can remember could be important."

"I know. I'll give my statement." But her voice didn't have the same enthusiasm it had earlier.

Travis couldn't blame her. She'd run from one high-intensity situation into another. The least he could do was support her. "How about I meet with you?"

"But you've been working all night."

"And you just gave us our first break in this case. I'm heading home now, so I'll get some sleep before we meet."

"Are you sure?"

"You bet. I'll set it up with the detective, then text you the details."

"Thank you." The lightness returned to her voice.

"Go back to sleep and I'll text you soon." He ended the call, then looked up Detective Astor's number. Natalia's news reenergized Travis. They needed to act quickly.

"Detective Astor," a groggy voice whispered.

"It's Trooper Wilkins with the Highway Patrol in Alkaline. Sorry to call you so late, sir, but I have a lead on the Marcus Elkhorn case."

"What's the lead?"

"He was spotted with Mary Russell at the Common Cents convenience store in Alkaline this afternoon."

"Who saw them?"

"Her name is Natalia Brynner."

"And she lives in Alkaline?"

"She lives in Sioux Falls, but she's visiting Alkaline."

"I'm headed up that way in the morning to search through the pickup. I'll stop by and talk with you and Natalia. I should be there by eight thirty. Where can I meet you?"

"The Prickly Pear Bistro on Golden Street."

"Tell Ms. Brynner not to be late."

* * * * * * *

Natalia checked the clock one more time. It was almost eight thirty, and she still hadn't seen Travis or anyone who looked like a detective. Rosemary nudged her shoulder before handing her a tray full of dishes. "Can you deliver these to table twelve?"

"Sure."

As Natalia delivered each plate, a man with Oakley sunglasses on his graying, brown hair, khaki pants, and a navy police department polo shirt stepped into the diner. On his belt, a badge sparkled next to his pistol. He carried a manila envelope under his arm. Travis, dressed in jeans and a black t-shirt, stepped in behind him.

Natalia untied her apron and tossed it under the counter. She grabbed a coffee carafe and two mugs, then approached them.

Travis placed his hand on her lower back. "Detective Astor, this is Natalia Brynner."

"Glad to meet you," she said. "I wish it was under better circumstances." She motioned to a clean table. "We can sit there." The detective slid into the booth and Travis sat across from him while Natalia filled their cups. "Would you like cream or sugar?"

"No, thanks." The detective held the mug with both hands.

"Can I get either of you something to eat?"

"We're good for now." Travis scooted over. "Sit and we'll get started" Natalia scooted in next to Travis and her arm brushed his, tickling her bare skin.

The detective pulled papers from the envelope and placed three pictures in front of her. "Is this the boy you saw?"

"Yes. That's him."

"And this was the lady with him?" Astor pointed to the picture of the woman Natalia had seen with Marcus. Reddish-brown hair curled around a heart-shaped face.

"Yes. She acted like his mom."

"That's Mary Russell, his foster mom. How about Caleb Russell? Did you see him anywhere?"

Natalia looked at the photograph of a man with a full beard and a buzz cut with a receding hairline. "He wasn't there. I've never seen him before."

Detective Astor narrowed his gaze. "Think back to your interaction with Mary and Marcus. Can you think of anything else that was said, even if it seems inconsequential?"

"Mary wanted Marcus to pick out a coloring book because she said Daddy was coming to get them. Then Marcus asked if he could go swimming."

"And how did Mary respond?"

"She said something like, 'if Daddy agrees.'"

The detective turned to Travis. "Where would they go swimming around here?"

"There are tons of stock dams and ponds, and a few creeks. Do you think they're staying near one?"

"Maybe. It's a place to start. I'll call Sergeant Black and we'll form a search plan." The detective glanced at Natalia. "Thanks for talking with me." He handed her his card. "If you see anything even remotely suspicious, or if you remember any other detail, give me a call. You both have a good day." The detective packed up his papers and slipped out of the booth, leaving Natalia and Travis sitting side by side.

"I wish I could have been more helpful," she said, tapping the detective's card on the table. She'd replayed the encounter a dozen times since Travis sent her the Amber Alert, but she couldn't think of anything she hadn't told the detective.

Travis yawned. "Sorry. I didn't get much sleep this morning."

And yet he'd met with her and the detective anyway. She leaned her head against his shoulder. "I should get back to work, and you could use a nap."

"Four hours just doesn't cut it at my age. I can't believe I used to pull all-nighters. What time are you off work?"

"Three. Want to help me put in a new toilet later?"

"That's what I live for."

"I doubt it, but maybe one of Rosemary's sweet rolls will make it more bearable."

They slid out of the booth, and Travis squeezed her hand. "I'll see you this afternoon."

Until then, Natalia would fight back her anxiety as she tried to remember every detail of her interaction with Mary and Marcus. His life might depend on it.

* * * * * * *

Natalia arranged the recliner so it faced the picture window, then placed a small, cherrywood table beside it. Now to clean the window so she could enjoy the view. As she wiped the glass, she admired the puffy white clouds floating through a soft blue sky that met golden fields. Cattle grazed on the grass while calves ran through a pasture that seemed to stretch for miles.

"Natalia, I need help."

She dropped the paper towels and hustled to the bathroom. Travis knelt next to the tub. His biceps flexed as he held the toilet.

"What can I do?"

"I need you to guide the bolts through the holes on either side."

Natalia squatted beside the sink and guided the porcelain onto the metal rods. Travis pushed down on the toilet. He'd insisted on oiling squeaky hinges and tightening loose cabinet pulls and light fixtures before setting foot in the bathroom. The man deserved a break and a reward.

She stood. "Want some peach pie?"

"I'll say. Let me finish in here while you warm it up. Do you have any ice cream?"

"I'll have to look. Rosemary stocked the fridge while I was finishing my shift." In the kitchen, Natalia washed her hands, then warmed two pieces of pie before checking the freezer. A tub of vanilla sat beside the ice cube trays.

"That should do it." Travis walked to the kitchen sink and washed up.

"Thanks. Rosemary will be excited when she sees it in the bathroom instead of the dining room. I think she was planning to hire a plumber to install it."

"Anything to help Rosemary. Getting paid with dessert is pretty sweet too." He winked as he dried his hands.

The microwave dinged. Natalia took out their pie, added the ice cream, and handed Travis his slice. They sat at the table before digging in. She took a bite. The perfect blend of sweet and tart.

Travis smiled at her. "Good, huh?"

"The best. Rosemary said she was sorry she sold out of lemon, but this is amazing."

"The lemon was for me. I've been partial to lemon-flavored anything since I was a kid."

"I wouldn't have picked you as a lemon sort of guy."

"It reminds me of a lady who lived across the hall from us when I was little. She kept a jar of lemon cookies on her kitchen table. After making us eat a PB and J, she'd give us one. They were the best." A slow smile covered his face. "When Rosemary found out, she started saving me pieces of lemon meringue when she could."

"You and Rosemary are close."

"Closest thing to a grandmother I ever had." He ate his last bite, then scraped the remaining filling into his mouth.

Natalia pushed her plate towards him. "I took too much. Want the rest?"

"Of course." He slid her plate closer without hesitation.

Her phone rang, so she left him to finish her piece while she answered it in the living room. "Hello?"

"It's Hayden."

Her pulse accelerated. Why hadn't she looked at the caller ID before answering it?

"Your next shift is Tuesday evening. Are you going to be here?"

The pie rolled in her stomach. "I have vacation days saved. I need to use them."

"Vacations have to be preapproved, and you can't use sick days unless you're sick."

"What about extenuating circumstances? You know what happened. Can I take a mental health day?"

"The department doesn't recognize those. You can meet with the police chaplain or a department psychologist. I'll email you their contact information. You still have to come to work though. We're short-staffed as it is."

"I don't need to see a psychologist. All I need is a break."

"You've got until Monday. If I don't hear from you, I'll have no choice but to terminate you."

Tears filled her eyes. She loved her job, but she wasn't ready. "I need more time."

"I'm sorry, but I can't give you any more than that. I have a dispatch center to run. If every dispatcher ran away after a horrific call, we'd never have anyone working. It's the job. You know that."

She walked to the window and rested her head against the glass. "I know."

Hayden hung up and she stared outside. What was wrong with her, running away because of a hard call? Every dispatcher had to deal with the tough stuff. If she couldn't, she might as well quit. Maybe her mom was right.

"Is everything okay?" Travis stepped behind her.

She turned to face him, wrapping her arms around her stomach. "That was my boss. He wants me back at work Tuesday night, but I don't know if I can do it."

"Why not?"

"I'm scared. I used to love my job. Every day was different but filled with excitement. I've helped people save lives and deliver babies. I calmed them when they were dealing with their worst moments. I don't want to walk away from that, but I keep hearing Officer Mason's panicked voice." She shivered.

"You have to take care of yourself. It's the only way you'll be able to cope with the trauma."

"Have you had to cope with trauma?"

He nodded.

"What did you do?"

He hooked his thumbs through his belt loops. "It helped when I rode my horse. Want to try it?"

The rock in Natalia's stomach turned to flutters. "I haven't ridden in years, but if you're okay taking a novice, I'd love to go."

"And I'd love to take you." He glanced at his watch. "My shift starts soon so I'd better head out, but I'll call you about the ride. Thanks for the pie." He tipped his head at her, picked up his tool box, and strode out the door. His footsteps echoed down the stairs.

She turned back to the window. Maybe a ride through the

country with a sweet guy would help. She hoped it would help. She didn't want to consider her other options.

CHAPTER 6

Saturday morning, Natalia limped two blocks down Golden Street to the mechanic's shop. Pain radiated from her blistered heels. The bell above the door jingled when she opened it. A group of cowboys stood in front of the counter drinking from steaming mugs and talking. She glanced at the wall clock. Rosemary expected her back in fifteen minutes, and she wasn't leaving without her sneakers. "Excuse me."

They laughed. She clenched her teeth. Her feet couldn't wait. Then she spotted Travis in a faded green John Deere cap. He'd help her.

She walked over to him and touched his arm. "If you don't mind, I need to get my car."

His eyebrows lifted and he stepped aside, giving her access to the counter.

"Thank you." She limped forward.

"It's lunchtime, Wilkins. You coming?" Someone behind her spoke.

"Meet up with you in a minute." He waved to the guys leaving the shop, then turned back to her. "Are you okay?" He leaned against the Formica top.

She shook her head and rang the bell. "I only have fifteen minutes before I have to be back at the bistro."

He rang the bell several times. "Sometimes you have to be pushy to get what you want." He smiled, and two dimples appeared.

Dimples? She'd spent hours with him yesterday. She wouldn't have missed those.

"There it is."

"There what is?"

He motioned to her face. "The moment you figured out that I'm not Travis. It's written all over your face." The familiar-looking stranger held out his hand. "Cole Wilkins, at your service."

"Natalia Brynner." She shook his hand. "Travis didn't mention having a twin."

"I'm not surprised. Everyone around here knows us, so there's nothing to talk about. But you're not from around here. Where you from?"

"Sioux Falls."

"And you're working at the bistro?"

"I'm helping Rosemary for a few days. It's a long story."

The garage door opened, and a lanky, older man in oil-smudged coveralls joined them. "How can I help you?"

"I'm Natalia Brynner. You called and said my car was ready."

"I called two days ago. Thing's taking up room in my shop."

She crossed her arms. "I came by yesterday, and you were closed."

He shrugged. "Been busy." He pulled out a three-ring binder and flipped through the pages. "Here it is. That'll be one fifty-eight."

She held out her credit card.

"Sorry, cash or check only."

"I don't have my checkbook or enough cash."

Cole put two hundred-dollar bills on the counter. "This should cover it."

She picked them up and held them out to him. "Thanks, but I can't let you do that. You don't even know me. I'll ask Rosemary to forward me the money."

"Take it, and get your car now. I'll meet you at the bistro and you can pay me back there if you're so concerned about it."

His brown eyes held the same warmth that Travis had displayed many times in the last few days. What would it hurt to borrow the money for a few minutes? "Okay. Thank you."

The mechanic took Cole's money, then gave him the change and Natalia's keys. "Pleasure doing business with you."

She grabbed the keys. "Thank you."

Cole opened the door for her. He matched her stride as he walked beside her. "How do you know Travis?"

"We met last week. He pulled me over for running a stop sign."

"And you're still talking to him?"

"He was just doing his job."

Out in the garage, Natalia went straight to her back seat and pulled out the gym bag. She threw her pumps into the metal trash can—she never wanted to see those torture devices again—then slipped on her socks and sneakers. Her feet practically sighed in relief. Facing Cole, she jingled her keys. "I'll meet you at the bistro, then?"

"Sounds good."

Two minutes later she parked in front of the picture window and her door opened. Travis, in a straw cowboy hat, moved back as Natalia stepped out of the car.

"You finally got your car. And your shoes."

"Thanks to your brother, actually. I didn't have enough cash, so he bailed me out." Cole appeared from behind a truck and leaned against the wall. Natalia smiled at him. "You didn't tell me you were a twin."

Travis shrugged one shoulder. "Didn't think it was important."

"A heads-up might have been nice. I thought he was you. Then he smiled."

"That's not the only difference between us."

When he didn't elaborate, she picked up her purse and locked her car. "If you'll excuse me, I've got to get Cole his money, and I'm already late getting back to work. See you inside?"

He smiled. "I've been dreaming of that buffet all night." He motioned for her to lead the way.

Cole beat them to the door and opened it.

"Thanks." She nodded at him as she stepped inside. Someone

put a hand on her lower back. She hoped it was Travis.

The hum of conversations, rattling of plates, and Rosemary's voice greeted Natalia. Pans of scrambled eggs, hash browns, and sausage steamed under heat lamps, and the aroma of caramel rolls made her mouth water. If there were any rolls left after her shift, she'd snag one. Or two.

She hurried over to the counter and put on her apron. Rosemary stood next to her refilling coffee carafes. "I'm sorry I'm late," Natalia said.

"Don't worry about it. I'm glad you got better shoes."

"Me too. I ran into a problem though."

"Is your car not ready?"

"No, I was able to pick it up. I didn't have cash to cover the tire though. Thankfully, Cole helped me out, but now I owe him. Could you lend me a hundred and sixty dollars and take it out of my paycheck?"

"Of course, love. Take the money from the till and write it down."

What had Natalia done to deserve such kindness? "You're the best." She rushed over to the register and counted out enough cash for Cole, then jotted down the amount on an order pad. She grabbed a carafe from Rosemary and went looking for Cole. He sat with the other cowboys she'd seen him visiting with at the mechanic shop, each of them with plates full of food.

Natalia handed him the money. "Thanks again for coming to my rescue."

"Anytime."

"Rescuing ladies in distress again, Wilkins?" The cowboy next to him elbowed Cole in the ribs.

"Shut up."

She walked around the table and refilled coffee mugs as they talked about cattle and crops. The table next to theirs emptied, so she swapped her carafe for a tray and started cleaning it when her gaze caught Travis's emotionless face. Why wouldn't he sit with his brother? Leaving the tray on the table, she walked over to him. "Is everything okay?"

"Sure. Why wouldn't it be?"

"You're sitting by yourself on the other side of the diner while your brother and his friends are laughing and having a good time."

He rubbed his eyes. "Sorry. I'm not in the best mood today. Switching from days to nights gets rough."

"Are you sure that's it?"

He sighed. "My brother and I don't get along. Seeing him tends to put me on edge."

"I get it. You know how I feel about my perfect brother." She took his empty plate. "I should get these dishes back to the kitchen."

"Before you go, how does Monday work to ride horses? Around ten?"

"Sounds perfect." She'd go horseback riding, then pack up and drive home. Back to her job. Her stomach churned as she headed to the kitchen. Hands shaking, she scraped food from the plates.

She loved waiting tables at the Prickly Pear, but it didn't satisfy her the way dispatching did. Giving first aid instructions to a panicked wife or talking with a suicidal soldier until help arrived. Then again, no one died at the bistro. What if another one of her officers was killed? The memory of Officer Mason's call still haunted her.

Natalia rinsed the last plate and tucked it into the dishwasher. By the time she dried her hands and walked into the dining room, the brunch crowd had disappeared. She helped Rosemary clean the tables, counter, buffet, floors, windows, and even a few chairs, then plopped onto a booth bench. Her stomach growled. She didn't think she had the energy to climb the stairs to her apartment, much less make herself a real meal.

"You survived your first Saturday buffet." Rosemary set two plates full of bacon, biscuits and gravy, caramel rolls, and scrambled eggs on the table, then scooted in across from Natalia.

"You are a godsend. I thought all the food was long gone."

"You can't run a successful business if you don't take care of your staff. I like to sit here, in the clean bistro, and enjoy a meal with my employees now and then."

Natalia took a big bite of the caramel roll. Soft and gooey, it did not disappoint.

"So, you met Cole today."

She nodded. "I'm surprised Travis never mentioned having a brother in town. They aren't close?"

"I don't see them together much since Hank died. They were eleven when they came to live with him. He never married, but he took in foster kids from time to time, always older boys. Travis and Cole were the only ones he adopted though."

Rosemary nibbled on a piece of bacon. "Cole took to Hank and his ranch from the start. Travis, on the other hand, got into more trouble than you could imagine. I thought he was a lost cause, but not Hank. He just poured love into that boy and gave him lots of chores. Probably figured if he worked him hard enough, he'd be too tired to make mischief."

"Did it help?"

"Sometimes. What probably did the most good was the example Hank set. If anyone complained about Travis's behavior, Hank'd ask them what they were doing to help him fit in. If you didn't have an answer, you'd best not bring any complaints to him. I'm sure Hank's proud of how well they both turned out. They were awfully heartbroken when he passed. What about you? Are your parents still alive?"

Natalia nodded and stuffed a biscuit into her mouth, hoping to avoid the topic.

"What a blessing."

Mostly.

"Tell me about them."

She forced down her food. "They're both teachers. My dad's ready to retire, but he's still working because of my mom. She worries about money, so he keeps working to ease her concerns."

"That's nice of him. Where do they live?"

"In Sioux Falls. Three blocks from my apartment."

"Do you see them often?"

"Whether I want to or not." She cringed. "I guess I shouldn't complain, especially after hearing about Travis's adoptive dad. I know my mom loves me, but she smothers me. I shouldn't be so hard on her."

Rosemary sighed. "I'd love to live that close to my daughter. She's in Arizona now, so I only get to see her for five months each year."

"What do you do with the bistro when you're gone?"

"Close up the place."

Natalia slouched against the booth as she looked around the dining room. What if she stayed and ran the bistro while Rosemary was gone? She could leave all the stress of her old life behind—how stressful could Alkaline be? And she could get to know Travis better too. Her stomach fluttered. Her mom wouldn't like it, but extra time in a quiet town with a handsome trooper might be worth the lectures.

CHAPTER 7

Birds chirped in the rustling branches of the trees that lined Golden Street. Long shadows stretched across the ground in the early morning sunlight. Natalia took a deep breath of the warm, flower-scented air, wanting to commit the town to memory before she left that afternoon.

Her phone rang, interrupting the peaceful moment. "Hello?"

"Nattie. I'm glad you finally answered one of my calls. How are things going?"

"Fine, Mom." She glared at the oak leaves overhead. Was it too much to ask for one more day?

"Your dad said you were coming home today. Said you sent him a text. What have I told you about that? A phone call is just as easy and far more polite."

"I know, but Dad doesn't mind me texting."

"Have you left yet?"

"Nope. Still have to pack. I'm planning on leaving around three."

"That's far too late. You don't want to drive when it's dark."

"It will barely be dusk when I get there. Don't worry."

"Why can't you leave earlier?"

"I have plans this morning."

"What kind of plans?"

"A friend is showing me around the area. It's a beautiful day, and I haven't had a chance to see everything yet."

"Who is this friend? You haven't been there long enough to make friends. You were never very good at it."

Natalia clenched her teeth. "Just because I wasn't as popular as

Mitch doesn't mean I can't make friends."

"I've never said anything about Mitch, but speaking of your brother, he's going to Peru for four weeks next summer on a medical missions trip. It's that wonderful?"

Of course he was. Perfect Dr. Mitch. "That's great."

"I called the administration office at the University of South Dakota. If you hurry, you'll be able to enroll for the fall semester."

Natalia's jaw dropped. "Why would you do that? I'm not going to college. I have a job."

"Dispatching is clearly too stressful for you. I think you'd make a wonderful teacher."

She took a deep breath as she prepared herself for their regular work-related argument. "Mom, please stop. I'm going back to dispatching." Eventually. "I'll send Dad a text before I leave. I'm sorry, I have to go. Bye."

She hung up before her mom could ask any more questions. Natalia was used to the meddling, but she had thought her mom would respect Officer Mason's death, not use it as ammunition against her. She didn't know if she could dispatch again, but she wasn't going back to college. She'd never done well in school. Why would she put herself through that again? And why did her mom have to push so hard?

A bird squawked overhead an instant before bird poop fell onto her shoulder. Lovely.

Abandoning her ruined walk, Natalia went back to the apartment. She changed into a clean t-shirt, then flopped onto the recliner and flung her arm across her face. Maybe she could squeeze in a nap before Travis arrived. After that phone call, she needed one.

Someone knocked on the door.

Or not. "Come in!"

Boots clomped on the wood floor. "Why isn't your door locked?"

Natalia rolled her eyes. "Because Alkaline has no crime rate."

"Even in Alkaline, you never know who could be snooping around. Locking your doors is a smart habit. Years back, there was a punk causing all kinds of problems. Stealing cars, burning barns, corrupting other kids."

Natalia chuckled as she stood. "I heard that he became a state trooper, so it worked out okay."

Travis stood in the dining room wearing a black Stetson with a turquoise, beaded hatband, a blue shirt with pearl buttons, a large silver belt buckle, and starched jeans. Even though he was off duty, he'd holstered a pistol to his belt. His chocolate-brown eyes captured her attention.

He winked.

Her cheeks warmed. She had just checked him out!

He returned the favor, then frowned. "You aren't ready yet."

She glanced down at her t-shirt and jogging shorts. "You're early. While I get ready, why don't you tell me about your brother?"

Travis strode to the recliner and plopped down. "That's going to take longer than it'll take you to change."

"You're not going to tell me?"

"Nope." He leaned back and pulled his hat over his eyes. "It's a beautiful day. Let's not waste it talking."

* * * * * * *

Amber grass stretching up to the middle of her calf crackled under Natalia's sneakers as she followed Travis through the pasture behind the peeling barn to where the horses grazed in the adjacent field. He'd draped lead ropes and halters over one shoulder while he carried a red bucket with his other hand. Overgrown daisies surrounded a yellow, ranch-style house on the other side of the gravel driveway.

"Is that your home?"

"It's where I grew up. Cole lives there now."

A robin whistled above them while grasshoppers fluttered around their feet. A warm breeze floated past Natalia as they neared the barbed wire fence. The air turned rancid and the ground softened. She looked down as her foot squished in a greenish-gray plop of manure. "Yuck!" She hopped away and wiped her shoe on the grass.

Travis turned and grinned. "You've got to watch where you're walking. We moved the cows from this pasture just recently. Their pies haven't hardened yet."

She glared at him. "Thanks for the warning."

He laughed. "Rub your shoe in the dirt to get the dung out of the cracks. We're going to have to find you some real boots."

"I'm not a cowgirl. These will do just fine."

He walked toward her and tugged the hat from his head, then placed it on hers. "Don't be so sure about that."

Her heart fluttered.

His rough fingers gripped hers. "Follow me. I'll keep you away from cow pies."

Travis led her toward the gate and shook his bucket. Two beautiful horses, one black and one brown, ran toward them, their nostrils flaring. He allowed the black horse a bite of oats, then handed Natalia the pail while he put on the halter and lead rope. The light-brown horse with a dark stripe down its back and a black tail and mane nuzzled her arm. She laughed and held the bucket out for it.

Travis wrapped the lead around the fence post, then haltered the brown horse. "This here is Wopila. She's a dun quarter horse and a princess." He petted her neck and whispered, "You are a spoiled princess, aren't you?" He turned back to Natalia. "She knows she's my favorite. Even when she's ornery, she'll turn to me with these big brown eyes and know I can never stay mad at her."

Natalia laughed. "You're a softy. What does Wopila mean? Spoiled one?"

"Just the opposite. It's Lakota for giving thanks. I'll ride her while you ride that patient guy over there." He pointed at the black horse, who swished his tail from side to side swatting away the flies. "His name is Dakota Peace and, unlike Wopila, he actually exemplifies his name. He's a calm, loving animal, which one would have to be to share a pasture with this filly."

Natalia patted Dakota Peace's neck. "You are a sweet one," she whispered. His ears twitched. "I have the feeling we're going to be great friends."

Once Wopila's halter was secured, Travis led the horses to the barn. Natalia locked the gate behind him, then joined him inside. In the barn, he tightened the cinch strap on Dakota Peace's saddle. "Why don't you hop up so I can adjust the stirrups?"

It had been several years since she'd been on a horse, and that realization sent nerves rumbling in her stomach. Ignoring them, she put her foot in the stirrup and swung onto the strong animal. Dakota Peace stood still under her weight.

"Have you ridden much?" Travis fastened the buckle and pulled until the strip reached the perfect length. Then he moved to the other side and repeated the steps.

"When I was younger, on my grandparents' farm. They had one stubborn old horse that my brother and I took turns riding."

"I put a hackamore bridle on Dakota because his mouth is too sensitive for a bit, so make sure you don't pull too hard on the reins. Also, the slightest pressure on his sides will get him going. He's truly an accommodating guy. I'm sure you'll charm him." He handed her the reins. "Lead him into the front yard. I'll be out in a sec."

Natalia squeezed her calves, and Dakota walked to the patch of grass in front of the barn. She rubbed her hand down his neck as he ate. "You're sure a pretty thing," she whispered.

A kitten ran across the yard to them and scratched her back against Dakota's leg. The horse kept eating. Natalia probably would have named him something clichéd, like Midnight, but Dakota Peace suited the gentle animal.

The horse's ears perked up as the low rumble of an engine approached. She looked around until she spotted Cole rounding the corner of the barn on an ATV. A white dog with black splotches followed, then ran ahead of him to Natalia and barked. Dakota kept eating grass.

Cole stopped next to her and killed the engine, then clapped. "Molly, quiet down!" The barking ceased as the dog ran to him. He leaned down and stroked her long fur, then grinned up at Natalia. "Well, aren't you a sight, looking like a genuine cowgirl?"

She touched Travis's hat. "It's the hat. What are you up to?"

He hopped off the ATV and dug into his pocket for a sugar cube. He held it out to Dakota Peace, then he wiped his hand on his jeans. "Just got done checking my calves in the northeastern pasture. Travis taking you out for a ride?"

"Yeah. He's saddling his horse. I can't remember her name." She cringed. "I sure hope that's not a cowboy faux pas."

Cole chuckled. "Travis picks odd names for his animals. It's Wopila."

"That's it."

He ran a hand down Dakota's belly and tugged on the cinch. "The native names are his way of staying connected to our Lakota roots."

"I didn't know you were Native American."

He raised an eyebrow. "You mean Travis hasn't shared with you the depth of our roots? I'm shocked."

She pressed her lips together as her chest tightened at his mocking tone.

"Make sure he takes you to see our calves, and there are a few foals further north."

Travis trotted out of the barn. "Cole. I borrowed your hackamore for Dakota. Last time I rode him the bit irritated his mouth."

Cole nodded then smirked. "You cleaned up for a horseback ride?"

Travis glared back. "What of it?"

"Nothin.' Have a nice ride, Natalia. I'm headed in for some grub." He whistled as he strode toward the house, and Molly ran alongside him.

"Follow me. I'll show you my favorite ridge." Travis clicked his tongue, and Wopila trotted west down a dirt path.

Dakota followed with Natalia bumping along in the saddle. When they slowed to a walk, she caught up with Travis. "Thanks for taking me on this ride. I've been looking forward to it."

"You bet. I'm glad you could come."

"Cole mentioned your Lakota heritage. Were both your parents Native American?"

"My mom was. Don't know anything about my dad."

"What about your adoptive dad?"

"Nope. He's white."

"Did the ICWA make it difficult for him to adopt you?"

"Doubt it. It's easy to approve an adoption outside the tribe when no one else wants you, and not too many families wanted a messed-up eleven-year-old. Hank saved my life. I'd probably be dead or in jail if it wasn't for him."

"Did he worry over you? My mom worries nonstop."

Travis shrugged. "If he did, he didn't show it."

"What was he like?"

"He was a simple cowboy. Worked hard all week from dawn to dusk. Went to church on Sunday morning and fishing afterward. He gave us a good life, died too soon, and left us his family ranch."

"Why did you choose law enforcement over ranching?"

A muscle in his jaw twitched. "Actually, I joined the army first. Couldn't get out of this town fast enough. I applied for the highway patrol after I was discharged."

Natalia pictured the quiet Alkaline streets and the daisies around the homey-looking ranch house. Everything about the place exuded charm. "Why did you want to leave so badly?"

"A girl I knew spread a bunch of lies about me, and it didn't take much for the town to believe them. Enough talking, now. More riding." He kicked his horse and galloped away.

CHAPTER 8

Miles of rolling hills stretched out around Travis. Spiky, green yucca plants dotted the expanse of the golden prairie spread out beneath the blue sky. He breathed in the sweetness of sage as he led Wopila along the fence of the western pasture.

Natalia laughed as a black foal with a white diamond on his head chased the buckskin foal around the pasture. "Have you named them yet?"

"These are Cole's. Not sure what he's going to call them."

Her nose scrunched. "Would now be a good time to ask about Cole?"

"First Hank, now Cole. Is there anything you don't want to talk about?" He enjoyed being with Natalia, but she was getting a bit too nosey.

"I'm just trying to get to know you better."

"Why don't we talk about your family first?"

She pressed her lips together.

"Exactly." He kicked Wopila a bit too hard and she jumped before galloping off. Making sure he heard the thump of hooves behind him first, he gave her free rein to run until they crested a hill. At the top, he pulled back on the reins until she stopped, shaking her head and ruffling her mane. He stroked her soft neck. "Sorry, sweetheart. I didn't mean it." Wopila nickered.

Natalia trotted up beside him. "What's she saying?"

"That she loves me, of course." The filly nudged Dakota with her nose, and the accommodating gelding stepped out of range. "She doesn't like you getting too close to us."

"Does she really not like me?"

"It's not you. She gets jealous easily. She's putting Dakota in his place."

Travis turned his horse around to look at where they'd just been. "This is my favorite ridge. Take a look at that view." The red barn and yellow house stood out in front of the deep-green cottonwood trees surrounded by yellow-green grass.

Natalia turned Dakota around. "Wow. It's beautiful. And peaceful. I can see why you like to ride out here."

He rested his hands on the saddle horn as he enjoyed the view. "When I'm out here, it's easier to forget life's chaos."

They sat together in silence. The wind whispered through the grass, but Travis didn't feel the need to make conversation. Instead, he glanced at Natalia. Her blonde hair blew across her back. She smiled at him and his throat tightened. His hat looked good on her. "Ready to keep riding?"

"Sure."

"You lead."

"Really?"

He smiled. "Of course."

"Try to keep up." She grabbed the reins and pressed her heels into Dakota's side. The horse cantered down the other side of the hill.

With a quick nudge, Wopila overtook Dakota, and Travis led Natalia into a gully and along the dry creek bed. He kept a steady pace as they twisted around the bends and curves. Hooves pounded behind him. He leaned forward and spurred Wopila up another ridge. When he reached the top, he slowed to a walk. Dakota leapt onto the ledge.

Natalia's cheeks, tinged pink, could barely hold her smile. Her chest rose and fell with shallow breaths. "That was fun."

"Thought you'd enjoy it."

Her smile warmed him. He wouldn't mind making her smile again.

They traveled through a pasture and up a smaller hill covered in flat, circular cacti. Ahead of them, his log cabin, partially surrounded by trees, came into view. The green metal roof peaked above large triangular windows supported by diagonal, wooden beams. Pillars framed the steps leading to the deck that ran the length of the front. A swing hung in front of one of the matching windows that framed the door. Two rocking chairs and a low, glass end table sat beside the swing.

"That's a cute place."

"Thanks." Sampson ran to them, barking. The collie's long white chest and belly hair contrasted with the black hair on his head, back, and tail. "Hey, buddy."

Her eyes widened. "This is *your* place?"

"Don't look so surprised."

"It's beautiful. That's the most trees I've seen all day." She pointed to two maple saplings tethered to t-posts with rope. "Did you plant those recently?"

"I planted the maples last fall, but I planted the cottonwoods and a few apple and pear trees in the back throughout the last five years. The rest were planted by Hank's grandparents over a hundred years ago. That oak tree was planted probably eighty years ago." He pointed to his favorite tree to the southeast of his home. It stood close to seventy feet tall with a canopy of green leaves.

"What a legacy."

"It's why I chose to build here. Hank's parents built the farmhouse and outbuildings so they could be closer to town, but I like it out here."

When he reached the cabin, he slid off Wopila, helped Natalia dismount, and handed her Dakota's reins. They led the horses to the paddock beside his shed. After unsaddling them, Travis offered Natalia his arm, then led her down the stone path toward the log cabin. He stopped about ten feet from the porch. "Look through those windows." He pointed to the windows near the roof.

She tightened her grip on his arm. "I can see the trees on the other side."

"Pretty cool, huh? I designed it that way so I could always see trees."

"You designed it?"

"And built it, with the help of a few professionals."

"Impressive. Do I get a tour?"

"Of course." His boots thumped on the pine steps as he guided her onto the deck. His collie brushed up against her. Travis bent down to push the dog away. "Sampson, stop flirting. It's pathetic."

"Sampson?"

"The name suits him. Just look at all that glorious hair. He's really quite vain about it."

"What's your other dog's name?" She pointed to his blue heeler, still manning his post by the front door.

"Jeeves. He's a bit more serious and likes to sit by the door to greet visitors."

"This place is amazing." She ran her hand along the smooth logs of the house.

Travis pushed the swing. "I bought all the porch furniture from a local, Lakota rancher whose father crafted each piece."

He unlocked the oak door and held it open for her. She put his hat on his head when she passed, and the scent of apples wafted around him. "Even in the middle of the prairie I lock my door," he said.

She glanced around the living room and sighed. "Oh, wow. I love it."

Travis looked at his home. In addition to books, Native American art and pottery filled the floor-to-ceiling shelves along the left wall on both sides of a river-rock fireplace. A brown leather couch with metal studs on the armrests sat against the far wall and faced the picture window while a matching recliner sat perpendicular to it and faced the fireplace. A woven rug with arrows in varying shades of brown covered the wood floor. Not liking cramped spaces, he'd left plenty of room to walk around.

Natalia strode over to the worn rocking chair next to the picture window. She sat and rocked. The cadence of the creaks calmed his nerves.

She closed her eyes. "It's so comfortable. I could fall asleep."

"Not before lunch. As soon as we get this tour out of the way, we can make some food. I'm hungry."

She opened her eyes and smirked at him. "Now I know why you're being so sweet. You just want someone to make you lunch."

"Am I that readable?" Travis's stomach chose that moment to growl. "My stomach has a mind of its own." He held his hand out to her. "Come on. I'll show you my favorite part of the house. The kitchen."

"You promised me a tour." Natalia placed her slender hand in his. He liked how it felt so he held on to it after he pulled her up.

"It's not a big place. Only two bedrooms and a bathroom. I'll show you on our way to the kitchen."

****

Natalia spread horseradish sauce onto a piece of French bread, then placed several slices of roast beef on top.

Travis set a jar of applesauce on the counter. "I got this at the farmer's market."

She put a healthy helping of green beans onto her plate, then a dollop of applesauce, and followed Travis onto the front deck. Jeeves sat by the door as Sampson bolted toward them. Soft mooing surrounded them as Natalia sat in one of the rocking chairs. Travis put a glass of lemonade on the table beside her, then sat on the swing.

She took a big bite of her sandwich and sighed. "For a man who claims he can't cook, this is amazing roast beef." She sampled the green beans. "Wow."

Travis laughed. "I stole them from Cole's garden yesterday."

"Not Trooper Wilkins? Speaking of Cole, why don't you like to talk about him?"

"You're rather pushy."

"It's what makes me a good dispatcher."

"Point taken." He pushed the swing and rested one leg over his other knee with a glass in one hand and his sandwich in the other. "We were close when we were younger. Cole watched out for me. Every time my mom got paid, she'd binge-drink and we'd wake up to a house full of passed-out strangers and no food. Cole would drag me over to the neighbor lady's apartment where she'd feed us. But after child protection took us, things changed."

"How old were you?"

"Nine."

"What changed?"

"I hated the foster homes but Cole liked them. I guess he liked having heat and food and a safe place to live."

"Why did you hate them?"

"I missed my mom. I figured if I was rotten enough, they'd give me back to her, but when I acted out they just moved us to another home. Two days before we moved in with Hank, I stole my foster father's car and ran it into a tree. Cole gave me a shiner after the social worker came to tell us we were moving again."

"How old were you when you moved in with Hank?"

"Eleven. He was different than the others."

"How so?"

"Nothing I did could get him to call the social worker. Once I stole beer from the drunk neighbor and threw a party in his barn. Not sure how it happened, but the barn burned down. I thought for sure Hank would throw us out. Instead, he pulled up to the house with a trailer full of lumber and told me I'd be rebuilding their barn." Travis looked at his cabin. "That's how I learned construction."

"How old were you when you were adopted?"

"Thirteen."

"That must have made you happy."

"Not exactly. The night I found out, I ran away, stole Rosemary's car, and found my mom. She was doing what she did best. Drinking. Once she discovered I had cash, she took Rosemary's car on a beer run. She was drunk, but I went with her anyway. She hit a car full of teenagers and killed herself, her boyfriend, and two of the kids in the other car. I broke both my legs and a handful of ribs."

Natalia stomach knotted up. "I'm sorry, Travis."

He shrugged. "After I recovered, Hank adopted us."

"But if it worked out and you got adopted, why would Cole still be mad at you?"

"He wasn't. We actually got along for a while."

"Until?" Though she wasn't sure she wanted to hear more of his tragic story.

Travis set down his food and clasped his hands on his lap. "The summer we turned sixteen Cole got a girlfriend. The three of us hung out swimming, fishing, riding horses. That sort of thing. One night I saw her walking down the dirt road from our house. She was crying and had a split lip. Her dad hit her when she came home after curfew. She didn't want to see Cole, so I took her to Rosemary's instead. Apparently, she told her dad that we'd been sleeping together. The lie spread throughout the town like a wildfire, and Cole found out. The next morning, he attacked me. By the time Hank busted up the fight, we were both pretty bloody and bruised."

"Why would she lie about that?"

"Not sure. Rosemary was the only one who believed me. She thinks his girlfriend was trying to protect Cole from her father. I had such a bad reputation, I guess it was easy for people to believe her lie about me."

Sampson whined and put his head on Natalia's lap. She stroked his soft fur.

"Sorry you asked?" Travis picked up his sandwich and shoved it into his mouth.

How could he eat? Her stomach was rock hard. She and Mitch weren't as close as some siblings, but she couldn't imagine thinking he'd betrayed her for more than a decade. "Have you tried to talk to Cole about it since then?"

Travis shook his head. "We've managed a sort of truce in the

last few years, but I have no plans to drudge up old grievances."
He leaned forward. "You gonna finish that sandwich?"

She shook her head and held the plate out to him. "Thank you
for telling me about your past. I wish there was something I could
do to make things better."

"Don't worry about it, just don't go poking around in it. You
can't fix it. Please don't try."

Natalia nodded, but her chest ached. Now her complaints
about her childhood and pushy mom seemed petty. If Travis could
return to a place where everyone believed the worst about him,
maybe she could face the pain of her past. But would she be ready
to stop running and head home in three hours?

CHAPTER 9

Travis slowed his horse and waited for Natalia to catch up. They had ridden south of his home for the last quarter of an hour as they explored the property. He led her to a dirt road and pointed to a trail that veered off to the left. "This road leads to the cabin. Those tire tracks lead to my favorite fishing hole. Would you like to see it?"

She nodded.

He fidgeted in the saddle as he let Wopila lead the way. Why had he told Natalia about Hank and Cole? He didn't want her pity.

Grasshoppers popped up around them as the horses walked down the path. As they got closer to the aspens that surrounded the pond, the tail end of a camper peeked through the branches.

The hairs on his neck stood up. "That's strange."

"What?"

"I've never seen that camper. I doubt Cole would bring it up here. He hasn't been this far east in years. This is still our property, though, so I'm going to check it out. You stay here."

"I don't have a good feeling about this. Maybe we should call the police."

"I *am* the police. If I call it in, I'll just have to turn back around and check it out. I'll save myself the trip."

"At least then you could get your body armor."

"I'm trained for this, and I have my gun with me. Stay here so I won't worry about you."

He hopped out of the saddle and gave the reins to Natalia. Then he snuck near the camper. His heartbeat accelerated. He checked the windows, but all the curtains were drawn. At the door, he stopped. Something rustled inside.

He pounded on the door. "State trooper! Anyone in there?"

A child cried. Someone murmured.

He banged again. "State trooper! Slowly open the door."

The cries turned into a wail. He stepped back, giving himself the safest angle. Someone fumbled with the handle. When the door opened, the bawling intensified.

"With your hands raised and visible, slowly come out."

"I can't. I'm holding my baby." A woman's shaky voice rose above the howling.

"Who's in the camper with you?"

"It's just me and my son. He's only three. Please don't hurt us."

Travis unhooked the leather strap securing his Beretta and grabbed the handle. He didn't want to scare the woman, but he also needed to be ready. "Do you have any firearms or other weapons in there?"

"Yes. My husband's rifle is in the bedroom."

He had to get her away from it. "Slowly walk out where I can see you. Keep your hands visible."

A young woman poked her head out. Her chin quivered when her eyes locked onto his gun. She whispered to the child as she walked down the metal stairs.

Even with the woman's long hair pulled into a ponytail, Travis recognized Mary Russell. He looked at the toddler in her arms. Travis couldn't see the boy's face, but it had to be Marcus. Goosebumps covered his arms, and he relaxed his grip on the gun. "Where's your husband?"

"He went to town."

He approached the petite woman, and patted her for weapons. "Are you aware that you're on private property?"

She shook her head.

"I need you to sit on the ground. Keep your hands where I can see them. Can I search the camper?"

"Sure, I guess."

Travis climbed inside. The ceiling was so low he had to crouch. A few dishes sat drying in the tiny sink. A basket of toys sat on the floor. A coloring book and crayons covered the table beside a paperback novel.

Opening a narrow closet, he found only coats. He walked through the living area and pushed aside a crib. A bed filled the back room. He rummaged through a cabinet near the ceiling until he found the rifle, then he checked the narrow vanity in the bathroom. Baby soap, bath toys, and a little train toothbrush.

Finding no other weapons, he carried the rifle outside. Natalia stood near the camper with both horses. Her hands were on her hips as she watched the woman. The boy sat on Mary's lap sucking his thumb.

Travis knelt beside them. "Are you hurt?" The boy shook his head, then laid it on Mary's shoulder. "What's your name, ma'am?"

Tears ran down her face. "Mary Russell."

"And the boy? What's his name?"

"Marcus."

"Last name?"

"Elkhorn," she whispered.

Travis smiled as relief coursed through him. The search was finally over. "You all have been hard to find."

She hiccupped. "Please don't take my baby." Her arms tightened around Marcus.

"He's not your baby."

She hugged Marcus closer to her.

"Do you have an ID?"

She shook her head. "It's with my husband. In the pickup."

Travis stood and motioned Natalia closer.

She grabbed his arm. "They're the ones I saw at the store. You found the kidnapped boy?"

He nodded. "We'll have to celebrate later. Right now, I need your help. I don't have cell service out here. Leave Wopila with me, then follow the dirt road back to my cabin. There's a landline in the kitchen. Call dispatch, tell them we've found Marcus Elkhorn and his foster mom, and have backup sent to Old Settlers Road. Then go to the end of the road and wait for them."

Her eyes widened. "Yes, of course. I'll hurry." She handed Wopila's reins to him, then mounted Dakota. They took off as soon as she was seated.

Travis turned his attention back to Mary. He rubbed the back of his neck to relieve the tension, but he wouldn't be able to relax until the Russells were in jail and Marcus was safe.

Wopila stepped closer to him and whinnied. She stomped her hoof as she nudged him with her nose. "Hey there, princess. You need to be patient."

The toddler reached toward the horse. Mary pulled him away. "Don't get too close to its mouth. It might bite."

"Wopila is harmless. She'd only hurt a fly, and that's because they bother her." Her tail swished from side to side. "See, she's swatting them away."

Marcus giggled. He tried to squirm out of Mary's grasp. "I want to pet the horsey."

"Horses are dangerous. Sit still."

He settled down but watched as Wopila wandered to a patch of grass and chomped the tall weeds. Travis released the reins.

A diesel engine rumbled in the distance. Travis's muscles tensed. "Keep a tight grasp on the boy." He stood in front of Mary with his hand on his pistol and waited until the vehicle came into view. Mud caked the sides of a silver Ford pickup.

It stopped, and Travis drew his sidearm, making eye contact with the driver through the open driver's side window. "I'm Trooper Wilkins with the South Dakota State Patrol. Turn off the engine and throw the keys out of the truck. Then let me see your hands."

The driver complied.

"Slowly open the door and walk backwards to me."

The man exited the vehicle. His nostrils flared as his fists tightened. He wore a tan t-shirt, camouflage pants, and black tactical boots. His military attire couldn't mask the full beard and buzz cut. Travis Wilkins, the screwup from Alkaline, had found Caleb Russell.

"Hands on your head, then turn around and walk backward to me."

The vein in Caleb's forehead throbbed.

"Now!"

He pivoted, folding his fingers together and putting them on the back of his head. His pockets lay flat and his shirt was tucked into his pants. No weapons were visible. Travis exhaled.

The man inched his way closer to Travis. "Mary, are you and Marcus okay?"

"We're okay." Her voice shook. "I'm so sorry, Caleb."

"Please be quiet, Mrs. Russell. Just keep Marcus with you. Sir, what's your full name?"

"Caleb Ray Russell. Don't hurt my family. I'll do whatever you want."

****

Out of breath and covered in sweat, Natalia slid off Dakota Peace. She ran into Travis's house and dialed 9-1-1.

"Meade County Dispatch. What's your emergency?"

"Go ahead, Officer Mason."

"Shots fired!"

Natalia's heart skipped a beat. "All available units respond. Shots fired." She typed in his address. Who was available?

"SO 225 responding."

"HP 355 responding."

She dispatched medical. Two ambulances responded.

"Officer Mason, do you copy?"

No response.

"Officer down."

"No! Recheck him. He can't be down." Natalia squeezed her

mouthpiece.

"What's your emergency?" A voice broke through her fog.

Shaking, Natalia leaned her head against the cabinet. Her pulse beat in her ear. She took a deep breath and looked around. Travis's kitchen. Not the dispatch center.

"Do you have an emergency?" An annoyed voice spoke though the receiver.

"This is Natalia Brynner. Trooper Wilkins needs backup. He's on Old Settlers Road, east of Alkaline. Send a unit, hot. I'll meet an officer at the turnoff—"

"Please stay on the line. HP 352 is requesting backup on Old Settlers Road? What's the situation?"

"He's off duty, but he found the little boy who was kidnapped. Marcus Elkhorn. He's holding the foster mom."

"Is anyone hurt?"

"Not when I left him."

"I have units responding. I'll need you to stay on the line until they arrive."

"I can't. I'm not at the scene. I need to meet the officers so they know where to turn. Travis—Trooper Wilkins—wants me at the turnoff."

"Is there a cell number where you can be reached?"

"I won't have service. Please hurry." Natalia slammed the receiver onto its cradle, ran for Dakota, and prayed they'd arrive before it was too late.

CHAPTER 10

"Where are your IDs?" Travis stood in front of Caleb who sat next to Mary in the dirt.

"My wallet is in the glove box and Mary's purse is on the passenger side floor."

Travis retrieved their licenses and put them in his pocket. Then he paced along the trail in front of them. Marcus cuddled in Mary's arms with his head against her shoulder.

Travis's chest tightened. The situation could get difficult when he had to separate Marcus from Mary. These weren't the first parents he'd had to arrest with children watching him.

The sun beat down on them as the seconds ticked by. He glanced at his watch. Only twenty minutes had passed since he sent Natalia for help. He hated waiting. If he had his radio, he'd know how far away backup was.

"Gashopper!" Marcus tried to jump out of Mary's arms.

"Sit still." She pulled him to her lap and hugged him.

Sweat dampened the boy's black hair. Travis took his hat off and put it on the boy's head. "Now you're a cowboy."

Marcus took the hat off, crushed the top, and put it back on with a smile.

Tires crunched over the dirt. Travis turned around as a white patrol car with the Meade County Sheriff's logo careened around the bend. His shoulders relaxed. The Charger skidded to a stop, spraying Marcus and the Russells with pebbles. A burly deputy climbed from his car and strode toward them.

"I'm Trooper Wilkins." Travis pulled out his law enforcement ID and the Russells' licenses. "Caleb and Mary Russell are under arrest for the kidnapping of Marcus Elkhorn. You can handcuff them."

The deputy nodded and handed Travis his ID back, then placed the other two in his pocket. He stepped over to Caleb as he pulled out his cuffs. "Hands behind your back." The deputy clicked the cuffs around his wrists and led him to the patrol car.

That left Mary. Travis knelt close to where she sat with Marcus.

"Where Daddy go? I want my daddy!"

Travis took a deep breath. "Mrs. Russell. Please make this easy on Marcus."

She nodded. "What do you want me to do?"

"Gently hand him to me."

She pushed Marcus away, but he clung to her shoulders. She tried to pry his fingers from her shirt. When he squealed, she sagged. "I can't do this."

Bile coated Travis's throat. He dreaded having to take Marcus by force, but he didn't have a choice.

"Is there anything I can do to help?"

He looked over his shoulder at the sound of Natalia's voice. She stood with Dakota a few feet from the patrol car. The perfect distraction. He motioned her over.

When she was close, Dakota licked the toddler's cheek. Marcus giggled and reached for the gelding. Dakota licked him again. Mary leaned away, but Marcus scrambled to his feet. "Horsey!" He danced around. Mary reached for him, but Travis pushed her hand back.

"Hey, buddy. Do you want to go on a horseback ride?" he asked.

"Yes! Horsey ride!"

"Give your momma a hug, then my friend Natalia will take you on a ride."

Marcus's chubby arms wrapped around Mary's neck. She glanced at Travis. "Thank you."

Natalia mounted Dakota. Travis picked up the toddler and set him in front of her. Marcus waved at Mary.

"I love you, baby."

As soon as Natalia turned Dakota toward Travis's house, the tightness in his chest eased.

Mary sobbed.

"Are you ready for me to take her?" The deputy returned with another pair of handcuffs.

Travis hauled Mary to her feet. "It's time to take you in."

"Where?"

"You're under arrest for abducting Marcus. The officer will take you to the jail." After the deputy handcuffed her, Travis opened the car door and guided her onto the seat.

"Promise you'll take care of him," she said.

"He's safe now." Travis slammed the door. *And you're going to jail where you belong.*

The deputy slapped his back. "Looks like we get to be the heroes."

"I'm just glad the boy's safe. Contact dispatch and Child Protection Services, then have Detective Astor join me at my house. It's the cabin at the end of Old Settlers Road."

The deputy nodded.

Travis mounted Wopila and headed home.

****

Natalia brushed the hair from Marcus's brow as he slept on Travis's bed. How could the three-year-old ever process the day's events?

One dog howled. Then both of them. Afraid they would wake Marcus, Natalia slipped out of the room to quiet them.

Outside, Travis said something to the dogs and the barking ceased. The front door opened, and he entered the house with a petite woman barely old enough to be out of high school. The woman's cropped black hair shone in the sunlight. Her plaid suit coat and skirt and large, black purse implied professionalism. Meanwhile, dirt covered Travis's jeans, sweat darkened his shirt, and his hair stuck out in six directions. He acknowledged Natalia with a lift of his chin.

"Hi, I'm Margo, the Pennington County case worker sent to check on Marcus Elkhorn." She held out the ID badge that hung from her neck.

"I'm Natalia Brynner. Marcus just fell asleep. Do you need me to wake him?"

"You don't have to wake him yet, but I do need to look in on him."

"I'm going to clean up a bit, then grab us some ice water." Travis headed for the kitchen.

Natalia led Margo to the bedroom where Marcus slept. The case worker nodded once, then motioned back to the living room.

Once they were seated on the plump couch, Margo took a binder out of her purse. "He looks like he's doing fine considering the day he's had. The detective from the Rapid City Police Department is on his way. We'll let Marcus sleep until he gets here. They wanted me to do a welfare check on the child as soon as possible. As far as health goes, does he need medical attention?"

Natalia shook her head. "He seems to be healthy."

Margo sighed. "Thank goodness. I've been out of my mind envisioning the worst."

Travis walked into the room with two glasses of water. He handed one to Natalia and set one on the table next to Margo. The dogs barked again. Travis answered the door and led Detective Astor into the living room. "Do you want a drink, detective?"

He shook his head. "I need to see Marcus."

Margo jumped to her feet and spun around. "Drew. I can show you, but he's sleeping."

Travis sat beside Natalia and grabbed her hand. "Are you okay?"

"Exhausted, but so happy that Marcus is safe. I hope he'll be okay."

Margo and Detective Astor returned. He sat in the recliner and pulled a spiral notebook from his pocket as he looked at Travis. "Tell me what happened." While the detective took notes, Margo pulled out a computer and typed away.

Travis wrapped up his story as Margo's phone rang. "Hello … He's good … You can't? I'll take him to the office for now. Call me when you find someone."

Natalia's body tensed at the tone of Margo's voice. "Is there a problem?"

"That was our placement worker. She's having trouble finding a foster home for Marcus."

"What are you going to do?"

"I've been doing this for three years, and we always manage to find homes for our kiddos. Eventually."

"And if you don't?" Travis walked to the picture window. He ran a hand over the back of his neck "Will you send him to a group home?"

Margo frowned. "That, of course, would be the last option."

Travis turned from the window and faced Natalia. "What about you?"

"Me? What can I do?" With the sunshine behind him it was hard to see his expression. Was he serious?

"You're a licensed foster parent."

Margo smiled. "Are you really?"

"In Minnehaha County, and only for respite care. I've taken care of my brother's foster kids before, but only for two days. I haven't got a clue how to help Marcus process the trauma of losing the only parents he's ever known."

"We can provide a counselor." Margo's eyes sparkled.

Natalia leaned against the couch. Her boss expected her at work tomorrow. If she stayed to help Marcus, she'd lose her job. But what if Marcus ended up in a group home? This was her chance to help someone she could see and touch, not just a voice on the other end of a call. "How long would you need me?"

"They've already started looking for a long-term placement. Maybe a week."

Natalia tried to run through the details in her mind. "I'll have to ask Rosemary if I can keep working for her, but I'd still have to find a babysitter for him while I'm there."

"Is there a licensed daycare in Alkaline?" Margo looked at Travis.

He shook his head. "Not that I know of, but I can help. I have some vacation days saved up. I'll take time off if I need to."

With Travis's help, it could work. "I need to talk to Rosemary first." Natalia walked to the kitchen for some privacy.

"Prickly Pear Bistro, this is Rosemary."

"It's Natalia."

"I hope you didn't leave town without stopping to say goodbye."

"I haven't left yet. Something came up." Rosemary listened while Natalia told her the whole, crazy story. "Is it okay to move things out of the apartment to make room for Marcus?"

"Of course." Rosemary clucked her tongue. "Oh dear. I wish I hadn't been such a lazy bird and cleaned out the apartment already. You can move out whatever you need, but we'll have to find a place to store it. I have a couple of sets of sheets at my house that I can bring over."

"Can I keep working for you until they find a place for Marcus?"

"I'll take you as long as I can get you, love."

"Thanks. Travis said he'd watch Marcus when he can, but do you know anyone else who can help when he has to work?"

"My pastor's daughter, Hannah, might be able to. I'll call her."

"Thanks, Rosemary." Natalia ended the call, then scrolled through her contacts until she found Hayden. Her finger twitched over his name. It didn't matter if she called him now or later, she'd still lose her job. She'd call later. Stuffing her phone back into her pocket, she returned to the living room and sat beside Travis. "Okay. I'll take him."

Margo sagged into her seat. "Oh, thank you. Who's your licensing worker? We'll need to get in touch with her. Then I'll have to do a home safety inspection." She shoved her computer into her briefcase as she looked around the room. "This is a lovely house. I doubt you'll need to make too many changes."

Shocked, Natalia shook her head. "This isn't my home. I don't live here." She looked at Travis for help, but he simply smiled.

Margo looked between them. "I'm sorry. I assumed …"

Natalia shifted away from Travis. "We're friends."

He chuckled.

"My place is in town, but it's going to take some time to get it ready for a toddler. The spare room is being used for storage."

"I can store what you don't need in my trailer," Travis said.

"Great. I'll call my supervisor." Margo walked to the window to make her call.

Detective Astor rose and shook Natalia's hand. "Thanks for stepping up. If you need anything, please call."

As Travis walked him to the door, Natalia's mind whirled. What if she couldn't give Marcus what he needed? What if he hated her, or worse, ended up scarred for life because of her? She rubbed her temples. What if she went insane with worry and turned into her mother? A moan rumbled in her throat.

When he returned, Travis sat beside her and grabbed her hand. "How are you doing?"

"I'm scared."

"I think you're brave," he whispered.

"I don't feel brave. What if I hurt him more?"

He squeezed her fingers. "That's not going to happen."

"I'm sitting here because I ran away from a stressful situation and ended up in the middle of an even crazier one."

"Your foster care training will kick in and you'll figure it out. And I'll help. I know the circumstances aren't great, but I'm happy you're staying a while longer."

"You are?" Her stomach fluttered.

He nodded.

"Mommy?" Marcus's soft voice broke her heart. Natalia rushed into the bedroom. Marcus sat on the bed looking around the room. "Where's Mommy?"

She sat beside him and patted his leg, afraid she'd say the wrong thing. Should she blurt out the bad news like she did with adults or soften the blow? He had no idea who she was. Would it be better if his case worker told him? "Do you remember Margo?"

He nodded.

"She's here. Let's go see her." She helped him down from the bed and held his hand. Feeling like a coward, she led him into the living room.

"Marcus." Margo walked over and laid her hand on his head. "It's good to see you."

He held his hands up to her. "I want Mommy. You take me to Mommy?"

Margo carried him to the rocking chair. "Mary." She cleared her throat. "Mary made some bad choices. She took you away from me and that worried me. I want you to be safe."

"I see Mommy?"

She shook her head. "You can't see Mary, but you're going to live with my friend, Natalia." She motioned for Natalia to come closer.

"You can call me Nattie."

Travis walked over and knelt beside Marcus. "Did you like your horsey ride?" Marcus turned his head into Margo and pushed Travis away.

Margo silently mouthed, "Sorry."

Travis nodded once, then walked to the foyer.

Natalia followed him. "Are you okay?"

"I'm the bad guy who made his mom cry and scared his dad." He pinched his nose. "I hope he'll be able to forgive me."

"Give him some time." She wrapped her arms around her stomach and admired how fine he looked even when he frowned. "You were amazing today."

"Just doing my job." He leaned toward her. "So, do I get to call you Nattie too?"

"If you want." She couldn't deny him that small request. He was adorable. And kind. And helpful. The desire to kiss him simmered. Grateful he couldn't read her mind, she looked away.

"I'll take the horses back to the barn, then grab the trailer. I'll meet you at the apartment if you want to ride with Margo and Marcus. Will you lock up before you leave?"

"Of course. A lawman once told me that locking your doors is a smart habit."

He chuckled. "Was that just this morning? What a day." He kissed her cheek, then grabbed his dusty, black Stetson, and whistled as he left.

Her heart lurched. If a peck on the cheek caused that much pleasure, what would a real kiss do to her?

The excitement of the day left Travis exhausted as he led both horses into the barn. He was relieved Marcus was safe, but a whole new set of worries weighed on him. Had he made a mistake talking Nattie into caring for the boy? *Nattie.* The nickname suited her. He hoped she wouldn't regret getting involved.

Cole stepped out of a stall and took Dakota's lead. "You've lost a rider."

Travis uncinched Wopila's saddle. "Checking up on me?"

"Maybe. I saw you ride in without Natalia. Where is she?"

"We ran into a bit of excitement."

"Is she okay?"

"She's fine. We found the boy who was kidnapped. She's taking him to her place."

"Is he okay?"

"He's fine." They unsaddled the horses and put up the tack in silence. Travis wouldn't have asked Cole for help, but he wasn't going to refuse it either. He could get to Nattie's in half the time thanks to his brother. In the tack room, Travis grabbed a couple of curly combs and handed one to Cole. "Since you're here, will you help me hook up the horse trailer after we're done?"

"Why do you need the trailer?" Cole asked as they returned to the horses.

"We're moving Rosemary's stuff out of the apartment to make room for the boy." Dust swirled around as Travis combed Wopila's coat.

"Why doesn't he go with his parents?"

"He's in the system, and the foster parents kidnapped him.

Have you been in a hole this week? It's been all over the news."

Cole's eyes widened. "*That* boy? That's crazy. Glad he's safe."

"Me too."

They worked quickly and silently. After they finished, Cole helped Travis hook the horse trailer up to his truck. Travis double-checked the trailer hitch and lights, then slipped back into the driver's seat. The passenger door opened and Cole jumped in.

"What are you doing?" Travis asked.

"Thought I'd come help."

"Suit yourself." Unease filled him. What was Cole up to acting helpful for the first time in years?

When they pulled up to the apartment, boxes and furniture lined the back wall of the bistro. One of the retirees carried a large box out the back door. Travis parked along the curb, backing the trailer to the door as closely as he could.

Cole hopped out before Travis shut off the truck. By the time he made it to the back of the trailer, Nattie had appeared with Marcus propped on her hip. She walked to Travis and smiled. "Isn't this great? Rosemary called some people to help clear out the room." Marcus laid his head on her shoulder.

"He seems comfortable with you." He hoped that was a good sign, that the adjustment would be easy for them.

"He's pretty clingy."

"Is that a good thing?"

"I wish I knew." She patted his back.

Cole sauntered toward them. "Travis told me about your exciting ride. I thought you could use some help, but it looks like the whole town showed up." Three retirees loaded boxes into the trailer while two cowhands carried a dresser over.

"Excuse me."

Travis pulled Nattie out of the way as Rosemary's pastor stepped outside with another box.

"Is that everything?" she asked him.

"Only things left in that bedroom are a dresser, the twin bed, and a rocking chair."

"Thanks so much. I owe you all."

Travis left Nattie by the door to help load the trailer. He only had to carry one armload before everyone else had the trailer full, so he shut and latched the doors as Rosemary poked her head out of the bistro's back door.

"Free coffee and pie for all you hard workers."

Everyone filed into the building.

She winked at him. "If you don't hurry, there won't be any lemon meringue left."

He looked around for a familiar head of blonde hair. "Do you know where Nattie is?"

"She's in here waiting for Hannah."

"Let her know I'm taking the trailer home. It'll be out at the ranch if you need anything."

"Hurry back, because I'm saving you some pie."

He hated leaving Nattie without saying goodbye, but too much of the day reminded him of his own childhood. The crowded bistro, full of people who'd seen him at his worst, was the last place he wanted to be.

* * * * * * *

Natalia held Marcus's hand as they approached the counter. Rosemary stood next to a brunette woman with light-pink glasses.

"Natalia. I'd like you to meet Hannah. She has some extra clothes and toys for Marcus."

"It's a pleasure to meet you." The women smiled at each other. "I hope these will work." Hannah lifted a large, black tote to the counter and opened it. Small, colorful clothes filled one side of the box. Stuffed animals filled the other.

"This is amazing. We were able to get some of Marcus's things from the camper, but there wasn't much." Natalia helped Marcus stand on a stool, anchoring him with her arm. "Hey, buddy. I see a dinosaur in there that could use a friend. Do you want him?" He nodded. She pulled out a two-foot long stuffed toy. He grabbed it and crushed it to his chest. "I think he likes it. Thanks so much."

"It's no big deal. You can keep everything or send it with Marcus when he goes to a permanent home. I put my contact info in there because Rosemary said you might need a sitter, but you're welcome to call if you just need a friend too."

"You've got a deal." In her peripheral, Natalia noticed someone waving from the other side of the dining room. She glanced over and spotted Margo motioning for her. "I wish I could stay and chat, but I need to meet with Marcus's caseworker."

"No problem. You've got my number if you need anything." Hannah put the lid back on the tote.

"You can leave that right there," Rosemary said. "I'll have someone carry it up so it's out of the way."

Marcus bent over and tried to grab the pie from the cowboy next to them.

"That's not yours." Natalia pulled him away.

"I've got an extra piece of chocolate silk pie if he wants to hang out with me," Rosemary said.

"I'm not sure if he'll stay with you. He's been attached to me since we left Travis's house." Natalia helped Marcus sit on the stool. "Would you like to stay with Rosemary and have some pie?"

Rosemary set a sliver of dessert in front of him. He gripped the spoon and shoved a scoop of chocolate filling into his mouth. She laughed. "I guess that settles it."

"Thanks for watching him." Natalia strode over to Margo and slipped into the booth across from her.

She glanced up from her computer. "I'm just finishing up the placement agreement. Then I'll look at the apartment."

"I still need to run to the hardware store to get outlet covers."

"That won't be a problem. Before we go upstairs, do you have any questions for me?"

A million, but Natalia didn't think Margo had the time to answer all of them. "I'd like to know a little more about Marcus.

Where are his parents?"

"His father's serving fifteen years for armed robbery and assault, and his mother died shortly after giving birth."

"The Russells took him as an infant?"

Margo nodded.

"Can you tell me what the long-term plan is?"

"We're looking for an adoptive family."

"Will it be hard to find one?"

"It might be because he's Native American."

"But that will only take a week, right?"

"I hope so."

"What if you haven't found a place for him by next week?"

Margo snapped her laptop shut. "We're looking for a long-term placement at the same time. Something should open up by then."

Natalia wished she had Margo's confidence. If they couldn't find something and Marcus ended up in a group home, she'd be giving up her job for nothing.

****

That night, Natalia's nerves fluttered as she dressed Marcus in his pajamas and helped him brush his teeth. What if he was afraid of the dark? She should have picked up a nightlight at the hardware store.

She led him to his bed, then pulled the blankets over him and his dinosaur before kissing his forehead. "Goodnight."

"Night." He curled onto his side.

She turned off the light and shut the door. That was easy. Maybe now she could call Travis and finally thank him for all of his help throughout the day.

"Mommy!"

Natalia opened the door, splashing the hallway light across Marcus's face. "What do you need?"

"I want Mommy!" He started to cry.

Fear paralyzed her. She had no idea how to help him.

"Sweetheart, don't cry." She rushed to his side and knelt beside him. "Close your eyes. I'll stay until you fall asleep. Okay?" His crying turned to sniffles. He nodded.

She stroked his head and softly sang the only song that came to her mind—John Legend's "All of Me." Marcus didn't seem to mind. His breaths deepened as she rested her head on the mattress.

Her phone vibrated in her pocket, waking Natalia. She sat up and looked around. She was still on the floor next to Marcus's bed. Ignoring her stiff back, she pulled the blanket over him again, then snuck out of the room.

She glanced at the caller ID. Hayden. Her stomach tightened. She sat on the recliner and called him back.

"You were supposed to call."

She winced. "I know, but something's come up and I won't be able to make it to work tomorrow."

"This isn't like you. What happened?"

"I'm fostering a little boy. It's only for a week."

"It doesn't matter if it's only for a day. You've given me no choice. I'm going to have to let you go."

"I know."

"I'm sorry, Natalia."

Her chest tightened. "It's okay."

Hayden hung up.

That settled it. She was no longer a dispatcher. She couldn't tell how she felt about that. She'd left those responsibilities behind, but a whole new set slept in her guest room. Travis had offered to help with Marcus, though. At the memory of his dark eyes, warmth spread through her limbs. Maybe things weren't so bad after all.

She glanced at the clock. It was only nine but she was exhausted. After changing into a t-shirt and running shorts, she slipped into the cool sheets and scrolled through Facebook, stopping to read the press release about Marcus from the highway patrol. The comments were full of well wishes and prayers for him.

Her phone rang. *Mom.* How could she have forgotten to call

her parents? "Hello."

"Where are you?"

"I'm still in Alkaline."

"You said you were leaving at three."

"I ran into some trouble."

"Are you okay?" Her mother's voice pitched.

"Yes, I'm good. Did you watch the news tonight? They found a little boy who'd been kidnapped."

Mom sighed. "I saw that. What does that have to do with you?"

"I was with the trooper who found him, and now I'm fostering him."

"Have you lost your mind? You don't even live there."

"They were going to send him to a group home. He's only three."

Mom clicked her tongue. "I knew getting your fostering license was a bad idea."

"How can you say that? You supported Mitch and Judy when they did it."

"They're married. These kids need a mom and a dad."

"I'm all he has right now. I don't expect you to understand." Natalia yawned. "I need to get some rest. I know you don't approve, but would you at least overnight some of my stuff?"

She huffed. "Text your father what you want. You have him wrapped around your finger anyway." Her mother hung up.

There was no making that woman happy. At least Natalia had bought herself an extra week away. If she could find a place in Alkaline that didn't have cell service, she wouldn't have to avoid any more phone calls while she was there.

Travis's house didn't have cell service. She closed her eyes and pictured the cozy, peaceful cabin. She could sit in front of the fire, snuggled against him, without a single worry.

****

Travis searched the bookshelf until he found *Buffalo Woman*. On the cover, buffalo kicked up yellow dust around a Native American man, woman, and child dressed in traditional clothes. With the book tucked under his arm, he strode onto the porch. The dogs followed him out and lay next to the door.

The insects' chorus battled with the beating of his heart. In the light of the full moon, a barn owl swooped down over the prairie.

He sat in a rocking chair under the dim light and flipped through the pages he'd read so many times that he knew the story by heart. A great hunter who loved a beautiful woman from the Buffalo Nation. They married and had a son, but she fled with the boy because they were unwanted among his people. The hunter searched for them, but they had turned back into buffalo. The hunter loved them so much he was willing to die for them. In the end, he won the respect of the Buffalo Nation, and they made him a buffalo too.

He and Cole used to pretend to be the great hunter, although they never found the beautiful woman. Maybe this time Travis had.

Jeeves barked. Travis stood, dropping the book onto the glass table and reaching for his gun. His fingers skimmed his empty belt. A figure approached. Jeeves growled.

"Who's there?"

"It's only me." Cole stepped into the light and held his hands up as he climbed the stairs.

Jeeves ran to Cole and sniffed his leg. Cole let the dog lick his hand before petting him.

"What are you doing here?" Travis sank to the chair and rested his ankle on his knee. He hoped his posture gave the impression he was relaxed even though anxiety coursed through him.

"Wanted to know how Natalia and the boy were doing."

"Could've called." Five years he'd lived here, and Cole had never visited. What did he really want?

"Stopping by annoys you more." He sat on the swing and pointed at the table. "Reading children's books now?"

"I wanted to give it to Marcus. Unci used to read it to us when we visited."

"Yeah, after she fed us. She's the reason we're alive."

Travis nodded. They owed her a debt they could never repay.

"Looks like Natalia's going to be sticking around a bit longer."

Travis shrugged. "Guess so."

"Are you two dating?"

The hair on his arms stood up. "I just met her a few days ago."

"So? Are you dating her?"

"That's none of your business."

"Hey, I'm trying to do the honorable thing and find out if you're interested in her before I ask her out. Would hate to steal her from you. That's your MO."

"What's that supposed to mean? I've never stolen a girl from you."

Cole snorted. "Audrey."

"That was ten years ago, and nothing happened."

"That's not what she said."

"And, of course, you believe her over me. After all we've been through, why would I betray you like that?"

"Why don't you tell me?" Cole stood and stared him down. Nothing Travis could say would change his brother's mind. It hadn't a decade ago, why would it work now?

"I guess that means Natalia's fair game then." Cole stomped off, his boots thumping on the wooden stairs. The grass rustled as he charged away.

The old anger simmered. It hurt that the entire town believed Audrey over Travis, but Cole's unbelief wounded him far deeper.

CHAPTER 12

Caleb Russell twisted open a bottle of Budweiser and took a swig. The bitter fizz soothed his aching throat. His body relaxed into his worn recliner in the living room of his four-bedroom, split-level home. Pictures of him, Mary, and Marcus dotted the wall next to him. Taking them down would probably help Mary, but he couldn't do it. He couldn't admit Marcus was gone.

He turned on the flat screen TV to drown out Mary's cries, but he couldn't focus on the programs. The shower turned on, muffling her sobs. Twenty minutes later, his wife, wrapped in a robe and her hair twisted in a towel, appeared. Her hollow gaze locked with his, and pain shot through his chest.

He rose on shaky legs and followed her into the bedroom. "I'll fix this, Mary. I promise."

She lay on the bed with her back to him. "How?"

"I'll figure out a plan."

"Like the last one?"

"It wasn't a bad idea. It just took too long to sell my truck. We should have left the area sooner." He leaned against the doorjamb. "I'll get Marcus back, I promise."

Her body shook.

"Please, Mary. Don't start crying again. I can't take it. The last time, when that dumb social worker told us she was looking for another home for Marcus, you cried for weeks. It about killed me."

"I want my baby back." Her weak voice pierced his heart.

"I'll find a way. Don't give up. We'll get him back." Caleb shuffled back into the living room and fell into his chair. His heart couldn't stand to hear Mary's cries, but the alcohol wasn't enough anymore. He pulled his cell phone out and dialed a number he knew better than his own.

"Caleb, old buddy, whatcha need?" his high school friend asked. "Your usual?"

His fingers shook. "Not pot. I need something stronger."

"Crystal?"

"Yeah."

"Thought ya gave it up at your bachelor party."

"Things have changed. Also, I need information. Do you know anyone who works at Child Protection Services?"

"Maybe. If you're willing to pay."

"Of course. I'd like to know where they've placed Marcus Elkhorn."

"I can get the address by tomorrow, but it's going to take a few days to get the rest. I'll text you the meet location and price."

"Fine." He hung up and grabbed the last beer in the case. The lukewarm bottle shook in his hand as he held it to his lips. The now-tasteless alcohol slid down his throat and numbed his mind. He let the empty bottle slip from his fingers as he laid his head back. The room spun even after he closed his eyes.

When he pried his eyelids open, light streamed into the living room. His head pounded. Six empty bottles surrounded him. He hadn't consumed that much alcohol since his wedding five years ago. His stomach protested, so he closed his eyes and allowed the nausea to settle.

"Look what I found." Excitement filled Mary's voice. He forced an eye open and found her beside him, a blue blob in her arms.

"What's that?"

"It's Beary Bear. Marcus lost it weeks ago, and I found it under some dirty laundry." She hugged the toy close. "Can you take it to him?"

"I don't know where he is."

Her face crumpled. "He'll be scared without Beary Bear."

Caleb ran a hand over his hair. That little boy needed his

mommy. "I'll find him, and I'll make sure he gets it." And he didn't care who got hurt in the process.

CHAPTER 13

The few customers Natalia had were enjoying their meals as she drummed her fingers on the counter and waited for Hannah to answer the phone. Cole sat a few seats down from her eating a caramel roll. He met her gaze and winked. She smiled.

"Hello?"

"Hannah, it's Natalia."

"Hi. How are things going?"

Natalia stifled a yawn. "We're both still adjusting to each other. Are you free to watch Marcus tomorrow morning to mid-afternoon? Travis couldn't get out of work tonight, and I don't think he should be watching a toddler with only three hours of sleep."

"I wish I could, but I have a dentist appointment tomorrow. Is there another day you need help?"

"Would Friday work?"

"It sure will. Text me the time and I'll be there."

"Thanks." Natalia ended the call and looked at the table of retirees. Marcus sat with them eating pancakes. Maybe she could bring him to work again tomorrow.

He grabbed the salt shaker, twisted off the cap, and dumped the entire contents onto his plate. The old ranchers next to him kept on talking to each other.

Or maybe not.

She scurried over and swooped Marcus into her arms. He squealed as he reached for his plate. "You're done." He whined and wiggled as she carried him to the counter and set him on a stool. "Here." She opened a cartoon on her phone and handed it to him.

With his attention glued to the screen, she sagged onto the stool beside him and laid her head in her hands. Clearly bringing him to work wasn't a great option.

"You've got your hands full."

She looked up. Cole stood beside her.

"I'm sorry." Natalia jumped up, straightening her apron. "Can I get you anything? A refill?"

"No, I'm good. Are you okay?"

"It was a long night. Marcus woke up five times."

"That's worse than calving season."

"Now I'm having trouble finding someone to babysit him tomorrow. Rosemary was kind enough to let him hang out here today, but we can't do this again. Do you know anyone who might be available?"

"I could watch him." A half smile revealed one dimple.

"Don't you have to work?"

"There's always work on a ranch, but you've caught me between harvest and branding. Marcus can tag along with me. It'll be fun."

"Marcus is very active. Do you have much experience with kids?"

He lifted an eyebrow. "As much as Travis."

She rubbed her itchy eyes. He had a point, and what other choice did she have? "Thanks, Cole. Can I drop him off around six thirty?"

"Works for me."

"Bailing me out is becoming a habit of yours."

He handed her a twenty. "And it's becoming my pleasure." This time, a full smile and double dimples filled his handsome face.

She rang up his coffee and roll, then held out his change.

"Keep it. See you tomorrow." He winked before strolling out the door.

****

Natalia finished loading the commercial dishwasher and turned it on, then she started another pot of coffee. The clock on the bistro's kitchen wall showed ten forty-five. Lunch customers would start trickling in anytime. The scent of meatballs simmering in tomato sauce reached her and her stomach growled. She had been too busy chasing Marcus to eat breakfast.

She peeked into the dining room. He sat at a booth coloring a stack of paper menus. With his attention elsewhere, she picked up a tray of salt shakers and slipped back into the kitchen to fill them.

Rosemary put a pan of bread into the oven. "You look like you're about to fall over." She stepped beside her and tightened a shaker lid. "Why don't you quit early and you can both take a nap?"

"I'd hate to leave you without help."

"Tuesdays aren't busy, and there's not much cooking on my schedule, with meatball subs as the lunch special and spaghetti with meatballs for dinner. That frees me to help in the dining room."

"That would be amazing. Margo is coming at one for her twenty-four-hour home visit and the place is a mess."

"I'll box up some chicken strips and fries for you to take with you. Go collect Marcus."

Natalia placed the full shakers on a tray. "Thanks." She delivered the salt to the tables, then walked over to Marcus. Black crayon marks covered the white table top.

Her face heated. "I thought you were drawing on the paper." She banged the tray onto the table. Marcus jumped. "Look at this mess." She collected the crayons, then crawled under the table and picked up the torn pieces of paper. She should have known his quiet playing was a façade. Tears threatened her tired eyes.

"Natalia. Come on out from there." Rosemary's soft voice sounded behind her.

"No. I'm staying here. Maybe for—" Emotion clogged her throat.

"Come on. You're tired and stressed. I'll clean his mess while you take Marcus home. Don't even worry about straightening the apartment. I'm sure that social worker has seen far worse places."

Natalia scooted out and held up her handful of trash. With Rosemary's help, she stood, then dropped her mess onto an empty tray. "I'm sorry about the table," she said. "I'm a sorry excuse for a foster parent. I can't even handle one toddler."

"I remember those days, trying to parent with little sleep. And your situation is extra stressful. Go rest. Your lunch is on the counter."

Natalia nodded and grabbed Marcus's hand, gently pulling him from the booth. "Tell Miss Rosemary sorry for making a mess."

His upper lip stuck out. "Sorry, Miss Rosie."

Rosemary ruffled his black hair. "You're forgiven. You listen to Nattie, okay? I put a special treat in the bag for you. You can have it after you take a nice long nap."

His eyes widened and he nodded.

"From your lips to God's ears." Natalia gave Marcus a tug, but he went limp.

"I want Rosie!"

Pain split through Natalia's head as she hefted him onto her hip. "If you keep this up, I'll eat your treat." Probably not the best parenting technique, but it stopped his whining.

She grabbed their lunches, left the bistro through the back door, and trudged up the stairs.

****

Natalia handed Margo a glass of water and escorted her to the living room. They sat on the plush furniture while Marcus sat at the kitchen table eating the cookie Rosemary had given him. The nap had refreshed them both.

"He's adjusting well." Margo placed the glass on the table and pulled out her computer. "I have to admit I was a bit worried he'd cause you problems."

"Why's that?"

"Mary spoiled him a bit."

"We've had some struggles. He woke up quite a few times last night crying for his mom."

"That's understandable."

"You mentioned counseling before. Is that still a possibility?"

"Yes, of course. I'm working on getting him in for play therapy. Appointments for most places are scheduled two weeks to a month out."

"Two weeks? But he's only supposed to be with me a week." Poor thing had to suffer an ill-equipped caregiver with no extra help.

"About that. We've run into an issue finding him a long-term placement. We have a family interested in adopting him, but they're out of state and we don't want to move him to a home just to move him again in a few weeks. We always try to keep the placements at a minimum. It's better for the children."

Natalia's muscles tightened. "But this is a temporary arrangement. I have responsibilities back in Sioux Falls. I can't keep him indefinitely. How much longer were you thinking?"

"Hopefully only another week."

Another week without sleep? Her throat tightened as anxiety rushed through her. "I'm already having problems finding sitters for him. I can't expect people to keep helping for free."

"I'll email you a list of state-licensed providers. There should be one close." She typed away on her computer.

Marcus hopped off his chair and disappeared into his room. Natalia was about to check on him when he ran back into the living room with his dinosaur under one arm and a book under the other.

"What have you got there?" Margo set her computer on the table and lifted him to her lap. "Firefighters?" She opened the book and started reading.

Natalia should offer to read to him so Margo could work, but she didn't want to reignite Marcus's clinginess. It had only been one day and she wanted to quit. Could she make it two weeks?

CHAPTER 14

The next morning, Natalia pulled up to Cole's house at six thirty sharp. Dew clung to the grass and sparkled in the morning light. She stepped out of the car and opened the back door. Marcus pushed his stuffed dinosaur into her face and growled when she tried to unbuckle him.

"I can't see, sweetie." She took a deep breath and lifted him to her hip. She pointed to the red and brown cows munching on grass in the pasture. "Marcus, do you see the cows?"

He giggled. "Mooo!"

A cow bellowed. Marcus squirmed until she set him down. She grabbed his bag out of the car. When she straightened, he was running toward the barbed wire fence. She dropped the bag and took off after him. "Marcus, come back here!"

Cole burst from the house. His long legs ate up the ground. Two feet from the fence, he snatched Marcus before he ran into the sharp wire prongs.

Natalia skidded to a stop beside them and heaved a deep breath. "You can't take off like that. You scared me." She plunged her fingers into her hair, pulling strands from the braid. "I'm not sure I'm cut out for this." Cole put Marcus down, and Natalia grabbed the toddler's hand.

"You're doing fine," he said. "See? No harm. He's okay." He crossed his tanned forearms, his John Deere hat shading his face, and stared down at Marcus. "You can't be running around on a ranch. Those cows may look nice, but if they get riled up, you could get hurt." He squatted to Marcus's eye level. "How about I teach you how to be a real cowboy? Would you like that?"

Marcus nodded.

"I think the best place to start is with a good ol' cowboy breakfast. What do you say? Do you like eggs and bacon?"

He nodded again.

Cole tousled his hair, then looked at Natalia. "Would you like to join us?"

"I can't. Rosemary is expecting me back. Can we exchange numbers?"

"Of course." He dug his phone out of his pocket and handed it to her.

Natalia added her information to the contact list, then sent herself a text from his phone. "You're sure he won't get in the way?" She handed the phone back to him.

"I'm used to herding cattle. How different can kids be?"

"That's not too comforting, but you'll probably do better than me."

"I doubt it. Don't be so hard on yourself."

Natalia couldn't help it. Mothering didn't come naturally to her. Maybe that's why her mother gave her such a hard time—maybe it didn't come naturally to her either. "You'll call if you have any problems?"

"Sure, but we'll be fine."

A dog barked. Marcus whipped his head around as Molly bounded toward him from the barn, almost knocking him over as she licked his face. Marcus giggled. When the dog ran toward the house, he pulled out of Natalia's grasp and followed.

Not again. She took a step toward them, but Cole grabbed her arm. "Molly will keep an eye on him." Marcus pivoted toward the pasture and the dog ran in front of him, herding him back to them. Cole swooped him up and put him on his shoulders.

"I'll get his stuff." Natalia picked the bag up off the ground, then went back to the car for his dinosaur, a teddy bear, a blanket, and a sippy cup.

Cole stood behind her. "He's just staying the day, right? Looks like he's moving in." He put Marcus down before slinging the backpack around his left arm and securing the rest under his right.

"There are a couple of changes of clothes in his bag. He's potty-trained, but he's had a few accidents, especially at nap time. I wrote out his schedule on an index card in the front pocket. There are some snacks in there too."

Cole laughed. "We'll make do. I promise he'll be alive when you come back."

"That's a relief. My shift is usually over around three thirty."

"Enjoy your break, not that work is much of one."

"I will. Thanks for this." She hugged Marcus before letting him chase Molly again. As she slid into the driver's seat, she watched them walk toward the house. Marcus motioned to Molly, then the cows, then a hawk gliding through the air. Cole nodded a few times. At one point, Marcus knelt in the dirt driveway, and Cole followed as they studied the ground.

Natalia took a deep breath. Her shoulders relaxed. Marcus wasn't her responsibility for the next nine hours, and she was going to enjoy every second of it.

****

At a back booth, Natalia took a bite of her club sandwich, enjoying the low hum of conversation and the clinking of dishes from the remaining lunch patrons. The morning had been carefree, fluttering from table to table, talking with the customers. She was tired, but surprisingly fulfilled.

Her phone pinged. She pulled it from her apron pocket and set it on the table. A text from Cole lit her screen. *Marcus is asleep. Wore him out chasing chickens, I mean collecting eggs. Hope your day got better.*

She tapped on the keyboard. *Glad he's sleeping. Thanks for the update. I'm taking a break myself.*

She leaned back and rested her head against the booth, sipping her iced tea and closing her eyes. Another bad dream had plagued her last night between Marcus's crying spells.

"You aren't sleeping on the job, are you?"

Travis's voice made her smile. "Maybe."

The vinyl bench across from her creaked. "Can I join you?"

She peeked over at him. His black hair was wet, and he wore a faded red t-shirt. "Looks like you just did." She sat up and pushed her plate toward him. "Would you like half my sandwich?"

"Sure." He took one half while she finished the other. "How's it going?"

"Marcus woke up four times last night. How was your shift?"

"Now that Marcus is safe, pretty routine. Stopped a few speeders and arrested a drunk driver. Working is back to being fun again. I'm not sure how detectives handle the stress of cases like Marcus's all the time. It's not for me."

"What about your job do you love the most?"

"Driving fast."

She raised her eyebrows.

Travis chuckled. "Busting drug runners. One day, I'd love to catch the mother lode coming through the state. I applied for Drug Recognition Expert training last month. Hopefully I get accepted. There's a promotion for a K-9 handler opening soon too."

"With your experience with animals, you'd be great as a K-9 handler."

"I hope so. Why's Marcus waking up so often?"

"He misses Mary. He cries for her and won't go back to sleep unless I stay with him. Last night, after the second time he cried, I curled up next to his bed and tried to sleep. And now it's going to be another week before they can move him. I'm starting to think he'd be better off in the group home with people who know how to take care of kids. Maybe it's time for me to go back to Sioux Falls."

Travis grabbed her hand and squeezed it. "Trust me, a group home wouldn't be the best place for him. Some of the kids there have deep emotional needs and can't function in a family setting.

You're doing fine. You and Marcus are learning as you go."

"I guess."

"Will going home make you feel better?"

"No, I'd feel guilty for abandoning him, but it's hard."

"Sticking around and working through the hard times makes us stronger. Hank taught me that. He also taught me it's not weak to ask for help."

That was encouraging, if it were true. Oh how she wanted it to be true, but when things got tough in her life, the only thing that seemed to get stronger was her anxiety. "My mom always wants to help, but that usually makes things worse. All I can think about is escaping the situation."

"Do you run from them a lot?"

Natalia evaluated her life. As she continued to think back over the years, she couldn't ignore the pattern. "In high school, I wanted to be on the school newspaper staff, but they put me in charge of ad sales. Back then I was pretty shy, and I couldn't sell anything. I should have talked to our advisor, but it was easier to quit. Then, in college, I wanted to be a nurse. I struggled in chemistry, though. I guess I could have gotten a tutor, but I dropped the class and changed majors to elementary education instead."

"How did you end up dispatching?"

"A family friend told me that as a dispatcher she helped save a man's life by talking his wife through CPR. I was inspired, so I dropped out of school and applied with Metro Communications. I've been there ever since." She sighed. "Until it got hard and I walked away."

"Why *did* you leave? Did you have a plan for what you'd do next?"

She shook her head. "I just needed to get away. I was so anxious that I couldn't breathe."

"How many bad calls have you abandoned?"

"None," she said, starting to get uncomfortable with all of his questions. Where was he going with them? "When I'm taking a difficult call, the adrenaline takes over, and I do my job, but once it's over the anxiety makes me want to crawl out of my skin."

"Weren't some of them tough to stick out?"

"Of course, but I wouldn't leave a person in need. I had a job to do."

"And how many lives have you saved?"

"I stopped counting. How about you?"

He pulled his wallet from his back pocket. He took out a worn business card and handed it to her. A man smiled at her from beside a realtor's logo. On the back, tiny pen marks had been grouped in fives.

"I arrested that man's son for a DUI when I was new to the job. The dad screamed at me when I called, saying I was ruining his son's life, that he'd never get into a good college or get a decent job. A week later, he left his card with a note at the office. The night I arrested his son, he'd been on the way to meet his buddies. They got tired of waiting for him so they left one party for another and rolled the car. All three were killed. The dad apologized for his behavior and thanked me for saving his son's life. We can't know for sure that he would have been killed that night, but every time I arrest a drunk driver, I put a mark on the back. Maybe that's another life saved."

She counted more than sixty marks.

"When I clear a fatality, especially the ones involving alcohol, I pull out this card and think about the lives that were spared, not the ones that weren't. If you dwell on the tragedies, you'll fall into a pit." He laced his fingers with hers. "Tell me about your favorite call."

There had been so many great ones. Telling a babysitter how to perform the Heimlich maneuver on a choking boy. Talking to a hysterical teenager who'd gotten lost and stranded in an unfamiliar part of the city. Helping a young child stay calm after she'd woken up alone while dispatching an officer and social worker to her home. But picking her favorite was easy.

"A man called because his wife was in labor on the side of the road. I dispatched medical and the nearest officer but there wasn't time. I walked him through the delivery, but the baby wasn't breathing when he was born. I talked him through infant CPR. That baby's cry was the sweetest sound I'd ever heard. I visited them in the hospital, and the dad hugged me so tightly I thought he was going to crack a rib." Natalia laughed.

"If you'd run away after your first bad call, you wouldn't have been able to help that dad. And if you run now, you won't be here to help Marcus."

She hadn't thought of it like that. "Thank you. You're pretty amazing." And handsome and wise.

He squeezed her hand, then let go. "I'm glad you think so."

With the moment broken, Natalia stretched her back. "I think my break is over. Are you still able to watch Marcus tomorrow?"

"Yep. I'll pick him up here. I've got a full day planned for us. I think we're going fishing."

"You don't think he's too active for that? He'll probably fall in and scare away all the fish."

Travis shrugged. "Good thing our future nourishment doesn't rest on our ability to catch food. Speaking of food, do you want to come over for supper after you get Marcus from Hannah's?"

"Hannah had a dentist appointment so Cole's watching him."

Travis straightened, frowning. "How did that come about?"

"I was having problems finding a sitter so he offered. He's always at the right place when I need him."

"Yeah, it's almost like *he's* the first responder."

Natalia laughed, but it quickly died down at Travis's blank expression. "Marcus is safe with him, isn't he?"

"Yes, of course. Cole wouldn't hurt a fly. He's the golden boy."

"That's what I call my brother too." Natalia stood. Travis followed. "Thanks for your pep talk. I feel better." She leaned in for a quick hug, but his arms settled around her waist. She rested her head on his shoulder and inhaled his spicy scent.

"Anytime."

Natalia stepped out of his embrace and smiled up at him. His gaze intensified as his eyes studied her face. Her stomach fluttered. A plate crashed and Natalia jumped back. "I should go help."

"Supper tonight then? I can grill an amazing steak."

"Can I take a rain check? I'm going to Sturgis. I need a few things and so does Marcus."

"Tomorrow night?"

"That's perfect. I'll bring Rosemary's potato salad and some coleslaw."

"Just don't bring Cole."

She shook her head. "You two. I'll see you in the morning."

He kissed her cheek, then walked over to Rosemary.

Natalia took a deep breath as a new energy pulsed through her. When she reached for her empty plate, she realized she'd been touching her lips. Maybe next time. She picked up the plate and spotted the business card. When she looked up, Travis was gone, so she put it in her pocket to give him tomorrow.

CHAPTER 15

The next evening, Natalia set containers of baked beans, coleslaw, potato salad, and cheesecake on her car roof so she could unlock the door. After nestling the food in the passenger's seat, she noticed a worn blue bear under the windshield wiper. She shut the passenger door, then removed the one-eyed toy. She searched for a note but found nothing. Not wanting to keep Marcus and Travis waiting, she tossed it in the backseat. She smoothed out her light-yellow sundress as she slid behind the wheel. Hopefully Travis liked yellow.

The sun shone brightly in the western sky as she rolled down her window and headed toward Travis's house. In the fields outside of town, tall grass swayed in the warm breeze. She crossed the Alkali Creek bridge and the asphalt turned to gravel. After a couple of miles, she drove past wild raspberry bushes. The fresh fruit would taste divine on Rosemary's cheesecake. Maybe they could walk down later and pick a bucket full, now that she had the energy to pick berries. Marcus hadn't woken up last night, and she had been nightmare free. Maybe talking with Travis really had helped.

Finally, she turned onto Travis's driveway. As she neared the house, he and Marcus came into view in the side yard. She parked under the canopy of the big oak tree, grabbed the food, then picked up the bear. She'd say hello first, then toss it in the garbage.

Natalia walked to where Marcus ran toward a baseball. He picked it up, reached as far back as he could, and threw it about two feet ahead of him. He dashed after the ball, giggling. He grabbed it again. Then Travis chased him, caught him, and threw him into the air. Marcus squealed. What a sweet sound. Travis was good with him.

Jeeves barked from the front porch. Travis turned around and his gaze collided with hers. He put Marcus on his shoulders and, with a wide grin, strode over to her.

"Nattie!" Marcus leaned toward her. Travis set him on the ground. He charged Natalia and hugged her legs, knocking her off balance.

"Whoa, buddy. You're going to plow her over." Travis steadied her with a firm grip on her arm.

Marcus tugged on the bear. "Beary bear!"

Travis took the containers, so Natalia knelt and looked Marcus in the eyes. "It's not polite to grab things from other people. You need to ask."

"Pease?"

"It's kind of dirty. Why don't I throw this one away and I'll get you a new one?"

"No!" Marcus threw himself on the ground. "My beary bear!"

Desperate to avoid a tantrum, she sat in the grass and pulled him into her arms. "It's okay. You can have the bear. You don't need to cry for it, but can you apologize for grabbing it?"

"Sorry," he whispered.

She gave him the bear and he ran off. Travis pulled her up. Her sandal caught in the grass, and she fell to his chest. His arm wrapped around her waist.

"Aw. Just where I want you. You look very pretty." He brushed his lips past her cheek, barely making contact yet leaving his spicy, woodsy scent to weaken her knees.

She stepped back and pivoted, lifting her heel-less sandal. "Guaranteed not to irritate my wounded feet, but apparently not good for off-roading."

"And cute." He winked.

"So you like the color of my dress?"

He stepped back and looked her over. "You can't go wrong with safety yellow."

She gasped. "It's not that bright." Before he could argue, she stood on her tiptoes and kissed his stubbled jaw. "Stick to the law and leave the fashion to me."

Travis leaned forward, his eyes on her lips.

Marcus screamed. She peeked around Travis. Sampson had the bear's leg in his mouth as Marcus pulled on its head.

Travis straightened. "Sampson! Drop it!"

The dog opened his mouth and lowered his head. Marcus grabbed the toy and swung his fist, hitting Sampson's nose.

Natalia ran over to them. "Marcus, don't hit him. He was only playing." She tried to take the bear to see if the tug-of-war had done more damage to the mangled toy.

Marcus pushed her hand away. "Mine."

Travis stopped beside her. "Real cowboys are nice to ladies and animals."

Natalia looked at Travis. "Did he get a nap? He's awfully cranky about that bear."

"Yeah, he passed out watching cartoons after lunch. Go wash up, cowboy." Marcus ran toward the house, dragging his bear behind him. Travis took her hand and led her to the front deck. "We had a busy day, so I doubt his thirty-minute nap was enough."

"Probably not. He usually takes a two-hour nap."

Travis cringed as he held the front door for her. "Sorry. I probably should have turned the TV down once he dozed off."

Natalia squeezed his hand before letting go and entering the foyer. "He'll sleep well tonight. What did you do today?"

"We went fishing while it was still cool this morning."

"Did you catch anything?"

"Nothing worth keeping, but Marcus had fun throwing rocks into the pond. Then we took Dakota on a ride before heading back to the cabin for lunch."

In the kitchen, Marcus stood on a chair washing his hands at the sink. "Did you have fun fishing and riding horses?" Natalia asked.

He jumped down with wet hands and wiped them on his dirty jeans. "Yeah! I caught a fishy." He hopped up and down. "Then we threw it in the water and it swimmed away. I want to swim too."

Natalia grabbed a towel from the counter and dried his hands. "That would be fun. Is the pond big enough to swim in?"

Travis took the lids off the food containers and added serving spoons. "It's a stock pond for cattle, so it's not clean enough for swimming, but there's a pond near Cole's place that we could try out."

Marcus pumped his fist. "We go swimming?"

"It's time to eat, and we already had a busy day. Maybe next time." Travis handed two containers to Natalia. "We'll eat at the table on the back deck." He opened the kitchen door for her and she stepped outside.

Travis had left this view off when he gave her a tour on her last visit. Fruit trees grew along the edge of a small lawn with a round, stone fire pit in the middle. Two wooden benches and a couple of chairs surrounded the pit. A small, raised, overgrown garden sat to the left of it.

She put the food on the glass table. Travis had already set it for dinner, complete with a Mason jar of purple flowers with frosted green leaves. She bent over the bouquet, breathing in its unique sweetness.

"That's wild sage. Marcus and I picked them for you." He opened the grill where two T-bones sizzled. He flipped the steaks over. "How do you like your steak?"

"Well done, please."

He turned around and snapped the tongs at her. "Come again? You want me to turn your prime grade South Dakota Angus beef into leather?"

"Medium?"

"How about medium rare? Trust me, you'll love it."

****

"How was the steak?" Travis eyed Nattie's empty plate. It boosted his ego that she liked his cooking enough to eat it all.

"Tender and juicy. You might have to give my dad some grilling lessons." She started stacking plates and silverware.

He took the dishes. "I'm on cleanup crew tonight. Do you want more iced tea?"

"No, but I'll take some coffee if you have decaf."

"You've got it."

With a pretty girl and a huge piece of Rosemary's chocolate cheesecake waiting for him, Travis made quick work of the coffee. While it brewed, he loaded the dishwasher and plated three pieces of cheesecake, then searched his cupboards for the tray Rosemary had given him. After he had the tray loaded, he stepped onto the deck.

Nattie cuddled Marcus as tears streaked his face.

"Dude, what happened?" He set his bounty on the table.

"He fell and scratched his knee. Do you have a bandage?"

"Spiderman?" Marcus's small voice tugged at Travis's heart.

"I'm fresh out of Spiderman, but I'll see what I can find." He went back inside and dug through his first aid kit for a bandage and ointment. On his way outside, he picked up a pen and drew a cowboy on top of a bucking horse on the bandage, then joined Nattie and Marcus outside.

"I've got just the thing a cowboy like you needs," he said. "Let me see that scrape." Travis held Marcus's calf and examined his knee. "I think we can save your leg, but you were lucky this time." He put antibiotic cream on the scrape and Marcus cringed. "I found a super-special bandage for you. It's a rodeo star on a bucking bronco."

Nattie smiled. "Isn't that sweet?"

He rolled his eyes. "It's not sweet. It's tough. How about some cheesecake? It'll make any cowhand perk up." He unloaded the tray and pushed Nattie's and Marcus's slices closer to them.

She gave Marcus a bite. He scrunched his nose and stuck out

his tongue. "Yuck!"

"You won't mind if I eat the rest then?" Travis slid Marcus's piece onto his plate.

Marcus buried his face in Nattie's shoulder. She smoothed back his hair, then took a bite of cake. "This is amazing." As she rocked him, her blonde hair fell over his black cowlick.

Travis took another bite and chased it with coffee, then leaned back in his chair, savoring the cozy picture they made. This beat a warmed-up can of soup in front of the TV any night. Even though Nattie had her doubts, she was doing a fine job caring for Marcus.

Marcus squirmed on her lap, bumping her arm and spilling coffee on the table.

Travis glanced around, looking for something to distract the toddler so Nattie could enjoy her dessert. Roasting sticks stuck out from a box at the end of the deck. "Hey, buddy. How about we roast some marshmallows?"

Marcus jumped up. "Yay!"

Nattie set her cup down and swiped the spill with a napkin. "Marshmallows? Haven't we eaten enough?"

"It'll be fun. Let's go get them."

Marcus, with the bear in his grip, followed him into the kitchen. Travis took a bag from the cabinet and handed it to him. "Don't squish them." Back outside, he snagged a butane lighter from under the grill and stuffed it into his back pocket, then he grabbed the roasting sticks. "Give Nattie your bear so you can help me haul firewood."

Marcus threw it onto her lap, spilling her coffee again, and ran behind Travis.

Nattie sighed. "Be careful."

"I forgot the newspaper. Would you mind grabbing some from the pile by the back door and meeting us by the fire pit?"

"No problem. I think I'll refill my coffee too." She grabbed both of their mugs and disappeared into the house.

Travis and Marcus descended the deck stairs and walked to the woodpile around the side of the house. Travis placed one split log in Marcus's outstretched arms, then picked up a few more. He led the way along the path to the fire pit. "Be careful here. These stones are uneven, and I don't want you to fall again."

Marcus bent to look down and the log fell from his arms.

Travis picked it up and gave it back to him. "There you go, cowboy."

Marcus grinned and followed, slower than before.

At the fire pit, Travis set down the roasting sticks and marshmallows before kneeling to stack logs across each other. The toddler knelt down too.

The back door slammed shut and footsteps echoed across the deck. The scent of coffee reached him just before Nattie did. She held coffee mugs in each hand, newspapers under one arm, and the bear under the other. Her yellow dress flowed around her legs. Travis's chest tightened. She was a pretty sight.

She handed him his coffee, then the paper.

Travis wadded up a page. "Marcus, crumple up a few pages for me. Like this."

Marcus crinkled the paper, and Travis stuffed it between the logs.

"That should do it." He lit the kindling. Smoke floated toward them, then orange flames consumed the paper, heating his face. Marcus put his hand on Travis's shoulder. Travis draped his arm around the boy's back and pulled him to his side. "You need to be careful around fire. If you touch it, you'll get hurt."

The toddler nodded.

"It's a nice night for a fire." Nattie sat on one of the benches and held her hands toward it.

Travis picked up a roasting stick as she handed him a marshmallow. He stuck it onto the sharp end. "Are you ready, cowboy?"

Marcus grabbed the stick, and Travis covered his hand, guiding the marshmallow to the flames. It bubbled golden brown on one side. "Let's turn it so we can roast the other side." He turned his wrist, then looked over his shoulder at Nattie. "I think we have a professional roaster here."

Flames reflected in her eyes. He hoped he'd have another chance at a kiss. Maybe if Marcus fell asleep.

The wind shifted, and smoke blew into his face. He focused on the marshmallow as a blue flame danced on it. Travis blew on it until the burnt surface smoked.

Marcus crossed his arms over his stomach and stomped his foot. "It's black."

"It's not ruined though. You'll still like it." Travis pulled the warm, gooey mess from the prongs. "Go sit by Nattie."

The boy ran over and jumped beside her. Travis handed him the cooled marshmallow, which he bit into, smearing goo all over his lips. He roasted another one and offered the golden perfection to Nattie.

"I'm full, but thanks." She rubbed her legs.

"Are you cold?" He popped the sweet treat into his mouth and sat beside her.

"A little."

Marcus yawned and lay across her lap, hugging the ugly bear.

"He sure is attached to that thing. Where'd you get it?" Travis laid his arm across the back of the bench.

"It was tucked under my windshield wipers after work."

Travis sat up. "Do you know who put it there?"

"I have no idea. There wasn't a note. Why?"

"It's probably nothing, but I think you should be careful until we figure out where it came from." He didn't want to worry Nattie, but there was a small chance the Russells were out on bail. He'd call the State Attorney's office in the morning to find out. He doubted the Russells could discover where Marcus was placed anyway.

"Okay." Nattie shivered.

"I'll get some blankets." He grabbed the marshmallow bag on his way into the house.

In his bedroom, he pulled on a gray highway patrol hoodie, then grabbed a fluffy black blanket from the closet. Under it was his denim patch quilt. He hurt for the scared nine-year-old boy he had been when the social worker had given him that blanket. He took the heavy blanket down and inhaled its musky scent. This was what home smelled like. He'd love for Marcus to use his blanket and feel the warmth it had provided Travis all those years.

When he returned to the firepit, Marcus was asleep. "I'll take him so you can get warm," he said. When Travis lifted Marcus, the boy moaned, then settled against his chest. Travis handed Nattie the fluffy blanket before wrapping Marcus in his quilt and laying him on the other bench.

Nattie covered her legs. "That's quite the blanket. Where did you get it?"

Travis sat next to her. "When I first entered foster care. They give you a bag of things, like a toothbrush and toothpaste, clothes that don't fit, a couple of toys, and a blanket. That was mine."

"And you've kept it all this time. Is it special or practical?"

"Both. I took it to every foster home. I even hid it in the bottom of my trunk at the police academy."

She laughed. "Really?"

"It was my lucky charm, if you will."

"Why?" She laid her head on his shoulder.

"We often went without heat when we lived with my mom, so blankets were like gold to us. Cole got a Batman fleece." Travis chuckled. "I thought mine was way cooler because it looked like a grown man's quilt."

The fire flickered as the sun finished its descent. Bright pink strips of sky soon faded to black. The wood crackled and the insects fluttered and chirped. Travis breathed in Nattie's apple scent, content beside her. Until she shivered again.

He pulled his sweatshirt off and handed it to her.

"Won't you get cold?"

"No, I'm fine. I've got thick skin."

"Thanks."

The glow from the fire illuminated her face. He admired its curves and contours, but admired her more for staying to care for Marcus, even when it scared her. The brave, kind lady next to him stirred his heart. A desire to kiss her returned, coursing through him. He sucked in a breath and ran his finger down her smooth cheek and across her jaw. Her gaze met his.

When she leaned toward him, he touched his lips to hers. Her hand grabbed his shirt as he deepened the kiss. Warmth spread through him as the burning wood popped.

Nattie pulled back.

Not wanting to end the kiss, he scooted closer and rubbed her arm. She pushed him away. Gasped for air. His eyes snapped open. She stared at him with wide eyes, her hands clawing at her throat.

Travis pulled her hands from her neck. "What's wrong? You're going to hurt yourself."

She panted.

His heart pounded. "You're going to hyperventilate if you keep breathing like that."

She took another quick breath.

"Nattie, slow down. You're okay."

Her eyes widened as she shook her head.

"Look at me," he said and her gaze met his. "Good, now breathe in with me and hold it. One… two … three … four, breath out. Again, breath in. One…two…three…four and out." He breathed with her a few more times and rubbed her back until her breathing slowed. "How are you doing?"

She laid her head against his shoulder. "Embarrassed."

"What happened?" he asked, thankful for his training.

"It sounded like a gunshot. Then I was at Officer Mason's side, and he was bleeding from his neck."

His stomach fell. A flashback. He knew all too well how terrifying they were. "You're safe."

She slumped against the bench. "That was awful."

He wanted to lighten the mood, help her forget her embarrassment, so he crossed his arms and huffed. "It's been a while, but I didn't think the kiss was *awful*."

Nattie covered her mouth. "Oh no! That's not what I meant, I—" Her eyes narrowed. "You're teasing me."

He winked.

She dropped her hands to her lap. "It's not you. I enjoyed kissing you. I think there's something wrong with me."

"Why?"

"I've been having nightmares pretty regularly."

"About what?"

"Officer Mason or you getting shot on a traffic stop, or Marcus gets kidnapped and I get shot."

His chest tightened. "Why didn't you tell me?"

She shrugged.

"Maybe you need to talk to someone about it. A professional. Getting help is a good first step to healing."

"If I have to seek help, doesn't that mean my mom was right all along and I'm not cut out to be a dispatcher?"

Travis grabbed her shaking hand. "I haven't ever told anyone this, but when I came back from Iraq, I saw a shrink."

Her eyes widened. "Did it help?"

"It did. He dug into my past with my mom as well as the war. Showed me some coping mechanisms too."

"I feel so stupid. You've survived so much. All I did was answer a call."

"A very traumatic call. You heard an officer lose his life. Don't downplay your experience because of mine." He kissed her cheek. "You can't run from trauma or things will only get worse."

CHAPTER 16

Natalia shivered and blinked back tears. If Travis could ask for help, maybe she could too. "I think I'm overreacting, but I guess I'll try it." The fire had died to a low glow. Darkness covered the yard and house. "It's getting late. I should get Marcus home."

"Are you okay to drive?"

"I'm fine." Other than the lingering embarrassment. She stood and folded the blanket. She was shivering by the time she completed the task. Hopefully he would think it was only from the cold.

Travis nestled Marcus's sleeping body close to his chest. "I'll put him in the car."

She matched Travis's long strides across the yard. After he set Marcus in the car seat, the toddler rubbed his eyes but was asleep again before Travis shut the door.

"Can I keep your sweatshirt until I see you next time?"

Travis squeezed her arms. "Of course. It's a guarantee that I get to see you again."

She hugged him. "Thank you for a wonderful evening. I loved almost every minute."

"I'm sorry about the kiss."

"I'm not." She stepped back to look at him. "My boss sent me the name of the department psychologist the day after the shooting. I'll call her in the morning and set up an appointment."

"I think that's a great plan. Are you working tomorrow?"

"Yep. Hannah's watching Marcus. What time do you work tonight?"

"Ten until six."

"That's brutal. What time is it now?"

"Nine fifteen. I'll finish cleaning up, then get ready. It should be a quiet night. Hopefully, I'll get my paperwork done."

"When can I see you next ... to give you back your hoodie?" She stepped closer to him, wanting to drag the moment out a bit longer.

"I work tomorrow night, but I'm free on Saturday. We could go swimming." His fingers trailed down her cheek.

"I promised Rosemary I'd go to the auction at the school with her. I think it starts at one. Would you like to come?"

"If I can get up in time. Then we can go swimming afterward." He pulled her into his arms and kissed her neck.

Warmth spread through her, and she stifled a groan. When Travis stepped back, a cool breeze hit her. He stroked her jaw. "Call me when you get home?"

She smiled. "Sure."

As she drove away, she watched Travis's silhouette in her rearview until she rounded the curve. Excitement bubbled as she replayed his kiss and caresses. His touch certainly perked her senses, but it was his kindness that tugged at her heart. Despite his past—or maybe because of it—he'd grown into a confident man. And she loved how playful he was with Marcus. She sighed. If only she hadn't ruined their kiss with her panic attack.

Ten minutes later, Natalia pulled up to the back of the bistro. The light above the back door flickered, then went out, leaving the area dark. She tucked her keys into her purse before draping it over her shoulder.

As she carried Marcus inside, the strong odor of cigarette smoke hit her. She flipped up the stairway light switch, but it remained dark. The hairs on her neck stood up.

She hadn't locked her apartment when she left. What if someone was in there? The person who left the bear? Pressing Marcus to her chest, she ran to her car, climbed into the passenger's side, and locked the doors.

Marcus continued to sleep as she fumbled in her purse for

her phone and dialed Travis's number. The ringing increased her nervousness. How many times had he told her to lock the door? He'd told her to be careful, but was she overreacting by calling him? Voicemail picked up. She laid her head against the headrest and hung up.

This was stupid. The hallway light was probably as old as the outside light. They probably went out on their own. At the same time. And anyone could have stepped inside to light up, then stayed inside to smoke even though Rosemary forbade it. Maybe.

Her phone rang, and she glanced at the caller ID. "Travis."

"Hey, sorry I missed your call. Did you make it home okay?"

"Yep, we're here. I was just about to head upstairs." Her voice trembled. "Would you do me a favor?"

"Sure."

"Could you stop by on your way to work? The outside light and hall light went out. And … I didn't lock the apartment before I left, so now I'm nervous about taking Marcus in. I'm probably being paranoid, but since you're starting your shift soon, would it be too much trouble?"

"I'm getting into my patrol car now. Where are you?"

"We're in my car. I locked the doors."

"Good. Sit tight. I'll be there in ten minutes." He ended the call.

She started the car to keep her and Marcus warm, then sang quietly along to the radio until amber lights flashed in the side mirror. Travis parked beside her and shone his spotlight on the building. Natalia stroked Marcus's hair until Travis, dressed in his uniform, knocked on her window.

She turned off the car and opened the door.

He took her keys. "Who has access to the stairwell?"

"Everyone. Rosemary locks it before she leaves, then opens it in the morning. It's a fire hazard to keep it locked during business hours. All the lights in the bistro were off when I drove by. Rosemary should have locked up a couple of hours ago." Nausea rolled in her stomach.

"You stay here while I go inside."

"But—"

He closed the car door. "Lock it."

He lit the backdoor with his flashlight before disappearing into the building. Her heartbeat increased as she locked the car. She pressed her cheek to the glass, straining to see her apartment windows from such an awkward angle. What was taking so long? The dining room light came on. Please be okay! It seemed like forever before a beam of light appeared in the back doorway. Then Travis appeared. She finally relaxed and climbed out of the car.

"All clear." He took Marcus from her and held him to his shoulder.

"I feel stupid for making you come over."

"I'd rather you call if you feel nervous. Sometimes our imaginations can run wild, but sometimes our instincts are right on point." He carried Marcus up to his bedroom, kissing the boy's head before lowering him to the mattress. Strong and tender. It melted her heart.

Travis grabbed her hand and led her to the apartment door where he released her. "I'll lock the outside door when I leave. You lock this one behind me."

"Thanks, Travis." She gazed into his dark eyes, wishing he could stay longer.

He leaned down and kissed her. She stepped onto her tiptoes, enjoying the feel of his lips against hers. Energy pulsed through her. She stroked the hair at the back of his neck as his hands gripped her waist. Breaking contact with her lips, he laid his forehead against hers. "I'm glad we got to redo that," he whispered.

She smiled. "Me too."

After one more quick kiss, he left, shutting the door behind him. His boots echoed on the stairs. She locked the door, then fell to the sofa, her lips still tingling. If her paranoia gave her those results, maybe it wasn't all that bad.

* * * * * * *

Natalia splashed warm water on her face. Her head pounded and her stomach rolled. Images of another nightmare flashed through her mind.

A seven-year-old girl crying. Her mom dead in a pool of blood. Her dad coming after her.

It didn't matter that Natalia hadn't been there—her mind created images as vivid as if she had been—but that call was years ago. Why was she dreaming of it now?

She stumbled back to her bed and covered her head with the sheet. Anxiety crawled over her skin.

She needed to talk to someone. Travis was working, and she'd already burdened him enough today. She grabbed her phone and scrolled through her contacts. Mom. Hayden. Maybe she could call dispatch and see who was working. Before she lost her nerve, she pushed the nonemergency number.

"Sioux Falls Metro Dispatch Center, how can I help you?"

"Janey, it's Nattie." Her voice shook.

"Nattie. How have you been, girl? We miss you."

"Is it a busy night?"

"It's not too bad. Are you okay?"

Natalia closed her eyes. Of course, Janey would know she was upset. She had more than a decade of experience dispatching calls. Somehow that knowledge comforted Natalia, and the tears flowed down her cheeks. "I'm scared."

"Are you in danger?"

"No, I'm safe. I shouldn't be bothering you. I need to sleep, but I'm having nightmares. Every time I close my eyes, I see crime scenes of some of the worst calls I took."

"Our imaginations are usually worse than the actual scenes. I can't talk right now, but can I switch you over to the officer wellness hotline?"

"No. I'll be fine."

"Nattie, they have psychologists and chaplains on call twenty-four hours a day. I'd feel better if you talked with someone now."

"They're for first responders. I'm just a dispatcher."

"Nonsense. I'm switching you over, then calling you back tomorrow to make sure you talked to them. Don't make me come all the way to your house."

"Okay." Her nerves calmed. "Thanks, Janey."

"Anytime. I'll talk to you tomorrow. Stay on the line."

Natalia sighed. These services were for responders. All she did was answer phone calls. She didn't get shot at or see bloody crash victims. She was supposed to be strong for her officers, not break down in tears because of a bad dream.

The hold music ended. "Hello, I'm Dr. Drakeford. The dispatcher told me that you're having a rough night."

Natalia sat up. Heat infused her face. The room spun. "I don't think I can talk about it."

"How about you tell me your name?"

"Natalia Brynner."

"And you're a former dispatcher for Sioux Falls Metro?"

"Yes. I left last week and have had nightmares ever since."

"How long were you a dispatcher?"

"Two years."

"First, you're not alone. Every dispatcher struggles with a call from time to time and a third experience burnout, especially at the two-year mark."

"Really?"

"Yep. And secondly, seeking help is the best thing you can do. Being a dispatcher is a high-stress job, and you need to be able to process these feelings with a professional but also with a peer group."

Natalia closed her eyes and leaned against the headboard as relief coursed through her. She wasn't alone or overreacting. "Thank you, Doctor."

"I need to ask. Have you thought about hurting or killing yourself?"

"No. Not at all."

"Have you ever thought of a plan on how to kill yourself?"

"No, I only want the nightmares to stop."

"When was your most recent nightmare?"

"Tonight." She shuddered. "It was from a call years ago, but the scene was so vivid."

"It's not uncommon to experience dreams from years past."

"I'm so tired, but I'm afraid to sleep. I'm taking care of a toddler, and I have to work in the morning."

"Where are you working now?"

"At a local café. I'm waitressing."

"For tonight, I'm going to talk you through some relaxation techniques. Then I want you to call my office in the morning and make an appointment for further treatment."

"But I'm living hours away for another week at least."

"We'll start with a phone session until we can meet in person."

Despite her initial hesitation, Natalia relaxed. "Thank you, Dr. Drakeford." Tears choked her voice.

"It's my pleasure. Now, lie somewhere comfortable and close your eyes. Focus on your breathing."

For the first time in a week, the thought of sleep didn't scare Natalia. She settled onto the soft mattress, closed her eyes, and listened to the doctor's soothing voice.

CHAPTER 17

In the back of the crowded gymnasium, Natalia stepped up to the bake sale table. Trays of brownies, cookies, cupcakes, and even a few pies covered the white tablecloth. She perused the desserts at one end of the table as Rosemary and Marcus checked the other. She decided on a large brownie to share with Marcus, then paid a teenage girl sporting orange and black braids.

Rosemary motioned toward the bleachers. "The auction starts in ten minutes. I'm going to go get some seats. This place is filling up quicker than I thought."

Marcus pointed to a fire truck cookie. "Pease, Nattie."

"Sure, why not." She paid the girl again, handed Marcus the cookie, then wrapped the brownie in a napkin and stuck it in her purse.

"You're going to spoil his appetite," someone said from behind her.

She looked over her shoulder at the handsome, dark-haired man. He smiled. Dimples. She returned his smile. "He just ate lunch, and what three-year-old can resist a fire truck cookie?" She glanced at Marcus, who already had red frosting on his cheeks. She took a stack of napkins and put them in her purse.

Cole motioned to the drink table. "Can I interest you in a strong cup of coffee? The firefighters made it."

"You bet. How about some lemonade, Marcus?"

He nodded, so they walked together to the next table. She gave Marcus a half-filled cup of pink lemonade while Cole poured coffee into a Styrofoam cup. He handed it to her, and she squeezed in at the end of the table to add cream and sugar.

"This place is packed," she said, trying not to spill.

"Everyone who can comes to the fire department auction. It's their biggest fundraiser. They had to move it here from the firehouse a few years ago."

"I'm surprised the school is this large. Are there enough kids in Alkaline to support it?"

"Sure, considering all of the grades are under one roof and it's the only school in the district. They bus in kids within a twenty-mile radius."

"Horsey!" Marcus pointed to a ferocious orange-and-black horse head on the back wall.

"That's the Alkaline Mighty Mustang."

"Did you and Travis go to school here?"

"We did, although it has undergone some renovations in the last ten years. Air conditioning being one of the better ones."

Natalia took in the high ceilings, championship banners, and multiple retracted basketball hoops. Had it been hard for Travis to start a new school as a teenager? Had he played basketball in this very gym? "What was Travis like as a child?"

"A delinquent. He was smart, but he got into a ton of trouble."

They headed for the bleachers, but several more people had filed into the gymnasium, making it difficult for her to see Rosemary. Natalia took Marcus's sticky hand. "We'd better find our seats."

"This way." Cole led them through the crowd. "Marcus seems to be doing well."

"I hope so. He doesn't cry for his mom at night anymore, but he asks about her a lot. I never know what to say."

"That has to be hard. I doubt he'd understand no matter what you tell him. Travis hoped our mom would find him, until she died."

"Didn't you think she'd be back?"

"I was more terrified she'd find us and take us back to the foodless dumps we lived in." He weaved his way through the crowd.

Natalia followed, towing Marcus behind her, her heart aching. When would Marcus finally realize his mom was never coming for him?

"Over here!" Rosemary waved from the middle of a large section of folding chairs.

They scooted along the row to the three empty seats in the middle.

Rosemary wiggled her white auction paddle. "I've got my paddle, and I'm ready to win."

Cole and Natalia sat with Marcus between them. She set her things on the floor, then pulled some napkins out of her bag. "Did you like the cookie?" she asked Marcus.

He nodded and smiled, showing red teeth.

"The cookie certainly liked you." She wiped his face, then leaned toward Rosemary. "What do you have your eye on?"

"There's a beautiful mahogany plant stand with carved leaves, a couple of china cabinets, and a juke box I think would look great in the corner of the bistro. What about you, Cole? What are you bidding on?"

"I didn't see anything I needed. There's a livestock auction in a couple of months I'd rather save my money for." He tapped Natalia on the shoulder and leaned toward her. "What are your plans for this evening?"

"Travis and I are taking Marcus swimming after the auction."

Marcus looked up at Cole. "I got sharks on my trunks." He pretended to bite him with his hands.

Cole fought him off. "Those sound scary."

"Travis said he'd try to stop by the auction, but it depends on when he wakes up."

"I see."

Should she ask him to come with them? She'd promised Travis she'd stay out of their relationship, and she didn't want Cole getting the wrong idea. She liked him, but her feelings for Travis had grown beyond friendship. The last thing she wanted was to create another reason for them to fight.

****

Travis squared his shoulders. He was a state trooper and an army veteran. He had been in combat and lived through many life-or-death situations. Yet standing outside his high school building, sweat beaded on his lip. He wasn't a helpless kid anymore. He could do this.

He entered the foyer of the school and the cool air sent a shiver down his spine. Ceramic tile had replaced the green carpet, but the place still reeked of old paint and smelly socks. He'd spent many afternoons of detention in the office in front of him. To the left was the elementary wing, and the secondary education wing was to the right.

His boots thumped on the tile as he walked to the gym, just past the office. Gripping the silver handles, he rolled his shoulders, then opened the doors. The auctioneer's rapid chant rose above the dull chatter. He was about to slip onto the chair nearest the exit when he spotted Nattie sitting with Rosemary and Marcus and … Cole. Ignoring the empty seat in front of him, he made his way through the crowd toward Nattie.

When he reached her, she glanced at him and smiled, then scooped Marcus onto her lap. He sat in the empty chair beside her.

Cole grunted. "Smooth, brother. Real smooth."

Travis smirked.

Nattie's warm hand gripped his. "I'm glad you came."

She'd pulled her hair back into a bun. Silver earrings dangled from her ears and caressed her exposed neck as she tilted her head. Her blue eyes sparkled. He couldn't resist a light peck on her gloss-covered lips.

Cole cleared his throat so Travis elbowed him in the gut.

Cole pushed him back.

Nattie leaned forward. "Do I need to separate you two? Stop acting like kids."

Cole snorted. "We were kids the last time anyone forced us to sit together in school."

The two gray-haired ladies in front of them turned around and glared. Oh, great. Of all the places he could be sitting, he ended up behind his seventh and eighth grade teachers. Their lectures were legendary. Travis squirmed in his seat.

On the stage, two cowboys set down a large, brown cabinet.

"Look at this gorgeous, antique, china cabinet." The auctioneer started chanting.

Rosemary lifted her paddle.

Nattie leaned toward him. "I can't believe she's bidding on that. It looks like the one we moved to your trailer."

Rosemary lifted her paddle again, then glared at Nattie. "Mine doesn't have those rounded doors and cherry finish. Now you hush." She lifted her paddle again.

Nattie pressed her nose to his arm and snickered.

"Sold!" The auctioneer pointed at Rosemary, who beamed. "That concludes our Alkaline Volunteer Fire Department auction. A mighty thanks to everyone who contributed. The bake sale still has plenty of homemade goodies left, and firefighter boots are set out throughout the room for donations. Have a nice day, folks."

Travis cupped Nattie's elbow, but she was talking with Rosemary. Mrs. Thorpe turned around and faced him with her usual pinched expression. "Travis Wilkins. Came back to the scene of the crime now, did you?"

His stomach clenched.

Mrs. Wilson slowly turned around. "Of course. He's here because of the pretty girl." They both looked at Nattie. "That's just his way."

Despite the years, they still couldn't see him as anything other than their rowdy student. Well, he refused to let them intimidate him again. "Was that your grandson I arrested last month for minor consumption, Mrs. Wilson?"

She gasped, then narrowed her eyes. "You don't have us fooled.

Just because you wear a badge doesn't mean you're walking the straight and narrow."

"I'm sure Dad would be tickled pink if he knew Travis was serving Alkaline as a state trooper." Cole smiled at the retired teachers. "What a lovely dress, Mrs. Wilson."

Mrs. Wilson grinned as she touched the collar of her paisley dress. "Oh, you. It's about as old as you are, young man."

Travis rolled his eyes.

As she and Cole talked, Travis tensed with the same anxiety he'd felt in class. Not wanting to run into another childhood nemesis, he snatched up Marcus, squeezed past Cole, and found a side door that exited to the playground. Travis hoped Nattie would see them leave, but he didn't bother to check. Once outside, the sunshine warmed his skin.

Marcus squirmed, so Travis put him on the ground. The boy ran after two kids about his age.

A hand looped through his arm. "I'm so glad you came today."

He glanced down at Nattie. Her grin thawed what remained of the frost he had experienced in the school. He returned the smile. "Sorry I missed most of the auction."

"I understand. I saw you talking with Mrs. Thorpe and Mrs. Wilson. Aren't they sweet? You should have seen the way they played with Marcus at the bistro last week."

"Mrs. Thorpe and Mrs. Wilson are battle-axes. Always have been."

Nattie gasped. "They are not. They've been nothing but nice to me since I met them."

"Posers," Travis mumbled, surprised she could be fooled so easily.

"It doesn't matter. They're only two in the crowd. Most of this town respects you. I can tell by how they talk about you at work." She squeezed his forearm and pulled him toward a bench. Kids shouted and giggled around them.

Travis examined the sky as they sat. "Those clouds"—he pointed to the dark thunderhead to the northwest—"look like they're going to ruin our swimming plans."

"Oh, no. Marcus was looking forward to it."

"Does tomorrow work?"

"Sure. If we go early, I can pack a lunch for us."

Marcus ran toward them with a clump of dandelions in his hand. Their yellow heads bobbed on bent stems. He held the bouquet to Nattie's nose. "I picked fowers."

She took his gift and kissed his cheek. "Thank you, Marcus. I love them."

"Is that all it takes to get a kiss?" Travis plucked a weed from the ground and handed it to her.

She wrapped her free hand around his neck and kissed his lips. Fire flashed through him. Children's laughter registered through the smoke. When he pulled away, he realized more kids had filled the playground, adding shrieks to their laughs. It probably wasn't the best place to be kissing Nattie, but she snuggled closer to him and laid her head on his shoulder anyway. Not a bad way to spend the afternoon.

Caleb stood in the shadow beside a large bush. Its full, green leaves provided the perfect hiding spot, only a few yards from his boy. He watched Marcus chase the other children. His son stopped to throw grass, then followed a little girl with brown pigtails. They walked toward him.

His palms itched. Just a few more feet and he could grab Marcus. The couple on the bench was practically making out. They were supposed to take care of his son, but they weren't even watching. It would be so easy.

How long would it take before the trooper noticed Marcus was gone? Was the man carrying a weapon? Caleb squinted. One of the trooper's pant legs bulged more than the other. He grunted. All of his guns had been confiscated.

As much as he wanted to, he wasn't ready to take Marcus. That wasn't the plan, but he was so close.

Marcus stopped by the bush and looked at Caleb, then he smiled. Caleb put a finger over his lips. His little boy nodded. With a quick glance at the distracted couple, Caleb knelt down and motioned Marcus toward him.

When his boy was in front of him, Caleb ruffled his hair. Marcus reached into Caleb's shirt pocket and pulled out a sugar baby. He popped the candy into his mouth. "Mommy?"

"She's at home sleeping. She's sick, but when she's better I'll come get you. We'll be together soon."

Marcus took another candy.

"Now run along and play. But remember that Daddy is coming. Be a good boy, and don't tell anyone you saw me."

Caleb stepped back into his camouflage as Marcus ran toward the tramp who was sniffing the weeds his son had given her. Marcus pointed at Caleb. The cop stood.

Caleb's heart raced as he pushed his way through the bushes. The twigs scratched his face and arms until he burst through, running down the street as fast as he could. His lungs burned. When he made it to his pickup, he slid into the driver's seat. This time he'd failed, but as soon as his buddy got him a pistol, he'd be ready.

Something squealed. Natalia sat up, her heart pounding. Sunlight seeped around the bedroom blinds. She grabbed her phone from the nightstand and peeked in the living room. Toys lay scattered on the floor. Her used snack plate sat on the coffee table, and a basket of unfolded clothes was on the couch. Everything looked normal.

Someone banged against the door. Her finger hovered over her phone, ready to call for help. "Who's there?"

"It's Travis."

Relieved, she shuffled through the apartment and swung the door open. He stood on the landing with a drill in his hand.

"What are you doing?"

"Fixing the door." He pointed to a half-inch hole in the hardwood.

She gasped. "It wasn't like that last night."

"I did it a minute ago. You need a peep hole."

"Why? Do you really think it was Caleb on the playground?"

He shook his head. "They're probably still in jail. Besides, there's no way for Caleb to know you have Marcus. We don't know who put the bear on your car, but someone was smoking in the hall. That alone is a good reason to be cautious."

"Did you ask Rosemary before you drilled a hole in her door?"

"Of course. Do you think she could say no to this handsome face?"

Natalia shook her head. He did look adorable with his stubble and backwards baseball cap. "What was the banging?"

He cringed. "I dropped my drill. Sorry."

"All this noise woke me up. Might as well check on Marcus."

"Don't bother. He's downstairs devouring flapjacks with the retirees."

Her heart clenched. How could she have slept through someone sneaking Marcus away? "How did you get in?"

"I was showing Rosemary what I wanted to do when we heard Marcus crying, so she took him downstairs. She left a note on his bed. Don't worry. We won't tell anyone about the log-sawing coming from your room."

Emotion clogged her throat. What kind of a mother was she to sleep through someone taking Marcus? She crossed her arms, hoping Travis didn't notice how upset she was. "I do not snore." She sighed. "I finally have a night without nightmares, and you wake me up with all this noise."

"Sorry about that, but I couldn't wait any longer for you to emerge from your coma. I'd already replaced the bulbs outside the back door and here in the hallway. Hopefully you'll sleep better after I install a deadbolt. The lock on the door knob is pathetic, but neither of them will work if you don't use them."

"I usually do, but thanks for beefing up security."

"You bet." He set the drill down and drew her to him. "You sure look cute first thing in the morning."

More like a mess. She'd rushed out without a thought to her snarly hair or morning breath. She covered her mouth. "I need to go get ready."

"Sure. Want to meet downstairs in an hour to go swimming?"

Keeping her hand on her mouth, she nodded. He leaned in and kissed her hand. She giggled and fled into the apartment, stepping on something sticky. She hopped to the recliner, plopped down, and pulled a caramel from her foot. Where had that come from?

The drilling resumed. This time the squealing comforted her. How did Travis manage to help her without making her feel inadequate? And could he teach her mom how to do it?

* * * * * * *

Natalia squeezed stinky water from her hair into the grass, then sat on an old, plaid blanket and tucked her legs beside her. She would need another shower tonight, but it was worth it. With the sun bright in the sky, at least she'd dry quickly. Giggles, twittering birds, fluttering insects, and splashing water were becoming her favorite sounds.

The nearby creek jingled as it flowed into the pond surrounded by cottonwood and elm trees. In the pond, Travis threw Marcus into the air. He giggled before falling into the dirty water. Natalia grabbed her phone and snapped a picture just as Travis threw Marcus again. Over and over again. A familiar warmth returned. Marcus seemed the happiest when he played with Travis.

Travis held Marcus in his tanned arm, their black heads touching. They looked good together, like father and son.

While she loved being an aunt, she'd never desired to be a mom. To be responsible for another person's life scared her. Ironic that she'd become a dispatcher.

Travis carried Marcus out of the pond and set him on the grass. He tried to run back into the pond, but Travis grabbed his shoulders and turned him back around. "Let's take a break."

A grasshopper landed on Natalia's knee. She cupped her hand over it. It jumped around, sending shivers down her spine, but she wanted to show Marcus. He ran to the blanket and slid to a stop on top of his knees.

"I have a surprise for you," she said.

"Pease?"

"Get ready. It's not going to stick around for long." She moved up her hand. The grasshopper stood still. Marcus squealed and reached for it but it hopped away. She laughed as he ran after it.

Travis chased after Marcus, caught him, and set him on the blanket beside her. Water glistened on his smooth chest. He pulled on a green t-shirt and sat with them. "I'm hungry. Is there anything left to eat?" He reached for the cooler and pulled out Marcus's half-eaten ham sandwich. "Want your sandwich, cowboy?"

"No. Cookie pease?" He scooted closer to Travis.

"You can only have one, okay?" Natalia wrapped a towel around his shivering body.

Travis gave him a chocolate chip cookie. Marcus fell to his stomach and ate a mouthful. Natalia stroked his wet hair, and he laid his head down, closing his eyes. His half-eaten cookie fell from his grip.

"I think you wore him out," she whispered.

"He wore me out. We've been out here for two hours." Travis leaned onto his arm, stretching across the length of the blanket at Natalia's feet.

She loved watching Marcus sleep, almost as much as she loved his joy when he played with Travis.

"How've you been sleeping recently?" Travis covered her hand with his.

She turned her hand over and laced her fingers through his. "I'm still having nightmares."

"I wish I could help."

"You did. I took your advice and called the police psychologist."

"Did you make an appointment?"

She nodded. "We have a phone session set up for tomorrow, but I'm nervous about it."

"Why?" He sat up.

"I don't know. She was kind on the phone, but I don't like telling a complete stranger my problems. What if she thinks I'm weak?"

"Why would she think that?"

"It's how my mom makes me feel, like a child who can't make her own decisions. When I do, I fail, and Mom rubs it in."

Travis scooted next to her. "Maybe you can talk to the psychologist about your mom." He wrapped his arm around her shoulders. "It's hard to lay it all out there, but you won't regret it. Trust me. In our line of work, we have to hold it together when someone's world is crashing down. We have to be the strong ones. But you can't hold it in forever."

She shifted and leaned her back against his chest. How did she get so lucky to make such an amazing friend when she needed one the most? And a handsome one at that.

A warm, sweet breeze blew over them. He kissed her head. "I'll help you through this however I can."

While she felt a little better about her upcoming counseling session, it also had her on edge. It might help her get rid of the nightmares, but it also might confirm her biggest fear: that her mother had been right all along.

CHAPTER 20

Travis whistled as he stepped into the Sturgis squad office Monday afternoon. He waved at the secretary as he walked past. After grabbing some supplies and coffee, he headed toward his cubicle. A quick check of his messages and he'd be back out in the perfect, seventy-five-degree day within fifteen minutes.

"Wilkins. Need a minute with you." Sergeant Black stepped out of his office and smoothed down his short, brown mustache.

"Sure, Sarge." So much for quick. Travis followed him into the office.

Sarge ducked as he walked through the doorframe. He was tall but also wide, reminding Travis of a linebacker. "Close the door."

Travis's stomach tightened. He hated closed-door meetings. They reminded him of being sent to the principal's office.

"Have a seat." Sarge sat behind his oak desk and put on readers, then shuffled through some papers.

Travis sank onto the hard chair. "What's up?"

He held up a paper. "I read through your report on the Russell apprehension. We suspected the Russells were in the area with the possibility of being armed, yet you approached the camper by yourself while off duty with your personal sidearm. Why didn't you call it in?" Sarge stared at him over his glasses.

"It's my property. I don't have to call it in." Even though that was true, Travis's face heated.

Sarge leaned back. "And the Friday before, why didn't you wait for backup before approaching the Russells' vehicle?"

"Backup was fifty miles away."

"You're kidding, right? We've had extra manpower in the area all week. You're part of a team. Playing the lone wolf is going to get you killed. If you violate officer safety policy again, I'll write you up and disciplinary measures will be given. Is that clear?"

Frustration rolled through Travis, but he gave a sharp nod.

"Good. You're dismissed. And it wouldn't hurt you to share a meal with other troopers occasionally. Maybe if you'd spend some time with them you'd learn to trust them."

"Is that an order too?"

"Watch it, Wilkins."

Travis shoved the door open. It hit the wall and slammed shut behind him. He jumped, then cringed. His temper wasn't going to win points with his superiors.

Back in his cubicle, he plopped onto his chair and opened his laptop. As it booted up, he pinched his nose. If he called for backup for every little thing, he'd accomplish nothing. Didn't Sarge trust him to do his job? Since he'd found Marcus, he hadn't been complimented once, not that he expected it, but to be lectured for it? What a thankless job. He slammed the computer shut, grabbed it and a ticket book, then stormed out.

The sun blinded him, but he didn't slow down. Switching his load to his left arm, he reached in his pocket for his keys. Then his phone rang in the opposite pocket. He grunted. When he tried to reach it, the ticket book fell to the ground, spilling tickets everywhere. His jaw clenched as he held his computer to his chest and answered the phone. "Wilkins."

"Trooper Wilkins. I'm from the State Attorney's office, returning your call on Caleb and Mary Russell."

"Thanks. What's the status of their case?"

"It looks like they were arraigned on Tuesday, August twenty-second and released on bail. Caleb pled not guilty to kidnapping in the second degree, and Mary pled not guilty to kidnapping in the third degree. The trial date is September sixth at two o'clock."

"What are the bail conditions?"

"Caleb and Mary Russell are allowed to live together at their home. They must be home between seven at night and six in the morning. They must stay in Pennington County and have no contact with Marcus Elkhorn, Margo White, or any other Child Protection Services employee. Do you have any other questions?"

"Are they wearing ankle bracelet monitors?"

"Not at this time."

"Thanks for the information." Despite the state's conditions, the hair on the back of his neck still stood up as he juggled his phone, laptop, and ticket book. The Russells were free. Maybe Marcus really had seen Caleb last Saturday. Travis should have searched better. What if Caleb was still in Alkaline?

Travis ran to his car and threw his supplies inside. His hand shook as he called Nattie and waited for her to pick up. It went to voicemail. Dropping onto the driver's seat, he tried her number again. Voicemail. He dialed the café.

"Prickly Pear Bistro, this is Rosemary."

"Is Nattie there?"

"May I ask who's calling?"

"It's Travis. Is she there?"

"She left after her shift at three."

"Do you know where she went?"

"Sorry, love. I don't. Is everything okay?"

Maybe. Maybe not. Travis didn't want to worry Rosemary though. "Have her call me if you see her, okay?" He didn't wait for an answer as he slammed his door and peeled out of the parking lot, trying Nattie's number again. When she didn't answer, he floored it.

* * * * * * *

Natalia trudged up the narrow staircase juggling a basket full of raspberries and a sleeping toddler. When she reached the landing, she shifted Marcus higher onto her hip. His eyes popped open. She nuzzled his neck, kissing him just under his ear until his yawn turned to giggling. She set him down and dug out her keys. "Sit still, and I'll have us inside in a minute. Then we can taste the fruit of our labor."

As she swung the door open, her cell phone buzzed on the kitchen counter. "Whoops. Nattie left her phone here. I wonder how many calls I missed in the hour we were gone." She winked at Marcus as she hurried to answer it, closing the door behind her.

"Candy!" Marcus ran around the room.

She reached her phone as it stopped. Five missed calls from Travis. She dialed his number and grabbed Marcus as he ran by. "You need to calm down."

He shook a yellow box, rattling its contents. "Daddy!"

Travis's voicemail answered. "Hey, Travis. It's Nattie. Sorry I wasn't—"

The front door bounced open with a bang. Natalia's heart leapt as she spun around. Marcus froze.

"There you are." Travis scowled as he strode to her, then hugged her, pressing her against the hardness of his bulletproof vest. He inhaled a deep breath and held her tight.

She leaned back to look at him. "You're scaring me. What happened?"

His face, a mere inch from hers, bridged the gap. The smoothness of his lips brushed hers. Heat rushed through her body. When he pulled back, she leaned forward. With a moan, he deepened the kiss. His hands roamed over her back until they reached her hair. He ran his fingers through the strands, draping them over one shoulder and allowing the air to tickle her neck. When she slid her arm around his back, he moved his lips to her forehead and hugged her close. His heavy breathing warmed her skin.

"Are you okay?" he asked, his voice hoarse.

She smiled. She was more than okay. She was elated. She laid her head against his shoulder and sighed. "Of course I'm okay. What's going on? I assume you didn't stop by just to kiss me."

He chuckled. "No, that wasn't the plan. But I can't say I'm too upset by it."

She stepped away and tucked her hands into her back pockets. "What happened?"

"I heard from the State Attorney's office," he said, lowering his voice. "Caleb and Mary Russell were released on bail."

What? Why would a judge grant bail to kidnappers? Would they try to take Marcus again? She had to keep him safe. "Marcus?"

The front door swung on its hinges.

"Marcus!" As she hurried for the door, a strong arm wrapped around her waist.

"Calm down, Nattie. He's here." Travis shut the door, then led her to the kitchen and lifted the table cloth. Marcus lay curled between the chairs, asleep. He clutched a box of Sugar Babies in his hands. Travis scooped him up. She pried the candy away before Travis carried him to bed.

While he did, Natalia looked in the box. Half empty. Where had Marcus found them? She put them on the counter.

When Travis returned, he stepped behind her and massaged her neck.

Natalia pointed at the box. "Did you bring him candy?"

His hands stilled.

So did her heart. She reached for the box.

"No. Leave it on the counter. I'll have it tested and the box dusted for fingerprints. If it was Caleb or Mary, they violated the conditions of their bail. They aren't allowed any contact with Marcus." He pulled rubber gloves from his duty belt, put them on, and examined the box. "Will you get me a plastic bag?"

She found a bag in the kitchen drawer and held it open for him.

He placed the candy inside. "Hopefully, they'll be able to get a print from it."

Natalia sank onto a dining room chair as thoughts whirled through her head. "Where did he find that candy?"

Travis sat in the chair next to her. "Maybe you should move back in with Rosemary."

The idea tempted her, but Natalia shook her head. "Rosemary's house only has two bedrooms. Marcus needs his own room, and I don't want to impose on her more by making her share a room with me." She looked at Travis. "Caleb has no idea who's fostering Marcus, right? Why would he suspect me?"

"I don't know. I'll have to make some calls." Travis squeezed the bridge of his nose.

She grabbed his hand and held it between hers. "You do that whenever you're frustrated. Did you know that?"

"Do what?"

"Pinch your nose."

He sighed. "It eases the pressure so I don't get a headache."

"It's endearing." She kissed the spot.

"That eases all my aches and pains." He kissed her until her heart pounded.

She took a shuddering breath. "Let's not start that again."

"Just promise you'll be more careful. Lock your door and take your phone with you."

"I locked the door this time."

"That's my girl."

* * * * * * *

Natalia's stomach tightened as she dialed the number. Hopefully Marcus would stay asleep for the next hour.

"Dr. Drakeford's office, how can I help you?"

She rocked in the recliner. "It's Natalia Brynner. Dr. Drakeford is expecting my call."

"One moment, please."

A moment for her nerves to increase.

"Hi, Natalia. This is Dr. Drakeford. How have you been?"

"Okay. I guess."

"Any more nightmares?"

"None as bad as the other night. I had one last night, but it was more weird than terrifying."

"Tell me about it."

She swallowed, her throat dry. "I was in the home of a teenager when a huge deer crashed through the window. While it tried to ram her, I calmly asked questions—like what's your address, where are your parents, is anyone hurt?—even though I was right there in the room. Then my mom appeared and told me I was asking the wrong questions. I needed to find out what kind of deer it was or how else would the officer be able to shoot it. It didn't work, though. I still couldn't help the girl."

"Why couldn't you help her?"

"My body was frozen in place. It's like that in all my dreams. I can only talk or scream."

"It's like you're a dispatcher, but on scene. Are all your dreams work related?"

"Yes. Some of them are horrifically graphic, even though I've never been to the crime scenes."

"It's human nature to imagine the worst. It might help to see pictures of the scenes after a disturbing call to process them accurately. The officers get to arrest perpetrators, and sometimes attend their sentencing or visit victims in the hospital, but you move on to the next call. Often dispatchers don't get closure."

"That makes sense."

"Back to your dream. Does your mom often criticize you?"

"Constantly. It seems I can't do anything right."

"How do you usually respond to that criticism?"

"I try to ignore it, but sometimes the anxiety gets to be too much, and the only thing that helps is leaving."

"Is that how you ended up hours away from home?"

"Yeah."

"When do you think you can meet in person?"

"In two weeks, at the earliest."

"That will give me enough time to develop a treatment plan so we can get you back to dispatching."

Natalia's peripheral vision darkened. Six long computer monitors appeared in front of her. Their screens shone bright white.

"Help! There's a fire!"

She typed as fast as she could, dispatching engines from the nearest fire department. A yellow house engulfed in flames filled the monitor in front of her. A baby's cries rose above the roar of the fire. A baby! Her heart pounded. She sucked in breath after breath. The baby was going to die!

"Natalia. Natalia, are you there? It's Audrey. Dr. Drakeford. Can you hear me?"

She closed her eyes.

"Natalia. Slow your breathing. Can you hear me?"

A baby cried. It was burning. "I have to help the baby."

"The baby's okay, but I hear it too. Is your child crying?"

"I don't have a child. It's a baby. He's burning in a fire."

"No, he's safe. There's a child near you but he's okay. Take a deep breath and slowly let it out."

Natalia sucked in a large gulp of air, let it out, and opened her eyes. Rosemary's apartment. Marcus crying in his room.

"Natalia. Can you talk to me?"

What just happened? "I have to get Marcus. He's crying." She ran into his room. He sat up when he saw her and lifted his arms. When she sat next to him, he laid his head on her lap. She wanted to do the same thing. "I'm sorry, Dr. Drakeford."

"What did you see?"

"All of a sudden I was at my console taking a house fire call. Then a burning house appeared with a crying baby. But I guess the crying was Marcus."

"Who's Marcus?"

"He's my foster boy, and he was just waking up from his nap. I'm sorry I spaced out like that." Embarrassment and exhaustion swirled in her. "I can't control when they come."

"Those are flashbacks. How many have you had?"

"That was the third."

"That's a symptom of burnout and post-traumatic stress disorder."

Her body tensed. "You think I have PTSD? Soldiers get that, not dispatchers."

"Anyone who has experienced trauma can develop PTSD, but having a few flashbacks doesn't mean you have it. Have the flashbacks affected your ability to work or function in society?"

"No, but I hate them." She stroked Marcus's hair, wishing she could escape. But where could she go that her flashbacks and dreams wouldn't follow?

"I can help you, Natalia. Even if you don't go back to dispatching. We can get you healthy again."

She hoped so, because she was running out of places to run to.

CHAPTER 21

Tuesday afternoon, Natalia sat on the couch next to Margo as the caseworker finished reading a puppy book to Marcus.

"Is everything okay with his case?" Natalia asked.

"I've got good news," Margo said, setting the book aside. "I think we have an adoptive family for him."

Natalia smiled as an unexpected sadness rippled through her. She would miss him, but his new family had to be better at caring for him than she was. "What happens now?"

"We take our time and let Marcus meet his new family a few times before he goes to live with them."

"What are they like?"

Margo took a black binder from her bag and pulled out a picture, then handed it to Natalia. "These are the Freemans."

A family with wide smiles stood in front of a gray backdrop. The man had slicked back, black hair and wore a brown suede, fringed jacket with a black, button-up shirt. His arm was around a tall, slender, woman with long, straight hair, a turquoise sweater, and a wide silver necklace. Her hands rested on the shoulders of a boy in a black dress shirt and turquoise tie. In front of the man was a girl in a turquoise-and-white-striped dress with her black hair in braids.

Margo pointed at each family member. "That's Rich. His wife is Etta. Rich is a high school principal and Etta is a photographer. Their oldest is Estella, but they call her Essie. She's nine, and her brother, Brody, is eight."

Natalia showed the picture to Marcus. "What do you think? Would you like to meet them?"

He took the picture and crinkled it. "The boy pay with me?"

"I bet he'd love to." Natalia handed the photo back to Margo. "Sorry about that."

"You can keep it." She shut the binder. "The Freemans live in Omaha, which is a day's drive from here. Since school doesn't start for a couple more weeks, now is the time to make the adjustment. They're going to drive to Sturgis on Thursday, but they won't meet Marcus until Friday. On Saturday morning, he can go on an outing with them. If everything goes smoothly, we can try for an overnight at their hotel."

"You'll be moving him this weekend?" So soon?

"Actually, would you be able to keep him another week? I know I told you it would only be two weeks, but it's better if we can wait and move him from your care to the adoptive family."

"Things have changed back home, so I can keep him until he's ready to move."

"Great. If everything goes according to plan, I'll drive him to Omaha the following weekend. Normally, we like the adoptive family to have three visits, but, because of the distance, it just isn't feasible. We'll let Marcus video chat with them throughout the week."

"Then no more contact from me?" A sharp pain sliced through her chest.

"That's entirely up to the Freemans. We recommend waiting at least a month so Marcus can adjust." Margo touched his knee. "We've come a long way, haven't we?" She gathered her things. "I'll bring the Freemans over Friday afternoon."

Natalia walked Margo to the door, locking it behind her, then turned to Marcus. He flipped through his book. Even though her mom was hard on her, Natalia always felt safe and cared for. She wanted Marcus to know that type of security and stability too, but she sure was going to miss him. It had been a rough start, but now that the end was in sight, sadness settled in. First because of losing Marcus, then because of herself. Without him to care for, she'd have to figure out what she was going to do with her life and her growing feelings for Travis.

* * * * * * *

Natalia filled Cole's mug with coffee. He sat at the counter eating scrambled eggs. Other than him and the retirees, who filled their usual table in the center of the bistro, the place was empty. The cook clanked around in the kitchen, preparing the lunch special.

"Where's Marcus?" Cole asked.

"Rosemary takes Thursday off, so she's entertaining him at her house. They were going to work in her garden."

"You and Travis seem to be hitting it off."

Natalia didn't know how to respond to that.

"Are you dating?"

Dating? Not exactly. Kissing? Most definitely. Heat crept up her neck. She turned around to avoid eye contact and put the coffee pot on the burner. "We haven't defined our relationship yet."

"I hope you'll be happy."

"Thanks." She picked up a rag and wiped syrup from the counter.

Cole bent over, then placed a wooden box the size of a shoe box onto the counter. "I brought these for Marcus."

She dropped the rag on the counter. On the box's lid, someone had carved *Travis* and *Cole* in crude letters. She traced the grooves of Travis's name.

"Dad helped us make it when we were eleven." Cole opened the lid. Toy cars filled it. "I thought Marcus would like to play with these."

"That's really special. Thanks." She set them under the counter. "I'll make sure he takes good care of them."

Cole stood and threw a ten onto the counter. "Make sure Travis takes good care of you too." He put on his John Deere hat, tipped his head at her, and left.

* * * * * * *

Friday afternoon, Natalia walked through the apartment fluffing pillows, plucking lint from the floor, and wiping fingerprints off the picture window. Marcus, dressed in a dinosaur-print polo shirt and matching green shorts, drove his toy cars around the swirly designs on the area rug. After she checked his room one more time, she inspected the bathroom. Still clean.

As she paced, the clicking of her heels kept time with the pounding of her heart. She picked a piece of fuzz off her black capris and pulled at the hem of her maroon blouse before running her fingers through her hair.

Why was she so nervous? She wasn't the one up for adoption.

Someone knocked and Marcus jumped up. He ran to the door. "Travis?"

Natalia grabbed his hand. "No, it's the Freemans, remember?"

Armed with a nervous smile and all the bravery she could muster, Natalia opened the door. Travis stood there in black jeans, a blue button-down shirt, and black boots. He smiled as he stepped into the apartment. "I hope you don't mind if I join you."

"Travis!" Marcus lunged for him.

Travis scooped him up. "Hey, cowboy. If it's okay with Nattie, I thought I might stay."

"Of course it's okay with me. I'm relieved actually." She took his hand and squeezed.

When Travis put Marcus down, the boy ran back to his toys.

"Remind me to give Cole a hug the next time I see him. He brought Marcus your box of toy cars, and they've entertained him all afternoon."

"I'll do nothing of the sort." Travis wrapped his arms around her. "If anyone is getting hugs from you, it will be me. You can sock him in the arm instead. Means about the same thing."

She laughed, then laid her head on his firm shoulder, her nose just inches from his freshly shaved jaw. She breathed in his spicy aftershave, allowing the scent to relax her. Travis rubbed circles on her tense shoulders. "I'm glad you came. I'm calmer with you here."

Another knock. She looked at the rug. "Where's Marcus?"

"I'll get him. You let them in."

At the door, she grabbed the doorknob and took a deep breath. "Please, let them be amazing." She opened the door to Margo and four smiling faces. "Hi, I'm Natalia Brynner."

Mrs. Freeman offered her hand. "I'm Etta. So nice to meet you."

Natalia shook her hand. "It's nice to meet you. Come on in." She stepped aside so the group could file into the apartment.

"I've heard so many wonderful things about you from Margo. You're such a sweetie to give so much to Marcus." Etta's warm, brown eyes settled Natalia's remaining nerves.

"It's been my pleasure watching him."

Mr. Freeman put his arm around his wife's shoulders. "I'm Rich. We've been excited to meet you and Marcus. When they called us, we could hardly keep the kids from hitchhiking out here. I think Brody had his bags packed Monday."

"Nattie, can you come here for a second?" She turned to see Travis in the door to the bathroom.

"Of course. Please have a seat." She pointed to the living room. "I'll be right back." She hurried to the bathroom.

Marcus sat on the bath mat with black smears around his eyes and down his cheeks. Bright pink streaks covered his lips and chin. Powder coated his clothes.

Travis held up a makeup-covered washcloth. "It won't come off. The harder I scrub, the more it smears."

Natalia knelt next to Marcus. "Why did you get into Nattie's makeup?"

"I wanna look petty like Nattie." His smile about melted her heart.

Travis put the cloth in the sink. "Cowboys don't wear makeup." Marcus's smile fell.

"Unless they're rodeo clowns. Were you trying to be a clown?" Marcus giggled.

"Oh, my."

Natalia jumped at Margo's voice. The social worker stood in the doorway, her eyes wide.

"Mago!"

"Is everything okay?" Etta poked her head in.

Natalia wished the floor would gobble her up.

Etta laughed as she pushed past Margo. "This must be the sweet boy we've heard so much about. Looks like you need a bath."

Natalia stood. "This is Marcus. Marcus, this is Etta, the woman in your picture."

Marcus waved. "Hi. This is Nattie."

Etta held her hand out to Marcus. "How about you come with me to meet some special people, then you can take a bath?"

He took her hand and pulled her out of the bathroom with Margo following.

Natalia faced Travis. His smile, which quickly disappeared, reappeared seconds later even bigger. "It's not funny," she said.

"It's going to be okay. He's a little boy. He's going to make messes." He chuckled as he led her to the living room.

Marcus sat on Rich's shoulders holding a foam basketball just high enough that Brody couldn't reach it. Marcus giggled as Brody jumped and missed the ball. When Rich swung Marcus down to the floor, he chased Brody around the table.

After the rest of the introductions were made, Natalia caught Marcus. "I'll give him a bath. There's a cheese-and-cracker platter, veggie tray, and lemonade in the fridge."

"I'll take care of it," Travis said.

After Marcus was bathed and dressed, he ran into the living room with Natalia close behind. Rich and Travis sat at the table talking about crime in Omaha. Marcus ran to Brody, who was driving cars on the carpet, and drove a car behind Brody's. Etta sat on the couch leaning over the phone Margo held. And Essie sat in the recliner looking through a magazine. Unsure of what to do, Natalia grabbed the dirty plates from the table and headed into the kitchen.

Etta joined her. "Can I help you?"

"There's not much to clean up."

"You didn't need to do any of this." She grabbed a Tupperware lid and snapped it onto the veggie dip.

"I mostly did it to keep myself busy. I was kind of nervous about this visit."

"I think we all were."

Natalia picked up a sponge and wiped the counters. "Can you tell me about your family? Margo didn't tell us much."

"Rich is from Pine Ridge and belongs to the Ogalala Sioux Tribe. I'm from Aberdeen and belong to the Cheyenne River Sioux Tribe. I met Rich at the University of Omaha, and we've been married for almost twenty years. How about you and Travis? Are you together?"

Natalia blushed. "I've only known Travis a short time. I'm originally from Sioux Falls. He was the first person I met in Alkaline. Have you been trying to adopt for long?"

"Actually, we've already adopted twice. Rich and I have been foster parents for twelve years. Essie came to live with us halfway through our second year."

"How old was she?"

"Two days, and my heart attached to her the minute I held her. Her mom found out she was pregnant the second month of a seven-year prison sentence. They didn't know who the father was, and the mom's parental rights were terminated three months later. There were no suitable relatives to adopt her, so we made it official when she was nine months old.

"Brody is Rich's cousin's boy. CPS placed him with us as a baby after his mom left him home alone to make a beer run. She was arrested for a DUI. Thankfully, she told the police she left her baby home. For the first year, he had weekly visits with her, then she decided to leave the state for a few months. When she came back, her rights had been terminated for abandonment."

Natalia couldn't imagine that kind of childhood. "They're blessed to have you both. I was a 9-1-1 dispatcher until recently, and I took a few calls of child abuse and abandonment. I rarely find out what happens, but I would have loved to see those kids get adopted."

"Have you fostered children before?"

"No, but my brother and sister-in-law have, and they adopted through foster care too. I wasn't working the day their girls came into the system, but I made sure to give the dispatcher updates on their case."

"What a tough job."

"Like being a foster parent."

Etta nodded. "I'm not sure which is worse, when you don't know what they're going back to or when you do know and there's nothing you can do about it."

"I can't imagine. I'm glad I'll get to see Marcus settled in a good home."

"The timing is perfect. My mother recently had a health scare, and she might need to move in with us at some point. If we can get Marcus settled before she needs more help, it would be far less stressful for all of us."

Natalia shivered. She didn't think she would survive living under the same roof as her mother ever again. She pushed that thought away. "Would anyone like some coffee?"

Travis raised his hand. "Is there any pie to go with it?"

Rich raised his hand too. "I'll take coffee if there's pie."

Margo shook her head as she answered her phone and stepped into the hall.

Natalia reached into the fridge and pulled out a cherry pie. "My boss gave me this for the occasion. Travis must have missed it in there."

Etta took it from her. "I'll dish it up if you want to make the coffee."

"Deal." Natalia started the coffee pot as Etta called the kids over for dessert. The coziness of it all calmed Natalia's nerves. She liked the Freemans, and Marcus seemed to as well.

Travis stepped beside her. "What are you thinking about?"

"How great the Freemans are. I'm glad I've been able to be a part of Marcus's life, even for this short time. I thought I was doing him a favor, but this has been good for me too. Thanks for talking me into it."

He squeezed her shoulder. "I've enjoyed spending time with him too. He's a great kid."

Coffee splashed into the pot, releasing a rich aroma. Natalia filled three mugs. When she turned around, the Freemans had moved into the living room. They patted their legs while Essie led them on a pretend bear hunt. A huge grin spread across Marcus's face. Peace filled Natalia's soul, confirming that this family was perfect for him. She could move back to Sioux Falls with a clear conscience. She glanced at Travis sitting at the table eating his pie. The problem, now, was that she didn't want to leave *him*.

She joined him at the table and sipped her coffee, watching Marcus's animated expressions change with the story. When the hunt was over, Rich and Etta took the other seats at the table and dug into their pie as Margo stepped back into the apartment.

"Sorry about that," she said. "Thanks so much for hosting us, Natalia. What time works for tomorrow?"

"Our plans are open," Etta said.

"I can bring Marcus to your hotel in Sturgis. Where are you staying?"

"At the Sleep More Inn."

Brody ran into the kitchen with Marcus chasing him. "There's a pool with a waterslide."

Natalia smiled. "I'll pack Marcus's suit."

Margo typed the information into her phone. "Perfect. I have some meetings later that day, but it should work if you can be there by nine."

"That shouldn't be a problem. I'll call when I leave to make sure the timing still works."

Rich motioned to the living room. "Brody, go help Essie clean up the books."

Brody trudged toward his sister with Marcus tugging on his shirt. When Brody knelt near the bookshelf, Marcus hugged him until they fell over laughing.

Natalia escorted Margo to the door. "Today went better than I thought."

Margo handed her a card. "Here's the play therapist's information. She has an opening on Wednesday at one, if you can take him. If not, I'll send someone to pick him up."

"I'll check my schedule. Thanks for setting it up."

"He'll only get to see her once, but she'll help him process this move. I've asked the Freemans to find a therapist for him in Omaha as soon as possible."

Margo said her goodbyes, then the Freemans met Natalia at the door. Marcus, holding his bear, rushed to Essie's side and lifted his arms. She picked him up but struggled to hold him.

Etta took Marcus from her daughter. "You're a sweet, sweet boy. We'll see you tomorrow."

He leaned over and kissed Natalia's cheek. "Bye, Nattie."

"You're not going with them now." She held her arms out, but he shook his head and tightened his grip on Etta.

Etta rubbed his back. "We'll see you tomorrow. We can go swimming at our hotel. Doesn't that sound fun?"

"Swimming!"

"Now, go to Nattie, and she'll bring you to us in the morning." Etta handed him over to Natalia.

Marcus screamed and went limp in her arms. "Swimming!"

"Sorry." Etta shooed her kids out of the door, then waved at Marcus. Rich chuckled and followed them down the stairs.

Travis shut the door. Natalia set Marcus on the floor where he continued his tantrum. He threw the bear at her as he flailed about.

She wanted to scold him, but what did she expect when he'd only napped for thirty minutes? Before she could respond, Travis picked him up and took him to his room. Natalia plopped onto the couch.

Travis closed the door, then sat beside her, draping his arm around her shoulders. "We'll let him cool down on his bed."

Someone knocked at the door. Now what? She sighed.

Travis stood. "I'll get it. You rest." He opened the door, and Rosemary walked in carrying a large, striped tote bag.

"How did things go? You look wiped." She set the bag on the table.

"It went well," Natalia said. "The Freemans are amazing. We got off to a rough start when we found Marcus covered in makeup. Turns out Travis isn't skilled at removing it."

"What do they make that stuff out of, engine grease? The more I scrubbed the worse it got."

Rosemary laughed. "I thought the visit might be emotionally draining, so I came up with the most brilliant plan. You two are going to go enjoy the evening, watch the sun set, and do some stargazing, or whatever you kids are calling it these days. I brought food for you to take with you. I'll feed Marcus and put him to bed, then curl up on that old couch and read my book."

A night out with only Travis? Energy jolted through Natalia. The days were passing so quickly that she had to grasp what little time with him she could. "Thanks, Rosemary. An evening out sounds amazing."

Rosemary waved her off as she handed Natalia the bag. "Don't hurry home."

N atalia nestled beside Travis in the bed of his pickup and held out her phone. He leaned closer, and she took a picture.

"Text that to me." Travis kissed her cheek.

Yellows and oranges streaked across the sky behind a darkening hilltop. The lake in front of them mirrored the brilliant colors. "It's beautiful."

"The Lakota name for the mountain is Mato Paha, or Bear Butte, and the lake shares her name. It's a sacred place for Native Americans."

"I can see why."

"I'll take you to the top some time. It's a great hike."

Natalia wanted to go on all kinds of adventures with Travis, but how would they make it work?

"Marcus leaves next weekend. What's your plan after that?"

She shrugged. "I wish I knew. I'd love to stay here and work for Rosemary, but she's closing the bistro in a month. Plus, I have an apartment in Sioux Falls and rent is due soon. I don't think my waitressing salary will cover it and my car payment."

"You don't need two apartments. Let the other one go."

"And do what?"

"I haven't figured that out yet, but I'd like you to stay."

She ran her finger over his rough jaw. "You would? Why?"

He kissed her finger. "I kind of like you."

"I kind of like you too." Excitement flipped her stomach. If they could figure out the logistics, could they make a relationship work?

Travis threaded his fingers around hers. "The Meade County

Sheriff's Office is looking for a dispatcher. You could move to Sturgis or commute. It's only a forty-five minute drive."

A lump formed in her throat. "Go back to dispatching? I don't know if I can. I don't know if I can take another call like Officer Mason's."

"Sure you can. You're a brave lady."

"I've never done anything brave."

"That's a lie. Reciting last call, taking in a traumatized boy, and seeking help for yourself all take courage. If you want to go back to dispatching, I know you'll find a way to do it."

"How did you get so smart?"

"You have no idea the turmoil and chaos I've had to work through, but it's possible. I want you to be free from yours too. To find peace."

She sighed and snuggled in next to him as the light faded. She had never felt more peaceful than at that moment.

****

Travis walked Nattie up to her apartment, stroking her hand with his thumb. What would it take to keep her there? Circle S Ranch was hiring for their large cattle operation, although she wouldn't make much of a wrangler with her novice horse-riding skills. Maybe the school had an opening. Better not suggest that idea, with her mom pushing her to become a teacher.

When she stepped on the landing, he stopped on the next step down. She turned to him, her eyes even with his. She wore his flannel shirt, her hair stuck out in disarray, and black makeup had smudged under her eyes. She was adorable.

"Thanks," she said. "Not just for the evening, but for everything. I'm one fortunate lady."

He ran his knuckle down her cheek. "If you haven't figured it out yet, I think you're kind of special. I'd like to take you on a real date. Dinner and dancing."

Her eyes widened. "You dance?"

"This is cowboy country. Not much else to do growing up but go to barn dances. I know a mean two-step. How about it? Next Saturday, after Marcus leaves."

"I'll need some cheering up at that point."

"We both will. Whaddya say?" His gut tightened. Did asking a pretty girl out ever get easier?

"I'd love to, but I'm not much of a dancer. I feel awkward on the dance floor."

"Then you haven't had the right guy leading you." He leaned in to kiss her. As soon as his lips met hers, his phone rang. He touched her forehead with his as he dug it out of his pocket. "Wilkins."

"It's Peters. We've got a hostage situation in Sturgis. The deputies served a felony warrant, and the guy started shooting. His girlfriend is in there with him. Captain called out SWAT."

"Are the deputies okay?"

"Yeah, so far no one's injured. We're getting the armored vehicle ready now."

"I'll be there as soon as I can." He stuffed his phone back in his pocket. "I've got to go. They called out the SWAT team."

"Is anyone hurt?"

"No, and we aim to keep it that way." He kissed her again, pulling her close. Her moan ignited a fire in him. How could he leave her? His phone buzzed and he pulled away.

She grabbed his hand. "Be careful, and let me know when you're safe."

* * * * * * *

Caleb was watching prime time TV in the living room when the front security light went on. He looked out the window as the old detective walked up his driveway. He glanced at his watch. Nine fifteen. Kind of late for a house call. He had some place to be in half an hour, and he couldn't be late, so he opened the front door and leaned against the doorjamb before the detective could knock. "What do you want?"

"Hello to you too. In case you forgot, I'm Detective Astor." He showed him his badge. "I need to know where you were Saturday afternoon at three."

"Took the wife to the movies. Is that a crime now?"

"Do you have any proof?"

Caleb growled. These officers were so stupid. He pulled out his wallet and handed him the ticket stub. "It's all I've got."

Astor examined it. "This doesn't prove you went to the movie, just that you bought a ticket for that time."

Caleb shrugged. "Doesn't prove I wasn't there either. Thought I was innocent until proven guilty?"

"Can I speak with your wife?"

"She's asleep, but by all means go wake her up. It's not like you haven't already ruined her life." He stepped aside.

The detective entered the house. Caleb led him to their bedroom and flipped on the overhead light. Mary lay curled on her side. He gently shook her shoulder. "The detective needs to ask you a question."

She moaned and rolled to her back, her eyes still closed.

"Go ahead and ask," he said as the detective stood in the doorway.

"Mrs. Russell, you need to wake up." She slowly opened her eyes and the detective stepped into the room. "Where were you Saturday afternoon at three?"

"Saturday?"

"Remember where we went, dear?"

The detective cleared his throat. "Let her answer on her own."

Mary blinked a few times, then sat up. "Did we go to the movies?"

Caleb nodded. Thatta girl. Then he glared at Astor. "Anything else you want to bother us with?"

He grunted. "No, but I'll be back if I do."

As soon as the detective left the room, Mary fell asleep. The sedative Caleb had slipped her earlier must have kicked in.

Astor stopped at the front door. "It won't take much to get ankle monitors on you both. Watch that you don't violate your bail."

Caleb watched the detective's car until it disappeared. Then he hopped into his car. Twenty minutes later, he pulled up to a small house with a yellow light shining onto a broken screen door. The door opened, and a hunched figure in dark baggy clothes approached his car. His buddy climbed in accompanied by the stench of cat pee. He handed Caleb a heavy, brown sack.

Caleb opened it and pulled out a black pistol. "A twenty-two caliber." He grunted. That wouldn't do much damage. "Is this the best you got?"

"Yep. Take it or leave it."

He laid the gun on the center console before dumping out the rest of the contents. A small bag of crystal and a slip of paper landed in his hand. "This the number from your guy at child protection?"

"Yeah, but he says he's done getting me info. He's not willing to lose his job, even for crystal."

"I've got all I need now." Caleb handed him a white envelope with seven hundred dollars.

"Pleasure doing business with you."

CHAPTER 23

Natalia lay in bed staring at the dark ceiling. She closed her eyes and saw Travis in his SWAT gear, shot through the head. She sat up and turned on the lamp. Her throat tightened. She'd already imagined him shot, stabbed, beaten, and even blown up. How much longer could her mind torture her? She grabbed her phone. She had to talk to someone.

She hadn't known Travis was on the SWAT team. Surely, his gear and training would protect him, although it hadn't saved Officer Mason. Her stomach rolled. She took a deep breath and tried to remember Dr. Drakeford's relaxation method.

Her phone buzzed.

Scene's clear. Will be here another few hours. All ok. Good night.

Relief poured through her.

The phone rang. The caller ID said unknown caller. "Hello?"

"Don't do it." The gruff male voice caused her skin to crawl.

"Who is this?"

"My boy needs his mommy."

"Caleb." The breath left her lungs. "You—you're not supposed to call me. You have to stay away from us." Her voice cracked.

"He's my boy! Give him back or you'll regret it." The line went dead.

Her fingers trembled as she dialed Travis's number, but she pushed end before calling him. He couldn't help from Sturgis, and if she called him now, he'd worry about her instead of the scene. She hurried to the front door and made sure both the handle and deadbolt were locked. Then she looked in at Marcus, who slept curled on his side.

Something crashed outside. Natalia rushed to the window and peeked around the curtain. The vet clinic next door looked normal. She ran to the dining room window. The newly replaced back light was out. Her pulse accelerated. Travis wasn't available, but he wasn't the only one who could help.

****

Travis rubbed his itchy eyes and yawned as he drove his patrol car down Alkaline's deserted roads. Lights illuminated the main street. He'd sweep down the alley behind the bistro, then head home.

The lights were on in Nattie's apartment. What was she doing up at two in the morning? The back light was out and an unfamiliar sedan was parked near the back door. Caleb!

He jerked to a stop behind the empty sedan. Fear propelled him from the car and he flew into the building. His boots echoed on the stairs while imagining Nattie hurt and crumpled on the floor. He kicked the door open.

A figure appeared to his left. Travis sprang toward it, tackling him to the ground. The intruder rolled, pushing at Travis, but Travis maneuvered him to his stomach and cranked his arm behind his back. "I'm Trooper Wilkins! Stop resisting!" Adrenaline pumped through him.

"Get off me!"

"Where are Nattie and Marcus? If you hurt them, I'll kill you." Travis tightened his grip.

"Dude! You've got major problems!"

The voice pushed through Travis's anger, and something registered. "Cole?" He hopped off. His twin sat up, rubbing his shoulder.

"Travis! What are you doing?"

He glanced up at Nattie's wide eyes, then back at Cole who glared at him. "I thought he was Caleb. Sorry, man." He held his hand out to help Cole up, but his brother hit it away and struggled to his feet. Travis pinched his nose. What was he thinking barging in like that? Stupid, rookie move.

"Why would you think Caleb was here?" Her lip trembled.

"There's a strange sedan parked out back. I didn't know Cole got a different car."

Cole's hand dropped from his shoulder. "I didn't. I'm parked out front."

Travis stilled. "Why are you here?"

Nattie stepped closer. "I was scared, and I didn't know who else to call."

"What scared you?" His jaw tensed.

"Caleb called me tonight. He wants Marcus back."

His gaze collided with Cole's then Nattie's. "Where's Marcus?"

"I just got him back to sleep. I'm surprised you didn't wake him up with all that fighting."

"Go into his room and stay there." Travis ran down the stairs and out the door. The car was gone. Cole stopped next to him, heaving. Travis pointed at the stairs. "Stay with Nattie."

He jumped into his patrol car and took off. Why had he attacked Cole? Those were precious minutes lost while Caleb got away. He drove through the streets of Alkaline and down a few country roads before returning to the apartment empty-handed.

He trudged up the stairs feeling like a hot-headed failure. At the landing, the apartment door hung from the bottom hinge and the frame was splintered around the lock. Great, now his impulse had left Nattie even more vulnerable.

When he reached Marcus's room, he tapped on the door. "Nattie, it's Travis."

The door opened, and Nattie fell into his arms. Was she trembling or was he? He couldn't tell as he tightened his grip around her. He looked past her to Cole sitting beside Marcus, who was still asleep.

He led Nattie to the couch. Cole followed them and stood by the table, concern etched on his face. "Was that Caleb's car?"

"I'm not sure. I tried to find it, but it's long gone. Is your shoulder okay?"

Cole rolled the joint and winced. "It's sore."

"I'm really sorry."

"That's the thanks I get for racing over to rescue your girlfriend."

Nattie stiffened. Travis stood. "Thanks for coming when she called. I owe you one."

Cole's eyes narrowed. "I didn't do it for you." He looked at Nattie. "I'm going to take off. Call me anytime, no matter what. It's a risk I'm willing to take."

"Thanks for coming over." Nattie followed Cole to the door and gasped. She turned to Travis. "My door is broken!"

Guilt nagged him. "Yeah, sorry about that. I'll move a dresser in front of the hole for now and fix it tomorrow."

"What if Caleb does come? I don't feel safe without a locked door."

"I'll stay for tonight."

Her eyes widened.

"I'll sleep on the couch. Don't worry. I'm a light sleeper."

"Okay." But she didn't look convinced.

Travis closed the distance between them and lifted her chin. "I feel like an idiot, attacking Cole and scaring you."

"I hope his shoulder is all right."

"Don't worry about him. He gets rougher treatment from the steers he brands. It'll keep him on his toes."

She hit his arm. "Don't joke about this. I can't imagine this will help things between you."

"I doubt much could hurt it at this point." He pulled her into his embrace. "Speaking of relationships, I liked him calling you my girlfriend." Maybe too much. He stroked her hair as she relaxed against him.

"And all the complications that go with it?"

"Nothing we can't figure out." His insides tightened. "Is that a title you want?" The seconds passed like hours.

She leaned back and looked at him, then she smiled and he

could breathe again. When she nodded, he kissed her, savoring her sweetness. As foolish as he'd felt earlier, this felt right. Reining in his passion, he reluctantly stepped away. "While I'd like to stand here kissing my girlfriend all night, I'd better secure that opening." And get some sleep. He had a sedan to find.

CHAPTER 24

Natalia rolled over and checked the time. Five thirty. The scene from last night replayed in her mind. She'd been terrified when she heard the door burst open, thinking it was Caleb. What a coward she was to hide in Marcus's bedroom while Cole had to fight off his attacker. Only when Travis shouted his name had she dared to sneak out.

She lay on her stomach and closed her eyes, needing another hour of sleep. Instead, she giggled. She was Travis's girlfriend. Giddiness danced inside her, then disappeared behind her insecurities. Was that the best idea? There was no way she could financially stay in Alkaline, and long-distance relationships were hard. Her brother had struggled when he went to medical school and his future wife stayed in Sioux Falls, and they had already been dating for a year. Natalia and Travis were just beginning their relationship. Would it fizzle out before it even began? Did she make a mistake saying yes? She moaned into her pillow, wishing she could see the future.

Two restless hours later, she gave up on sleep and got out of bed. After getting herself and Marcus dressed, she held him close as she tiptoed into the kitchen. Travis slept on the couch in black fatigues with his service belt still hugging his waist. That couldn't be comfortable, but she didn't want to wake him.

She scribbled a quick note that she and Marcus were meeting the Freemans, then they crept to the doorway. And the dresser.

She set Marcus down and leaned close to his face. "We need to be quiet because Travis is sleeping. Okay?" she whispered.

Marcus held his swimming bag in a fist. "I go swimming?" he whispered loudly.

"I'll take you swimming. Go sit at the table while I move the dresser." She pushed on the side of the dresser, but it didn't move. Travis had made it look so light last night. Repositioning herself, she put her backside against the side, braced herself against the floor, and pushed with all her strength. It moved a foot. Victory! She motioned for Marcus to come to her. The opening was wide enough for them to squeeze through.

Downstairs, patrons filled the bistro. Natalia sat Marcus at the only free counter stool and handed him a lemon poppy seed muffin. William, an elderly rancher, occupied his usual spot next to Marcus. "Can you watch him?" she asked.

"You bet." He handed Marcus a crisp piece of bacon. "Here. You need a real man's breakfast."

Natalia slipped into the kitchen in search of Rosemary. The cook flipped hotcakes on one griddle and fried omelets on the other while the server scurried around pouring coffee into carafes. The savory smell of bacon floated around Natalia.

At the far end of the kitchen, Rosemary pulled a pan of caramel rolls out of the oven. She flipped the rolls onto parchment paper. Gooey caramel slid down the sides.

Natalia's mouth watered. "You're an artist. I might have to have a bite."

"You need more than a bite." Rosemary set a roll on a plate and handed it to her.

"My pants are already tight." Still, she took the plate and sat on the stool in the corner. "Do you have a minute to talk?"

"If you can talk while I work."

"I think it's time to go back to Sioux Falls."

Rosemary froze. "I knew this day was coming. What about Travis?"

That was the million-dollar question. "He asked me to be his girlfriend last night."

"You don't look happy about it."

"One moment I am, and the next I'm scared. With all I'm

dealing with I'm not sure a long-distance relationship is what I need, and I don't know if it's fair to Travis. Marcus is leaving next weekend, and I still have no idea what I'm going to do afterward."

"I could use your help."

"Until you leave in October. Maybe I can keep the bistro open year round?"

"I can't see how it will make enough money without the summer traffic."

"Yeah, it was a crazy idea." Besides the slow traffic, Natalia didn't know the first thing about running a restaurant.

Rosemary patted her hand. "Don't worry about tomorrow. Today has enough worries of its own."

Natalia rolled her eyes. "That doesn't help. I've got to figure this out. Isn't it stupid to uproot your life for a guy you met two weeks ago?"

This time Rosemary hit her hand with the spatula. "Don't put yourself down around me. If Travis asked you to be his girlfriend, that means a lot. He doesn't trust easily."

"I know." She shoved a giant piece of caramel roll into her mouth. "I have to take Marcus to Sturgis to meet with the Freemans by nine, then I can come back and work for a few hours."

"You best get going or you'll be late."

"If I can't figure out what to do, I might drive to Arizona, get pulled over, and pretend to be stranded."

"You go right ahead, love. You'll find me at the Sandy Beach Resort. Poolside." Rosemary took her platter of rolls and stepped into the dining room. Cheers erupted.

Why would anyone ever want to leave these amazing people? Natalia found Marcus at the counter under a big cowboy hat drinking chocolate milk.

"Thanks, William." She handed him his hat as she scooped up Marcus.

"The boy's no problem." He squeezed Marcus's knee until he laughed. "Those giggles breathe life into these old bones."

Natalia carried Marcus out to her car and got him settled in. She climbed in and smiled at him in the rearview mirror as she started the car.

The passenger door opened and Caleb Russell fell into the seat. He slammed the door shut.

"Get out!" Natalia reached for her purse.

He grabbed her bag.

"Daddy!" Marcus clapped.

"Drive." Caleb's voice sent chills down her spine. The stench of ammonia filled the car.

Her heart pounded. "You're not supposed to be here."

He pointed a gun at her.

"You wouldn't hurt me in front of Marcus." She tightened her fingers around the steering wheel, hoping she sounded more confident than she felt.

Caleb's hands trembled. Red rimmed his eyes. His pupils dilated. "I said drive."

Natalia pulled onto the road. She searched the area for someone who could help them, but the streets were deserted. As she drove toward the edge of town, she remembered her training. She had to keep calm and think.

"Daddy! Daddy! Candy?" Marcus's singsong voice floated through the air.

"Hey, son. No candy this time. Do you want to go for a drive with Daddy?"

"Yeah! We see Mommy?"

"We'll see her soon. She misses you so much. I can't get her to stop crying." His voice shook. "I have to save her."

"Caleb, you don't want to do this. I'll pull over to let you out. We'll pretend the last few minutes never happened." Her insides quivered, but she kept her voice steady.

"You brought this on yourself. I begged you to give me my boy back."

He pressed the gun against her ribs. Her eyes watered. She

didn't know if it was from the awful smell or fear. She blinked away the tears and glanced in the rearview mirror. A beat-up pickup approached her. She searched the dash for some way to signal the driver, slowing to a crawl and gently tapping her brakes.

"Go!" Caleb growled and slammed the gun into her.

Pain radiated through her side as she stepped on the gas pedal. The pickup still trailed them. Hope welled up in her. She had to find a way to signal him! Could she turn on the emergency flashers without Caleb noticing? If she slammed on her brakes, would the truck driver call the police? Would a fender bender hurt Marcus?

Her pulse echoed in her ears. Caleb watched the road. She glanced once more at the truck in her mirror. It turned down a gravel road.

Her stomach dropped as the town disappeared from view.

* * * * * * *

Travis entered the bistro with a pounding headache and an aching back. It had been five years since he'd slept on a couch but never in his vest and duty belt.

He slipped into a booth and signaled the waitress. "I'll take a large black coffee and the special."

She nodded and hurried away.

He leaned his head against the vinyl seat and closed his eyes. After breakfast, he'd take a nice long nap and hot shower.

Something banged against the table. Travis jolted upright.

"Hey!" He opened his eyes to find Rosemary cringing.

"Sorry. I didn't realize you were sleeping. I heard there were some developments with you and Natalia last night."

He grinned. "Nattie must have stopped in. Was she happy when she told you? She seemed hesitant last night."

"She worries too much. I'm sure you'll find a way to make the distance work."

"Unless I can find a way to keep her here."

"I hope you can. I'll get your order."

"Add a side of ibuprofen, please."

Rosemary patted his arm. "Sure."

He pinched his nose as he waited for the pills. Someone slid a plate in front of him. He didn't bother looking up to find out who. Halfway through his ham and cheese omelet, his phone rang. "Hello?"

"Hey, Travis, Margo here. Have you seen Natalia? She said she'd call when she was on her way, but I haven't heard from her and she's not answering her phone."

Travis sat up, his heart pounding. He'd slept harder than he'd expected. Could Caleb have snuck into the apartment and forged the note? Or maybe she had another flat tire and was out of cell phone range. "I'm heading out now to look for her."

"Thanks. Will you call me as soon as you know something?"

"Sure." Travis threw a ten on the table and jogged to his car, calling state radio on his way.

"Northern Hills State Radio."

"This is HP 352. Have there been any crashes or motor assists on Highway 34?"

"No activity on Highway 34."

"Thanks." He tried Nattie's cell. It rang but went to voicemail. He shoved his cell phone in his pocket and switched on his radio. Where was she?

****

Natalia's grip on the steering wheel made her fingers ache, but she couldn't loosen them. She needed to be ready. She glanced at Caleb. His hand shook even more, but he had lowered the pistol from her side. Hopefully, he didn't know the area well enough to catch on to her plan.

They sped past pastures, a graveyard, a farmhouse, and over a bridge. The pavement turned to gravel as she drove toward Cole's ranch. Would he be home?

"Daddy! I have to go potty!" Marcus squirmed in his seat.

"There's no bathroom out here."

"But I hafta go bad!" He started to cry.

"Shut up!"

Natalia jumped. Marcus sniffled. Tears ran down his cheeks. Caleb's whole body trembled.

Pastures stretched as far as she could see on both sides of the road. Once they passed a long row of mailboxes, Natalia knew they were near the turn off to the Wilkins Ranch. She drove up a hill and spotted Cole's barn. If she and Marcus were going to run for it, now was the time.

She slowed the car. "Can we stop and let him pee? It won't take long."

"No. He's fine."

"But he'll wet his pants. He's only three, and he can't hold it."

"It won't kill him. Drive!"

Natalia steadied her nerves. "We don't have extra clothes. He can't sit in a urine-soaked car seat."

Caleb huffed. "Fine. You have two minutes."

She stopped the car and hopped out, keeping an eye on Caleb as she unbuckled Marcus and carried him to the side of the road.

Caleb opened his car door and stretched.

Her heart pounded as she searched the cow-filled pasture. Cole's house was just over the hill. She could see the roof of his barn. Her arms tightened around Marcus and she waited. Caleb turned his back toward them.

She ran. She raced through a ditch, then veered toward the fence. Caleb swore. She dropped in the tall grass and scooted under the barbed wire, pulling Marcus after her. He cried. Weeds scratched her skin. On her feet again, she lifted him and took off.

"Stop, you stupid—" Caleb cussed. "I'll shoot you!"

Profanity bellowed from him. She ran through cow manure. Her arm cramped.

A thud sounded behind her. She looked over her shoulder. Caleb struggled to his feet, the gun in his hand. If she could just get to Cole's barn!

Her lungs burned. She pumped her legs up a hill. Footsteps thundered behind her. Sweat ran down her face. An ache shot through her side and her hold on Marcus slipped. His cries grew louder.

Another thump behind her.

"Cole!" She ran toward a wooden fence. It wasn't tall. She could jump it. Maybe. "Hold on, Marcus."

He squeezed her.

She jumped. A hand grabbed her ankle, pulling her back. She twisted. Her side hit the ground, her cheek sliding along the grass. Dust flew in her eyes. She tucked Marcus close and rolled under the boards. Tears and dirt stung her eyes as they struggled to their feet.

"Stop, or I'll shoot you!" Something clicked behind her.

Natalia froze, her lungs heaving. She slowly turned around, pushing Marcus behind her legs and keeping her body between him and Caleb.

Caleb rose onto his knees. He pointed the pistol at her. His gaze bore into her. The gun steadied in his hand.

Marcus wailed.

"You're scaring him," she said.

"You did that! Come here, boy."

Marcus sniffled.

She held him in place. "No. Stay here, Marcus."

Caleb jumped the fence and pulled Marcus's arm.

"Owie!"

Natalia tackled Caleb's legs. When he hit the ground, she took a fistful of dirt and threw it into his eyes. "Marcus, go find Cole!"

Caleb swore.

"Marcus, find Molly!"

An explosion blasted. A ball of fire burst in Natalia's chest, knocking her onto her back. Her head bounced against the dirt. Heat spiked through her chest with every breath. Something gurgled and her legs went numb. Above her, puffy clouds swirled in the pure blue sky as beams of sunlight streaked toward her. Her vision spun, turning white then fading into blackness.

CHAPTER 25

Travis turned onto Highway 34 toward Sturgis. His radio squawked. "Attention units and stations, we have a report of someone with a gunshot wound at Wilkins Ranch five miles north on Omega Place."

Cole! His stomach dropped. He pushed the radio button. "HP 352, I'll be en route from Highway 34."

"10-4. 352."

He flipped on his lights and sirens, then pushed the accelerator. The scenery whizzed by. His phone rang. Without slowing he answered. "Wilkins."

"Travis, it's Cole. Natalia's been shot."

What? Why was she at the ranch? "I'm coming. I'm twelve miles away."

"We're in the south pasture four hundred feet from the barn. I've got to go. Dispatch is calling me back."

Travis dropped his phone. Who would have shot Nattie? He took a shortcut, barely keeping all four wheels on the ground. Within minutes, he turned into the pasture and raced toward the barn. Cole knelt on the ground. Molly sat nearby.

Travis skidded to a stop beside them and jumped out. Cole pressed his plaid shirt to Nattie's chest. Blood soaked through.

Kneeling next to Nattie, Travis grabbed her wrist. He couldn't find a pulse. Panicked, he leaned over her mouth and listened. Shallow, labored breathing. Relief hit him. "Nattie. I'm here." He stroked her pale face. "What happened?"

"I don't know."

A black pickup pulled up beside the fence.

Travis put his hands on top of his brother's. "I'll take over. Go see if that's the EMT. Tell him everything you know."

Cole moved his hands, and Travis applied pressure to the warm, wet cloth. Seconds crept by.

The EMT draped a blanket over Nattie, then knelt at her side and opened his bag. He cut through her clothes and placed a clear plastic square on the wound, taped it onto her skin, then covered it with gauze. "Hold her while I check her back for an exit wound." He lifted her shoulder, and Travis held it while he examined her back. "The bullet must still be inside." They lowered her to the ground.

In the distance, the steady beat of the Life Flight helicopter sent a sliver of relief through Travis. "They're almost here, Nattie. Hold on." He looked at Cole. "Wave down the chopper."

The EMT checked the pulse on her wrist. "It's rapid, weak, and thready, but it's there. That's good."

Chopping drowned out all other sound. The wind picked up. The helicopter landed about fifty feet away.

"They're here, sweetheart," Travis whispered close to her ear. "Nattie, you have to fight. Do you hear me?" He couldn't lose her. Her eyelids fluttered but remained closed. "I love you."

The medical team pushed Travis aside. He stood and took a few steps back. The blue jumpsuits of the two flight nurses blocked his view. He rubbed his sticky fingers together. Dark, drying blood covered his hands. Nattie's blood. A wave of nausea crashed into him. How could this have happened?

A strong hand squeezed his shoulder. Cole stepped beside him.

The nurses put Nattie on a gurney. Travis followed as they loaded her into the helicopter. One of the nurses turned to him. "Excellent job! We've got it from here!"

His throat tightened. "Take care of her! She's mine!"

She nodded, then jumped into the helicopter and shut the door. Travis backed up. He didn't move until the chopper disappeared.

He had to be there when she woke up, and she *would* wake up.

He couldn't lose her. He sprinted to his cruiser. Cole stood next to Molly, but Travis wanted him by his side. The past was history. He needed his brother. "Get in."

Cole pointed at Molly. "Go home."

As they climbed into the car, Travis's phone rang. "Wilkins."

"Trooper Wilkins. It's Detective Astor."

"Can't talk right now. Nattie's been shot. I need to meet Life Flight at the hospital."

"Is she going to be okay?"

His chest ached. "I don't know."

"Who shot her?"

"Not sure. My brother found her in his pasture, but he doesn't know what happened. Caleb called her last night and threatened her."

"That's why I'm calling. Mary called a few minutes ago. Caleb told her he was going to get Marcus and to meet him at the Flying J truck stop in Rapid City. We have a BOLO out for him."

Travis hit the steering wheel. This couldn't be happening. Then reality struck. He looked at Cole. "Where's Marcus?"

"I didn't see him. Do you think he's back at the ranch?"

Dread filled Travis. "Astor, Caleb must have Marcus. I've got to go." He hung up and called his boss.

"Sergeant Black."

"It's Wilkins. Marcus Elkhorn's foster parent, Natalia Brynner, has been shot. Marcus is missing. There's a BOLO out for Caleb Russell because he told his wife he was going to get Marcus. Sarge…" His throat tightened. "Natalia's my girlfriend."

He swore. "I'm calling out every available unit. What's your location?"

"I'm still on scene. I suspect this is where Russell took the boy. I'm going to search for Marcus."

"You head to Rapid. We've got this covered."

"I know this area better than anyone."

"We'll find him. Go be with your girlfriend. That's an order."

Travis threw his phone on the console. "I've been ordered to go to the hospital."

"Good. Then we can check on Natalia."

"We're no help to Nattie. I'd rather be looking for Marcus."

"Don't you trust them to find him?"

"Not in the least."

****

Travis found a spot in the corner of the crowded Emergency Department waiting room. He stared through the large windows at the construction crew building the new hospital wing. Beside him, Cole sat with his back straight and arms crossed.

The anxiety was eating Travis. He hated feeling helpless.

A nurse approached him. "Who are you here to see?"

He stood. "Natalia Brynner."

"We'll need next of kin signatures as soon as possible."

"I'll call her parents. How is she?"

"We're prepping her for surgery now. They intubated her and gave her a blood transfusion. Her vitals have improved. You can wait in the ICU surgery waiting room on the third floor. You'll receive updates there."

"Do you know how long it will take?"

She shook her head. "It depends on how much internal damage she sustained."

"Thanks."

Travis's legs went numb as he and Cole walked to the next waiting room. Smaller and emptier than the ED waiting room, a few windows along the far wall allowed for some natural light. Compact couches, chairs, and end tables dotted the room. A round table with six chairs filled the corner of the room. Magazines covered most of the tables.

"Coffee?" Cole asked.

"Sure."

"I'll be right back."

Cole left, so Travis sat in an uncomfortable chair, dug out his phone, and called dispatch. "It's HP 352. I need the number of a Mr. Brynner out of Sioux Falls." He pulled a pad and pen from his pocket.

"I've got a number for Maximilian Brynner and one for Mitch Brynner."

"Go ahead with Maximilian." He jotted down the number as she rattled it off. "Thanks."

No trooper wanted to make this call, but he fought the dread creeping through him and dialed it anyway. His stomach cramped as the phone rang.

"Hello. This is Max Brynner."

"Mr. Brynner, this is Trooper Travis Wilkins. Is Natalia Brynner your daughter?"

"Yes. Is everything okay?"

Nothing was okay. Travis squeezed his eyes shut. "I'm a friend of hers. Where are you?"

"At home, why?"

"Is Mrs. Brynner with you?"

"She's shopping with our granddaughters. Where's Nattie?"

Travis inhaled. "Nattie's hurt. She was shot in the chest."

"What? No! Where is she?"

"She's at Rapid City Regional Hospital, in critical condition. They're prepping her for surgery. That's all I know. I'm sorry I don't have any more information."

"I've got to make some calls. And pack. And the dog. I've got to find someone to watch the dog. Martie! I've got to tell Martie."

"Wait until she comes home to tell her. You don't want her driving upset."

"She could be out all day!"

Travis gripped the phone tighter. "Just tell her she needs to come home because you have some news. She'll be worried, but that's okay. Are you going to be able to drive out here?"

"Of course."

"Drive safely. I'll call when I have an update."

Travis slumped in the chair. *Fight, Nattie. Don't run away this time.*

Cole walked into the room with two Styrofoam cups and sat next to Travis, handing him a cup.

"Thanks." Travis didn't think his stomach could handle the black liquid, but the aroma soothed his frazzled nerves more than the stench of bleach.

Cole's hand shook, sloshing coffee over the side.

"Are you okay?"

"I keep replaying it in my mind. I was working on the fence in the north pasture when I heard the gunshot. I thought maybe the neighbor kids were target practicing again. Thankfully, I had Molly with me. She ran straight to Natalia. I wouldn't have seen her otherwise." Cole shuddered.

"Was Marcus there? Did you see Nattie's car?" Why hadn't he thought to question Cole before now?

"No, she was alone." Cole ran trembling fingers across his brow. "There was so much blood."

"You saved her life." An unfamiliar feeling spread through Travis as every bitter and angry thought he'd had about his brother melted away. He nudged him with his arm. "I don't think I'll ever be able to repay you."

"She's got to make it."

Voices rumbled in the hallway. Rosemary led a group of people through the waiting room doorway. Travis and Cole stood.

She pulled them into a tight hug. "Is Natalia going to be okay?"

"She's in surgery now," Travis said loud enough for everyone to hear. "All we can do is wait."

She clucked her tongue. "Where's Marcus?"

"Missing. They have every available unit looking for him."

Deputy Jackson clapped him on the shoulder. "Missing? Any idea where he disappeared?"

"We think Caleb took him from Cole's ranch. He's armed and

dangerous, so you should let law enforcement handle it."

"Of course I will, but it wouldn't hurt to drive around those bluffs a little bit."

"Don't. You could make the situation worse. Scare Caleb into doing something desperate."

"Don't worry, son. I haven't forgotten all my training." He walked over to a group of five other retirees. They nodded and left the waiting room. Travis pinched his nose, hoping they didn't get themselves or Marcus killed.

Mrs. Thorpe gave Cole a hug, then turned to Travis. He straightened his back. He didn't have the energy for his old teacher today.

She smiled and placed her wrinkled hand on his cheek. "I was wrong about you. I told Hank you'd amount to no good, I told him he was a fool to waste his time, but I was the fool." Tears filled her eyes.

"Hmph!" Mrs. Wilson pulled on Mrs. Thorpe's arm. "You're certainly making a fool out of yourself now."

"It might do you some good to eat a little humble pie too. I'll serve you up a piece." Mrs. Thorpe led Mrs. Wilson away.

Mrs. Thorpe's heartfelt confession inspired Travis. If she could forgive him, he could certainly forgive them. If Mrs. Wilson wanted to stay angry and bitter, he wouldn't hold it against her. Life was too precious. The past hour he'd realized just how precious.

"I brought rolls," Rosemary said. "Would you like one?"

He shook his head. The thought of food knotted his stomach.

Soon the residents of Alkaline filled the round table with pizza, fruit platters, brownies, coolers, and pots of coffee. Chatter filled the room. Why were they all here? For Nattie or Cole? For him? Did they feel the same as Mrs. Wilson, that they'd been wrong to judge him a fool, or were they like Mrs. Thorpe, holding on to their unjust prejudices? He wanted to trust them but doubt nagged him.

Travis stepped into the hallway to process his thoughts. Leaning against the wall, he slid to the floor and rested his head against his knees. Sorrow rippled through him. If Nattie didn't make it, he wouldn't stick around. He couldn't stand their pity. It still haunted him after Hank's death.

But he couldn't run away either. He'd stopped running after his mom died. And how many times had he told Nattie to face her problems? She'd just have to make it. He'd find a way for them to be together, even if he had to transfer to Sioux Falls.

CHAPTER 26

"Are you Trooper Wilkins?"

Travis looked up. An older version of Nattie with short blonde curls stood beside a tall, middle-aged man. "Yes, ma'am."

"I'm Martie, and this is Max. We're Nattie's parents."

He rose, his body protesting, and Mrs. Brynner hugged him. He stiffened, awkwardly patting her back. How long had he been in the hallway? He glanced at his watch. "How did you get here so fast?"

Mr. Brynner squeezed his shoulder. "A friend flew us over in his plane. Any word on Nattie?"

"No. She's been in surgery since I called you, but that was two hours ago, so we should hear something soon." He hoped.

Mrs. Brynner grabbed her husband's hand. "What happened?"

"We're still investigating. She was threatened by Marcus's foster dad last night, so he's a suspect. There's a BOLO—be on the lookout—for him now. Every available officer and some locals are searching for them. I'm sorry I don't have better news, Mrs. Brynner."

"You'll call me Martie."

"And please call me Max." He shook Travis's hand.

"I wish we could have met under better circumstances."

Martie wrapped her arms around her stomach. "How could something like this happen? She should have come home when I told her to."

"That hardly helps, honey."

Travis motioned to the waiting room. "Let's go find you a place to sit."

Martie peeked inside. "It's packed. It must be a busy day for surgeries."

"They're all here for Nattie. Come on. I'll introduce you." Travis led them into the room and whistled, silencing the crowd. "These are Nattie's parents, Max and Martie Brynner."

Rosemary stepped forward and ushered them to a vinyl couch. "I'm Rosemary. Would you like some coffee?" They both nodded. She waved at one of her employees. "Will someone get Natalia's parents some coffee?" Then she handed Martie a basket of creamer. "These are the best the hospital has. When Nattie's better, you'll have to come by the bistro and have a better cup. I'll even throw in a couple of my famous caramel rolls."

"Thank you."

"Trooper Wilkins?" A nurse in blue scrubs stood at the door.

"Here." He walked to the nurse, then motioned for Nattie's parents to join him. "Natalia's parents are here too."

"I'll take you to a consult room." They followed her to a sitting room with two small couches and a chair. The beige windowless walls featured a lone picture of a lighthouse on a cliff. "Have a seat. The surgeon will meet with you here."

"Is the surgery over?" Max asked as he and Martie sat.

"Yes. Natalia is in recovery and will be moved into the surgical ICU through the doors at the end of the hall."

Relieved, Travis fell into a chair. The nurse left them alone.

Max sighed. "Thank God."

Martie wiped at her eyes.

The door opened and another woman in scrubs entered the room. She sat opposite the Brynners. "I'm Doctor Wienkler. Natalia's in recovery, and her vitals are strong. The bullet lodged in the seventh rib on the left side. It barely grazed her left lung, but it was enough to puncture it, causing a pneumothorax."

"A pneumo-what?" Travis asked.

The doctor smiled. "A collapsed lung. Thankfully, it was a small bullet. Unfortunately, she was shot at close range. We gave her five units of blood before surgery, but we had no complications during the procedure, so there was no need for more. Right now, we're concerned with infection and pneumonia, so we have her on a strong antibiotic."

"Is she going to have permanent lung damage?" Max asked.

"There is a possibility, but the rib did its job and took most of the impact. It saved her vital organs. If she can take it easy and allow her body to heal, she should make a full recovery." The surgeon stood. "You'll be able to see her in about an hour. Since she'll be in ICU, we ask that only two or three visitors be in her room at a time. Please let us know if you have any more questions."

"Thank you, doctor." Max shook her hand.

Travis escorted the Brynners back to the waiting room where they updated the town on Nattie's condition. While Rosemary helped Nattie's parents settle in, Travis's gaze found Cole's, and he tipped his head toward the hall.

The twins met outside. "What's up?" Cole asked.

"Now that I know Nattie's going to be fine, I'm going to search for Marcus. Will you come with me? Between the two of us, we know every place to hide around Alkaline."

"Of course." Cole squeezed his shoulder. "You don't even have to ask."

* * * * * * *

Travis drove his ATV over the dry creek bed and through the narrow twists of an orange-tinted gully. Cole's ATV roared behind him.

He followed the natural livestock trail to the top of a grassy ridge and stopped. Cole pulled up beside him and took off his helmet. Covered in red dust from riding Travis's tail, Cole took a drink from his canteen, then handed it to Travis. He gulped the cool water. The sun shone slightly from the west. A blanket of amber grass covered the rolling hills and valleys. He scanned the bumpy horizon where it met the pale blue sky. Nothing! Travis checked his watch. Almost three thirty. Ninety minutes of searching and no luck.

Travis passed back the canteen, then grabbed binoculars from his pack. The shadows from the gully walls made it difficult to spot anything other than brush and dirt. Then the sun reflected off something far off and to the left.

The flash rekindled his hope. He offered the binoculars to Cole. "What do you make of that shiny object at ten o'clock?"

His brother looked through the binoculars, shrugged, and handed them back. "Let's check it out."

They packed their gear, then headed down the gulch and through the gullies. As they rounded the bend, Travis recognized Nattie's car wedged between the sandstone walls. Relief and worry battled inside him. They were on the right track, but where could Caleb be?

Travis parked behind the car and hopped off his ATV, throwing his helmet into the dirt. He drew his gun and slowly approached the vehicle. He pushed his anxiety aside as he focused on his surroundings. When he was close enough, he peeked through the rear window then climbed over the car, touching the hood. Cool.

He holstered his gun as he grabbed his hand-held radio. "Northern Hills. HP 352."

"Go ahead HP 352."

"I've located Natalia Brynner's vehicle ten miles west of Old Settlers Road. Requesting backup."

"10-4."

"What was he thinking to take a car through these gullies?" Cole shook his head.

"Desperation." Because of the shape of the gully, only the bottom two feet of the car were wedged between rocks. The driver's side windows were rolled down. Travis crouched on the steep embankment, leaned into the back window, and found Marcus's dinosaur, but nothing to cause him alarm. In the next window, he grabbed the keys from the ignition and pocketed them, then slid down the dirt to the front of the car. He clawed at the gully wall and dirt fell. "Do you think we can get our ATVs around the car?"

"The ground's too loose there, and it's a steep incline, so I doubt we'll be able to get up this way. We'll have to backtrack. Keep up if you can." Cole jumped onto his ATV as Travis reached his.

Travis followed in reverse until they found a trail up the dirt wall, then he throttled past his brother up the incline. Relieved to be going forward again, he drove along the edge of the ridge, scanning the area for any sign of Caleb or Marcus.

A loud blast echoed through the trenches. Travis stopped, and Cole pulled up next to him. He ripped off his helmet, killed his ATV, and motioned for Cole to do the same.

"Was that a gunshot?" Cole's eyes widened.

Another blast rang out.

Travis slammed his helmet on and sped down the gully. His pulse beat against his eardrums. The sandstone walls rushed around him as he pushed his ATV to its limits. Why was Caleb shooting, and where was Marcus?

Something squeezed Natalia's arm. She forced her eyes to open. Brightness shone overhead. A blood pressure cuff released the pressure a little at a time as a monitor beside her bed beeped.

A nurse walked into her room holding a bag of clear liquid. The strong scent of hand sanitizer followed her. "Hello, Natalia. Glad to see you awake." She replaced the empty bag on the metal stand with the full one. "Now, between one and ten, with one being no pain and ten being the worst pain you've been in, where would you rate your pain?"

Natalia held up three fingers.

"You should try speaking. Get those voice muscles moving again."

"Three," she whispered.

The nurse smiled. "Good. How about I get you a sip of water? I'm sure your throat feels like someone scrubbed it with sandpaper."

"Thanks."

"Your parents want to visit if you're up to seeing them."

"My parents … are here?" Confusion swirled in her mind. What happened?

"Sure enough. Would you like to see them?"

Natalia nodded as she closed her eyes. The monitors beeped. People talked around her.

"She's sleeping. Can we wait here until she wakes again?" her mother whispered. A phone rang. "She's going to be okay," her mother whispered again. "It's going to be a long road to recovery … I can't believe she was shot either."

Somebody shot me? Natalia opened her eyes. Tubes ran from her hand to a bag hanging above her head. She moved the blanket from her chest. More tubes stuck out from the side of her hospital gown. Beside her, her mom faced the window.

Caleb! Her memory returned, and Natalia grabbed the bed rails. Where was Marcus? She had to find him. She pulled at her IV.

"I've got to go." Her mom set down her phone. "Nattie, lay still. What are you doing? You're going to pull out your chest tube." She knocked her mom's hand away, but her mom came back and pushed her onto the bed. "Nattie. You're going to hurt yourself more. Nurse!"

Natalia pushed against her mom's arm. "Marcus."

The nurse ran in. "Natalia. Calm down. Grab her hand."

Her mother pinned one arm to the bed. The nurse kept a hold of her other.

"Where's Marcus?" Natalia's chest ached with each deep, quick breath.

"Slow down your breathing, Natalia. Easy now." The nurse demonstrated slow even breaths.

"Nattie, please listen to her."

She wanted to fight, but her body rebelled. She tried to stay awake as exhaustion engulfed her. Her lids drooped.

The aroma of coffee roused Natalia. When she opened her eyes, her dad stood next to her bed with a mug in his hand. "She's awake," he said over his shoulder.

"Hi," she whispered.

He patted her leg. "Hi, baby girl. You gave us quite a scare. How are you feeling?"

"My throat burns and my chest hurts."

"Do you remember what happened?" He sat beside her.

The fog lifted a bit. "Caleb got into my car and pointed a gun at me. I drove to Cole's ranch. He let us out so Marcus could pee." She sat up. "Marcus! Where is he?" The room spun. She dropped to the mattress.

Her mom stepped up beside Dad. "He's missing. Everyone's

looking for him."

Natalia's chest ached, but not from the gunshot. "I want Travis. Is he here? I need him."

"I'm sorry. He's looking for Marcus. Should I call him?"

She shouldn't bother Travis while he was looking for Marcus, but she needed to hear his voice. Her breathing sped up.

Her mom tapped on her phone.

The nurse returned. "The doctor prescribed a sedative for your anxiety."

"I don't want to sleep. I want to know when they find Marcus."

Her mom pulled a chair up to the bed. "I promise to update you as soon as you wake up."

"It's important for your recovery that you sleep and not worry." The nurse injected something into the IV.

Natalia prayed for Marcus until she drifted off to sleep.

* * * * * * *

Travis sped through the dry creek bed. Plants and cacti dotted the hills on both sides of the gully as it opened into a wider valley.

A movement up the hill to his left caught his attention. Caleb jumped down the hill, waving his arms. His screams cut through the rumbling motor. Travis followed him up a steep embankment, but the man disappeared behind a boulder.

His heartbeat increased. He turned his ATV sideways before stopping about twenty feet down and ten feet back from the boulder. He turned off the engine, signaling for Cole to do the same as he crouched behind his vehicle and drew his pistol.

"Northern Hills. HP 352. Be advised, we have Caleb Russell at gunpoint seven miles west of Old Settlers Road."

Cole crept up next to him. "What's the plan?"

"Stay hidden. I'll try to secure the threat." Travis peered over the four-wheeler. "Caleb! Where's Marcus?"

"He needs help." Caleb's voice shook.

"Throw down your gun!"

Caleb stepped out from behind the rock holding Marcus's limp body.

Every muscle in Travis's body strained against the need to rush forward. "Stop! Throw down your gun!"

"He's hurt!" Caleb stumbled. When he reached the bottom, he knelt less than five feet from Travis. "He was bitten by a rattler. Please help him."

"When was he bitten?"

"I don't know. They kept coming at us." Caleb pointed his gun at the boulder and shot it. Dirt sprayed out. Marcus flinched. Caleb shoved the gun behind him.

Travis jumped and tightened his grip on his pistol. "Kick your gun over here. I'll take Marcus to the hospital."

"He needs help. He's going to die. Will you help him?"

"Of course I'll help him, but you need to throw down your gun!"

Caleb set Marcus on the ground and stood. "Tell my wife I love her." He sprinted through the valley and disappeared around the bend.

Travis holstered his pistol as he ran to Marcus. The boy arched his back and moaned. "Hey, cowboy. Hold still while I look at your injury."

Marcus's eyes opened. They were glassy and red-rimmed. A few scratches covered his arms, but it was when Travis pulled up the boy's left pant leg that he howled. His lower calf was swollen twice the size of the other and turning purple.

Pebbles rolled down as Cole ran up to the boulder.

Travis grabbed his radio. "Northern Hills. HP 352. We need a medevac team for a snakebite victim. There's a flat area to the east of these coordinates. I'll meet Life Flight there with the patient." His voice shook. He had to keep calm so Marcus wouldn't panic.

"Looks like he was bit by this rattler." Cole approached with the tail end of a snake dangling from his fingers. "Caleb must have shot its head off. It's stiff. This snake's been dead for hours."

"Are there more up there?"

"I only saw this one."

Fear coursed through Travis. He didn't know if Caleb was hallucinating or if there were more than one snake, but he had to get Marcus to the hospital now. He carefully lifted the boy into his arms. His whimpers turned to sobs.

"It's going to be okay," Travis said. "We're going on a four-wheeler with Cole, then a helicopter ride." He rushed over to Cole's ATV. "I'll hold Marcus, you drive."

Travis climbed on and laid Marcus across his lap, holding his head up with his arm. He scooted to the back of the seat. Marcus leaned over and vomited into the dirt. Travis's fear intensified as Cole mounted in front of them.

They sped up a shallow bank. By the time they reached the pasture, Travis could hear the helicopter blades.

"It's going to be okay," he said, checking Marcus's pulse. Too fast. "The helicopter is coming. Can you hear it?" Marcus cried, breaking Travis's heart. He hated seeing him in so much pain. "Shh." He pushed black hair from the toddler's clammy forehead. What could he say to keep a child calm and slow the venom? "You're being a brave, tough cowboy."

The chopping sound eased Travis's nerves. A black dot appeared in the southwestern sky. As it grew, the noise increased. Wind from the propellers sprayed them with dust as it landed. Two nurses jumped from the helicopter and wheeled the gurney to them. Travis helped them load Marcus onto the bed.

The female nurse checked Marcus's vitals. "Do you have the snake?"

Cole pulled the reptile out of his bag. The male nurse held out a plastic bag, and Cole dropped the snake into it. They secured Marcus to the gurney, then loaded it into the helicopter.

Travis turned to Cole. "I'm going with them. Can you wait for the deputies and show them which way Caleb ran?"

"You bet."

Travis could only manage a nod as he climbed into the chopper.

The medics started an IV, then cleaned Marcus's purple skin before bandaging the twin puncture wounds.

Marcus focused his teary eyes on Travis. "I want a cowboy Band-Aid."

"Anything for a brave cowboy." He grabbed the pen from his pocket and drew a cowboy and a bucking bronco on the bandage. Marcus's hand went limp hand as they lifted off. Travis hoped they weren't too late.

****

In her hospital room, Natalia lay on her side. Her dad watched *I Love Lucy* in the chair beside her. His chuckles sent spikes of annoyance through her. How could he laugh when Marcus was missing? "Can you turn that off?"

"Do you want to rest?" He turned off the TV.

"I want Marcus to be found and Travis to be safe."

"Should I go get your mom?"

"No. She'd somehow make this all my fault."

"She means well. We want you to be happy."

"You do. She wants me to be obedient."

"She loves you."

Natalia turned her head and watched the nurses work at their station. Did Mom really love her, or did she want a perfect puppet? A nurse answered the phone, then looked at Natalia.

She hurried into the room. "They found him! Your little boy. He's on his way to the hospital now."

Joy and relief exploded inside Natalia. She closed her eyes. Thank God! But wait … why were they bringing him to the hospital?

CHAPTER 28

The medical team wheeled Marcus into the Emergency Department and into a plain, white examination room brightened by the harsh, overhead lights. Travis stood inside the door as the staff swarmed around Marcus. He wore a tiny hospital gown, and a blanket covered him to his waist.

One nurse held his arm while another nurse took a vial of blood. Marcus cried and tried to pull away, but the nurse held his arm in place.

"Almost done." She pulled the needle out and wrapped the puncture. "Would you like a puppy sticker?"

He nodded. She handed him the sticker, then left.

Travis pulled a chair to the right side of Marcus. "I'm here."

Beads of sweat dotted the boy's forehead. He closed his eyes, whimpering. Travis rubbed the back of his hand, wishing he could take his pain away.

A middle-aged man wearing a white lab coat entered the room. "I'm Dr. Hash."

Travis nodded. "Trooper Wilkins."

"And this must be Marcus Elkhorn."

Marcus turned his head away from the doctor.

"I heard you fought off a wild animal." Dr. Hash sat on the stool and scooted to the other side of Marcus. "That lady who took your blood is called a phlebotomist. She takes it to our lab so we can figure out how to make you feel better." He looked at Travis. "We're checking his hemoglobin and clotting factors. Once the antivenin reconstitutes, we can administer the first dose."

"When will that be?"

He looked at his watch. "It's a quarter to five now, so we have twenty-eight minutes to go. We'll have to do a blood draw before and after each dose." He uncovered Marcus's leg and examined it. "He has significant swelling. He'll need two vials every six hours for eighteen hours."

Travis rubbed his eyes. They were in for a long night and poor Marcus for a lot more pokes.

****

An hour later, Travis sat in a green recliner in Marcus's room on the pediatric floor. Pictures of lions, tigers, zebras, and elephants covered the light-green walls. An empty bed sat near a window that overlooked the parking lot. Travis flipped through the TV channels until he found cartoons. Marcus giggled at the animated sea creatures.

The phlebotomist entered the room.

Marcus whimpered and turned away. "No."

Travis gripped his hand. "I know it hurts, but she's going to take your blood to get tested."

"It's just a pinch, and I'll be quick, then you can see what happens with Sponge Bob. I bet he does something silly." She rubbed his arm with a cotton ball.

Travis turned Marcus's face from her and pointed to the screen. "What's he doing with that spatula?"

She poked Marcus and he flinched, but he kept his arm steady while she filled her vials. "All done. Now you can rest for a bit." She left with her supplies.

They watched cartoons until Marcus's eyelids closed. Dried tears streaked his face. Travis relaxed into the hospital chair, letting his eyes drift close. With both Nattie and Marcus safe in the hospital, his worries from the last eight hours melted away.

"There's Marcus."

Travis opened his eyes at the familiar voice.

Margo rushed into the room and sat on the other side of the

bed. "I didn't mean to disturb you," she whispered. "I'm sure you're exhausted. I'm completely worn out, and all I've done is sit at a desk and worry."

Travis took a good look at her. Her black hair was a bit ruffled, and she wore jeans and sneakers instead of a skirt and heels.

"How's he doing?"

"It's been a rough day. They administered his first dose of antivenin fifty minutes ago. He'll need more in five hours. Can you sit with him for a while? I'd like to check on Nattie, and I don't want him to wake up alone."

She smiled. "Yes, of course, and the Freemans are on their way."

Travis's gut clenched. He was going to miss this kid. He slipped out of the room and navigated the labyrinth of hallways until he found the ICU. The double doors opened, and Nattie's parents walked through.

"Travis!" Martie waved at him. "How's Marcus?"

"He's resting. I'm on my way to see Nattie."

"That's not a good idea. She just fell asleep. We're going to get some dinner. Would you like to join us?"

"I think I'll wait with her until she wakes up."

"I told you, she's sleeping."

Max took his wife's arm. "Martie, Travis can go see Nattie. She's been asking for him all day."

"Okay, but try not to wake her."

He pulled her toward the elevator. "Stop lecturing him."

Travis took a deep breath and headed toward the nurses' station. They pointed to a room across the hall. He squirted hand sanitizer onto his dirty palms and entered her room. Nattie lay in the bed, tubes running from her chest and arm. They didn't distract him from her beautiful, sleeping face though. The sight of her—alive and healing—released the tension that had plagued his muscles all day.

He walked to her side and sank into the hospital chair. He picked up her smooth hand. Without adrenaline to fuel him, his strength drained away.

****

A sharp jab seared Natalia's chest. Rhythmic beeping soothed her as she waited for the pain to subside. A soft snore interrupted it. She opened her eyes. *Travis.* He slept in the chair beside her. The faint whiff of sweat filled the air. Dirt covered his uniform and face. Dark stubble shadowed his chin. Warmth filled her.

"Travis." Her voice cracked. "Hey, Trooper Wilkins, naptime is over." He jerked awake, scanning the room with wide eyes. "I'm sorry, I didn't mean to startle you."

His face softened, and his shoulders relaxed. "Hi, beautiful."

She grinned.

He leaned forward, grabbing her hand and squeezing her fingers. "You scared me."

"I've never been so scared. I thought he was going to kill us."

"I thought I'd lost you. There was so much blood." He shook his head. Pain filled his eyes. "Then to watch the helicopter fly off with you. It was awful."

"My first helicopter ride, and I don't remember any of it." She pushed a button on the bed rail and moved the head of her bed so she was sitting. She leaned near him. "I wanted to see you all day."

He kissed her nose. "You should have woken me before you left this morning. I would have gone with you to take Marcus. Then that"—he pressed his lips together—"Caleb wouldn't have taken you."

"The next time a madman wants to kidnap my foster son, I'll make sure to bring you with me." She squeezed his fingers. "Where's Marcus?"

"They admitted him to peds."

"Why? Is he hurt?"

"No one told you? He was bitten by a rattlesnake."

"What? Is he going to be okay?" Her poor boy!

"It sounds like it, but he's going to need shots all through the night. He was sleeping when I left. Margo's with him now."

"I'm so glad you found him."

He leaned forward. Their lips touched and her stomach flipped. "Do you remember anything after getting shot?" he asked.

She tried to think back. "I remember Caleb grabbing Marcus and pointing the gun at me. Then it felt like a ball of fire exploded inside my chest. It was the worst pain I've ever experienced. The last things I remember were the clouds. Is that weird?"

"A little. Were you floating towards a bright light?"

She chuckled. "Nothing like that. The clouds floated past as I concentrated on breathing."

He ran his hand through the strands of hair at her temple. "So you don't remember what I said to you right before the medics took over?" His gaze softened.

"What did you say?"

"Only that I love you."

Natalia sucked in a deep breath. Her chest exploded in pain. She clenched her teeth until the pain eased.

"What is it? Are you okay?"

Travis reached for the call button, but she grabbed his wrist to stop him. "You can't go around dropping L-bombs. You shocked me."

"I'm sorry. I had no idea you'd be so surprised."

He couldn't love her after only two weeks, could he? And all that time she'd been a crazy mess. Was it love or his desire to protect and help her? "Do you mean it?"

"Of course I do. Don't you believe me?"

"I do, but we've had a long day and you're tired. I would understand if you're confused."

He kissed her again. "I'm not confused."

"We brought you some food, Travis." Her mom's voice startled her.

He groaned, pecked her lips, then sat back.

Mom stepped near Natalia's shoulder and held out a white

paper bag. "I figure you can't go wrong with a cheeseburger and fries."

"Maybe he's lactose intolerant." Dad walked to the chair by the window and sat.

Mom's smile fell. "Are you? We can take the cheese off."

Natalia sighed. She didn't have the patience for their bickering.

"I'm not allergic to anything. Thanks. I'm starved." The bag crinkled as he pulled out the wrapped cheeseburger.

"Did you bring me anything?" Nattie asked.

"The nurse ordered your dinner before we left. You'll need your strength if you want to get better, and with all the blood loss, you'll need to replenish your iron. I hope they ordered you an iron-rich meal."

Natalia controlled her eye roll. "Why don't you check with the nurse to make sure they know what they're doing?"

"I think I will." She left the room.

"That wasn't very nice," Travis whispered, then took a bite of his burger.

"She's going to drive me crazy, thinking she knows everything."

"I meant to the nurses."

Travis cringed as Nattie glared at the green gelatin. "I can't eat any more," she said, leaning back against the bed.

"There isn't much left." Her mom held up a spoonful.

Nattie shook her head and pushed the tray away. "I don't want it." She turned to Travis. "Could you find them a hotel room?"

"That would be fine for your father, but I'm staying with you. I can sleep in the chair." She pointed to the green, vinyl recliner her dad was sprawled in reading the newspaper.

Nattie widened her eyes at Travis. He shrugged. How was he supposed to convince Martie to leave if Nattie couldn't? Maybe the nurses could help. He walked over to their station. "Natalia Brynner is having a problem. Her mom insists on staying the night with her, but Nattie would rather be alone."

The nurse smiled. "I'll handle it."

"Thanks." While the nurse handled Nattie's family, Travis needed to touch base with his. He pulled out his cell and nervously called Cole. They had acted like a team today. Would Cole revert back to his cold attitude now that the emergency had passed?

"Hello?"

"Hey, it's Travis. Where are you?"

"I'm at the ranch. How're Marcus and Natalia?"

"They're both on the mend. I'm with Nattie now, and I'll swing by Marcus's room in a bit."

"I'm almost done with chores, then I thought I'd come in. Do you need anything?"

"Could you bring me some clothes and my shaving bag? I'm going to get a couple of rooms at the Holiday Inn across the road for Nattie's parents and me."

"You got it."

Cole had been there for Travis, like he had in their childhood. Travis needed to take the first step in mending their past. "Thanks for helping me out today."

"Of course, although I didn't do much."

"Just being there was a lot."

"Sure. I'll see you soon."

Travis leaned against the nurses' station and stretched his back. The terror of the day would remain in his memory for a long time, but maybe some good could come from it too.

His phone rang. Sergeant Black. "Hey, Sarge."

"Wilkins. What's the status on Natalia and Marcus?"

"Natalia is awake and going to be fine. Marcus had one dose of antivenin and will need another in two hours. Did they catch Caleb?"

"Not yet. That guy knows how to hide but we'll get him."

"Let me know when you do."

As he hung up, Martie approached him, scowling. "That nurse is something else. She kicked us out."

Max followed. "It's her job to look out for Nattie's best interests. She was nice but firm."

"The hotel across the street has hospital rates. I'll reserve us some rooms." Travis tapped his information into the website. "It's under my name. Why don't you go get settled? I'm going to tell Nattie and Marcus good night before I head over."

"Better watch out. The nurse is still in there." Martie pulled the strap of her purse higher on her shoulder. "We can meet up for breakfast in the morning."

They walked away, so Travis went back to Nattie's room.

The nurse finished taking her vitals, then winked at Travis. "Now, you'll be able to get some rest tonight."

Nattie sighed as the nurse left. "Thanks. I couldn't handle her all night."

He held her hand. "I'm glad I didn't have to be the bad guy. I'd hate to get on your mom's bad side."

"What a smart man you are. Will you stay with me a little longer?"

"I've got an hour. Marcus is getting another vial of antivenin at eleven thirteen. I'd like to be there for that."

She ran her fingers over his arm, leaving tingles. "That's sweet. Can we video chat while you're with him so I can see him?"

"That's a great idea."

Her eyelids drooped. He stroked her hair back, and she smiled. He continued until she fell asleep. She had doubted his confession of love, as if he didn't know the difference between love and adrenaline. Nothing could be further from the truth. He'd never felt this way about anyone. He was trusting her with his heart, and she didn't believe him. He hoped he wouldn't regret it later.

****

Travis held his phone steady so that Marcus could see Nattie.

"Hi there, Marcus. I miss you."

"Hi, Nattie." He smiled as he lay against the pillow. "A mean snake bite me."

"I'm sorry. I bet it really hurts."

"Daddy shot you."

Travis groaned. How was he going to forget that?

"He did, but I'm okay now. The doctors and nurses fixed me and have taken good care of me. I need lots of sleep to get better, though. You're going to need lots of sleep too."

The doctor walked in. Travis leaned his head next to Marcus so Nattie could see him. "The doctor's here, so we have to go."

"Okay. Bye, Marcus. Get better. I love you." She blew him a kiss.

"Love you, Nattie."

Travis turned the screen so it was facing only him.

She swiped one side of her hair behind her ear, but the other side hung limp. Her face was still pale, but her eyes were brighter than earlier that evening. "Keep me updated. He looks so tired."

"He's going to be fine. You need to get some sleep. I'll see you in the morning." He smiled, hoping she couldn't see how worried he was.

"'Kay. Bye."

Travis turned off his phone and looked at the doctor.

"Let's take a look at that leg of yours." The doctor pulled the blanket back. Travis cringed. It looked bigger than it had earlier. The doctor pinched Marcus's big toe. He howled. When the doctor touched the leg, he cried out, tears streaming down his face. "I'm sorry, Marcus. I won't touch it again. Okay?"

He whimpered.

"Can't you give him something stronger for the pain?" Travis patted Marcus's hand, hoping he wasn't causing more pain but wanting him to know he was there.

The doctor looked at the chart. "We're giving him the strongest dose of morphine we can. His pain levels and swelling are concerning. I'll order a few more tests. Once we get the results, we'll know more."

Travis pinched his nose as the doctor left, then he sent Margo a text.

The doctor is concerned about Marcus. I need to get a shower and some sleep, but don't want to leave him alone. Can you sit with him?

Yep. On my way.

Thanks. Call me if there are any changes, k?

Got it.

Twenty minutes later, Travis walked into the hotel lobby. Munching on a cookie, Cole sat on a bench across from the front desk with a black duffle bag at his feet.

Travis joined him. "Where'd you get that?"

Cole pointed to the tray of cookies between a water cooler and two coffee makers. Travis filled a mug of decaf and grabbed a chocolate chip cookie, then sat beside his brother. "That my stuff?"

He motioned to the bag.

"Yeah." Cole kicked it over to him. "You need me to stay with you tonight?"

"If you want, but I'll be okay. Going to get a few hours of sleep then head back to the hospital. Marcus is in some serious pain."

"That's too bad. If you don't need me, I'll head back home. I have chores in the morning. I already brought Sampson and Jeeves to my place, so don't worry about them."

"Thanks." Travis and Cole finished their cookies. Cole's kindness was eating at him. What had changed? He was too tired to dig into anything deep, but he had to know. "What gives? You're acting like we're best friends all of a sudden."

Cole shrugged. "You asked me to help earlier. There was a room full of people and you asked me. I figured that meant something."

"It does. Despite everything, I trust you. Nothing can change our past, but I'd like to move forward. Together."

Cole stood and squeezed his shoulder. "Me too."

Travis stood and held out his hand. "See you tomorrow?"

Cole stared at it, then shook it with a firm grip. "Yep. I'll stop by and see the patients." He walked away, and Travis felt the weight he'd carried lighten a smidge.

****

The shrill ring of his phone jolted Travis awake. Nattie! He fumbled for it on the nightstand. "Hello?" He blinked, trying to adjust his eyes to the darkness.

"Travis, it's Margo."

"What's wrong?" Travis glanced at the clock. Five thirty.

"It's Marcus. His swelling increased even after more doses of antivenin. The doctor said he's developed acute compartment syndrome."

"What's that?"

"An increase in pressure within his leg muscle. It's causing nerve damage. They're going to try to fix it with surgery and are prepping him now. He's asking for you and Nattie."

Travis took a deep breath. "I'll be right over."

"Thanks."

He pulled on clean clothes, then hurried over to the hospital. Fifteen minutes later, Margo met him as he stepped off the elevator on the surgical floor. She handed him a cup of coffee.

"Thanks. I'm going to need this."

"This way. They said we can wait in pre-op."

"Did you get any rest last night?"

"A little. I woke up every time they woke Marcus up." He followed her down a narrow hall to double metal doors. She pushed a silver button and the doors opened. After passing several drawn curtains, Margo pulled back one and entered. Marcus lay motionless on the bed.

Travis sat in the chair next to him. "Hey, cowboy. I'm sorry you're not feeling well."

Marcus's eyes flickered open then closed tightly. Tears trickled down his pale cheeks.

Travis squeezed his arm. "I'll be here when you wake up." His stomach tightened.

A nurse entered the room. "Time to go." She smiled. "We'll keep you updated on his progress."

"Appreciate it." Travis stood beside Margo as they wheeled the bed out of the room. "And now we wait."

They made their way to yet another waiting area where Margo refilled her coffee. An hour later, after flipping through every magazine he could find, Travis threw down an outdated *Better Homes and Gardens* and stretched. He couldn't sit there any longer. "I'm going to search out some grub. You want anything?"

Margo shook her head. "I don't eat breakfast. Thanks, though."

"I'm going to swing by and see Nattie too."

"I'll text you if I hear anything."

After scarfing down a quick breakfast in the cafeteria, Travis headed to Nattie's room. It wasn't even seven o'clock, but she sat up in bed eating oatmeal. "Hi, beautiful."

She held her spoon halfway to her mouth and glanced up. "Good morning. You're looking more rested."

"Got a full six hours." He sat in the chair beside her.

"That doesn't seem like enough."

He looked at her breakfast and cringed. "That looks gross."

"It's not Rosemary's caramel rolls, but I've had worse. The nurse said if I eat it all they'd let me take a walk around the pod. Perhaps I could find a handsome cowboy to step out with me."

"Anything for you. But first …" There was no easy way to tell her about Marcus that wouldn't upset her.

"What's wrong?" She grabbed his hand from where he'd been unconsciously pinching the bridge of his nose.

"Marcus is in surgery to relieve the swelling in his leg."

"Is he going to be okay?"

"He's in great hands."

"What if he's not okay? What's the worst-case scenario?"

Travis knew, but he didn't want to worry her any more. If the worst happened, how could he help her when he'd be just as devastated? And how could he reassure her when he had doubts himself? "Finish that gruel, then we'll take a walk. We can't help Marcus by worrying."

Five minutes later, with the nurse's help, Travis escorted Nattie into the hall. She leaned against him through each slow, unsteady step. For the first time in his life, he didn't mind a turtle's pace. They walked around the nurse's station, then back into the room.

"Do you want to sit in a chair?"

"For a bit." She eased into the recliner and sighed. The nurse straightened out the IV.

Travis sat beside her. "I'm impressed. Less than twenty-four hours after being shot in the chest and you're out of bed. I'd be milking this injury for all the attention I could get."

"Let me know when you're ready to get back into bed." The nurse took the food tray as she left.

"I forgot to ask. Have the Freemans seen Marcus yet?" Nattie asked.

"I don't know if they made it, but I know they left today."

"I wonder how this will affect his adoption. I doubt he'll be ready to move next weekend."

"I wish I knew. What about when they release you? What's your plan?" His gut tightened, fearful that she would leave too soon.

"No one's brought up the subject, but I'm sure my mom expects me to leave with them. I'm trying not to think about it."

Avoidance was better than running, for the moment. Another hour of small talk passed before Margo texted him.

Marcus is out of surgery. Sent Dr. to N's room to update you. He sat back in the chair and tried to look calm.

A short man in scrubs stepped into Nattie's room. "Are you Trooper Wilkins?"

Travis nodded.

"I'm Dr. Montgomery, Marcus's orthopedic surgeon. We had some complications with the surgery. I'm sorry, but we had to amputate below the knee."

Everything stopped as the words replayed in Travis's head.

"Marcus's leg is gone?" Nattie's voice wobbled. "What happened?"

"We're guessing the snakebite occurred almost six hours before the antivenin was administered. Because of that, it was too late to prevent extreme nerve damage, which caused the swelling and pain. He was given a transfusion of platelets, but his count is still low. He's in recovery and should be waking up in about an hour. We'll let you know when you can visit."

"Can I see him too?" Nattie asked.

"That's up to your physician."

"What does his recovery time look like?"

"That depends on how quickly he heals. We're going to monitor his hemoglobin and platelet levels. From my experience, kids tend to be quite resilient. I know you're worried about him, but you need to take care of yourself, or you'll be useless to Marcus."

The doctor left, but questions remained. What would Marcus's life look like with a prosthetic leg? He already faced challenges because of his trauma. How would he bounce back from this extra hurdle? And would the Freemans still want to adopt him? If not, Nattie wouldn't be able to care for him in her condition. Would he need another foster home?

"What now?" she whispered as tears fell down her cheeks.

Travis kissed her temple. "We'll take each day as it comes." He slid his chair beside her and held her while she cried.

Monday morning, Natalia held Marcus's hand as he slept in the pediatric intensive care. A glass wall separated his white room from the nurses' station. "What's next for him?"

Margo looked up from her phone. "I've been updating the Freemans periodically. It's hard on them to be so far away. Obviously, this will delay moving Marcus into their home. If they aren't able to meet his medical needs, we'll need to find him a medical foster home until he's sufficiently recovered."

"I wish I could help."

"You have a long road to recovery yourself. I know how quickly you bonded with him, but there's no way the state is going to let you keep him. We have foster parents who are trained to care for sick kids. We need to place Marcus where he'll get the best help."

Natalia went numb. She wanted what was best for him too, but she was going to miss him so much that it hurt just thinking about it. For the first time in years, she didn't feel any anxiety about staying and facing a challenge, but this time she couldn't.

"Nattie." Her dad poked his head into the room. "Your new room is ready. I'll take you there."

She glanced at Margo. "Keep me updated?"

"Of course."

While her dad pushed her down the hall, she dialed Travis's number. It went to voicemail.

* * * * * * *

Travis walked into the Prickly Pear Bistro for his five o'clock dinner break. He chose a booth at the back of the diner and slid into the seat with his back to the wall.

Rosemary set a cup of black coffee in front of him as she dropped a menu on the table. "How are Natalia and Marcus?"

"Healing. I'm headed back up there when my shift is over in an hour."

"Give them my love. What can I get you?"

"The special."

"You got it."

As she walked away, Cole slid into the booth opposite him. "How's Natalia?"

Travis smiled. "Good."

"I'm sorry about Marcus."

"Yeah, it's tough." Travis stared at his coffee, uncomfortable having small talk with Cole.

"Everything that's happened recently has me thinking about Mom. She always liked you best, said you were such a good helper and that I should be like you."

Travis chuckled. "She was manipulating you. She used to say the same thing to me about you."

Cole rolled his eyes. "She was something else, wasn't she? Always looking out for herself. Why do you think she bothered hiding us from all those social workers? Wouldn't it have been easier to give us up?"

"Who knows? Maybe the extra welfare money, or maybe she had a warped view of love."

"And you always wanted to go back."

"Is that part of the reason you're still mad at me? Getting us kicked out of foster homes?" Travis tapped his foot, not sure he wanted to have this conversation but too far into it to stop.

"Could be when it started."

Travis cringed. "I'm sorry about that. I was stupid to think they'd give us back to Mom if they ran out of homes."

"But it brought us to Hank and the ranch, so it's all good."

"Then why have you hated me for the last ten years?" Blood

rushed to Travis's eardrums.

Cole cleared his throat. "Audrey."

Heat crawled up his neck. Not this again. "I didn't sleep with her."

"That's not what she said. She practically told the whole town."

Travis slammed his fist onto the table. "She lied!"

"Calm down." Cole growled. "I'm willing to let it go, but I need to know the truth."

"After all these years and you still don't believe me. I found her walking away down the driveway, beaten and bloody. Her dad had hit her. I tried to take her to you, but she said her dad would kill you if he found her there, so I took her to Rosemary."

"But you didn't come back until dawn. Where were you all night?"

Travis squirmed. He'd kept the secret for ten years and look where it had gotten him? Maybe it was time to confess. "I dumped Audrey off, then met up with Gretta Perkins. We stole a six-pack from her dad and spent the night at the bluffs."

Cole's eyebrows shot up. "Why didn't you tell me before?"

"Are you kidding me? I've always known what everyone in town thinks of me. If I admitted I was with Gretta, they'd think those things about her too. Plus, I wasn't going to give you ammunition to rat me out. I couldn't believe you bought Audrey's lie. There's a lot I did that I'm not proud of, but I would never betray anyone, not Gretta and especially not you."

Cole ran his hand through his hair. "Why would Audrey lie?"

"She wanted to protect you." Rosemary set a plate of food in front of Travis. "Her daddy showed up with a shotgun. He didn't know who she was with that night, but he was drunk and looking for a fight. She lied and said it was Travis. Her dad tried to take her home, but I told him the police were on their way, and he left. Thankfully, he never found either one of you that night. If I'd realized this was what got between the two of you, I'd have told you years ago." She walked away shaking her head.

Cole cringed. "Maybe it was a good thing you were out all night."

A drunk, ex-bull rider with a shotgun wasn't someone Travis wanted to meet up with now, much less when he was sixteen. But that didn't solve the whole puzzle. "Why does the whole town think I slept with her?"

"Her dad was ranting about it for weeks, how Hank's no-good boy seduced his little girl. I tried to tell people it wasn't true, but you never denied seeing her that night, so I started to believe it."

"It didn't take much for the town to believe I was that bad, to steal my brother's girl." No wonder they all hated Travis, but he didn't care about the town. Only Cole's opinion mattered now. "Do you finally believe me?"

Cole stared at his hands, then nodded. "Yeah. It's hard to believe Audrey would lie like that, but I believe you. I'm sorry I ever doubted you."

A long-forgotten emotion stirred in Travis's chest. Before he could analyze it, his phone rang. "Hey, Sarge."

"A deputy has Caleb Russell trapped in an old building five miles north on Stoneville Road. I'm on my way, but you're closer."

"Got it. Leaving now." He turned his radio up so he could hear the situation and squished the meatloaf between the toast. "I've got to go. Glad we finally hashed this out."

Cole stood and offered his hand to Travis. Travis pulled him in for a hug.

"Stay safe, bro."

Travis stepped back and took a bite of his sandwich. "Always." He hurried out to his patrol car and headed out of town.

Fifteen minutes later, Travis drove through a pasture so fast he barely felt the bumps. He couldn't get there quick enough. Caleb had hurt two of the most important people in his life—he was going to pay.

Travis sped up a hill until he saw the red and blue flashing of the county squad car in front of a weather-beaten, wooden homestead.

The tail end of a brown sedan stuck out to the left of the small house. He pulled perpendicular to the deputy, placing his patrol car as a barricade. He grabbed his M16 from the rack above him and squatted behind the passenger side door.

"Have you had any contact with him?" he asked Deputy Davis.

"Initially, he was yelling at me that he wanted his wife. I haven't heard anything in a while."

"How long have you been here?"

"About twenty minutes. I noticed the sedan from the BOLO. He was headed northbound on Stoneville Road, and I followed him here. I've been waiting for backup since then."

Travis mounted his rifle on the hood, then squinted through the scope. A dark figure moved across the window. "Is he alone?"

"I believe so."

Caleb stopped in front of the window.

Travis pushed the button on his shoulder mic. "HP 352. I'm on scene, and I have a clear shot of the suspect. Am I approved to take it?" Travis held his breath and steadied his finger on the trigger.

"Negative. Stand down." Sarge responded. "I'm two miles away."

Travis growled. This was his chance to serve justice. To make sure Caleb never hurt another person. Caleb moved out of sight. If he started shooting, Travis could shoot back.

"Caleb!"

The door creaked open. "I told you I want my wife."

He shifted his aim to the door. "It's Trooper Wilkins. You shot Nattie."

"I didn't want to hurt her, but she wouldn't give me my boy." His voice shook.

"Marcus lost a leg and it's your fault."

"What are you doing?" Davis scowled. "You're going to make him do something stupid."

That was the plan. "Marcus could have died. Come out, Russell."

"No! I want Mary."

An engine roared behind Travis. He gritted his teeth. His chance was gone.

Sarge pulled up next them and ran over. "Get your less-lethal."

"What? Why?"

"That's an order." Sarge knelt next to Travis and drew his gun. "SWAT and a negotiator are on their way."

Travis clenched his jaw as he exchanged his rifle for his shotgun. Instead of heading back into position, he crouched behind the back of his car. It could be his only chance to make Caleb pay for hurting Nattie and Marcus. Sarge might be fine waiting all day for backup, but Travis was itching to end it right then, right there.

He ducked down and crept beside his car where Sarge couldn't see him. Davis was just far enough forward that he could see Travis. He looked at him with wide eyes. Travis shook his head. The homestead door inched open. Travis aimed his shotgun at the crack, his heart pounding. *Come out, you weasel.*

The door shut. His hand sagged. The window exploded as shots hit Travis's patrol car. He fell to the ground, covering his head. More shots rang out. He was a sitting duck!

"Get out of there, Wilkins!" Davis shouted and fired at the homestead. Then everything went still. Travis scooted to the back of his car, heaving. He wiped sweat from his forehead with his arm.

"I'm going to kill you, Trooper! We were fine until you took my boy! It's your fault he lost his leg!"

"Give it your best shot!"

"Shut up, Wilkins," Sarge yelled. "Caleb, throw out your weapons! We'll take you in so you can stand trial."

"I want to see Mary!"

"The only way you can see her is if you come out now!"

Travis tried to steady his breathing as they waited. He would do anything to see Nattie, but how desperate was Caleb?

"Okay. I'm coming out." The door to the house opened, and a gun hit the ground.

"Keep your hands above your head and step out." Sarge's command was met with silence.

The door creaked. Caleb, dressed in a khaki t-shirt and camo pants, walked out with his hands in the air.

Travis gritted his teeth. Without waiting for instructions, he edged closer. This might be his last chance. When he was by his wheel well, Caleb locked eyes with him and stiffened. His arms lowered. A second later, he charged at Travis. Gun fire and shouting erupted around them. Travis dropped the shotgun and reached for his pistol. Too late. Caleb tackled him to the ground.

Pain shot through Travis's jaw. Caleb was on top of him, punching with one hand and grabbing for the gun with the other. Travis tried to roll to the side. He had to keep his gun away from Caleb! He pushed Travis's head up by the chin. A soft snap, and movement at Travis's side. He turned and looked into a gun barrel.

Shots exploded.

Caleb flew backward.

Travis's heart stopped, then his pulse surged to life. Davis appeared over him and helped him sit up.

Sarge kicked Travis's gun away. "Call for medical."

Travis sat in the dirt, his mind racing and thankful to be alive.

"Are you hurt, Wilkins?"

"No." Stunned and feeling stupid? Yep.

Sarge knelt and felt Caleb's neck. "Cancel medical. Request the coroner."

The deputy complied. Travis's legs shook as he stood and walked toward Caleb's body. Blood oozed from his chest. Other troopers arrived. Sarge talked on the phone as he paced. "Get a hold of DCI. We need them on scene."

Davis approached Travis. "Why would you do something so reckless? He could have killed you."

He had been reckless. And an idiot. And Davis still covered him. "You saved my life."

"Even though you were stupid, I've got your six, brother.

Always." He patted Travis on the back.

In a rush, it hit him. Travis had only been after Caleb. Davis had been trying to do the same while protecting Travis the whole time. When it mattered the most, Travis had put them in danger while the deputy protected them.

Davis shook his head. "It could have been bad, man. Why would he attack you when we had him at gunpoint?"

"We have history. I shouldn't have egged him on. I put you and Sarge in danger."

"Maybe next time you'll stay where it's safe."

Sarge strode over to them. "The forensic team and DCI are on their way. They're going to be investigating you both, so plan on sticking around."

Travis nodded. Caleb's lifeless body could have been his. If it weren't for Davis, it would have. He'd relied on himself for so long that it felt weird trusting anyone else, but maybe Sarge was right. Maybe it was time to let the lone wolf go.

****

At six o'clock Tuesday evening, Travis walked into the hospital. He couldn't wait to see Nattie. When he reached her room, the lights were low. She was on her side facing away from him. He knocked on the doorjamb, but she didn't move, so he snuck around to the other side. Asleep. He'd go check on Marcus.

He found Marcus sitting up in bed eating mac and cheese. Margo sat next to him using her phone, and an older lady with tight, gray curls sat next to her. Cartoon music blasted from the TV.

"Hey, cowboy. You're looking good."

Marcus waved. "Travis!"

Margo looked up. "Pull up a chair."

Travis grabbed the last chair and sat on the other side of the bed. "How are you feeling?"

"Good." His attention moved to the TV.

"This is Dotti." Margo motioned to the lady beside her.

Dotti smiled. "It's nice to meet you. Marcus and Margo have talked a lot about you."

"She's going to be caring for Marcus when he's released."

Concern crept into Travis's mind. "Can't the Freemans do it?"

Margo scrunched her nose. "The Freemans aren't able to provide Marcus with the care he needs. Etta's mom's health is deteriorating, and they feel like taking care of both her medical needs and Marcus's will be too much, so they pulled their adoption application. Dotti is a retired nurse. She'll be able to navigate the medical appointments Marcus will now need."

Another foster home for Marcus. Travis's heart ached for the boy. He looked at Dotti. "Will you be able to adopt him?"

"I'm far too old to raise a boy. I'm not even sure how much longer I'll be able to foster kids, but I had to help when I heard about Marcus."

"So you're back at the beginning, finding him an adoptive family."

Margo nodded. "It's going to be even more of a challenge now."

"Does Nattie know?"

"Not yet. I haven't seen her since talking with the Freemans."

It was going to break her heart.

"How's my favorite patient?" Dr. Hash entered the room and picked up Marcus's medical chart. "I thought I'd check in before I head out for the day."

Travis ruffled Marcus's hair. "As long as everything's okay, I'll take off."

"He's recovering nicely. He should be good."

Travis nodded, thankful that not everything he had to tell Nattie was bad. "I'm on my way to see Nattie, so I'll give her the news."

"I appreciate that," Margo said.

He took his time returning to Nattie's room as he tried to figure out how to tell her. She didn't need any more stress, but he couldn't avoid it. He wanted her to hear the news from him.

When he finally entered Nattie's room, she was awake and eating applesauce. A bowl of soup and a few saltine crackers sat untouched. "Not hungry tonight?"

She pushed the tray across the table toward him. "You can have it. I'm not hungry."

"Why not?"

"I'm sick of being cooped up here. I want to see Marcus, but my mom won't let me, and I hate arguing with her. It's easier to give in."

"I have some news." He took her hand and threaded his fingers with hers. "A deputy shot Caleb today. He died instantly."

Nattie trembled. "It's over."

"How do you feel?"

"I'm not sure. Mostly angry."

"That's not uncommon. You'll feel better when you can forgive him."

"Maybe. If I can."

"I think you should. He's not worth your resentment." He squeezed her fingers. "There's good news too. Cole and I talked. I think we're going to be good."

She beamed. "I'm so happy for you."

"There's more. I just came from Marcus's room. Doc says he's recovering nicely." Nattie smiled and he took a deep, fortifying breath. "But I also learned that the Freemans have withdrawn their adoption application."

"What? Why?"

"They don't think they can meet his new needs, so he's going into a medical foster home."

Tears welled up in Nattie's eyes. "This isn't fair. It took a year to find the Freemans. How much longer will it take to find another family, especially now that he has a disability?"

"I wish I knew. Until then, he's going to live with a retired nurse named Dotti. She's with him now. She seems nice."

"And thanks to Caleb I can't care for him anymore." She pulled her hand from his and stared at the ceiling. "And you want me to forgive him. It doesn't matter. I'm going home soon, so I can't take care of Marcus anyway."

"When?"

"I think I'd like to be alone." She turned toward the wall.

"Nattie, don't run from me."

But it was too late. She had already fled.

CHAPTER 31

Wednesday morning, Natalia sat on the edge of the hospital bed as her mom brushed her hair. Without her mother's lectures, Natalia could enjoy the soothing strokes. Until Mom pulled her hair as she braided it.

"Ow. That's a little tight."

"It needs to be tight if you want your hair to stay in a braid. It's been a mess."

"I was shot, Mom. People will understand."

She twisted the hair tighter until she tied off the braid and moved around the bed to inspect her work. "Your face wouldn't look so long if you cut some bangs."

Natalia rolled her eyes. "Got it."

A woman in dark-blue scrubs walked in. "Natalia, I'm your case worker. I'll fill out your discharge papers, go over next steps, and help you dress." She looked between Natalia's parents. "Now, who are you going home with today?"

"My parents. Max and Martie Brynner."

"Excellent. Does their house have many steps that you'll need to navigate?"

"No." Mom scooted a chair closer to them. "We have two steps that lead into the kitchen from the garage."

"I'm not going to move back in with you. I have my own place."

"You can't go back to your apartment. Who will care for you? Plus, you have two flights of stairs. I told you not to move into a place without an elevator."

Natalia took a deep breath. "I want to go home."

The case manager tapped on her tablet. "Natalia, I have to

agree with your mother. I'm concerned about you staying by yourself right now. We'll set up physical and occupational therapy appointments for next week, but your therapists will need to clear you to live on your own."

"I'm twenty-five years old. I don't want to move back in with my parents."

"I understand," the case worker said, "but it's only temporary. The only other option is transferring to a rehab center. We can look into one for you if you prefer."

Mom clucked her tongue. "That's ridiculous. You're moving in with us. I think it might be best to give up your apartment for the time being. You're wasting money paying rent on a place you aren't staying in."

Natalia gritted her teeth.

The case manager looked from Natalia to her mom. "I think permanent decisions should be made after you've met with the therapists. Are you okay moving in with your parents until then?"

She wasn't okay with it in the slightest, but what choice did she have?

****

Natalia petted the stuffed golden retriever on her lap as she sat in her wheelchair outside Marcus's room. Even though she'd had second thoughts about being a foster parent, she hoped he wouldn't forget her. The pain of her incision was dull compared to her heart breaking.

Wheeling herself inside, she found a familiar form sitting on Marcus's bed with his back to her. Her heart stuttered. Marcus flew a toy helicopter around his head, his cheeks glowing. "And they flied me into the air, and gave me an ugy Band-Aid, but Travis gave me a cowboy one."

Cole. Her heart relaxed as she rolled next to Marcus's bed. "That's quite the story," she said.

"Nattie! Look at my 'copter!" He flew his toy around her head making helicopter noises.

"They finally let you put on some real clothes?" Cole said.

"They had to. I'm leaving today."

"So soon?"

"After lunch."

"I hope this isn't goodbye forever."

Sadness welled up in her. Cole had been a good friend, and she would miss him. "We'll stay in touch. I'm glad our paths crossed."

"I hope so." He gave Marcus a fist bump. "Stay strong." Then he gave Natalia a hug. The tapping of his boots faded down the hall.

A pain shot through her chest as she pushed herself up and sat beside Marcus. He landed the helicopter on the nearby table and scooted onto her lap. Leaning her face against his smooth cheek, she inhaled the sweet scent of baby shampoo.

"You are such a brave boy."

Marcus pointed at his shortened leg. "The doctor took my leg. Now they're gonna gimmie a new one, like my 'copter."

Natalia laughed. "What kind of leg is like a helicopter?"

"That's what Cole said. A metal leg like my 'copter. Then I can fly."

She hugged him close. "Sorry, you won't be able to fly. But don't you think it would be silly to fly with your leg in the air, anyway. You'd be upside down and probably get dizzy." She tickled him until his laughter filled the room. "You're going to have to work hard to learn to walk again. If you do, you'll be able to run to me the next time I see you."

Marcus frowned. "You going bye-bye?"

She nodded. "My mommy and daddy are taking me home. I have to get lots of rest so that my owies get better. Dotti is going to take good care of you."

"Grandma Dotti has a cat and a bird, and I can pay with them. She's gonna teach me to walk on my new leg."

"You're going to do great." Natalia reached into the wheelchair and grabbed the stuffed dog. "I brought you this doggie so you'll remember me."

Marcus hugged the golden retriever against his chest.

"Are you ready to go?" Her dad popped his head into the room.

She kissed Marcus's cheek, then sat back in the wheelchair. Sadness gripped her as she rolled herself out of the room. When she reached the doorway, she glanced back at Marcus. He took the dog on a helicopter ride around his head. She smiled, thankful he'd been a part of her life, even for a short time.

****

Travis was parked in his patrol car in the median at the edge of Alkaline typing out a report when his phone rang. "Wilkins."

"It's Sergeant Black. Captain wants to meet with you at D300 ASAP."

Travis's stomach dropped. A meeting at District Headquarters with the captain was not his idea of a fun afternoon. "10-4. I'll be there in an hour."

He hightailed it to Rapid City. He'd been on Sergeant Black's radar for too long and had made some stupid choices before Caleb was killed. Had the investigation come back already? Was he being charged? Caleb had the upper hand during the fight so Travis hadn't used excessive force, but they wouldn't have been fighting if Travis had kept his cool.

Forty minutes later, he pulled into the parking lot. He entered through the back door of the stone building, walked past closed officer doors, and knocked on the captain's door.

Sarge opened it. "Come in, Wilkins."

"Have a seat, Travis." The captain motioned to the leather chair in front of his desk. Sergeant Black leaned against the window sill with his arms across his chest. "How's your girlfriend?"

Travis sat on the comfortable chair, though the atmosphere was anything but comfortable. "Natalia is healing. They should be discharging her soon."

"That's great news. And the boy? How is he?"

"They had to amputate his leg."

"I'm sorry to hear that." The captain cleared his throat. "Let's get down to business. You've been with the highway patrol for eight years now, and we've never had any major issues with work performance. It has come to my attention, however, that you first met Natalia, whom you are now dating, on a traffic stop. Is that correct?"

"Yes. I stopped her for speeding and failing to stop at a stop sign."

"Then you asked her out on a date?"

"No, of course not. I stopped her, and she was quite upset. Then she got a flat tire that couldn't be fixed until the morning. I merely offered to get her some food and a place to stay for the night. It was all very innocent."

"Yet you just admitted that she's your girlfriend, correct?"

"Yes, but, like I said, it started innocently."

The captain narrowed his eyes. "Innocent or not, it's against policy."

The acid in his stomach churned. "Yes, sir."

"Sergeant Black said he's already talked with you about approaching the Russells' vehicle without backup."

Travis's jaw tightened. "Yes, sir. I shouldn't have taken that chance, especially since Natalia was with me."

The captain's eyebrows shot up. "I didn't know that particular detail." He made a note in the file in front of him.

Travis cringed.

"Finally, you once again disobeyed a direct order and went searching for the kidnapped boy."

Heat climbed up Travis's neck. "If I hadn't searched for Marcus, he would be dead right now."

"We have a chain of command in place for a reason."

Travis leapt to his feet. "Marcus would have died if I had obeyed that order."

The captain raised a hand. "Calm down, Wilkins. We know all about that. And Sergeant Black told me what happened with Caleb Russell. Still, we can't ignore these issues. That's why we've decided to transfer you to Rapid City, where backup will be minutes away and you'll be under direct supervision."

"But I live in Alkaline."

"If you want to continue to work for the highway patrol, you'll need to move."

"For how long?"

"You'll be on probation for six months. After that you can try to transfer, but I can't guarantee you'll get approved anytime soon. Any more questions?"

He clenched his fingers. "No, sir."

"You're dismissed."

His mind whirled as he left the office and drove to the hospital. He didn't care if his shift wasn't over yet. He was going to see Nattie. Maybe she could help him make sense of all of this. He was trained to make split-second decisions. He didn't need his supervisors to hold his hand.

But he loved his job. Could he really move to Rapid? Where would he live? He wasn't about to sell his cabin, but he'd have to find a place that would let him bring his dogs. Would it be fair to bring them into the city?

At the hospital, he walked through the lobby and headed to the elevators when he saw Nattie sitting in a wheelchair outside the gift shop. "Nattie!" He jogged over and kissed her cheek.

"Travis, what are you doing here? I thought you were working today?"

"I'm technically still at work. I just met with the captain and Sarge. I'm in trouble for saving a boy's life."

"Why?"

"Because I'm not a team player. Now they're transferring me to Rapid City."

"Are you going to have to move?"

"If I want to keep my job. I'm so frustrated."

"I'm sorry."

He pinched his nose. "Enough about me. How are you?" He glanced down and noticed her tennis shoes, sweatpants, and t-shirt. "You're dressed. Are you going somewhere?"

She blushed. "I've been released."

Already? He pulled out his phone. "There aren't any missed calls. Were you going to leave without telling me?"

"I was going to call." But she wouldn't make eye contact.

"When you were halfway home? What's going on? Why didn't you call?"

"I didn't know what to say."

She didn't have to say anything. Her actions spoke loud enough. "Please don't run away from me."

"I'm not running away. The doctor discharged me, and my parents are taking me back to Sioux Falls."

"That doesn't explain why you didn't tell me."

She stiffened her shoulders. "I need some space. I'm an adult who has to move back with my parents. I have no career and no purpose. I'm just … existing."

"What about us?"

"We need to break up." She finally looked at him. "We never should have let it get this far. You knew I wasn't going to stay here forever."

But he'd hoped. He wanted to make her understand that she wasn't just running away from life, she was running from something special. He wanted to beg her to fight for them, but to what end? He couldn't make her change her mind. "Okay. Whatever you want." He turned and strode away, slamming his palm against the wall as he walked past. Pain shot through his hand, but it was nothing like the pain Nattie had caused.

****

From the back of the parking lot, Travis sat in his patrol car as the nurse pushed Nattie to a black Suburban. He closed his eyes and squeezed the bridge of his nose until his eyes watered. When he opened them, Nattie was gone.

Pain sliced through him. She had actually left. He'd fallen in love with her, but she'd left. Didn't that mean anything to her?

His phone rang. He grabbed it from the center consul and glanced at the caller ID. His brother. Good, he needed a distraction. "Hey, Cole."

"It's Dakota Peace. He's lying down in the pasture behind the barn, and I can't get him to stand. The vet's on his way."

Fear rolled through him. How much more could he take? "I'm coming." He flipped on his lights as he sped out of the parking lot.

An hour later, he skidded to a stop beside the barn. The vet's black pickup and horse trailer sat in the pasture. Travis ran through the tall grass and jumped over the fence. Dakota Peace lay on his side. Sweat covered his coat, and he took quick breaths. Cole knelt at his back while the vet held his stethoscope to Dakota's belly.

Travis fell to his knees beside his horse and pulled his head onto his lap. "How is he?" He stroked the rough mane. He couldn't lose his beloved horse too.

The vet put his stethoscope back in his bag. "He's lethargic because I gave him a sedative for the exam. His pulse is regular, but his stomach is gurgling quite a bit. Looks like a mild case of colic." He pulled out a bottle with clear liquid, poked a syringe into the top, and pulled the liquid into the syringe. "I'll give him some Banamine for the pain." The vet leaned toward Travis. "Hold his mouth open while I administer it under his tongue."

Travis cradled Dakota's mouth in his hands and pried open his lips and teeth. He held his breath while the vet slowly pushed the liquid into his mouth.

The vet patted Dakota's neck. "Have you changed his diet recently?"

Cole stood. "I bought a new bag of oats, but it's the same brand I always use."

"That could be the reason. His bowels are good. I don't suspect any displacement or twists in the intestines. Let's try to get him standing."

Cole crouched beside Dakota's hip while Travis stood and crouched near his shoulder. When the vet was in place at Dakota's abdomen, he nodded, "One ... two ... three ... push."

Travis grunted as he pushed, his muscles straining under the pressure. Dakota lifted his body onto his legs. He pawed at the ground, kicking up dirt, then tried to lie back down. They pushed again until Dakota stumbled upright. Travis stroked his nose. "I know you're hurting. We'll get you feeling better soon."

The vet jogged over to his truck and returned with a five-gallon bucket. "I'll need to intubate him to administer mineral oil, but I think he's going to be fine."

Travis sighed as the tension eased from his back and shoulders. "Looks like you're stuck with us a bit longer." He should let Nattie know about Dakota. He pulled his cell phone from his pocket, but when he saw Nattie's number, his finger froze over her name.

Why should he call her? She was the one who'd walked away. If she cared so much, she would have stayed, or at least asked Travis to visit her. If she wanted to know about Dakota, she'd ask. He closed his eyes and leaned against his horse's neck. "At least you're not leaving me."

CHAPTER 32

As they pulled into the driveway, Natalia swallowed down her disappointment. She'd pretended to sleep the first hour of the trip to avoid talking to her parents, but she must have fallen asleep because the next thing she knew, they were driving down her childhood street.

Her parents' bluish-gray craftsman home with white trim and a covered porch greeted them. Two wicker chairs with blue striped cushions sat untouched on the porch. She couldn't remember anyone ever sitting in them.

Before the SUV stopped, she unbuckled her seatbelt so she could climb out as soon as her dad parked. She walked past the porch to the back door.

"Nattie, let me help you." Her mom scurried over and lifted Natalia's arm over her shoulder.

Natalia pulled away. "I can do it. It's only two steps." Once in the house, she shuffled through the kitchen to the living room. As soon as she stepped through the arched wall, her nieces ran to her and hugged her legs.

"Surprise! Welcome home." Seven-year-old Lacey smiled up at her.

Natalia squeezed them close. "What are you doing here?"

"Daddy wanted to make sure you were okay. He said you were hurt."

"I was, but I'm getting better, especially with you here. You girls give the best hugs."

"Girls, run along. Your aunt needs to rest."

"I'm fine, Mom. I slept the whole way here." She looked down at their blonde and brown curls. "Why don't you help me to the couch." Lacey took one hand while five-year-old Jasayla took the other and led her to the stiff, Victorian-style sofa. She sat with a niece on either side.

She tried to relax, but the entire room—from the thick cream-and-blue flowered curtains to the sculpted couch and matching chairs—screamed stiff and formal. The only comfortable furniture in the house, besides her bed, was in the basement family room, and she doubted her mom would let her down there anytime soon.

Her brother walked in from the dining room. "Nattie. You're home." He put Jasayla on his lap and sat beside her. "Let me see your wound." He reached for the hem of her shirt.

She pushed him away. Talk about intrusive. "No. I'm fine."

"I want to see if it's healing properly."

"I had a team of doctors. I don't need another one."

"Let your brother have a look." Mom scowled at her.

"Mitch, leave your sister alone. She doesn't want you looking at her chest." His wife, Judy, appeared from the hallway. Her black hair was pulled into an elegant bun, and she'd accessorized her jeans and sweater with a chunky gold necklace and heels. Her style resembled her personality: exuberant. Natalia envied Judy's ability to stand up to her mom and brother. "How are you doing, Natalia?"

"I'm alive and glad to be out of the car."

Judy clicked across the room and squeezed next to Mitch. She'd give Natalia an earful if she knew what she'd done with her black heels in Alkaline's mechanic shop.

Sadness hit her. She hadn't expected to miss Alkaline so much or so soon. Especially Travis. Why had she treated him that way? She could have left without dumping him. Then she could go to her room and call him.

Instead, her mother's flowery papered walls closed in on her. This time she couldn't run if she wanted to. She'd trapped herself.

* * * * * * *

Natalia lay on her bed flipping through television channels. After seventy-two hours of living with her parents, her sanity was slipping away. Her mom wouldn't let her do anything for herself, though she'd stood her ground when her mom insisted on helping her shower. And she was bored. She'd never been a great reader, social media had lost its appeal, and after binge-watching *COPS*, even television seemed tedious. She missed people, but the only ones she saw anymore were her parents. She couldn't wait for her next doctor's appointment.

It was nearly ten. Maybe she'd just go to bed. She trudged to the kitchen for a drink. Her mom stood at the sink holding out her pain meds. Natalia shook her head. "I'm going to take some ibuprofen instead. I haven't had any pain all day."

"That's because you're taking your medication. Believe me, if you stop, you'll feel it."

"I'll be fine without it."

"Nattie, you have to stay on top of the pain. Take the pills."

She held out her palm. It wasn't worth fighting over. Mom dropped the pills in her hand and she squeezed her fingers around them. "Night, Mom."

"Good night, dear."

Nattie shuffled to the bathroom and dropped the pills into the toilet, then brushed her teeth. Back in her room, she took a couple of ibuprofens and snuggled into her mattress. She hadn't missed much since moving out, but she had missed her pillow top.

* * * * * * *

Natalia sprung forward, gasping for air. *Travis!* She glanced around. She rubbed her eyes. The red numbers of her alarm clock blared three thirty-six.

Her dream had seemed so real. The gunshot and the pain.

The pain. Her wound throbbed. She took some more ibuprofen from her nightstand. Her mom was probably right about the pain meds, but she wasn't going to admit it. She lay back down and closed her eyes, but the nightmare haunted her. It was her first one since getting shot. Her first instinct was to call Travis, but she couldn't do that. She couldn't lead him on when she didn't know what she was going to do next. Instead, she lay down and closed her eyes, but the image of Caleb popped into her mind.

Would she ever be able to think of Alkaline without thinking of him? She wanted to go back to the time before Caleb hurt her, but she'd done her fair share of hurting people too. She hadn't called Rosemary until she got home, and Travis … no amount of pain meds could numb that ache.

CHAPTER 33

A week after coming home, Natalia sat in the passenger seat of her parents' SUV in silence as her mom navigated the streets of Sioux Falls. They passed the police department as a police car left the parking lot. Her chest tightened as they passed the Metro Communications building where she'd spent the last two years working. She missed it.

"Turn right on West Fourth Street," she said. "Then a right up here at North Main Avenue. Dr. Drakeford's office is in the health and human services building on the left."

Mom sighed as she turned. "I don't see why this is necessary. You're not crazy. Why do you need a shrink?"

Natalia rolled her eyes. Once her therapists cleared her to drive, she'd leave her mom at home. "It's that brick building. You can let me off out front."

"Nonsense. I'm coming in with you." She parked on the street in front of the building.

"No, you're not. I'll be out in an hour." Natalia hopped out and slammed the door before her mom could protest. Once inside, a black informational board listed Dr. Drakeford's office on the second floor. As she turned to the elevator, she spotted her mom climbing the steps outside the building. Natalia groaned. Would that woman ever stop smothering her?

Natalia changed directions and headed to the stairs. Her physical therapist would disapprove, but she was desperate. She ran up the first flight, then had to rest on the landing to catch her breath. Her chest ached, her muscles shook, and sweat beaded on her forehead. This was a mistake, but she was almost there. She climbed the next set of stairs at a much slower pace.

When she reached the next landing, she opened the door and trudged down the white hallway to a wooden door with *Psychological Services* engraved on a brass plate. She opened the door expecting to see her mom standing at the front desk, but instead a blond receptionist looked up and smiled. Relief filled her as she stepped up to the desk.

"Good morning. How can I help you?"

"I'm Natalia Brynner. I have a nine o'clock appointment with Dr. Drakeford."

"Please have a seat. She'll be out to get you in a moment."

Natalia turned to the waiting area. Three leather couches formed a semicircle with end tables at each corner. She walked to the water cooler in the corner and filled a cup. The first, cool gulp soothed her still-sore throat. She sank onto a leather couch and admired the large saltwater fish tank beside the receptionist's desk. A bright yellow fish swam at a leisurely pace while an orange-and-black fish chased a larger, blue one. Their swimming calmed her nerves. The front door opened again, and her mom stepped through. Natalia groaned. What twenty-five-year-old woman brought her mom to her doctor's appointment?

Mom sat next to her and frowned. "I'm not letting you do this alone."

Natalia drank the rest of the water before crumpling the cup in her hand. The staccato beat of heels on tile intensified until a tall, slender woman opened the inner office door and smiled. "Natalia?"

Natalia stood on shaking legs as her stomach fluttered. "Hi. You must be Dr. Drakeford."

"It's very nice to meet you in person. I'll show you to my office."

Natalia's mom stood. "I'm Nattie's mom, Martie."

Dr. Drakeford's perfect eyebrows rose. "It's nice to meet you too. I hope you'll be comfortable while you wait. There's water by the door or, if you'd prefer some coffee, there's some in the back room. I'm sure our receptionist can get you a cup."

"I'd like to join you. Nattie relies on me."

Natalia bit her tongue.

"I'm sure she does. Down the road we might have a family session, but Natalia and I need to get to know each other first. Have a seat, Mrs. Brynner." Dr. Drakeford guided Natalia through the door. "I'm down the hall. This way."

The doctor escorted her into an office with tall windows along the back wall. A brown suede couch and two puffy, navy chairs circled an empty coffee table. A print of van Gogh's "Starry Night" hung above the couch, and copies of Dr. Drakeford's degrees hung in a straight line above a glass desk.

"Have a seat."

"On the couch?"

"Wherever you'll be comfortable. Would you like something to drink? We have bottled water, juice, or coffee."

"I'm fine." Natalia walked to one of the chairs and sank into the soft material. Her body relaxed, but her stomach continued to flutter.

Dr. Drakeford sat erect in the other chair, crossing her long legs. "A lot has happened since we spoke on the phone. How are you feeling physically?"

"Until I decided to run up your steps to avoid my mother, I was doing pretty well." She rubbed her chest where the ache persisted.

The doctor dropped her leg to the floor as she leaned toward Natalia. "You didn't reinjure yourself, did you?"

"No. Just overdid it."

"Okay, but if you feel sick, please let me know. Should we start with your relationship with your mom?"

"I thought I was here to talk about my nightmares."

"We'll get there. I'd like to start with your mom though. The environment you were raised in affects how you process trauma."

"That's an onion with one layer smellier than the next."

Dr. Drakeford laughed. "Then let's start peeling. Tell me about her."

"I'm not sure where to start. She's overbearing, but she means well. I'm tired of being treated like a child. She contradicts every choice I've ever made, from my hairstyle to my career, and I can never measure up to my perfect older brother."

"I bet his life isn't quite perfect."

"You're right. His life isn't perfect—he and his wife have struggled with infertility for years—but sometimes I wonder if my mom knows it."

"Have you asked her why she compares you to him?"

She shook her head. The thought had never occurred to her. "I guess I thought that was her way."

"Try asking her. You might be surprised at her answer." Dr. Drakeford wrote something on a spiral journal. "Do you feel your mom loves you?"

"Maybe too much. She smothers me."

"From the short interaction with her in the waiting room, that would be my guess too. She looked terrified when I told her she couldn't come back with you."

"That's the only thing that keeps me from pushing her away."

"I dated an engineer in college. He fixed everything. If we went out to dinner and the chair he sat in was lopsided, he'd turn it over and tighten the screws, right in the restaurant. If my front door squeaked when he dropped me off, he'd grease it. He even tried to 'fix' me. The problem with a fixer is that people usually don't like other people trying to fix them. It makes us feel inadequate. We want to be loved for who we are."

Natalia sprang forward. "Exactly. I want her to be happy with me."

"Would it annoy you less if, every time she criticized, you thought of it as a helpful suggestion? Think of it as her showing love and concern for you instead of her finding fault. Often it's easier to change our perceptions of people than it is for them to change their behavior."

"I could try."

"Journaling would help too. Write down her offensive comments, then, under those, find a way it expresses her love or concern. For instance, what did she say about your hair?"

Natalia ran her fingers through her newly cut bangs. "She told me my face wouldn't look as long with bangs."

"And how do you feel about your bangs?"

"I hate them. They're always rubbing against my eyebrows."

"Do you like how you look with them?"

Natalia shrugged. "I don't hate it."

"Why do you think your mom cares if your face looks long or not?"

"She wants me to look my best, I guess. After I cut them, she told me how gorgeous I looked, but I also think she was happy because she got her way."

"Perhaps it was both. She thought you looked better with them cut, and that confirmed that she was right. Consequently, that will make her fight harder the next time she thinks you need to be persuaded to her side."

Natalia moaned. She was creating a monster.

"Don't look so discouraged. Try the journaling exercise and report back with the results next week."

"I'll try."

Dr. Drakeford tapped her fingers on her knee and tipped her head to the side. "How are you sleeping? Any more nightmares?"

Natalia closed her eyes and nodded. "Almost every night now. Sometimes they're weird, made-up crime scenes, but most of the time they're from calls. Last night, I dreamed that everyone in the diner I was working in was shot in the chest, and I was shot last so I had to see them all die."

"Have the breathing techniques helped?"

"They relax me enough that I can usually fall back asleep."

"That's progress. We need to spend some time defusing your dreams so they're not so scary though."

"How do you do that?"

"We'll make up non-scary endings, then rehearse them until we've recreated them to be less frightening. Let's practice with the dream you had last night. You said everyone was shot at the diner where you worked. Who shot them?"

"Caleb. The man who shot me."

"How did the dream start?"

Natalia shuddered as she replayed the scenario. "I was refilling a rancher's coffee mug when Caleb burst through the front door. First, he shot the rancher, then a group of retired men, then he shot Rosemary. I watched them all fall to the ground and I couldn't help them. He shot me last."

"Let's say Caleb came into the diner and, before he could shoot anyone, the police showed up. What would that look like in your imagination?"

"Travis is a state trooper. He could arrest Caleb. I even saw him do it once."

"Okay. Close your eyes."

Natalia squeezed her eyes shut.

"You're at the counter filling the coffee mug when Caleb bursts through the door holding a gun. He points it at the rancher, but before he can fire, the state trooper shows up. What does he do and say?"

"He tells Caleb to drop the gun."

"Caleb drops the gun. Then what?"

"He has him turn around and walk back to him slowly. Then he cuffs him and puts him in the patrol car."

"And the threat is gone. You can open your eyes."

As Natalia opened them, she felt better, even giddy that Travis got to be the hero in her made-up dream ending.

They worked through two more scenarios before Dr. Drakeford clicked her pen. "You'll need to rehearse the endings so your mind is focused on the new versions. You can do this with any dream." She wrote in her journal, then tore off the page and handed it to Natalia. "Here are a few online support groups you should look into. They'll help you feel like you're not fighting alone. Can we meet next week? I want to dig deeper into some of your hardest calls and recreate endings to some of your scarier dreams."

"I'm free. Except for doctor appointments, I have no plans." And for the first time since talking with Dr. Drakeford, Natalia was looking forward to their next conversation. "Thanks. I was nervous about meeting with you, but I'm so glad I came in."

"It was a pleasure to finally meet face to face. Until next week."

Natalia walked back to the waiting room feeling lighter than she had in years. For the first time in weeks, she didn't feel quite so trapped.

* * * * * * *

Travis led Dakota Peace around the pasture. In the last week, the gelding had improved so much that he was almost acting like his old self.

The dry, golden hay reached Travis's knees as he strolled through it. Soon he'd be helping Cole cut and bale it, if the weather stayed dry. Thankfully, only white clouds streaked across the afternoon sky. Staying busy with work, moving, and helping Cole kept him from dwelling on Nattie, which hurt far more than he'd ever admit to anyone.

When his phone rang, his heartbeat increased. A quick glance at the caller ID and it returned to normal. She'd been gone a week, How long would he expect her calls? "Wilkins."

"Hi, Travis!" Marcus's sweet voice soothed his raw nerves.

"Hey, cowboy. How are you feeling?"

"I go to Grandma Dotti's house today."

"That sounds fun. Are you excited to leave the hospital?"

"Yeah. Nattie can't come 'cus she's hurt."

"I know."

"Daddy hurt her," he whispered. "Why did Daddy shoot her?"

Travis twisted Dakota's reins around his hand until it tingled. No three-year-old should have to ask that question. "He's not your daddy."

Marcus breathed into the phone.

He shouldn't have said that. He was probably scarring the poor kid for life. "I'm sorry. He was your daddy, but he's not anymore. You're going to get a new daddy."

"Can you be my daddy?"

Travis's chest tightened. How was he supposed to respond to that? "You need a new daddy *and* mommy."

"Why?"

Good question. Travis scanned the horizon where the hills rolled into the horizon. This land was his because a bachelor with a huge heart opened his home to two hurting boys. Why couldn't Travis do the same?

Dakota whinnied.

"Horsey!"

Travis chuckled. "I'm walking Dakota Peace. Do you remember when you rode him?"

"Can I ride him? Can I ride him? Pease?"

"I don't see why not. You go home with Grandma Dotti, and when she thinks your leg is ready, I'll take you for a ride. Deal?"

"Yay! What? Grandma Dotti says to say bye."

"You be good for her, okay?"

"'Kay. Bye, Travis."

"Bye, cowboy." As soon as Travis ended the call, he scrolled through his contacts.

"Hello, this is Margo."

"It's Travis. What do I need to do to foster Marcus?"

* * * * * * *

Two days later, Travis glanced around his small rental house. He'd bought a navy futon, recliner, and flat-screen TV for the living room and brought over the small dining room table from the ranch. From his spot by the front door, he could see into the kitchen. It wasn't as big as his house in Alkaline, but he didn't need much space.

The doorbell rang and Travis's heart leapt. When he opened the door, Margo stood there holding a briefcase and smiling. Unlike their days together at the hospital, she was once again neat and tidy in a dress and high heels. "Come in." He held the screen door open.

"This place is quaint." She glanced around the room. "It certainly could use a bit more decorating."

"I didn't think decorations were a prerequisite for fostering kids."

"You're right. It's just so different from your cabin."

He didn't need the reminder. "Back here is my bedroom." He walked down the short hall and opened the door to the right. A new queen mattress sat on a box spring with the plastic wrap still on it. "I just moved in, and I don't officially have to live here until next week."

He backed away from her and opened the next door. "And this is the spare room." The scent of paint still filled the air. His denim quilt, plush blue pillows, a blue teddy bear, and a stuffed horse covered the twin bed that took up most of the floor space. A pine dresser from his childhood sat under a window framed with cowboy curtains. Pictures of horses and cows lined the blue walls.

"Oh, Travis." Margo followed him into the room. "I see where you've spent your time. This is wonderful. You know this is just the beginning of the process, don't you? Adopting Marcus is not a done deal."

"I know, but I get to foster him, don't I?" Had he gotten too excited too soon?

"I can't promise anything. We like to keep the number of homes a foster child lives in to the barest minimum, and Marcus has had three. Your chances are better because you're enrolled in a Lakota tribe, which fulfills ICWA requirements. Do you still want to go forward with your license?"

"Of course I do."

"Have you started the classes yet?"

"I start tomorrow and will go every other week for six Saturdays." What if he did all this work and they found a better family for him? One with a dad and a mom?

"Let's sit so we can finish your paperwork." She headed for the kitchen. He sat opposite her as she pulled out a stack of papers. "Fill these out. You'll need to be fingerprinted for the background check. Are there any arrests on your record?"

"Not since turning eighteen."

"And before?"

"Those records are sealed, but all that's there are a minor consumption and a few speeding tickets."

"Any recent drug use?"

Travis sat straight. "Of course not. I'd lose my job."

"After Caleb, I can't be too careful. I wish we could require our foster parents to do drug testing."

"I'm nothing like Caleb Russell."

"I know, but I'm not sure I'll ever be able to do another interview without thinking of him." She shivered.

Travis nodded. Caleb had changed all of their lives, but maybe something good could come from it. Travis couldn't help Nattie, but he could still help Marcus. And if CPS said no, maybe he could help someone else, like Hank had.

Natalia pulled her new Ford Fiesta into the parking lot behind Dr. Drakeford's office building. The insurance company had totaled her last car, which was fine with her. Too many bad memories.

She'd slipped out of the house as soon as Mom went downstairs, and now she was fifteen minutes early. She pulled out her phone. A notification of Marcus's birthday popped onto the screen. Perfect. She missed him, and this gave her an excuse to call.

She dialed Dotti's number. Marcus's chocolate-covered face filled her phone's screen. "Hello, Marcus. Happy fourth birthday."

"Hi, Nattie!" He smiled at her.

Dotti smiled over his shoulder. "I figured you wanted to talk to the birthday boy. He's enjoying a doughnut. Let me clean you up." She wiped his face, then handed the phone to him. The ceiling appeared, then Marcus.

"Did you get the gift I sent?"

"It's right here," Dotti said in the background. She handed Marcus the box with red wrapping.

"I open it?" He ripped some paper off.

Natalia laughed. "Looks like it. Go ahead."

Once all the paper was off, he tore off the lid and pulled out a stuffed German Shepherd in a police officer's uniform. "I love him." He gave the dog a hug, then pulled out a book. "It's a fire truck!"

"You can learn all about first responders."

"Thanks, Nattie. I love you." He held the phone up to his face so only one brown eye was visible.

"I love you too. I have to head in for my appointment soon, but I'll talk to you later, okay?"

"'Kay, bye."

She sure missed him. And Travis. Did she have the nerve to call him? He might not want to talk to her. She glanced at the dash clock. Five minutes until nine. She'd better get to her appointment. No use wallowing in the despair of her own making.

Ten minutes later, Dr. Drakeford ushered Natalia to her office. She wore a black pinstriped skirt and suit jacket, making Natalia feel underdressed in her frayed jeans and pink tank top as she slid onto the plush chair.

Dr. Drakeford scooted her office chair close and sat. "How was last week?"

"Good. I was cleared to drive so I snuck out of the house while my mom was doing laundry."

"Have things improved with her?"

"A little. I've been journaling. I list the grievance, then why I'm thankful."

"Can you give me an example?"

"Sure. Yesterday, I got the insurance check for my car and wanted to go car shopping. Mom said it was a waste of money to buy a car when she could take me anywhere I wanted. Even though I was frustrated, I didn't fight with her. Instead, I wrote it in my journal that I'm thankful my mom taught me how to budget so I can afford a car and that she doesn't mind driving me places."

"Did you go car shopping?"

"I did. My sister-in-law took me and I bought one. Now I'm thankful to have a little more freedom back."

"Sounds like you have the hang of it. How do you feel about it?"

"At first, I hated it because being thankful for my mom took away my annoyance of her, and sometimes it's easier to be annoyed, but once I did it a few times, it got better."

Dr. Drakeford laughed. "That's true. But is it helping with your relationship with her?"

"I think so. I still feel annoyed right away, but after I write down why I'm thankful, I truly feel grateful for her."

"That's great. Keep up the practice, and hopefully your outlook will continue to change. How about nighttime? How are you sleeping?"

Natalia's mouth dried as she thought about the previous night. "Last night was rough. I woke up from a nightmare around two. I went to one of the online support groups you suggested and shared it. The other dispatchers were really encouraging."

"How did they encourage you?"

"They told me about their experiences. A couple said they'd pray for me or that they understood what I was going through. One shared the Dispatcher's Poem with me. It was beautiful, and I'd never heard it before."

"I'm glad they helped. Did you try to recreate the ending of the dream?"

"Yes, then I slept peacefully the rest of the night."

"That's exciting progress. How is your physical therapy coming?"

"The therapist says I'm healing fine. The muscles still hurt from time to time, but I should be back to running in a few weeks."

"Exercise is crucial for mental as well as physical health. What other things are you working on?"

"I need to find a job so I can move out." She sank against the soft fabric. It still grated on her independent spirit to live with her parents at her age.

"What kind of job do you want?"

"I love people, and I want something rewarding. I enjoyed waiting tables in Alkaline. Maybe something like that."

"Have you given up on dispatching?" Dr. Drakeford lifted an eyebrow.

Natalia sighed. "I loved it, but I'm scared to go back."

"It's okay if you want to give up dispatching and find a less stressful job, but if you want to work through these feelings and try to dispatch again, I can help you set up a support system and stress management plan so you can go back with self-care as a priority."

Serving up Rosemary's caramel rolls definitely made people happy, but it couldn't compare to helping save a person's life. Could she really do it again? Excitement bubbled in Natalia's stomach at the possibility. "I'm willing to put in the hard work to get better, but I'm not sure if I can commit to going back yet."

"There's no need to commit to anything right now. Until you decide what to do, let's keep talking through your experiences. It should help you recognize your feelings and might alleviate the nightmares. There's one more thing I'd like to talk about." The doctor leaned forward. "How did you end up in Alkaline?"

Natalia swallowed. She hadn't prepared herself to talk about that. Dr. Drakeford had helped in every other way, though. Maybe it wouldn't hurt. "My supervisor asked me to give Officer Mason's last call, I was supposed to go to the memorial afterward, but I ran away instead."

"Why?"

"I don't know. I sat outside the auditorium for a while trying to make myself go in, but my stomach was in knots. I lost the nerve and ran to my car. The further away I drove, the looser the knots got, so I kept driving. Every time I thought about turning around, the knots tightened."

"Why did you stop?"

"I wasn't planning to, but I got pulled over for speeding, then I got a flat tire and ended up staying the night with a sweet older lady. That night I had a nightmare and my first panic attack. I started hyperventilating, but she helped me through it." Rosemary had been a light in the darkness, and Travis turned out to be the steel that kept Natalia grounded. "I want to go back there so badly."

"Why?"

"Because I felt safe there. Is that weird that I felt safe with a complete stranger?"

"What about this lady made you feel safe?"

"She comforted me and gave me sympathy instead of lecturing me. She said I could stay with her as long I needed, but didn't guilt me into doing things her way. I felt taken care of without feeling like a child."

Dr. Drakeford's eyebrows scrunched together like she was confused. Had she said something wrong? "Natalia, did you call your family at any point after the incident with Officer Mason to tell them how it affected you?"

She shook her head.

"During our last session, you told me you knew your mom loved you. Why wouldn't you tell her about it?"

Natalia choked out a laugh. "She would've told me she was right all along, and that I wasn't cut out to be a dispatcher." Her nose and eyes stung. What if her mom was right?

"Do you share *any* of your feelings with her?"

Tears flowed down her cheeks. A box of tissues appeared on her lap. She took three and wiped the moisture from her face. "No. I'm afraid she'll get mad at me."

"I know it's not easy talking about this, but instead of running away to find a safe place, we need to create a support system for you to lean on. I think it's time you had a heart-to-heart talk with you mom. She needs to know that her criticism hurts you and maybe she'll learn to be supportive. Do you think you can do that?"

"I'm not as sure as you are that she can be supportive, but I can try."

By the time she walked out of Dr. Drakeford's office, Natalia was emotionally drained. She said she'd talk with her mom, but now she wasn't so sure. If the conversation backfired, it could lead to the biggest lecture of all time. But if she didn't have it, she'd never learn to stay, and she was tired of running.

The golden morning light filtered through the cracks in the barn, highlighting the dust in the air. Travis set the saddle on Dakota Peace and cinched it around his belly. The weatherman had forecasted a great day. Travis could barely contain his excitement.

Cole sauntered up to them and patted the horse's rump. "He seems to have made a full recovery."

"Thank God. I was worried for a bit." Travis lifted the bridle around Dakota's mouth and looped it over his ears.

"Going for a ride?"

"Got an important guest coming." He led the horse out of the barn while Cole walked on the other side.

"Have you heard from Natalia?"

Tension tightened his muscles. "Nope."

"Have you called her?"

"She's the one who left. I'm trying to respect that and give her space."

"Too much space might not be a good thing."

"Leave it be." He clenched his jaw. He missed her so much that he'd had to talk himself out of driving to see her three times. He even opened a Facebook account to check on her. He was pathetic.

As they neared the gate, a white van pulled up to the barn. "Stay with Dakota." Travis handed Cole the reins and jogged to the van's side door. His hands tingled with anticipation as he slid it open.

"Travis!" Marcus reached for him.

"Hey there, cowboy. Heard it was someone's birthday today."

"My birthday! I'm four."

Travis unbuckled the car seat and picked up Marcus. After two weeks apart, it felt good to hold him again. "You've grown so much since I saw you last time. You're going to be taller than me soon."

Marcus giggled. "I'm strong." He flexed his arm muscles. Then he took Travis's hat from his head and put it on.

"Now you're a real cowboy. Are you ready to ride?"

"Yes!"

Dotti walked around the front of the van. "He's been talking about it all morning."

"Would you like to ride too? I can saddle up another horse."

She laughed and pulled on her long, flowery dress. "I'm certainly not dressed to ride, and these old bones would rather sit in a café with a warm cup of tea and a novel."

"There's the Prickly Pear Bistro in town. The proprietor is Rosemary. Tell her you're Marcus's foster mom, and she'll treat you like royalty. After our ride, we can meet you there for lunch. Rosemary would love to see Marcus again."

"That sounds perfect. I'll leave the car seat here for you."

"If you hold Marcus, I'll get it out."

"I can get it. He's raring to go." Dotti stepped closer to them and kissed Marcus's cheek. "Have fun."

"Bye, Grandma Dotti." He pointed to Dakota. "I go ride now."

"We're going." He carried Marcus over to Cole, who stood beside Dakota rubbing his nose. "Do you remember this beast?"

"Horsey!"

"No, that's Cole."

Cole groaned. "Watch it. Hey, Marcus. Happy birthday."

Marcus leaned toward Cole and hugged his neck, then reached for the horse's bridle.

Travis stepped back. "Gentle. Like this." He stroked Dakota's mane, and Marcus did the same. "His name is Dakota Peace. Why don't you go to Cole while I mount him, then he'll lift you up, okay?" He exchanged Marcus for the reins, which he looped over the horse's head. After he mounted, Cole tucked Marcus in the small space between the saddle horn and Travis. "All right, cowboy. Let's ride."

He squeezed Dakota's flanks, and the horse took off. Marcus's giggles warmed Travis's heart.

They walked along the dirt road that led to the eastern pasture. Cole caught up to them on his palomino and opened the gate. Travis urged Dakota into a trot, causing Marcus to laugh, which brought him a joy that he hadn't realized had been missing from his life.

He took Marcus to see the foals—the boy pointed and giggled when they chased each other—then they galloped around a few babies suckling their mommas. As they rode through the pastures, Marcus squealed and laughed at every little thing, from hopping grasshoppers to prairie dogs popping their heads from their holes to chirping swallows. Russian sage and ground clover sweetened the air as Marcus settled against Travis. Having seen everything he'd planned to see, he looped around and headed back to the barn.

Two hours later, Travis drove Cole and Marcus into town. Marcus still wore Travis's cowboy hat. If he liked his present, then maybe Travis could get his hat back.

When they entered the bistro, Rosemary was sitting in a booth across from Dotti. Her hands moved as much as her mouth, which didn't slow down as they approached. "And then he shot her in the chest. Point-blank. It's a miracle she's alive to—" Travis stopped next to the table, and her gaze met his. "Hi, boys."

He set Marcus beside Dotti, then scooted in by Rosemary as Cole grabbed a chair.

"If it isn't the birthday boy. How are you doing, love?" She reached across the table and squeezed his little hand.

"Hi, Rosie. I'm four."

"What a big boy! If Travis will let me out, I'll go get you all some menus."

"Not a chance. We're having a birthday party and you're invited. My treat." Travis waved the server over to their table.

Rosemary looked around the dining room. "I've been over here chatting for almost an hour. I should get back to work."

Cole set his chair at the end of the booth and put a gift bag on the tabletop. "There's no one else in here."

"Please stay, Rosemary." Travis winked at her, hoping she'd join them. "It wouldn't be a party without you."

"Okay, but dessert is on the house."

"Deal." Travis leaned back and draped his arm along the back of the booth.

The server took their orders and hurried back to the kitchen.

Marcus bounced on the seat. "I ride Kota so fast, up a hill and down. There were baby horsies running around the mommies. And tiny birds sitting on the fence. And a great big bird in the sky. And we saw turkeys. And cows. And grasshoppers. And a pond, but we couldn't go swimming. We have to go another day, right Travis?"

He chuckled. "That's right. What did we see popping out of the ground?"

"Doggies!"

"Prairie dogs. You want to open your gift from Cole and me?" Travis scooted the large, green gift bag toward the toddler.

Marcus scrambled to his knees and pulled out the tissue paper, tossing it to the floor. When it was out of his way, he pulled out a miniature black cowboy hat with a turquoise, silver, and yellow beaded hat band.

"That's beautiful." Rosemary ran her hand over the beads. "Did you have someone make it?"

"Yep. A Lakota lady who lives near Bear Butte. I wanted Marcus to have one just like mine." Travis reached across the table and took his hat off of Marcus's head, then put it on his own. With a huge grin, Marcus put on his hat.

"I need a picture." Dotti took out her phone.

Cole scooted away from the table as Travis slid out of the booth. When he picked up Marcus, the boy squeezed his neck in a tight hug.

"Look here, you two cowboys." Dotti lifted her phone.

Travis smiled as she took the picture. Could life get any sweeter than a moment with his matching cowboy? "Will you text that to me?"

"Of course."

Travis put Marcus back by Dotti and slid in next to Rosemary as the waitress brought their food. Once the meal was finished, she brought over a chocolate silk pie with four candles. Cole lit them, and Marcus beamed as they sang happy birthday. He blew them all out, and they cheered. Laughter flowed around them.

Despite the joy, something was missing.

Travis's chest tightened.

Rosemary patted his leg. "I miss her too," she whispered.

CHAPTER 36

Natalia arrived home after her physical therapy session exhausted and hungry for lunch. When she walked into the kitchen, her mom was sitting at the table. "Hi, Mom."

"Where have you been?" She tapped her fingers on the wood.

"PT. The therapist says my mobility has improved. He gave me a few more stretches to do at home."

"I told you I wanted to go to your appointments with you. How am I supposed to make sure you're doing the exercises right if I don't come?"

Frustration filled Natalia. *I'm thankful for my mom. I'm thankful she cares about my recovery.* The tension diffused. As long as her mom was there, she might as well get the conversation over with. "I met with Dr. Drakeford yesterday." Natalia plopped her purse onto the counter, pulled out a chair, and sat across from her mom. "We need to talk."

Her mother's eyebrows rose. "I would think so. Why won't you let me help you? I could have driven you."

"I was cleared to drive, you know that. I don't need my mom coming to my appointments with me."

"You don't need me, period." She folded her arms and sat back in the chair.

Natalia took a deep breath. "I need you to back off the criticism and support me. No matter what I decide to do."

"It that what your shrink has been telling you? That I'm the problem?"

"I need a support system, people I can trust, but every time I come to you, you get defensive. I want you to be part of my system, but if you can't support me, I'll have to find other people."

"I don't get it, Nattie. Your father and I have given you a great life. We want what's best for you. I'm only trying to be helpful."

"I know you have my best interests at heart, but I'm an adult. I want to make my own choices and suffer the consequences of my mistakes without you making me feel worse about my failures."

Her mouth popped open, but Natalia held up a hand.

"I don't expect you to change, but I wanted to warn you that I'm putting up boundaries. I've thought about it, and I'm going back to dispatching." A wave of peace flowed through her. Finally saying the words out loud encouraged her.

"You said you couldn't handle it anymore."

"I can't, not by myself, but I'm going to work with Dr. Drakeford to learn how to handle the stress better."

"And I'm supposed to be okay with my child setting herself up to be hurt again?"

What? Natalia blinked as her mother's words sank in. "Is that why you fought me on this? All of this time, you've been worried about me?"

"Of course." Mom's hands fell to the table and her shoulders slumped. "You've chosen such a hard path. Not a day goes by that I don't worry over you. Or your brother."

Her brother? "Why would you worry about Mitch? He's done everything you've ever wanted."

"I worried that he'd burn out from his studies and that he'd never find a girl who would put up with his OCD. Then, when they had problems having a baby, I worried they'd end up resenting each other and their marriage would suffer. When they became foster parents, I worried more than ever that their hearts would break when the kids left. Now, I'm worried sick he'll be injured in Peru."

"Why do you worry so much? We're capable people."

Her mom twisted the wedding ring around her finger. "When I was fourteen, my sister died from cancer."

Natalia had an aunt? "Why didn't you ever tell me?"

"I wanted to protect you. I watched her wither away, and there was nothing I could do. I didn't want to be that helpless ever again. If I can keep the people I love from making choices that will lead to heartbreak, how can I not try?"

"Oh, Mom." Natalia stood and pulled her mom into a hug. Her mom sniffled, so she squeezed harder. "I had no idea how scared you've been."

"I tried to hide it. I didn't want to pass my fears on to you."

She sat back down across from her mom. "I always thought you didn't trust me."

"Of course I trust you, but it's my job to make sure you're safe."

"Even when I'm twenty-five years old?"

"Always. But I am sorry that I made you feel like I don't support you. I'll try to do better."

"Thanks, and I'll try to be more honest with you."

"What haven't you been honest about?"

She brushed the bangs out of her eyes. "My hair. I got this silly haircut because you wanted me to, but I hate it."

"Really? I think it makes your face look rounder."

"But I don't want bangs."

"Then why did you get them?"

"Because *you* wanted me to."

"What, I'm not supposed to have an opinion?"

Natalia growled. "You've nagged me about so many things that I don't even argue with you anymore. It's not worth the fight. I need you to try to keep your opinions to yourself, at least on the little things. Can you do that?"

"I'll try … on the little things. I'm still going to give my opinion, but I won't push so hard."

Natalia relaxed. "That's all I'm asking. I want to be able to come to you with my problems, but I won't if I feel like you're going to judge me."

"I'd like that." Her mom pressed her lips together. "Why do

you like it so much? Dispatching? Why not let stronger people do that job?"

"Why don't you think I'm strong enough to do it?"

"Because your dad and I tried to shelter you and Mitch. We didn't let you watch adult shows or play violent video games. Your brother pitched a fit every time we told him no. I'm pretty sure he played the games at his friends' houses though. He was a sneaky one, unlike you, my obedient child."

Natalia didn't remember them ever telling Mitch no. Had she put filters on concerning her brother? "I was pretty sheltered when I started, but I'm not anymore. Thanks to Dr. Drakeford, I'm confident I'll be able to go back to dispatching, but this time I'll take care of myself too."

"I hope so. I've only ever wanted you to be happy." Her mother squeezed her hand. "I know I come off a little overbearing; at least that's what your dad says, but it's only because I can't stand to see you hurt. It doesn't matter how old you get, you'll always be my baby girl."

"I appreciate that, but I think I'm ready to grow up now."

CHAPTER 37

Almost two months after Nattie returned to Sioux Falls, she sprawled on her bed and stared at the Jonas Brothers poster she'd hung on her wall in high school.

A soft knock sounded on the door before her mom opened it. "Hi, Nattie." She carried in a load of clothes, clean and folded, and put them on her bed.

Nattie had been cleared to go downstairs for weeks now, so she really should take over her own laundry, but she hated that chore, so she didn't argue when her mom kept doing it. "Thanks for doing my laundry."

"Sure. You're back from counseling early. How's it going?"

"Good. We're still working on my nightmares."

Mom frowned and Natalia's stomach tightened. She braced herself for criticism.

"I didn't know you were having nightmares. Are the sessions helping?"

"I think so. I haven't had a terrifying dream since we started. The doctor says I need to keep rehearsing new endings to them."

"How's the job hunt going?"

"Not as good. I met with Hayden at Metro, but he won't hire me back. Said he couldn't take the chance I'd leave him short-staffed again. I tried to convince him that I won't burn out again because of the counseling, but he said he wouldn't risk it. I found a waitressing job downtown if I want it. It's not great, but I could at least move out."

"You're not ready to move out. You need to take your time." She perched her hands on her hips.

Natalia sat up as her insides churned. "Mom, you promised not to be so pushy. I'm going to move out eventually, but don't worry. I won't leave before I can afford it."

Her mom opened her mouth, then shut it. She huffed. "I'm trying. My therapist said I shouldn't ask you about it for a few more weeks, but you can see that I'm trying, right?"

Nattie's jaw dropped. "You're seeing a therapist?"

"You inspired me. I don't want my fears to keep pushing you away. I didn't know you couldn't trust me with your hurts or your nightmares. I never wanted that."

Her mom turned to leave, but before she could, Nattie hopped off the bed and pulled her into a hug. "Thanks, Mom." Her mom sniffed, then nodded as she stepped into the hallway.

Nattie dropped onto her bed and picked up her phone, flipping through the pictures she'd taken of Travis and Marcus at the pond and roasting marshmallows. Then the selfie of her and Travis when they'd watched the sunset in his truck bed.

She missed him, but she felt good about the progress she'd made with Dr. Drakeford. She wanted to call and tell him about it. Butterflies fluttered in her stomach. It really wouldn't be hard to call him to see how he was doing. Maybe apologize. She wanted to hear his voice.

Her phone chimed and the Facetime button appeared. Dotti. Natalia tapped the button and Marcus's face filled the screen. Joy bubbled in her. "Hi, Marcus. I've missed you. How are you?"

"Nattie! I lost a tooth." He smiled and revealed a gap in front.

"I see that. Did the tooth fairy bring you money?"

He nodded. "I got a dollar."

Dotti's face appeared. "The tooth came out because he fell out of bed and bonked his mouth on the dresser. He's going to have that gap for a while, but that's not why we called. Marcus has something he wants to ask you." She whispered into his ear.

"Will you come watch me walk?"

"Are you getting your new leg?"

He nodded again.

"Of course I'll come. When are you getting it?"

"Grandma Dotti, tell her." He disappeared and singing filled the air.

Dotti reappeared. "I guess he's done talking. November sixth."

Five days. "I'll be there. I'll go online and reserve a hotel room right now."

"Nonsense. You can stay with me. I have plenty of room."

"I might want to stay for a few days."

"Stay as long as you'd like."

Her kindness eased Natalia's nerves. Marcus had definitely been blessed with a great foster mom. "Thanks. Any updates on his case?"

"Yes. They found him a foster placement here in town. He'll be moving before the end of the month."

A mixture of emotions swirled in Natalia's chest. Marcus would finally have a stable, loving family, but that meant their relationship would probably fade away. Still, he deserved an amazing family, even if that meant she had to say goodbye. "What are they like?"

"I can't tell you more at this point, but I can assure you that he's going to a loving home."

"If you're okay with them, then I will be too. I'll see you next Monday. Tell Marcus I love him."

"I will. See you soon."

The screen went black, then the picture of Natalia and Travis popped up. She wondered if he would be there for Marcus's prosthetic fitting. She went to her contacts. His name topped her favorites list. She stared at it, wanting so badly talk to him. Losing courage, she tapped the text icon.

Marcus is getting his prosthetic leg on Nov. 6th. You coming?

Jitters fluttered in her stomach.

Working that day.

Disappointment rippled through her. Maybe it was just as well. Seeing him again would be awkward.

Dropping her phone on the bed, she looked at the Jonas Brothers poster again. She'd had such crushes on them in high school.

But she wasn't a teenager with a crush anymore. She was a woman who had fallen in love and tossed it away. She ripped the poster off the wall and crumpled it up. It was time to grow up. No more wallowing in self-pity. She had to at least try to fix her relationship with Travis. To do that, she needed to be closer. If she wanted to be closer, she needed a job. In Rapid City.

****

At five in the morning on November sixth, Natalia threw her suitcase into the trunk of her car. Light from the front porch bounced off snowflakes as they floated to the ground. The dark morning and cold weather didn't chill her excitement though. She would see Marcus soon!

Her mom stood on the porch in a long black coat with her hands on her hips. "I don't think this is a good idea. There's a storm expected today." Her breath puffed in front of her as she spoke.

"Not until tonight." Natalia walked over to her. "I want to see Marcus walk on his prosthetic. I know you're worried, but I'll be fine. I'll call when I get there." She gave her mom a hug before hurrying to her car.

As she drove across the state, houses, fenced lawns, and swing sets gave way to rolling hills covered in patches of white and brown. About fifty miles from Rapid City, snow blew across the road and covered the interstate lines. The wind picked up. At the top of a snow-covered hill, the Black Hills stretched across the horizon.

Despite the weather, peace filled Natalia. She felt like she was going home instead of leaving it. As she drove closer to the city, she followed the blue hospital signs off the interstate and through town.

Thirty minutes later, she pulled up to the ten-story, octagon building surrounded by parking lots. The rehab parking lot was full, so she drove around to the front of the hospital. Snow flurries blew around her as she ran into the building. After entering through the revolving door, she walked across the granite floor to the receptionist and smiled. "Which way is the rehab center?"

"After the gift shop, take a right, then a left. You'll need to follow the signs until you reach the elevators."

Natalia wove her way through doctors' offices and labs until she found the right wing. On the elevator, excitement fluttered in her stomach. She pulled out her phone and sent Dotti a text.

I'm here. Where do I go?

Then one to her mom.

Made it.

The elevator doors opened, and Dotti stood on the landing smiling. "It's good to see you. We're through here."

Natalia gave her a hug, then followed her into a room with exercise equipment, two sets of parallel bars, and large blow-up balls scattered throughout. Floor-to-ceiling windows lined the wall. Marcus sat on a chair with bars on either side of him, his back to her. A man in khakis and a blue polo shirt sat on a rolling stool in front of him holding the prosthetic leg. Two ladies stood behind him.

Natalia hurried along the padded floor. She didn't want to miss a second of Marcus's adventure.

When he noticed her, Marcus smiled, flashing his toothless gap. "Nattie! See my new leg? I got Spiderman shoes."

She knelt beside him and hugged him. "Hi, Marcus. I love your new leg and shoes. I'm so excited to see you walk."

His hair was cut short along the back and long on top, like Travis's hair. Her heart ached. She wished he'd come.

The man patted Marcus's back. "I'm Dr. Bradly and this is Amanda, his occupational therapist, and Mae, his physical therapist."

"I'm Nattie. I was his foster mom for a few weeks back in

August."

The doctor handed Marcus the leg. His stump was puckered on the end, but it looked healed. "I think we're ready. I'm going to have your Grandma Dotti sit beside you so she can see how to put on your new leg."

Natalia stepped back, letting Dotti sit next to Marcus.

The doctor rolled an orthopedic sock over the stump. "Now, you need to keep your knee steady as I push your leg on. Okay?"

"'Kay."

Amanda knelt next to Marcus and held his knee. The doctor pushed the leg on, rolling the stretchy, cream-colored material to Marcus's mid-thigh. "How does that feel? Any pain or pinching?"

He giggled and shook his head.

"Good."

Mae switched places with the doctor. "Okay. Hold on to the bars on both sides and slowly stand up."

Marcus gripped the bars and pushed himself up. A grin filled his face.

Natalia clapped as she tried to contain her excitement. "Good job!"

"Take a couple of steps in place," the doctor said, stepping a few times without moving. "Like this."

Marcus lifted his whole leg, then slowly lifted the prosthetic and put it back down.

"Good job." The therapist wheeled the stool back. "Now, take a step, then stop." Marcus took slow steps, the tip of his tongue sticking out the side of his mouth. He stepped forward, and the therapist rolled back. The next step was a bit quicker, then quicker again until they reached the end of the bars. "Now, turn around, and walk back to Grandma Dotti."

He swung his prosthetic leg around in one smooth motion but stumbled with the first step. His movements were slow and choppy, but when he reached Dotti, she kissed his cheek. He turned around and walked back to the therapist, then back to Dotti until his strides looked natural.

Natalia's cheeks ached from her uncontrollable smile.

Dotti motioned her over and they switched places. Her chest expanded with pride as Marcus walked to her, his face scrunched. He reached the end of the bars and launched himself into her arms.

"You're walking!" She picked him up and swung him around. Travis stood behind her, smiling. Her heart pounded. "You're here."

"Travis!" Marcus wiggled.

Dressed in his taupe uniform, Travis approached them with a half-smile. "Hi, Nattie. Good walking, cowboy." He held out his fist. Marcus bumped it. "Sorry I'm late."

The physical therapist handed Marcus some crutches. He took them and walked away with her, but Nattie couldn't tear her eyes from Travis. She hugged herself, trying to calm her nerves. She'd imagined seeing him again but she wasn't prepared. "You said you couldn't come."

"No, I said I had to work." He shrugged. "I wanted to surprise you. You look good. How are you feeling?"

She'd missed his low, smooth voice. "My doctor and therapist have lifted all my restrictions. Seems I'm as good as new."

Travis nodded then stepped beside her, but he kept his eyes on Marcus. The boy walked with crutches for a while, then moved on to a cane. When he could move without teetering, the doctor crouched down in front of him. "I think you're ready to walk by yourself. I'll walk beside you. If you feel like you might fall, grab onto me, okay?"

"'Kay." His first few steps were slow, but it only took a few laps before he walked from one end of the room to the other without assistance. Natalia couldn't believe how easy he made it look. She couldn't wait to see him chasing after the dogs again.

While Dotti talked with the doctor and therapists, Travis walked with Marcus to the windows. Marcus waved her over. "Nattie, come look. A 'copter!"

She joined them and watched Life Flight land on the helipad

below them.

He clapped. "I rode in a 'copter."

"I did too, but I don't remember my ride."

"Worst day of my life," Travis whispered.

She took a deep, pain-free breath. "Mine too."

Outside, the flight nurses unloaded a patient. Natalia shuddered.

"I think we're ready to walk out of here, Marcus," Dotti said. "You're going to have to hold my hand, though, so that I don't fall." When they turned around, she winked at them.

Marcus took the three steps to Dotti, then grabbed her hand.

"How about I treat you all to lunch?" Travis asked as he followed them across the room.

"Thanks for the offer, but we're going to have to pass." She patted Marcus's hand. "He's had a busy morning, so we'll hit a drive-thru, then take a nap. Why don't you join us for dinner?"

"I'll not turn down that invitation. What time?"

"Does six work for you, Nattie?"

"Sure." Her pulse quickened.

"Perfect. Marcus, give Nattie and Travis a hug."

Natalia bent low and squeezed his little body. "I'm so proud of you."

"Way to go, cowboy." Travis patted him on the back. "We're going to have to see how your legs look with boots."

"Yes!"

Dotti laughed as she led Marcus out the door.

Travis turned to Natalia. "How about you? Will you have lunch with me?"

She smiled as her stomach fluttered. "I'd love to."

"I need to ask the doctor something, then we can head out."

Natalia rocked on her heels while she waited, trying to not eavesdrop on their conversation. When they were done, Travis nodded toward the door. She kept pace with his long strides to the elevator. "I'm parked out front. Should I meet you someplace?"

He nodded. "The Colonial House is on Mount Rushmore

Road, only a few blocks away."

A few minutes later, Natalia parked in front of the brown-and-red stucco restaurant that had a metal frying pan with flames above the door. She stepped into the frigid wind. Travis opened the front door as soon as she reached it. Inside, she finger-combed her hair to hide the tremor in her hand.

Travis motioned for her to walk ahead of him. "I hope I don't get called out before we have a chance to eat."

The hostess led them to a table and handed them menus. Natalia sat across from Travis. Televisions on every wall showed football highlights without sound. "It feels weird to eat with you any place other than Rosemary's," she said.

"The Prickly Pear is all closed up for winter. Not much activity in Alkaline these days."

"I figured. Rosemary called from the pool last week. How's Cole?"

"Busy. He's getting ready to take a load of cattle to the feedlot. I'll help him haul them in a few weeks."

The waitress brought water. "What can I get you?" She looked at Natalia.

"Coffee with cream and sugar and a cheeseburger platter with fries."

"Coffee, black, and I'll take the roast beef special."

The waitress jotted down their orders, then left.

"I bet they don't have Rosemary's fancy coffee," Natalia said, smiling.

"Probably not." Travis stared at her, his face unreadable. "So … what have you been up to?"

Natalia unrolled her napkin and put it on her lap as she tried to figure out what to say. "Not much. I've been staying with my parents, so I haven't had to work. They've been taking care of me."

"How's your wound?"

She rubbed the scar on her chest. "Better. I've graduated from physical therapy, and all restrictions have been lifted."

"Are you still having nightmares?"

"Sometimes, but I'm learning how to handle them." Heat crawled up her neck as she thought of the endings where Travis was the hero, which were most of them.

"What's next for you?"

Excited energy raced through her fingers. "I have a job interview this afternoon."

"Really? Where?"

"The dispatch center in Rapid City."

Travis's eyebrows rose. "You're going back to dispatching?"

"I'm going to try. I have my therapist on speed dial, and I've joined an online support group. If I can't handle it, I'll look at other options, but I miss it. What about you? Have you moved yet?"

"Yep. I'm officially a resident of Rapid City. I'm renting a two-bedroom house on the south side. I left most of my stuff at the ranch and head there whenever I can."

"How do you like working here?"

He shrugged. "It's a lot like working in a fish tank with so many supervisors watching my every move. I'll get used to it. I hope." He reached into his coat and pulled out a white envelope "I'm glad you agreed to have lunch with me. I have a surprise." He handed it to her. "I wanted to tell you, but I didn't know if I should call."

She opened the envelope, and, with shaking fingers, pulled out a fancy piece of paper with a purple border. *South Dakota Department of Social Service: Certificate of License as a Child Welfare Agency. This is to certify that Travis Wilkins is hereby granted this license to conduct and maintain a Family Foster Home.* Her gaze shot up to his. "You've become a foster parent?"

He smiled. "My last class and home study were Saturday."

Pride and love for him filled her. "That's awesome."

"There's more. Marcus is moving in with me. I'm hoping to adopt him."

Natalia dropped the paper. Her eyes stung as she blinked back tears. How could she have walked away from this man? "I can't believe it. I'm so happy for you both."

He laughed. "I'm terrified. I never imagined doing anything like this."

"You're going to be the most amazing dad."

"It was a purely selfish move. The kid grew on me. I didn't want to lose him."

"When is he moving in?"

"A week from Saturday. If everything goes according to plan, his adoption will be official in six months."

She wanted to ask more—when had he decided to adopt Marcus, were they going to stay in Rapid City, was he seeing anyone—but their food arrived and the conversation lulled. As they ate, Natalia lost her nerve. When the waitress arrived to clear the table, Natalia pulled out her credit card.

"Put that away. My treat, remember?" Travis threw his card on the check.

"Thank you." In a few minutes, they'd go their own ways, but Natalia still had so much to say. When the waitress walked away, she summoned her courage. "I've missed you."

Travis stared at her, his face blank.

Her stomach sank. She stood and zipped her coat. "I'd better take off. My interview is in thirty minutes. I'll see you tonight."

Outside, the wind stung her face and the cold stole her breath as she ran to her car. All the way to the dispatch center she thought about Travis. She should have been mentally preparing for the interview, but what did Travis's response, or lack of, mean? She should have asked him but she ran, just like the old Natalia. She wouldn't make that mistake again. After dinner, she'd corner him and ask him if he had any feelings left for her, even if the answer might not be what she wanted to hear.

CHAPTER 38

Travis leaned back and rubbed his stomach. "That was some mighty fine fried chicken."

"Thank you. It's my grandmother's recipe."

He looked around the room as everyone else finished eating. Oak hardwood floors ran from the dining room into the living room. A painting of a white farmhouse, some weathered barns, and green fields hung on the far wall. A clear plastic tablecloth covered Dotti's polished cherry table. Beside him, Marcus dropped another forkful of food onto the table, and Travis considered asking her where she got the tablecloth.

Dotti stood and gathered the plates. "Now, who wants chocolate pudding?"

"Me!" Marcus raised his fork into the air. "Travis likes pie."

"I like anything with sugar."

"I can help with the dishes." Natalia took the stack from Dotti and went into the kitchen.

Travis watched her walk away. She'd laughed and talked through dinner like she had before Caleb. Her confession at lunch had stunned him, and if she'd stuck around longer, he'd have admitted to missing her too. He might still.

Marcus kicked the table and Travis smiled. "How do you like your new leg?"

He frowned. "I can't swim with it. Grandma Dotti said."

"That's true, but the therapist said you're doing a great job swimming without it."

"Marcus is learning to swim?" Nattie put a large bowl of pudding in front of Travis and a smaller one in front of Marcus.

"For a couple of weeks now. He's like a fish."

"I love swimming." He shoved a spoonful of pudding into his mouth.

Dotti joined them and handed Nattie a bowl before sitting. "It's his favorite therapy session."

"I'm so proud of you, Marcus." Nattie's smile lit up her face.

Travis dug into the pudding to keep from gawking at her.

She laughed. "I think we wore him out."

Travis looked at Marcus. The spoon dangled from his fingers. His eyes drifted closed, and he swayed to the side.

"Whoa, cowboy. You're going to fall over." Travis steadied him with a hand on his shoulder.

Marcus's eyes popped open. He took another bite before they drifted closed again.

"I think it's time for bed." Dotti took the bowl from Marcus. He opened his eyes but didn't protest.

"I'll get a washcloth to clean him up." Nattie hurried to the kitchen. When she reappeared a minute later, she scooted next to Marcus and wiped his face.

Travis breathed in her apple-scented hair. It had smelled like that after the auction, when they sat outside talking. Well, mostly talking, except for the few kisses they'd shared. He cleared his throat, uncomfortable with the turn of his thoughts. "I'll carry him to bed." He stood and lifted Marcus to his shoulder, then trotted down the hallway. Marcus giggled when he dropped him onto the bed.

"You're getting him riled up before bed." Nattie walked in and stood beside him. "But I guess it's none of my business anymore."

Travis squeezed her elbow. "You're right. I shouldn't horse around with him when he needs sleep. I have a lot to learn."

"I'm no expert either. Would you mind if I read him a story? I've missed cuddling with him."

"Not at all. I'll help you get him changed." He sat on the bed and lifted Marcus up by his arms while Nattie took off his shirt.

In a few minutes, they had him changed. Travis carried him to the bathroom, brushed his teeth, and helped him potty. Marcus was barely awake when he brought him back to bed.

Nattie pulled the blanket over him and kissed his cheek, her blonde hair and pale skin contrasting with Marcus's darker shades. "We can read a story tomorrow. Good night, Marcus. I love you."

Travis bent down and kissed Marcus's head. "Good night, cowboy," he whispered. "Sleep tight."

"Don't let the snakes bite," Marcus mumbled.

Travis chuckled as he led a wide-eyed Nattie into the hallway. "What did he just say?"

"One night he told me he wasn't scared of bugs, so I asked what he was scared of and he said snakes. I thought I'd try to make light of it. Do you think that's a mistake?"

She shrugged. "He seems to be okay with it. How's he doing with the whole thing overall?"

"He meets with a child psychologist once a week for play therapy. I'm thinking of meeting with her too. I'm at a loss for how to comfort him some days."

"A handsome state trooper once told me that seeking help is a good first step."

Handsome? Before he could say anything about it, she walked back to the dining room.

Dotti finished wiping off the table, then looked up. "I'm headed off to bed," she said. "Lock the front door after Travis leaves. And make yourself at home." She winked at him.

Heat spiked up his neck. "Good night. Thanks for supper."

"Anytime." She hugged them both before heading down the hall.

Travis checked his watch. It was only seven thirty. He wasn't comfortable hanging around someone else's house while they slept, but wasn't ready to leave Nattie either.

Nattie swiped the hair from her eyes.

"When did you cut your hair?"

She sighed. "That first week home. My mother insisted I'd look better with bangs, but they're annoying. I'm growing them out."

"They cover too much of your face."

She smiled. "Would you like to stay for a while?"

"Sure."

"Do you want something to drink?"

"I'm good." He followed her into the living room and sat on the leather sectional. Framed, scenic paintings hung next to pictures of Dotti's kids and grandkids on all the walls except the front one with a bow window. The lights were low and a fire flickered in the gas fireplace.

"Dotti's nice to let me stay here, but I feel weird playing hostess in a house where I'm a guest." Nattie sat next to him instead of the other side of the couch.

Pleased to have her near, he nodded. "She's a special lady. A couple of her grandkids live nearby, and they come over to play with Marcus on the weekends. That's one thing he's going to miss when he moves in with me. There aren't any kids in my neighborhood."

"He's old enough for preschool, isn't he?"

Travis shrugged. "I have no idea. That's another thing I'll have to look into."

She squeezed his arm. "I'm proud of you."

Tingles ran across his skin. "How did your interview go?"

"Good, I think. She said she'd let me know in a week if I got the job. The start date is November twentieth. That doesn't leave a lot of time to find a place to live, so I thought I'd start looking tomorrow, just in case. Dotti said I can crash with her for a while, but I don't want to impose."

He knew he should respond—he'd thought about seeing her and planned out what he wanted to say—but with the glow of the flickering flame casting shadows across the soft lines of her face, his mind went blank. She was so beautiful.

She dropped her hand to the couch, only a few inches from his. His fingers itched to touch her. Before he could move, she spoke.

"Travis, the last couple of months have been difficult, but, in a way, rewarding. I've been working on myself with my counselor, and even my mom is seeing a therapist. She said I inspired her to get help. And I got help because you encouraged me to. I can't thank you enough." She sucked in a breath. "I'm sorry for how I left. You didn't deserve it."

His chest tightened. *Please keep going.*

"Can you forgive me?"

"Done."

She leaned away from him, her expression confused. "It can't be that easy."

"Nattie, I know you were hurting. I'll admit I took it personally the first few days, but ..." He loved her too much to allow unforgiveness to sour his emotions. "Once my anger simmered, I realized that I couldn't fix this for you, no matter how much I wanted to. You had to do the work. And I'm so glad you did."

"Me too. I missed you and your wisdom from practically the minute I left."

"You could have called me."

"I was afraid to." Her eyes glistened. "I broke your trust."

"And I don't trust easily, but that's my fault, not yours." Nervous energy sparked through him. She'd set him up perfectly. "How about a redo on this relationship thing?"

"What if I hurt you again?"

He picked up her hand, stroking her soft fingers and palm. "You probably will. And I'll probably hurt you, but not on purpose. We can rebuild trust, but not if you run away again. You have to trust me too."

She laced her fingers through his and lifted his hand to her lips. "I want a redo more than anything."

He cupped her chin with his free hand and kissed her. Familiar, heated sensations roiled through him. He broke the kiss and scooted closer to her, wrapping his arms around her. "This is the best part of a redo," he said, and he kissed her again.

CHAPTER 39

The puffy headset against her ears, the comfort-engineered chair, even the cold coffee felt normal to Natalia. The room was dark but her console glowed. Six computer monitors faced her as she took 9-1-1 calls for the city. At midnight she was two hours into her first solo shift at the dispatch center in Rapid City. Even after a month of training, though, she literally sat on the edge of her seat.

A call came in. "9-1-1. What's your emergency?"

"Someone broke into my car!"

"Where was it parked?"

"In front of my house!"

Natalia rolled her eyes. "And what's the address?"

"Fifteen, fifteen Kellogg Place."

Natalia took the caller's information as he yelled at her, but even being yelled at didn't bother her. Not today. "Thank you, sir. We'll dispatch an officer to one five one five Kellogg Place. I don't know the exact time frame, but maybe in thirty to forty-five minutes."

"Fine."

"And thank *you*." Natalia ended the call and exhaled. As she took a drink of coffee, the nonemergency line rang. "Dispatch."

"Nattie? Is that you?"

Travis. She smiled. "It is."

"Can you call me when you get a break?" His low voice soothed the last of her first-day jitters.

"Sure. That'll be thirty minutes."

"Talk to you soon."

She clicked the disconnect button, but the emergency line rang before she could wonder what Travis wanted. She took three more calls then stretched her back.

"Natalia, time for your fifteen-minute break," her supervisor said as she hurried by.

She unplugged her headset from the console and slipped out of the center, excited to talk to Travis even if it was only for a few minutes. She grabbed her cell phone from her locker and called him.

"Wilkins."

"Hey, it's Nattie. How's it going?"

"Slow. How's your night?"

"We've been busy. I have to monitor the PD radios, but my pod is next to State Radio so I can hear a little of what you're doing."

"Keeping track of me, are you?"

"It's convenient, isn't it?" She laughed. "No, but it's comforting to know you're out there."

"Whatever helps. How are you doing?"

"So far, I've been able to stay pretty calm. I'm not sure I'll ever get back the confidence I had before Officer Mason, but I'm here."

"I'm proud of you. Maybe you'll be an even better dispatcher because you faced your fears."

Natalia's heart warmed. He always knew how to encourage her. "Thanks."

"When's your shift over?"

"Six."

"How about breakfast to celebrate your first night?"

"If you're buying, because I'm sure I'll be starving." Although she was too wired to even think about food at the moment.

Travis chuckled. "You got it. I'll meet you at the exit fifty-five truck stop."

"I can't wait."

"Enjoy the rest of your shift."

As she hung up, jitters bounced in her stomach, this time in anticipation of her date. It would be her first time alone with Travis since she moved to Rapid City a month ago.

As soon as she sat down after her break, a call came in. She didn't hesitate to answer. "9-1-1, what's your emergency?"

"I think someone's outside. My husband's gone, and I'm all alone," a woman whispered.

Natalia tensed at the fear in the caller's voice. "What's your address?"

"Thirty-eight Oak Street. Hurry. I'm really scared."

She typed in the address. "Help is on the way."

"ID 3829. Shots fired!" The radio next to her squawked.

The hair on Natalia's arms stood up. The dispatcher next to her typed, then Natalia heard a crash over her line. "What was that?"

"I think someone broke a window. Please tell them to hurry."

She typed the information into the database. "You're doing great. An officer is responding. Where are you in the house, ma'am?"

"My bedroom."

"Can you lock the door?"

"It's locked."

"Good. Do you know who could be at your house? Could it be your husband?"

"No. He's out of town until next weekend hunting."

Natalia covered her headset mic and glanced at the radio dispatcher behind her. "Could you get me the ETA of ID 677?" She glanced at the screen of the state radio dispatcher beside her as she waited for the police to respond.

"ID 677 at the door."

She refocused on her call. "Ma'am, the officer is at the door. Can you go let him in? I'll stay on the phone with you."

"Yes." Her voice shook. Metal jingled, then someone spoke. "It's the police." The line went dead.

"Officer down! Officer down! 2-2 send medical hot! East Watertown and Pine Street. Suspect fled on foot," an officer called over the radio.

"HP 352 on scene in foot pursuit." Travis's out-of-breath voice sent shivers down Natalia's spine.

"HP 352, your location?" The state radio dispatcher, Ava, asked.

"Northbound on Pine Street, just past Madison Street."

Natalia searched through her screen for Travis's number. Multiple units had arrived at the scene. Ava turned up her volume.

"HP 352. Suspect at gunpoint!"

"HP 352, your location?"

"Pine and Van Buren, new corner."

Natalia's pulse increased. What if he got shot? She'd never even told him she loved him. Why hadn't she told him?

Medical arrived at the scene of the injured officer.

The phone rang. Natalia answered. "9-1-1, what's your emergency?"

"Some jerk just rear-ended me."

"What's the location?"

"I'm at Fifth and Columbus."

Natalia typed in the information. "Is anyone hurt?"

"No. We're both fine."

"Are the occupants in the other vehicle hurt?"

"He's fine. He was texting. Dumb kid."

"What is your name?" Natalia's fingers shook as she took and typed his information while listening to State Radio for Travis's voice. She needed to hear his voice, but she needed to do her job. "An officer is en route."

"Thank you."

She disconnected the call. Her stomach tightened as she watched Ava's fingers fly across her keyboard.

"HP 352"—Travis!—"10-15. Code 4."

He had the suspect. He was safe. Tension flowed out of Natalia as relief poured in. Tears clouded her eyes.

Ava took off her headset and rubbed her eyes.

"Are you all right?" Natalia asked.

"I don't think my heart will ever beat normally again."

She knew the feeling. "Do you need a break?"

"I'm good for now." Ava put her headset back on and answered a call.

Natalia watched the call log until the ambulance with the hurt officer arrived at the hospital. Then Travis made it to the jail. She checked the clock. Only an hour before she could hug him and reassure herself that he was okay.

* * * * * * *

At the end of her shift, Natalia entered the bathroom and found Ava bent over the sink splashing water onto her face. Natalia handed her a paper towel. "That was some call. You did a great job."

Ava wiped her cheeks. "I hope the officer's okay. Have you heard how he's doing?"

"I haven't. We could stop by the hospital and see him if you'd like."

She shook her head. "We'd only be in the way."

"Every available unit from all three agencies is there. What're two more people?"

"We're just dispatchers."

"I used to think that too, but we're not 'just' anything. I'll drive you."

"Okay." As they walked toward the parking garage, Ava took a shaky breath.

Natalia understood. "I took a bad call a few months ago. I've been involved in an online support group for dispatchers since then. I really like it. It helps to process the tough calls with people who understand. I can send you the information if you want."

"I'd like that."

At the hospital, they entered the Emergency Department. "Can we see Officer Shaw?" Natalia asked the receptionist behind the glass.

"Are you family?"

"No."

"Family only."

"They're law enforcement. They can come back." Travis stepped up to the window.

The receptionist smiled. "Come on through."

The double doors buzzed, then slowly opened.

Travis walked toward them. "I'll show you his room. He's pretty ornery, so I'm sure he'll be okay. The bullet only grazed him."

Natalia relaxed, releasing tension she hadn't realized she was still carrying. "Thanks. Travis, this is Ava. She was dispatching the scene. Ava, this is Trooper Wilkins. He was on scene."

"Nice to meet you," he said.

Ava nodded but didn't respond. They turned a corner, and officers from the police department, highway patrol, and sheriff's office lined the hall. Travis stopped at a door and knocked.

"Come in." They entered the room. A man with cropped blond hair, broad shoulders, and a round face sat on the bed. "Wilkins."

"Shaw, this is Natalia and Ava. Ava was dispatching the last call for you."

"Are you okay?" Her voice shook.

Shaw nodded. "They tell me I'll live. Going to need a new uniform though. Punk kid tore a hole in this one. Thanks for your help today."

She smiled for the first time since the call. "I'm just glad you're okay."

Travis laced his fingers through Natalia's and led her into the hall, then to the waiting room. They sat in the corner away from everyone else. "Looks like I'm going to be late for our date," he said.

She grabbed his other hand. "That was crazy. How are you?"

"I'm good. The hothead who shot Shaw is going to prison for a long time though."

He wouldn't be able to threaten another trooper anytime soon, but there would always be someone else, and Travis would always respond. Before he did, Natalia had to tell him. "I realized something when you had the suspect cornered."

"What's that?"

Her heart swelled with an overabundance of emotions. She could try to deny it, but she couldn't—wouldn't—run from it. "I love you. I couldn't bear it if something happened to you and you didn't know."

His smile appeared, growing until his eyes creased. "About time you realized it. I seem to recall admitting my feelings months ago."

"I guess I'm not quite as perceptive as you."

Travis ran his finger across her jaw, then he kissed her. Heat spiked through her. She really, truly loved him.

"Wilkins. We don't pay you to make out with your girlfriend."

Natalia snapped back, her cheeks burning. A trooper with sergeant stripes stood in front of them.

Travis pushed his handheld radio. "HP 352. I'll be 10-7."

"HP 352. 10-7 at 0648 hours. Have a good day."

"Oh, I will." Travis winked at the sergeant, then kissed her again. Her lips melted against his as sparks tingled her skin.

When his kisses gentled, he rested his forehead against hers. "Nattie, I love you. I was going to do this at breakfast, but I can't wait. Our beginning was a bit rough, and I suspect there will be challenges in the future, but I want you beside me through it all." He reached into his shirt pocket.

Her heart leapt.

A rose-gold ring. Swirls of little diamonds surrounded a larger one. "Will you marry me?"

Jitters danced in Natalia's stomach as she scanned the courtroom. The judge's bench towered in front of her. She sat at a large oval table next to Marcus, Travis, and their lawyer. Behind them, Margo, her parents, her brother and sister-in-law, and nieces sat in the jury box. She smiled when she looked at them. They'd all come. Rosemary waved at her from the gallery with Cole on one side and Dotti on the other. The retirees, some troopers, and several other Alkaline residents lined the rows of seats behind them.

Natalia leaned forward and tapped Marcus on the shoulder. "This is it. Are you excited?"

He raised his little eyebrows. "We go swimming later?"

"Yes, you little fish, we can go swimming later."

Travis squeezed her hand. "That was a good idea renting the party room at the pool."

"I couldn't think of a better place to celebrate." She smiled as she imagined Marcus's excitement when he opened the new water-resistant prosthetic leg, flippers, and goggles. He was going to love them.

The bailiff entered through the back hallway. "All rise."

Natalia helped Marcus stand. The judge followed the bailiff in, then sat behind the bench between the American and South Dakota flags. Natalia's insides went crazy.

The judge smiled down at Marcus. "They tell me this is a special day for one amazing boy," she said. "Are you that boy?"

He nodded. "I get a new mommy and daddy and name, then I get to go swimming!"

"Then we'd better get started. Travis Wilkins and Natalia

Wilkins, will you raise your right hands?"

Natalia held up her hand and glanced at Travis. He faced the judge, his right hand steady beside his shoulder.

The judge raised her hand. "Do you solemnly swear to tell the truth, the whole truth, and nothing but the truth?"

"We do." Natalia and Travis spoke in unison.

The lawyer stood. "We are here today in the matter of the adoption of Marcus Elkhorn. Age four, born on September twentieth, twenty-thirteen." He faced Marcus, Natalia, and Travis. "We are asking the judge to grant this adoption and make it final so that Marcus will be a permanent child of your marriage. Are you prepared to take care of Marcus until he is at least eighteen years old and possibly further?"

"Yes."

"Can you tell the court your reasons for adopting Marcus?"

Natalia took Marcus's hand. "As I was caring for Marcus, I fell in love with him and I want to be his mommy. I want him to belong to our family forever."

Travis cleared his throat. "I was adopted when I was eleven. I hope that I can be as good a father as my adoptive dad was. I want to adopt Marcus because I love him and want to provide a life for him where he will always feel safe." He blinked several times, and Natalia's heart swelled. She loved that tough, sweet man.

The judge turned to Margo. "Miss White, is it the Department of Social Services' belief that this adoption is in Marcus's best interests?"

Margo stood. "Yes, your honor."

The judge flipped through her papers, then looked up at Travis. "And Marcus Ray Elkhorn's name will be changed to?"

Travis lifted his chin a notch. "Marcus Hank Wilkins."

She nodded as she examined the papers. "Marcus has been residing with Travis and Natalia Wilkins since February tenth, twenty-eighteen. A home study was completed and a written report by case worker, Margo White, is hereby accepted. There is no reasonable objection to the proposed change of the name of the adopted child."

"I would like to make a motion that the courts sign the orders of adoption," the lawyer said.

The judge smiled. Marcus bounced beside Natalia. Her eyes watered.

"It is hereby ordered that the petition of Travis Wilkins and Natalia Wilkins for the adoption of Marcus is allowed and approved, and Marcus will henceforth be regarded and treated in all respects as the child of the adopted parents. It is hereby ordered that the adopted child's name be changed to Marcus Hank Wilkins." The judge banged her gavel.

The courtroom erupted in applause. Tears flowed down Natalia's cheeks. She looked at the jury box. Her mom wiped at her eyes with a tissue. They shared a smile.

Travis wrapped his arm around her and squeezed Marcus between them until he giggled. "We're all part of the Wilkins legacy. There's no going back now."

"I think we're pretty happy right where we are," Natalia said. And just like she'd given her nightmares new endings, the adoption had given that date a new meaning. A year ago to the day, she'd recited last call for Officer Mason. Now, she looked over her son's head into the eyes of her husband. Aside from her wedding day, it was the happiest day of her life. She patted Marcus's head. "What do you think? Are you happy here?"

"We go swimming now?"

She laughed. "Soon."

"Now, come on up here, and we'll get some pictures," the judge said.

Travis scooted Marcus's chair back, freeing him to run to the judge's bench. He paused at the stairs and looked back at Natalia. She took a step toward him, but Travis wrapped his arm around her waist. "He can do it. He's been practicing."

Travis gave a stiff nod. Marcus mimicked him, then faced the stairs. He took the first step, wobbling a little, then stomped up the next two. The judge lifted him to her lap. He grabbed her gavel and pounded on the wooden block.

Travis kissed Natalia's cheek. "Let's go join our son."

CPSIA information can be obtained
at www.ICGtesting.com
Printed in the USA
LVHW100216030622
720427LV00002B/93

9 781645 262558

Quest
for the
Sublime

RICHARD BANGS

Quest

for the

Sublime

Finding Nature's Secret
in Switzerland

RICHARD BANGS

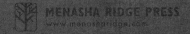

MENASHA RIDGE PRESS
www.menasharidge.com

Published by Menasha Ridge Press
Printed in the United States of America
Distributed by Publishers Group West
First edition, first printing

Library of Congress Cataloging-in-Publication Data

Bangs, Richard, 1950–
    Quest for the sublime: finding nature's secret in Switzerland/
by Richard Bangs. —1st ed.
        p. cm.
    Includes bibliographic references.
    ISBN-13: 978-0-89732-680-3 (alk. paper)
    ISBN-10: 0-89732-680-6 (alk. paper)
    1. Switzerland—Description and travel. 2. Bangs, Richard, 1950–,
—Travel—Switzerland. I. Title.

    DQ26.B36 2008
    949.4—dc22

                        2008029261

Cover design by Travis Bryant
Text design by Annie Long
Cover photograph © Loetscher Chlaus/Alamy
Other photographs by Walker Bangs, John Canning, Sara Givens,
    Laura Hubber, Didrik Johnck, and Small World Productions
Indexing by Rich Carlson

Menasha Ridge Press
P.O. Box 43673
Birmingham, Alabama 35243
www.menasharidge.com

table of contents

To the three marching mountains of my own Bernese Oberland:
Walker, Jasper, and Laura

FOREWORD

When you come right down to it, The Sublime is that state of being where the landscape you're witnessing has moved you toward tears, whether of joy or fear, exhilaration or love. You see The Sublime when the lenses behind your eyes have flipped scenery into rapture.

My own eyes are tuned to mountains. When a chiseled peak looms over me, I imagine myself crawling up its faces, crossing its ridges, chopping a snow ledge to spend the night on. When I'm in a car on a mountain road, my wife, Adele, always takes the wheel, because my eyes and heart are too busy measuring the intensity and beauty of every craggy wall and cloud-veiled summit. And when sunset paints its colored lights across another glaciated panorama, in my mind's eye I'm up *there,* on my way back from the summit, and the red glow warns me that soon only the stars and my headlamp will show me where to go.

Yes, it's hard for me to see mountains without getting a sublime jolt to the gut. For me, this landscape is visceral. Perhaps that's because I grew up in Switzerland. Or at least it feels like I grew up there. My Swiss years—ages seven to ten—seemed a complete lifetime, and in my heart it feels like I never left. A few memories: the sweet elegance of the first fat snowflakes of autumn floating past the windows of my third-grade classroom. The rim of peaks on every horizon, as viewed from our balcony. The ski jumps I built below our chalet, and the deep snow I landed in. The sound of cowbells in the spring as their owners

John Harlin III, about to attempt the Eiger, the mountain that killed his father
Photo courtesy of Didrik Johnck

returned from a winter in the valley far below. The feel of limestone
in my hands when Dad took me climbing. I was a Swiss mountain-boy
through and through, though born in America and to America
I'd soon return.

Above our village of Leysin, the ski lift rose to a spectacular 360-degree panorama, where off to the east one could see the
mountain that fractured our lives: the Eiger. In 1962, the year before we moved to Leysin, Dad became the first American to climb its
six-thousand-foot North Face, the highest in the Alps and the most
notorious in the world. In 1966 he returned to blaze a new, direct
route up the Eiger's north face. After a month on the wall, he fell
four thousand feet to his death when his rope broke. I was nine, my
sister eight, and with my mother we soon returned to the States.

So it shouldn't be surprising that the mountain whose outline is
etched into my soul is the Eiger. The Matterhorn always epitomized

perfect mountain beauty for me, but the Eiger is the embodiment of awe, a power dark and scary, a power that could eat your heart. I had to climb it to free myself from its shadow. Finally, in 2005, after many years of trying, I spent three days climbing up that wall. By the time I descended, the mountain had changed. The Eiger's Sirens had fallen mute, and my heart filled with soft acceptance, with love for the family I grew up in forty years before, and with love for Adele and our daughter, Siena, a family that is now growing up together.

It was at the foot of the Eiger that Adele, Siena, and I met Richard Bangs. We spent many storm-bound days together in Kleine Scheidegg playing Scrabble and cards, dining on *rösti* and drinking panaches. We hit it off immediately with Richard, discussing all manner of things, though most of all we talked about the mountains around us, and especially of the Eiger, and how my father died there and how I intended to live. These days were in many ways the culmination of my long affair with Switzerland. At the time we didn't know it, but our weeks together were just the beginning of Richard's journey into Swiss mountains.

Richard returned to Switzerland time and again as he tried to understand the sublime transformative effect that Swiss mountains have on people. In the process he discovered how these hills have deeply shaped the way Western culture relates to nature. This book, *Quest for the Sublime,* is the fruit of Richard's search.

John Harlin III
Editor, *The American Alpine Journal*
Author, *The Eiger Obsession: Facing the Mountain That Killed My Father*

INTRODUCTION

Dying for me would mean nothing—though the discomfort involved frightened me off.

—Ed Hillary, 1988

Nothing is more insistent, in the traveler's mind, than the will to transfigure the hell-bent into the heaven-sent.

It was the seventh day of a trek up into the Annapurna Himal in Nepal. Some years previous, in 1978, the throne room of the mountain goddess Annapurna was the objective of the first American women's expedition to an eight-thousand-meter peak. On October 15, after a long and perilous climb, Vera Komarkova and Irene Miller succeeded in reaching the summit. Two days later, two other members of the expedition, Alison Chadwick-Onyszkiewicz and Vera Watson, disappeared into a cloud of unknowing on the mountain, and their bodies lie entombed there still.

The weather had been unseasonable and unreasonable, and I resorted to looking at postcards to catch the grandstand views supposedly outside the tent door.

For the past several hours my team had passed a river of trekkers retreating down the trail, shaking heads and warning in a dozen accents that avalanches ahead made it impossible to continue.

Now, at Hinku Cave, as we stopped for thrice-brewed milk tea and hard-boiled eggs, Maureen, our trek leader, looked worried. She was hunched in solemn conversation with Ngati, our sirdar and veteran of three Everest expeditions, including one with legendary British mountaineer Chris Bonington. Ngati's flat, Apache-like face was leathery and lined from years in the mountains, and it now telegraphed intensity.

Finally, Maureen turned to us and announced the plan. Although her clients had traveled halfway around the world and paid upward of $2,500 each, plus airfare, to be guided up into the Annapurna Sanctuary, the dangers were too high. The heavy snow had created high-risk avalanche conditions in the final, narrow entrance to the sanctuary. Half a dozen major avalanches had already spilled into the gorge, and the lodge owners at the Machapuchare Base Camp had evacuated.

There was a communal sigh with the news. Most were ready to sacrifice time and money for some assurance of safety. But Maureen sensed my compulsion to continue, because just as my heart was sinking she turned her gaze on me and said, "I will allow one exception: Richard, who is the strongest, fastest hiker, can continue with the help of Ngati."

The rest of the group grew angry and questioned the preferential treatment; the group dynamic began to disintegrate. But by then I was gone, heading up the incline behind Ngati. We'd taken only a few steps when a young Englishman with a face the color of old bone came scrambling down the trail, carrying a sleeping bag under his arm. "Don't go any further," he implored. "An ice chunk came down and just missed me. My friends kept going, and they're crazy. I almost died."

Yet up we continued, into a dark cloud, and I realized I was feeling some pleasure in this stab of fear. As we approached the first swath of avalanche debris we saw a message scrawled in the snow: "No Pass." But Ngati computed the distance across, the freshness of the snow, and the angle of the sun, and he was willing to proceed. The rubble at our feet was from an avalanche a few days old, he said. It looked as if someone had rolled a bin of soccer balls off the ridge. The trail disappeared into this white riot of ice and snow.

Ngati told me to loosen my backpack so I could jettison it if another avalanche began and urged me to cross, if I could, in a *lung-gom* mode, a type of Tibetan mystic running. My passage, though, felt more like that of a pink-skinned tourist heading for happy hour.

When the trail reappeared, it snuck beneath an overhanging wall. As we started toward the overhang, a rumble split the unsullied

oxygen of this space, and a spume of ice and snow spilled off the rim
like a white waterfall, right onto the path. "Sir, that's where the Englishman was almost hit," Ngati said. "And two years ago a German
was caught by an avalanche here and died. But I have another way."

Ngati steered us off the trail into knee-deep snow. We crossed to
the east side of the river, the Modi Khola, and up a small rise, out of
the immediate way of the avalanches that slide down from Hiunchuli,
the dripping mountain we couldn't see that towers over the western
walls of the Modi Khola valley. As we waded upward we could see and
hear lethal spears of ice dropping on the path not taken.

After a couple of hours of hard trekking we could see Bagar and
its one building, the Gangapurna Lodge, named for the 24,458-foot-
high mountain that looms directly to the north, which in turn is
named for another Hindu goddess. At last we crossed the river and
stepped our way up to the red-lumber lodge, the last outpost before
the sanctuary. We were at 10,825 feet. At half past noon we opened
the door and discovered two other visitors and the innkeeper inside.
The foreigners were Nick and Nicolette, both from England, both
students in English literature, and both terribly unprepared for a
mountain expedition. They had no gaiters or waterproof outerwear,
and Nick had made it to this outpost wearing shorts. Still, our little
den had a vaguely exclusive air, dark and sumptuous with plight.

As we settled in for milk tea and cold yak-cheese pizza, we
heard what sounded like the low peak of organ music outside.
Another avalanche. The weather was getting nastier. Faint crow's-feet
nested under Ngati's chocolate eyes as he announced we wouldn't
continue farther that day. In fact, he said, he must head back to the
main group. "You're an experienced mountaineer. Why don't you stay
with us?" I appealed. "I'm sorry, sir," he answered. "I have four children now. I do not take risks anymore." And with that Ngati, as lean

and brown and hard-muscled as a snow leopard, disappeared into the whiteness.

We tried to relax in the little way station and prayed for better weather tomorrow. We settled back for an afternoon of hot lemon, card games, and small talk. Nick and Nicolette seemed delighted with the predicament. They told me they had been spending holidays in Switzerland, following in the footsteps of some of the great English Romantic poets, who had found inspiration among the Alps. Seeing the mountains through the eyes of Byron and Shelley motivated them to seek ever higher ground and ultimately brought them here. I confessed I didn't pay much attention to the musings of the mountains in my literature schooling. I grew up in the boggy flats of the Eastern Seaboard and went to college at the edge of Lake Michigan. The highest peak at the time was Mount Trashmore, an artificial slope in Chicago fashioned from landfill. There was nothing elegiac to be found in that heap.

With the dark we stepped outside for the short walk to the frigid meat-locker barracks of the Gangapurna Lodge. There was no electricity, so no reading lamp. I pulled an egg-shaped novelty candle from my pack and lit it to postpone the day's finish, and to read a card unrolled from my sleeping bag. It was from my wife, and it read: "Have a safe, sublime, sweet, serene, sure, and sacred trip." The alliteration notwithstanding, I sensed none of those qualities at that moment.

The morning didn't look much prettier, the sky like underexposed film with a bit of snow buzzing around. Aspersions were cast my way as I wolfed down a three-egg omelet. Three days ago, we had passed the rock shrine to Pujinim Barahar, the powerful mountain goddess who protects the Annapurna Sanctuary. Beyond the shrine no impure person should pass, nor any polluting foods, such as eggs. Violations risk the anger of the goddess, whose revenge will be sickness or death. In 1956, when Colonel James O. M. "Jimmy" Roberts

Life in the slow lane   Photo courtesy of Didrik Johnck

became the first outsider to enter this sacred ground, he left fifty eggs behind at the shrine. Between bites I reminded myself I didn't subscribe to such myths. "These eggs are sublime," I said with a grin to Nick and Nicolette, who recoiled at my words and choice of breakfast. Nick stared out at the snow, vigorously cutting his bread as though demonstrating the murder of Julius Caesar.

Our plan was to see if we could march the two hours or so through the pinched gateway of the sanctuary to the Machapuchare Base Camp. We knew the camp was abandoned and closed, but it was where we might rest before heading west another few hours through waist-deep snow to our ultimate target, the Annapurna Base Camp.

So we whiled away the morning with more card games and talk. Then, around noon, the sun finally broke through, and the world was briefly bent toward us. We rushed outside to witness the scene, a view up valley of Gangapurna's triangular, snow-and-rock face. Pastel waves of light cascaded off the sharp walls, and the world pulsed with possibilities. This was our chance. We hoisted our packs and headed out into the snow, up to where the mountains blush, toward the vestibule of the otherwise impregnable sanctuary.

After forty-five minutes trudging through the snow, we stepped over a lone black feather from a cinereous vulture, a bird seemingly as out of place at this altitude and landscape as we were. Minutes later we reached the remains of a colossal, recently triggered avalanche. It was several hundred yards wide, and, like a huge, pocked arm, it reached all the way across the Modi Khola to the far wall of the ravine. Upstream, less than a mile away, we could see the point where the trail squeezed through the steep-walled pass to Annapurna Sanctuary's restricted precincts. The Gurungs, the Sino-Tibetan ethnic group that has lived in the shadows of the Annapurna for centuries, believe this is the abode of Pujinim Barahar, the goddess who protects the Annapurna Sanctuary. The Tibetans, who view the range from the other side, say this is the home of Tara, the savioress of Tibetan Buddhism.

Then, as we stared into the chalky abyss of the avalanche, something roared behind us. We turned to see a shower of snow spraying off the east rim directly above us. Nick ran in circles with the noise, then made a series of superhuman flying leaps through the snow. I couldn't tell whether he was scared to death or in some state of exalted joy. The avalanche never materialized; it petered out a hundred yards short of us, and Nicolette laughed out loud at the spectacle.

When the sounds and snows settled, I took stock. The sky had darkened and boxed us in, and the Himalayan wind was whistling. It seemed as if we were standing at the threshold between the ordinary universe and the *bardo,* a sacred realm, but to continue was courting death. Many have died on Annapurna, most from avalanches. A porter had died recently right at this stretch. Nick and Nicolette agreed, though reluctantly, and so we retreated back to the little lodge.

At nightfall I lit my egg candle and lay awake for hours, wondering why the attraction to the flame of risk. What was it about the mountains that kittled and drew so irresistibly to some? I had no answers. At last the candle flickered and went out.

When I got up to relieve myself around midnight, I stepped outside into the snow and saw a sky so clear the starlight cast shadows on Machapuchare. So many sparkles and glitters and glints appeared above me, it looked as if an expensive bauble had been dropped and had shattered above this redoubt. I stood transfixed, shivering in silent wonder. The flatlands never inspired this.

Sometime before dawn I awoke to the ear-rending explosion of a plane crashing. And then another. And another. The clamor seemed to be coming from down valley, toward the Himalaya Hotel, where the rest of my group was camping, waiting for me. It was next to the Himalaya Hotel in the spring of 1989 that three Sherpa kitchen boys died when an avalanche rolled over their tent in the middle of the night. I got up to relieve myself once again and stepped out into the bracing shock of a blizzard. The sky had shut, flakes were flying, and almost a foot of fresh snow smothered the landscape. I cast about for the skyline, an outline, any line, but there was only whiteness in the roaring dark.

John Harlin II fell to his death four thousand feet down the Eiger's North Face in 1966.
Photo courtesy of Didrik Johnck

An hour later we gathered for a breakfast of frisson, but while I was solemn, Nick and Nicolette seemed positively blissful, in some sort of agreeable kind of horror. The owner of the lodge said that two years ago an avalanche from Machapuchare had rolled down and ripped off the roof. I retreated to pack. I heard the door creak as someone stepped outside.

Minutes after the owner's story, there was another cataclysmic roar, and a blast of wind pushed its way through the cracks. It lifted up the side of the roof a few inches, powdering me with snow and forcing me to shut my eyes. A scream followed outside. In ran Nicolette, pasted with snow, looking like the abominable snowwoman.

"That was sublime!" she announced, an arch smile across her face, as white as an arctic bear. Nick nodded in rigorous approval.

"How's that?" I asked. But Nick and Nicolette weren't forthcoming. We all finished our packing in silence and headed down to safety and our own separate lives, a groove of wonder now carved in my mind.

Not long afterward, I went snowshoeing in the Cascades with my son Walker and a friend, Anna Bezzola, an alpine guide of Swiss descent. After stepping through the fresh snow for a spell, we cleared a spot and sat down to a Swiss lunch of thick-crusted bread, Appenzeller and Gruyère cheese, and a rack of Toblerone chocolate. It was a perfectly beautiful day, but I was in a bit of a mood. I was in midlife and had many of the aspirational trappings—a beautiful home, a beautiful wife, a good job at a large corporation. Everything was proportional and predictable. But there was a dullness inside, as though all the beauty muted the real colors. I never shared these feelings, but rather let them simmer beneath the surface. At one point I took a big bite of Gruyère, and it was so smooth it poured down my throat like a light mead. "This is sublime," I oooohed to Anna. She didn't respond, her face blank with the moment. Then, behind us, higher up the valley, we heard a sudden peal, a question turning over in the sky's mind perhaps. We looked up to see the cascading spray of an avalanche. Walker's eyes grew wide, as, I imagine, did mine. For an instant I felt a stirring inside with the danger at a distance. "Now that is sublime," Anna corrected.

Anna went on to explain that The Sublime, as she understood it, having spent much of her life in the Swiss Alps, was not and could not be a tasteful bite, or a little moment of happiness, or even a thing of delicate beauty. That was some postmodern drivel, a vial of tincture that had lost its potency. The Sublime was large, overwhelming, and dangerous—like an avalanche. She mentioned that several of

the Romantic poets and artists of the late eighteenth and early nineteenth centuries ventured to Switzerland from England and other
parts of Europe and there found the inspiration for The Sublime. To
these early proponents The Sublime was greater than The Beautiful.
Beauty was light, fleeting, and charming. The Sublime was profound,
overwhelming, scary. Anna suggested that if I wanted to disinter this
concept, then I should take a trip through Switzerland—the Swiss
Alps were the temple of The Sublime—and with such a trip the tele-
ology would become evident.

When thrice there is a call, then heeded it should be. . . .

While in Berkeley, California, for an American Alpine Club
dinner, I found myself at the famous local bouldering site Indian
Rock with John Harlin III. John, the speaker for the evening, had
recently climbed the Eiger's North Face, following in the boot steps
of his father, who had died, falling four thousand feet on the Eiger,
thirty-nine years earlier, when John was nine. The account was
featured in an IMAX film, *The Alps;* in John's own book, *The Eiger
Obsession: Facing the Mountain that Killed My Father;* and on a Web
site I developed for Yahoo. After he finished a little clamber around
the rocks, he dropped down next to me. His craggy features, engraved by the mountain weather, were as calm as those of a head on
a coin. John's father took him climbing for the first time when he
was six, and he has been an axis in the climbing world ever since.

"For my dad, it was connecting with the deeper dimensions of
yourself and the outdoor world through exposing yourself to dangerous, risky situations. He wanted to be a participant in The Sublime,
and he succeeded."

John is the editor of the *American Alpine Journal,* so I guessed he
might have encountered citations of The Sublime in various articles
throughout the years.

"Today we often confuse the term with 'wonderful,' and writers and climbers do that too. But The Sublime is an appreciation for nature in its most awe-inspiring sense. It is more powerful than mere beauty; you feel like you're under the influence of something bigger than you. You feel the scale and power. It is intimidating and thrilling at the same time. It's not something that can be understood academically or through reading books; it has to be experienced."

"OK. How can I get a grasp of The Sublime?" I asked John.

There was, it seemed, in the spongy timbre of his speech the sound of great distances. "You need to go to Switzerland. You have to travel the Alps. Take a train, so you can see. Hike. Explore. Experience being inside this landscape. You could start in the east, in St. Moritz. Take a trip to the Eiger. And then go all the way to the west, to the Matterhorn, the most perfect icon of a mountain, more perfect than the pyramids of Egypt. The Matterhorn was my dream to climb when I was a kid. My dad promised to take me up it when I was fourteen, but he died when I was nine. I waited until I was an adult and then climbed it twice. I think it is the most beautiful peak in the world. It is the mountain that spurred The Sublime movement. If you traverse the spine of the Swiss Alps and finish at the Matterhorn, then maybe, just maybe, you'll understand The Sublime."

In 1735, the poet Sir Hildebrand Jacob penned an essay, "How the Mind Is Rais'd to the Sublime," in which he presaged John Harlin's evocation: "A Mind truly disposed for the Perceptions of that, which is great and marvelous, whether in nature or in art, is a product of nature and cannot be attained through study. All the vast and wonderful Scenes . . . which the Universe affords, have this Effect upon the Imagination."

RAPTURE AND FURY

a sense sublime
Of something far more deeply interfused,
Whose dwelling is the light of setting suns,
And the round ocean and the living air,
And the blue sky, and in the mind of man;
A motion and a spirit, that impels
All thinking things, all objects of all thought,
And rolls through all things. . . .

—William Wordsworth, 1798

Before packing, I rifle through my attic and find a musty copy of *Peri Hupsos,* or *On Sublimity,* attributed to Dionysius Longinus, left over from a college philosophy course. Rereading the slim, third-century volume, I find that this original Greek enumeration of The Sublime was mostly rhetorical; its purpose was to teach oratorical devices that empowered a speaker to move an audience. The author called The Sublime "the echo of a noble mind" and argued that "intensity" was greater than sobriety, that "living emotions" are higher than "good breeding," that "speed . . . , vehemence and power" compensated for lack of fluency, smoothness, and charm. He even outlined techniques, such as the "rhapsodic cadence," which includes repeating key phrases; repeating key phrases. It all sounded as if he were describing the oratorical magic of such legends as Julius Caesar, Daniel Webster, John C. Calhoun, Henry Clay, Indonesia's President Sukarno, Cuba's Castro, Malcolm X, the Reverend Jesse Jackson, John F. Kennedy, Barack Obama, and all others with the gift of open-vowel intonations. These were sublime rhetoricians who could inspire wonder, rapture, even ecstasy in a crowd.

But Anna's interpretation was somehow different. It seemed her take was that the poets and philosophers, the artists and aestheticians of the nineteenth century who passed through or spent time in Switzerland took this oratorical feeling, applied it to nature, and forged a new way to regard mountains and other bold landscape features.

So I click to Amazon and order a satchelful of tomes on The Sublime and several guidebooks about Switzerland. With them at hand, I settle back on a Swiss International Air flight from Los Angeles to Zurich to see if I can grok this concept. The appeal and satisfaction of a guidebook lies in its reticence, its incompleteness—in the gap it leaves for the imagination to fill pending arrival. But the

Zürich is the largest city in Switzerland and the main commercial and cultural center, and is widely considered to be one of the world's great cities. According to several surveys from 2006 to 2008, Zürich was named the city with the best quality of life in the world.   Photo courtesy of Walker Bangs

books on The Sublime are noisy and ill-behaved, prompting more questions than answers. Somewhere over Newfoundland, it becomes evident that cracking the doctrine of The Sublime is like playing Alice in Wonderland croquet, with the flamingo mallets curving around to stare at the player. There may be rules, but they bend in every direction, and there are beasts at every post.

On the approach, flying over the Swiss Alps, the view seems less an interpretation of The Sublime than a fly's sight of the wrinkled forehead of a very old man. But I know from years of aerial scouts of river canyons that what looks like a scar from high up is often a canyon of considerable awe once on the ground.

The twin Swiss passions for nature and technology are in ripe evidence at first moments. The runway is adjacent to a nature reserve, and the solar-powered terminal is so clean it could double as an atom smasher. As I ride from the gate to the baggage hall, the tram is filled with the sounds of cowbells, moos, and yodels. At one point there is a moving image of Heidi through the windows, created with the train as rotoscope.

From Zurich I rent a car and point south to look for the dragons of The Sublime. The first stop is Lucerne, in the heart of Switzerland. It widens like a horn to steep-sided mountains. Once a fishing village, it became an important commercial center between Flanders and Italy when the route over the St. Gotthard opened in the thirteenth century. Later it became a vital component to the Grand Tour, the European excursion fashionable in the seventeenth and eighteenth centuries which awoke certain well-heeled travelers to The Sublime. Lake Lucerne covers forty-four square miles in a complex shape with seven bays, the Alps looming on several sides. The city is also a hub for train, bus, and boat links, so it's an ideal starting point for this exploration. Lucerne was founded when Benedictine monks who had a settlement dating back to the eighth century handed over the parish to the city. The area was charitably described as "inhospitable" at the time, with running sewage and wild animals roaming the narrow streets within the city walls.

I check into the baronial Hotel Schweizerhof Luzern at the edge of the old city, a row of palm trees lining its frontage. It stands just yards from the northwestern shore of Lake Lucerne. In the vaulted lobby there is a stirring of the mood. The dramatist and essayist John Baillie, in his 1747 treatise, *An Essay on the Sublime,* suggests that a building can achieve, through architectural features such as columns, arches, and space, a kind of code that works like language to evoke a feeling of The Sublime. Here, between the neobaroque stucco marble columns, I meet co-proprietor Patrick J. O. Hauser, the fifth generation to run this property—prim, genteelly clad in striped tie and crisp, triangulated hand-kerchief, looking very much as though he had stepped here from another century. Patrick and his brother Michael grew up running the halls of the shining hotel and live here still. The Schweizerhof was built in 1845 as the first luxury hotel in the region. Though it's been renovated, it maintains an imperial-century splendor and has seen its fair share of notable guests who found inspiration. Leo Tolstoy wrote one of his works here; Wagner completed *Tristan and Isolde* and met with King Ludwig II here. Patrick says the hotel has always been a haven for artists, members of the nobility, and spies—everyone from Mark Twain to Roger Moore to "lots of kings and queens, even B. B. King." The bar has wooden tables painted with names of famed musicians and bands who've bellied up here—Seal, Deep Purple, Jimmy Cliff, Kool & the Gang, and Van Morrison. All of them trekked here to perform in the ripely named Blue Balls Festival, an annual midsummer jazz and rock do. It joins the classical music-oriented Lucerne Festival, founded in 1938 by Arturo Toscanini. Toscanini had hoped to build a festival to rival the one in Salzburg, which had fallen under Nazi sway. Now, Patrick has positioned the Schweizerhof as the "festival hotel." It has been frequented by a hit parade beyond those memorialized at the bar stools: Randy Newman, Al Jarreau, Billy Idol, Tracy Chapman, Keb' Mo', Bob Geldof, and on.

Lucerne's eight-sided Wasserturm (Water Tower) was once a defense post, an archive, a prison, and a torture chamber. It's now the headquarters of the Lucerne Artillery Association and a gathering place for corporate events.   Photo courtesy of Small World Productions

I check into a fourth-floor waterside room and pull back the curtains to see the lake set like a beveled pane of mirrored glass reflecting the surrounding Alps. Sixty percent of Switzerland is made up of the Alps. Twenty-six percent is covered by forest, and the country has some two thousand lakes, of which Lucerne in many minds is the most beautiful. It's not difficult to appreciate Wagner's sentiments in 1866. Writing to King Ludwig II, he proclaimed: "I do not know of a more beautiful spot in this world." And: "Nobody will get me out of here again."

After a spelt ale in the bar, I take a stroll up to the Reuss River, which sings and chuckles as it conflues into Lake Lucerne. A man and two boys are tossing bread crumbs into the water as flocks of swans and their cygnets dart about competing with ducks for the pieces. The ducks sometimes dive for lost morsels, heads down, bottoms up, but the dignified swans seem above that behavior until I unfold my hand without thinking and a stately bird dives into my palm and pecks his beak into my skin.

I cross the covered, 670-foot-long Kapellbrücke (or Chapel Bridge, named after the nearby St. Peter's Chapel), built around 1300, marketed as the oldest preserved wooden bridge in Europe. Only a bit less arch in its branding is the claim that in the fifteenth century, Lucerne was the only city in Europe to boast four bridges. Now the flower-festooned footbridge, with its gabled roof, is a camera-phone favorite, along with the Wasserturm, the octagonal stone Water Tower, which in its time was a defense post, an archive, the city treasury, a prison, and a torture chamber. It now is headquarters to the Lucerne Artillery Association and hosts corporate events.

The rafters of the bridge bend time and space together as neatly as the folds in an origami swan. Well, perhaps more a phoenix than a swan. In 1993 the bridge was damaged after catching fire, possibly from a nearby boat. The catastrophe elicited not only buckets of town tears but also fears of lost tourodollars. By the time the fire was put out, only thirty of the original Heinrich Wegmann–painted panels beneath the eaves remained. Another eighty were lost in the conflagration. Though there has been a righteous attempt at restoration, it is impossible not to notice the tinctumutation between the original depictions of saints and town history and the fresh, a livid tinge as if the paintings were bruised in a battle for survival.

After strolling up the river past the open-air cafes, I recross at the wooden Spreuerbrücke, named for corn waste. Back in the fifteenth century, when the enterprising millers of Lucerne diverted part of the swift-flowing Reuss River to power their water mills, they dumped their chaff into the river from this bridge. *Spreuerbrücke* is, literally, the "Chaff Bridge." Its most distinguishing feature hasn't changed much, I'm told: the rafters are adorned with sixty-seven "Dance of Death" pictures, grim depictions of everyday folk—a bride, a baby, a nun, a hunter, even the artist himself—on the edge of mortality, victims of the plague, facing the mocking smile of the figure of Death, all painted by Kaspar Meglinger in the seventeenth century. I study these grim panels one by one, as if they contain the answer to the riddle of why we find depictions of death so riveting, so sublime. I feel a seam open onto a void whose terrible content is the inevitability of finality, and it does indeed race the blood and evoke feelings of being more alive.

I meander past stalls filled with big wheels of cheese, which were once important historical records inscribed with dates of significance, from births and deaths and marriages to avalanches, floods, and miracles. I stop to sample fondue from a big, black pot. I sniff the bright-scarlet geraniums in a flower box and stoop for a drink from a water fountain—clear, crisp mountain water; nothing filtered here. They are all sublime sensations, I think, then catch myself. My cultural baggage is weightless, but impossible to leave behind.

I wander the cobbled streets, past the endless shops selling Swiss Army knives and mass-produced exclusive watches. I pass by beer gardens, ancient guild halls, some very old half-timber houses with colorful frescoes, fountains in squares, a Starbucks, a Gothic church, and a baroque cathedral with architecture that gestures toward the absence of something much greater. But one sight always draws my eyes upward, beyond even the toothpick steeples: the snowy tonsure of Pilatus. Even as I gaze at a dark bottle of Le Fasce Olio Extra Vergine di Oliva, there is a reflection of the jagged-toothed peak. My only acquaintance heretofore with Pilatus has been with its

In 1993 the Chapel Bridge was partially destroyed after catching fire. By the time the fire was put out, only thirty of the original Heinrich Wegmann–painted panels beneath the eaves remained. Though there has been a noble attempt at restoration, there is now a tinctumutation between the original depictions of saints and town history and the fresh. Photo courtesy of Small World Productions

namesake airplane, the Swiss-made Pilatus PC-6 Porter, the "Jeep of the air." I once chartered a floatplane version of the Porter to fly from Norman Wells in Canada's Northwest Territories to Willow Handle Lake, a feeder to the Mountain River, down which I made a canoe passage. Like all Swiss-made machinery, the high-winged, angular, dragonlike aircraft performed like a dream. But now here I am in the dense shadow of the eponymous mountain, and so I arrange the following morning to touch its sky.

Trek is the wrong word. Though there is a trail, it is not often employed. Rather, the preferred route to the top of the heaven-kissing hill is by way of what is billed as the "world's steepest cogwheel railway," one with a gradient that tilts in one section to a gravity-defying 48 degrees.

If there is a machine that qualifies as sublime, it is the train. Its tracks across the landscape marked the extension of frontiers and increased the democratization of movement across physical space. This occurred despite an early, pavid sentiment that trains might damage one's health—that such rapid movement would cause brain trouble for passengers and vertigo among those who looked at moving trains. For this reason, it was once recommended that all tracks in the Swiss Alps should be enclosed by board fences taller than the cars and engines.

With the introduction of trains, for the first time in history travelers could move faster than a galloping horse. Access to new vistas opened; new features appeared on the land, such as great spans, viaducts, bridges, tunnels, and switchbacks. The landscape boiled away to insubstantiality in the steam, smoke, and sheer speed of the train.

Perhaps no rail line in Switzerland is more sublime than the Pilatusbahn, more than a hundred years old and powered by steam until 1937, when electric cars were introduced.

And if there is a beast that could be called sublime, it is the dragon. The village of Alpnachstad and this mountain are festooned with the Pilatus logo, which though supposed to be a fire-breathing dragon looks more like a salamander with wings. There, at the Valley Station, I climb into a bright red, parallelogram-shaped railcar (designed to "lean" uphill) and hang on, back pressed against the seat, for the delightful horror of a thirty-minute ascent. Longinus wrote of poetry that was "ravishing and transporting," and this ride also qualifies, with its cadence of the thud-clack of the cog wheels locking onto the toothed track as we snail in and out of the mountain, over rushing creeks and dark gorges, past sheer cliffs and ogrelike outcroppings. There in the middle distance is a small herd of chamois, the protected, goatlike animal native to the Alps. Before the cult of the Romantics, alpine piles such as Pilatus were merely protuberances, barriers, and impediments to agriculture. When early geographers pointed at the peaks and asked what they were called, locals replied, *"Alpes."* But this referred only to the high-level pastures on which they grazed their stock. The old Swiss peasant name for the Alps is *Geissbergen,* literally "Goat Mountains," land purposeful only for pasturing tough meat.

HIC SUNT DRACONES

Placed on this planet since yesterday, and only for a day, we can only hope to glimpse the knowledge that we will probably never attain.

—Horace-Bénédict de Saussure, 1796

’ve penned a few books that have been placed in the category of "wilderness travel." But perhaps the first to stock this shelf was the eighteenth-century mountaineer Horace-Bénédict de Saussure, who wrote in his opus, *Voyages dans les Alpes,* that the chamois hunters of the Alps experienced a certain delight in their dangerous profession: "It is these very dangers, this alternation of hope and fear, the continual agitation kept alive by these sensations in his heart, which excite the huntsman, just as they animate the gambler, the warrior, the sailor and, even to a certain point, the naturalist among the Alps whose life resembles closely, in some respects, that of the chamois hunter." As someone who has spent some time exploring wild rivers in remote corners and who holds the distinction of having capsized on six continents, I know this notion—that life is more intensely lived the closer one gets to its extinction. We never feel so alive as when we have nearly died.

Upward we creep at six miles an hour on a track built on a wall of granite blocks. We move like an underwater runner from the dark and spiry pine forests of the base past the timberline to the snow-dusted, rocky outcroppings of the seven-thousand-foot shoulder. The continual agitation, the swaying rhythm of hope and fear, fear and hope notwithstanding, somehow it doesn't seem right to climb this high without any panting or pain. But travel by train does allow a feeling of something beyond the merely functional or utilitarian.

The mountain, however absurd it seems, is named for Pontius Pilate, the Roman governor of Judea who presided over the crucifixion of Jesus Christ and, according to tradition, later committed suicide in prison rather than face the prospect of death at the hands of Emperor Tiberius. Legend has it that each time the Romans tried to dispose of Pilate's body, weighed down with stones, in various

Before the cult of the Romantics, alpine piles such as Pilatus were merely barriers and impediments to agriculture. When early geographers pointed at the peaks and asked what they were called, locals replied, "Alpes." But this referred only to the high-level pastures. The old Swiss peasant name for the Alps is Geissbergen, *literally "Goat Mountains," or land purposeful only for pasturing tough meat.*   Photo courtesy of Sara Givens

rivers, including the Tiber and the Rhône, fierce storms swept in and wouldn't stop until the corpse was retrieved. The Romans considered the Alps inhospitable, difficult, horrid—*ocris, arduus, horridus.* The Roman poet and philosopher Titus Lucretius Carus, about a half century before Christ, called the Alps the waste places of the world, where nature had swept its rubbish. And so such seemed the place the Romans might rid themselves of this curse at last.

They carried the body up an isolated mountain in Switzerland, a peak then known as Frakmont, and left Pilate's remains in a dark lake near the top. For good measure, his wife, Procla, was tossed into a nearby pond.

But Pilate still caused trouble, and storms still blew, so Lucerne authorities banned the ascent of the mountain. When six clerics tried to climb the hill unaided in 1387, they were imprisoned. There was a belief that every Good Friday, Pilate's tormented spirit would float to the surface of the lake in an attempt to wash his hands of Jesus's blood. But it's hard to validate. Supposedly, all those who saw the specter died within a year.

Stories transcend history, and though dozens of mountain places in the Middle Ages boasted of the burial plot of the man behind the crucifixion, the claim of this one, with its evocative tales, took.

It wasn't until the sixteenth century that it was legal to climb the mountain's shanks, and to this day locals like to blame Pilate for the violent storms that not uncommonly break over the area.

Queen Victoria took on the beleaguered spirit of Pontius Pilate and assorted dragons in the summer of 1868, ascending halfway up the mountain in a sedan chair, the rest of the way on a pony brought from England. It was her first trip to the Alps. Still in mourning for Prince Albert, she was persuaded of the virtues of such an expedition by her doctors, who were concerned about her withdrawal from society. She knew of Albert's love of Alpine scenery (he had brought her a pressed alpenrose from the slopes of Mount Rigi) and eventually conceded the therapeutic qualities of the scheme.

She traveled incognito, pretending to be the "Countess of Kent." Arriving at the start of August, she settled into a pension in Lucerne and admired the vistas that were so much grander than anything on the isles. She wrote in her diary: "What am I to say of the glorious scenery of Switzerland; the view from this House which is very high is most wonderfully beautiful with the lake—Pilatus, the Righi etc. I can *hardly* believe my eyes when I look at it."

Her little adventure helped bleach the long-held taboo and inspired her subjects in ever-increasing numbers to come "take the air" of this and other alps.

Once we dock in the gaping maw of the terminal station, I head out and step onto the palisade, the wind sharp and moaning. Guides, with a wink, say the sound is Pilate's ghost as he wanders the slopes searching for a route to heaven. But the sensations of sound and wind do not dominate here; instead, it is sight. Seventy-three alpine summits and six lakes can be viewed from this vantage. Looking across a sea of clouds, I'm seized by a sober intoxication from the view of the marching mountains of the Bernese Oberland: the Eiger to the left, then the Mönch in the middle and the Jungfrau on the right. At the former, I spent time a year earlier covering the climb by John Harlin III.

Legend holds that the Mönch ("Monk") peak is protecting the Jungfrau ("Virgin") from the nearby Eiger ("Ogre"). But to me, here at this viewpoint, it looks to be the other way around. It is, after all, a leap year. "It is a good name, Jungfrau—Virgin. Nothing could be whiter; nothing could be purer; nothing could be saintlier of aspect," wrote Mark Twain on his 1891 visit. But when I read this uncharacteristically sincere sentiment, all I can think of is Mae West's line: "I used to be Snow White, but I drifted."

There is, not surprisingly, a less romantic version. Jungfrau likely got its name because a convent once owned pastures at the foot of the mountain. "Eiger"—denoting the mountain famous for its killer north face—could derive from the Latin *acer,* meaning sharp, or the old German *ger,* meaning a spear or javelin. And Mönch? Chances are its lower pastures were owned by monks.

Legends notwithstanding, this is an empirical domain, and the feelings evoked are powerful, at least to me at this moment. My insides seem to be filling with a froth of excitement and awe, as a punctured raft fills with cold river-water. But such regard was not always accorded here. For generations, the mountains signified only the deformed and execrable, thinly soiled, steeply sloped, bad for farming, disease ridden, ordeals to cross, the lairs of energetic demons and trolls. Adam of Usk was so petrified when he crossed Switzerland's St. Gotthard Pass in 1402 that he had to be blindfolded, and travelers after him would often close the carriage curtains to avoid the dreadful scenes of the Alps. Anything could happen in this icy semicircle of teeth that bit off Italy from the rest of Europe. Not only were the Alps scary, but also they were ugly, blemishes on the terrestrial globe, and people of good taste sought to avoid them. The classical notions of beauty called for purity, order, restraint, regularity, proportion—perfection. The Alps were disordered, irregular, chaotic, and bad-mannered. The seventeenth-century diarist John Evelyn thought them "horrid and fearful." (His sentiments were published posthumously when discovered in 1817 in a laundry basket.) The early-eighteenth-century essayist Joseph Addison wrote to his friend Edward Wortley, "I am just now arriv'd at Geneva by a very troublesome Journey over the Alps, where I have bin for some days together shivering among the Eternal Snows." The monk John de Bremble, one of the earliest English travelers to the mountains of Switzerland, was so horrified by his experience crossing the Great St. Bernard Pass that he prayed, "Lord restore me to my brethren, that I may tell them not to come to this place of torment." Bishop Berkeley, crossing the Alps in 1714, carped, "Every object that here presents itself is excessively miserable." In 1723, a Swiss fellow of the Royal Society, Johann Jacob Scheuchzer, penned a famous dracopedia, a detailed description of Alpine dragons.

31

(He even saw one.) He also discovered near Brig a superintelligent community, most of whose members shared the surname Supersaxo, who were fluent in German, French, Italian, and Latin, and descended from a sixteenth-century Italian count who had sired twelve sons and eleven daughters. And he believed that certain chamois possessed a stone in their bellies that rendered them immune to bullets.

What may be the first travel brochure for Switzerland, *Les Délices de la Suisse,* published by Abraham Ruchat in 1714, promoted the tidiness of the towns and the happiness and health of the cows but was dismayed with the "eternal snows" of the high Alps. "These great excrescences of the earth," it declared, "to outward appearance have neither use nor comeliness." Others cited the Alps as nature's shames and ills, as boils, blisters, warts, and wens, and even called the peaks the "Devil's arse" and the steep valleys "Nature's pudenda."

A German traveler in 1785 wrote, "What struck me most in Switzerland among the curiosities of nature were those horrid structures the Alps." Sir Leslie Stephen, the pioneering mountaineer and biographer, and father of novelist Virginia Woolf and painter Vanessa Bell, wrote in his 1871 book, *The Playground of Europe:* "Before the turning-point of the eighteenth century, a civilized being might, if he pleased, regard the Alps with unmitigated horror." And indeed in 1791 William Gilpin noted that "the generality of people" found wilderness dislikable. "There are few," he wrote, "who do not prefer the busy scenes of cultivation to the greatest of nature's rough productions." Mountains were things to avoid or, if one were a merchant, soldier, or pilgrim, to go around. Mountains, as a whole, were anathema.

So how did this mind-set change? Some of the shift, perhaps, had to do with the palpable deterioration of the cities of Europe, especially smoggy, coal-blackened London, with its rising fatigue and social atomization. The success of the agricultural revolution, with its crop rotation

and protective enclosures, created a steep upward curve in food production and in turn population. As more people flocked from the fields
to the economic opportunities that cities promised, sewage got worse,
crime increased, urban blight spread, and faith in a higher power that
looked after those in need faded. By 1847, England was the first country
in the world where more people lived in cities than in the countryside
and more were employed in industry than in agriculture. From this
claustrophobic urban cesspit the cholera epidemic broke in 1832, killing
fifty thousand people. Influenza, measles, scarlet fever, and diphtheria
became epidemic. Tuberculosis was spread effectively by the perfect
storm of the dense population, the damp climate, and the concentration
of smoke from factories and homes. By the middle of the nineteenth
century, tuberculosis in England accounted for one death in six.

In the wake of this corrosive wave there evolved the romantic
notion of the virtues of the simple, clean, and healthy life in nature;
the bucolic verve among the mountains that the Swiss seemed to exhibit found special appeal. It was, however, the industrial revolution
that led to vastly improved means of transport and to a chattering
class with disposable income. Those developments allowed and inspired travel to places such as Switzerland, where the high mountains
and contented people set the minds wandering, and perhaps got rid of
that nasty cough.

Alongside this gradual reassessment came a renewal in a biblical
belief that mountains, in all their horror, were manifestations of God's
work. Poets and artists called the feelings they felt when experiencing
the Alps sublime. Among these was the Swiss natural scientist Albrecht
von Haller, who, after exploring the Bernese Oberland, published in
1729 a poem called *Die Alpen* (*The Alps*) that contrasted the redoubt-
able Alpine peasant's natural way of life with the civilized lifestyle of
the metropolitan elite and concluded that the mountain life was better.

"Luck is much too poor to improve his well-being," von Haller rhapsodized about the Swiss peasant. In 1739, Thomas Gray took the Grand Tour, crossed the Alps, kept a journal, and wrote letters in which he used the adjectives "romantic" and "poetic" and the phrases "a sacred terror" and "a severe delight." With these words he planted the seeds that grew a movement. "Magnificent rudeness and steep precipices. . . . You can here meet with all the beauties so savage and horrid a place can present you with; Rocks of various and uncouth figures, Cascades pouring down from an immense height out of hanging groves of Pine-Trees, & the solemn Sound of the Stream that roars below, all concur to form one of the most poetical scenes imaginable." Mountain landscapes were not conventionally regarded as worthy of regard in Western literature from Virgil through Dante on down to Shakespeare and Milton. It was the rock-star Romantic poets who changed this. William Wordsworth, who called himself "an Islander by birth, a Mountaineer by habit," made a journey of three thousand miles on his first visit to the Alps, more than half on foot. Although the habit of pedestrian travel for pleasure in the mountains was becoming agreeable to many of the Swiss, walking for the rest of the Western world was the curse of the poor. Wordsworth and his friend Robert Jones followed the course of the Rhône and crossed the Simplon Pass into Italy. The result of the trip was a long poem, "Descriptive Sketches Taken during a Pedestrian Tour among the Alps," in which he shares his enthusiasm for a new type of therapy:

> *He holds with God himself communion high*
> *There where the peal of swelling torrents fills*
> *The sky-roofed temple of eternal hills;*
> *Or when, upon the mountain's silent brow*
> *Reclined, he sees, above him and below,*
> *Bright stars of ice and azure fields of snow. . . .*

The bright red, parallelogram-shaped railcar (designed to "lean" uphill) of the Pilatus-bahn, on the final stretch of its thirty-minute ascent.   Photo courtesy of Sara Givens

But while Wordsworth's poetry provoked a desire to see the Alps, politics stepped in the way. Napoleon seized the greater part of what today is Switzerland in 1798, creating the "Helvetic Republic," and few of the English were inclined to visit. But when in 1815 Napoleon was defeated at Waterloo and the Congress of Vienna guaranteed neutrality for Switzerland, the poets came once more, and were no less awed.

George Gordon Byron's take on The Sublime was that it was something distinct from the beauty so often extolled in English gardens: it involved violence and terror mingled with exultation. "Are not the mountains, waves and skies a part of me and of my soul, as I of them?" The Alps were "palaces of Nature," that "throned Eternity in icy halls of cold sublimity." They were the greatest manifestations on earth of the power that had created them. "All that expands the spirit, yet appalls, gather around these summits."

Percy Bysshe Shelley's tributes to grand nature were similar: "terrible, strange, sublime, awful." After experiencing the Alps, he wrote:

The everlasting universe of things
Flows through the mind, and rolls its rapid waves,
Now dark—now glittering—now reflecting gloom—
Now lending splendour, where from secret springs
The source of human thought its tribute brings. . . .

The idols of pattern, regularity, symmetry, restraint, proportion, and vocabulary were broken down and replaced by ideals of diversity, variety, irregularity, indefiniteness, and vastness, and the feelings they provoked. It was something on the other side of thought and language. The flocking of the Victorians to the Swiss Alps was not about growing crops, grazing animals, or extracting minerals. It was about observing, feeling, and articulating a personal response. "To me / High mountains are a feeling," declared the protagonist in Lord Byron's narrative poem "Childe Harold's Pilgrimage." Switzerland became a literary topography as much as a geographical designation. Poets and other artists provided a vocabulary of these landscapes, and the seekers came.

TRANSPORTED
AND AMAZED

I know that many fooles will jeere and frumpe,
That I dare come so neare the Divells Rumpe.

—John Taylor, 1639

take a tour of the top of Pilatus Kulm, passing a pack of young Chinese boys skipping like young rams, then a gaggle of women speaking Russian and wearing so much fur they're practically an ecological disaster. The mountains of the Bernese Oberland are forever tugging at my view. I pause once again to gaze and find myself standing next to a mother and infant, both transfixed by the distant scene. The little boy seems about the same age as my younger son, Jasper, and the look on his face is so familiar, one of wide-eyed astonishment. It seems a look of The Sublime. Anthony Ashley Cooper, third Earl of Shaftesbury, made the Grand Tour in 1686 and then in perhaps prescient advance of the Romantics wrote a rhapsodic account of mountains in *The Moralists*, published in 1709. But he saw The Sublime as a rhetorical term (like Longinus before him), describing a form of literature that appealed only to barbarians and children. He wrote: "'Tis easy to imagine, that amidst the several styles and manners of discourse or writing, the easiest attained and earliest practiced, was the miraculous, the pompous, or what we generally call the sublime. Astonishment is of all other passions the easiest raised in raw and unexperienced mankind. Children in their earliest infancy are entertained in this manner; and the known way of pleasing such as these, is to make them wonder, and lead the way for them in this passion by a feigned surprise at the miraculous objects we set before them." That may be true, and I am as guilty as all parents in this dynamic, but at this moment, on this ledge, with this view, there is astonishment that transcends all generations, all cultures. We all are experiencing what Shaftesbury described as that fine sight that is "amazingly beheld with a kind of horror and consternation."

I pop into the Dragon Shop, where I find a flyer called "History of the Conquest of Mt. Pilatus, an evolutionary success story." It is not

The Dragon Trail on Mount Pilatus tails into a cave dripping with icicles, looking very much like dragon's teeth. The grotto is pocked with window holes, invitations to goat-dizzying views of the mountain falling away into the white profound.
Photo courtesy of Small World Productions

an anticreationist creed but rather a timeline of the various tourism enterprises on the mountain, from the cog railroad to the hotels and restaurants on top. Then I make my way down the Dragon Trail, along a corridor cut into a cliff face. Here I meet the fire-haired Colette Richter, who works as a marketing manager for Mount Pilatus, and she is steeped in dragon tales. One goes that in the summer of 1421, an enormous dragon was flying to Mount Pilatus when it crashed close to a farmer named Stempflin, who fainted from the shock. When he recovered, he found a clot of blood containing a "dragon stone" and took it to the city, where the stone's healing powers were "officially" confirmed, as any ills his family suffered were miraculously cured. It was said to be a nostrum for "haemorrhage, dysentery, diarrhoea, poisoning, plague, and nosebleeds." It may be the source reason that so many pharmaceutical firms are based today in Switzerland.

Colette tells another story of a young cooper who went wandering the mountain in the autumn searching for rods with which to make barrel hoops. He fell into a deep cave and landed between two fire-breathing dragons. The dragons nurtured the drop-in through the winter, feeding him moon milk, whatever that is. When spring came, one of the dragons helped the cooper by holding out its tail as a bridge for him to scale so he could exit the dark cave. Then it flew the inadvertent guest on its leathern wings to a lowland meadow and carefully alighted. When the cooper got back to the city, he had the tale of his adventure embroidered on a silken tunicle, which remains today under glass at the Church of St. Leodegar in Lucerne.

Petermann Etterlin, one of the early sixteenth-century Swiss authors who told the tale of William Tell, also wrote of how regional Governor Winkelried killed one of the termagant dragons: he wrapped thorny branches around a long lance and pushed this into the dragon's open mouth; then he finished off the beast with his sword. A drop of poisonous dragon's blood fell on his hand, which somehow made his own blood freeze. The dying dragon exhaled one last poisonous breath on Winkelried, and that was the end of both.

On the morning of May 26, 1499, after a violent night storm, the townspeople of Lucerne gaped in amazement as a giant, wingless dragon lurched out of the River Reuss near the Spreuer bridge. They assumed it had washed down the mountain in the storm and was just trying to get home. As recently as 1649, the local sheriff said he saw an evil dragon come out of a cave on Mount Pilatus. He said that its head "terminated in the serrated jaw of a serpent" and that it flew about, "throwing out sparks like a red-hot horseshoe hammered by the blacksmith."

The trail tails into a cave dripping with icicles, looking very much like dragon's teeth. The grotto is pocked with window holes, invitations to goat-dizzying views of the mountain falling away into the white profound. Pilatus abounds in pterodactyl fossils, and it's easy to imagine them flying about this precipice. Now, though, the only flying creatures I see through the hole in the rock are the alpine dohlen drawing lazy naughts across the sky.

Then, after my lunch of *pastetli* (meat pie) and a tankard of Braugold, the local beer made with pure Pilatus water, at the 1900-built Hotel Pilatus-Kulm, the sky turns lurid. A cold vapor seems to be heaving in, like the breath of a dragon. Shadows of clouds smudge the snow at my feet. The valleys seem to be multiplying themselves in the mist. Of course, ghosts and medieval dragons and monks protecting virgins from ogres cannot exist here. Or can they? It's easy to believe in their reality here, no matter the pedigree of the skeptic. The Danish Nobel Prize–winning physicist Niels Bohr, who nailed a horseshoe above his office door for good luck, was asked by a colleague, "You don't really believe in this stuff, do you?" To which Bohr replied, "No, but I've heard it works even for people who don't believe."

And so I take the aerial tramway down the north side, the cable car floating like a sun-filled bubble into dense cloud to the station of Fräkmüntegg, developed as a sort of midmountain adventure theme park. There is the biggest suspension rope park in central Switzerland, a terrifying zip line, and the Frakigaudi Rodelbahn, the longest summer toboggan run in Switzerland, a shiny steel dragon's tail of a track almost a mile long down which a rider barrels on a wheeled sled.

John Baillie in his 1747 essay described sublimity as a "contradictory" sensation of pleasure and pain: "The Sublime dilates and elevates the Soul, Fear sinks and contracts it; yet both are felt upon viewing what is great and awful."

The key word here is "viewing." For Baillie there is a difference between being in the actual battle and contemplating it from afar. Where the former involves a real possibility of death, the latter is just the thought of it. And as I charge down this toboggan run at frightening speeds, at the edge of capsizing on the sharp curves, feeling the torque and rattle in my bones, my heart feathering through my breast, it occurs to me that this is a modern example of Baillie's sublime. It is pleasurable because I am reasonably certain that the groove down which I am plummeting will contain me from catastrophe. The toboggan run mimics the suicidal descent into the abyss, providing me with a glimpse of what a free fall down the mountain might really be like. Hurtling down this mountain track, banking through the sharp turns and shooting through tunnels like a bullet, I feel energized, vibrantly alive, and I can't stop myself from heading back up the mountain to be kicked downstairs three more times.

Hotel Pilatus-Kulm, constructed in 1900, straddles the dragon peak of Mount Pilatus. Photo courtesy of Sara Givens

Then I take the gondola from Fräkmüntegg to Kriens, the wind against the window like the beating of leather wings. Safely at the bottom station, I load up on postcards, one of my last analog ardors. In the late nineteenth century, when Switzerland introduced cards that could be mailed with color pictures covering one side, they were shortcuts to The Sublime and graphic harbingers of envy. What other purpose do they serve than to say, "I'm here and you're not"? I'm as guilty as any in employing these tidbits of schadenfreude, but I am in good company. Leslie Stephen wrote to an American friend in the middle nineteenth century: "You poor Yankees are to be pitied in many things, but for nothing as much as your distance from Switzerland."

Back to Lucerne for the night I head, driving through the blades and bars of moonlight. From the hotel window, I overlook a string of lakeside lanterns. Above, the full moon hangs minted against the sky like a bright Swiss five-franc piece. Outlined against the glow is the sleeping black cat of Pilatus. Legend links the name *Lucerne* (from the Latin *lucerna,* meaning "lamp") with an angel who, with light streaming from his fingertips, indicated to eighth-century Benedictine monks the site on which they should build the city's first chapel. It was Richard Price who, in an 1789 pamphlet called *Discourse on the Love of Our Country,* described his ideas of illuminating Europe: "Light becomes a liberating sublime, driving out the false, oppressive sublime of darkness and obscurity through which kings terrorize the people." The nineteenth-century painter-philosopher John Ruskin called it "the unfatigued veracity of eternal light." In that sense, Lucerne is the right kind of sublime.

LEADING THE MIND BEYOND WHAT THE EYE SEES

However great a man may be, there are always some subjects which ought to throw him off his balance; some, by which his poor human capacity of thought should be conquered, and brought into the inaccurate and vague state of perception, so that the language of the highest inspiration becomes broken, obscure, and wild in metaphor.

—John Ruskin, 1856

The day following, I decide to see how Lucerne has memorialized itself with museums. The first stop is a sort of poor man's Mount Rushmore, a carving in a sandstone cliff of a dying lion slouching toward a hushed water-lily pond. Danish sculptor Albert Bertel Thorvaldsen designed the beast, carved by his students. The thirty-foot-long lion protects the French lily coat of arms and commemorates the Swiss Guards (twenty-six officers and seven hundred soldiers) killed defending Louis XVI's palace in Paris in 1792 during the French Revolution. Mark Twain described the Lion of Lucerne as "the saddest and most moving piece of rock in the world," which even for the hyperbolist seems a bit of a stretch. Just beyond, I meet Peter Wick, director of Gletschergarten (Glacier Garden), a lost world of glacial sculpting discovered in 1872 by Joseph Wilhelm Amrein-Troller when he was renovating a wine cellar in Lucerne. It's a series of giant, glacially polished potholes and boulders, remnants of the last ice age, created some twenty thousand years ago. Dialing the Wayback Machine even further back, Gletschergarten includes fossilized mussels and palm-leaf imprints, collapsing time to some 20 million years earlier, when this grove in the heart of Switzerland was a tropical oasis with a palm beach. With a few steps, I feel robbed of any conventional grip on time; human history seems a momentary blink against the immense scroll of eternity embedded in the rock here. This, I believe, is a crystallization of the concept "sublime."

It's hard to find an uninspiring journey in Switzerland, even a simple walk, and time seems to shiver and swirl like wind-scattered leaves as I stroll along the Quaianlage (the lakefront walkway). I find my way to the Bourbaki Panorama, which seems to express The Sublime as Irish philosopher Edmund Burke essayed, in that it allows consideration of battle without participation. In a pre-cinema experience, the visitor stands in the middle of a giant, round diorama. A circular painting, created by Edouard Castres in 1881, is dimensionalized with twenty-one life-size figures, a railway carriage, fences, weapons, bandages, and blood. The frozen scene depicts an incident from the Franco-Prussian War, specifically the internment of the French Eastern Army under General Bourbaki during a brutal winter in 1871. The French, chased by the Germans, sought asylum and voluntary imprisonment across the border in Switzerland.

Burke's 1757 treatise *A Philosophical Enquiry into the Origin of Our Ideas of the Sublime and Beautiful* tried to account for the passions evoked in the human mind by what Burke called "terrible objects." He was interested in our psychic response to things—a rushing cataract, a soaring cliff face, an avalanche—that seized, terrified, and yet also somehow pleased the mind by dint of being too big, too high, too fast, too powerful, too uncontrollable to be properly comprehended. These sights inspired a heady blend of pleasure and terror; these were sights of The Sublime. In Burke's theory, beauty, which was about balance and grace, has a relaxing effect on the "fibers of the body," whereas sublimity tightens these same fibers. He wrote: "Whatever is fitted in any sort to excite the ideas of pain and danger, that is to say, whatever is in any sort terrible, or is conversant about terrible objects, or operates in a manner analogous to terror, is a source of the *Sublime;* that is, it is productive of the strongest emotion which the mind is capable of feeling." He went on to summarize that terror was a passion which "always produces delight when it does not press too close." So, as when riding on a mountain train or viewing a violent scene in a theater or reading a murder mystery, it is the suggestion of harm, melded with the knowledge that no harm will likely come, that induces the sensation of delightful terror. It's why we rubberneck while passing auto accidents, why we ride roller coasters, and why we take adventure-travel trips.

An Avalanche in the Alps

Because the mind is both attracted and repelled by a sublime object, Immanuel Kant identified The Sublime as a "negative pleasure"—a paradoxical pleasure. His versions of The Sublime include a violent storm, a rampaging avalanche, a raging lake—any powerfully frightening natural force or set of forces, all of which are in abundance in Switzerland. The Sublime, in this sense, contrasted with the picturesque. The picturesque was pretty, of a human scale; The Sublime was vast, powerful, forbidding, terrifying, and awe-inspiring, and held the possibility of death.

Some seasons back, I made a trip to Patagonia and immersed myself in the writings of Charles Darwin, who was influenced by philosophical articulations of The Sublime. At one point, from the deck of the *Beagle,* he stood in awe watching the eruption of Mount Osorno; on land, he felt earthquakes. It has been said that these intensely powerful geological events along the Chilean coast prompted his understanding of change. His reception of the mechanics of dynamic landscape was what later triggered his considerations on the transmutation of species. While on sail, he wrote: "How opposite are the sensations when viewing black mountains half enveloped in clouds, and seeing another range through the light blue haze of a fine day! The one for a time may be very sublime; the other is all gaiety and happy life."

A little later in the day, I take a walk over to the Swiss Museum of Transport, the most-visited museum in Switzerland. It promotes itself as "the most comprehensive traffic museum in Europe," a distinction that makes a difference when tackling transportation over, around, and through the Alps. It is showing the IMAX movie *The Alps,* which features John Harlin III's Eiger climb that I covered. Judging by the lines, I would say it is the most popular thing going at the museum. But the whole place is buzzing, and it is packed with cars, planes, bikes, and trains from the steamy past, including two of the original steam cars from the Pilatusbahn. But my absolute favorite artifact is a piece of machinery named for the Lord of the Nile, an original "Crocodile Train," a green-hided electric locomotive with a long snout at each end connected by an articulated center section. These Swiss Crocodiles were developed for pulling heavy-goods trains on the vertiginous tracks of the Gotthardbahn from Lucerne to Chiasso, including the forbidding Gotthard Tunnel.

The electric motors available at the time were large and had to be body-mounted, but flexibility was required to negotiate the tight curves of the Alpine routes and tunnels. An articulated design, with two powered nose units bridged with a pivoting center section containing cabs and the heavy transformer, met both requirements and gave good visibility from driving cabs mounted safely away from the point of any collision. These green machines served successfully until the 1980s but now rest as relics.

In the lengthening shadows of the day, I walk up the River Reuss into the old town to Wirtshaus Taube, a traditional Swiss restaurant, and meet Mark Meier, the overseas marketing manager for the Lucerne Tourist Board. After the wurst meal, a second bottle of wine is plunked onto the big wooden table, and Mark shares that there is no universal field theory of The Sublime, but that its tie-in to tourism is well recorded. He offers to give me a history of tourism in Switzerland.

Tourists, Mark explains, were pretty much unknown in the Swiss Confederation during the Middle Ages. Scenery was not a motivation. The early travelers stepping across Swiss soil included pilgrims on the way to Rome or Santiago de Compostela in Spain, Crusaders heading for the Holy Land, mercenaries en route to military service abroad, messengers and tradesmen journeying between markets, and smugglers and other criminals. Most of these voyagers avoided the "hills whose heads touch heaven," afraid of the uncanny powers that lurked within.

Still, the first stirrings of a Swiss "foreign-tourist industry" date back to pre-Reformation times. The mineral waters of the Alps began to appeal to Roman nobility seeking health and comfort at natural spas, and some made the trek to higher climes to cool off in the summer months. Switzerland became Rome's sanatorium.

In the Reformation era of the sixteenth century, daring naturalists started to poke about the upper landscapes of Lucerne. In 1518, four Swiss humanists undertook the ascent of Pilatus, as described in 1522 in Latin by one of the participants, Joachim von Watt. In the latter year a "tourist from a foreign land"—namely Ulrich, Duke of Württemberg—climbed Pilatus for the first time.

Following these "conquests," as they were oft called, more disciplines were drawn to the upper reaches. In 1541, Conrad Gesner of Zurich described the splendor of the Alpine world and the pure, noble pleasures of mountaineering ("*de admiratione montium*") in a letter to his friend James Vogel: "Men dull in mind find no cause for wonder anywhere; they idly sit at home instead of going to see what is on view in the great theatre of the world; . . . therefore I declare that man to be an enemy of nature who does not esteem high mountains

The author at the Swiss Museum of Transport, "the most comprehensive traffic museum in Europe"—a significant distinction when tackling transportation over, around, and through the Alps.   Photo courtesy of Small World Productions

worthy of long study. Of a truth the highest parts of the loftiest peaks seem to be above the laws that rule our world below, as if they belonged to another sphere. Up there the action of the all-powerful sun is not the same, nor is that of the air of the winds. There the snow is everlasting and this softest of substances that melts between our fingers cares nothing for the fierceness of the sun and its burning rays. So far is it from disappearing with the lapse of time that it passes into hardest ice and crystals that nothing can dissolve."

Gesner was one of the first thinkers to propose the idea that the world of the Alps constituted a world apart: an upper realm where physical laws operated differently and conventional lowland ideas of time and space were upended and unhinged. The terrestrial mountains, in other words, were as fantastic as the moon.

Then, on August 20, 1555, Gesner and a few friends, carrying a "sustaining quantity of wine," climbed Mons Pilatus and summited without incident. With a bellow of his alphorn he celebrated their survival. Yet it took another thirty years before anyone made another attempt. In 1585, Pastor Johann Müller of Lucerne made the climb and deliberately cast stones into the gray waters of the lake in provocation of any supernatural entities that might have been lurking there. The waters didn't erupt, the ghost of Pilate did not rise, and no cataclysm overtook Lucerne. The emblematic exorcism is now credited by some scholars as being the beginning of the banishment of superstition from Western imagining of the mountains.

It was no coincidence that this period witnessed the appearance of several detailed descriptions with appended maps of the then-Confederation. In 1538, a first outline map of Switzerland, by Aegidius Tschudi, was published. And then, in 1547, Johannes Stumpf published a thirteen-volume description of the Confederation, with an overview map and detailed accounts of journeys over the Alpine passes. A land was being defined, demystified, and, by some, celebrated.

DELICIOUS SHUDDER

The Alps are broken into so many steps and precipices that they fill the mind with an agreeable kind of horror, and form one of the most irregular, mis-shapen scenes in the world.

—Joseph Addison, 1701

Travel during this era was adventurous and really available only to a few members of the upper classes and the avant-garde, mercenaries and explorers. Roads were dirt poor and largely neglected, and the scantiest of infrastructures awaited travelers in the few hostelries. In 1520, Erasmus of Rotterdam's notes on the inns included these comments: "If you arrive at about 4 o'clock in the afternoon, it will be 9 o'clock before you dine," and, "Even if a weary traveler wants to go to bed immediately after the meal, he is expected to wait until the others retire," and, "The sheets were last washed maybe six months ago."

After a lengthy period of stagnation following the Reformation era because of the damper of wars and religious clashes (the Thirty Years' War and the famines that followed, the peasants' revolts, and the Counter-Reformation movement), travel to Switzerland experienced a revival about 1700. A number of aristocrats, scholars, poets, painters, and pedants traveled through the Confederation, giving euphoric accounts of their impressions. The first major impetus emanated from Johann Jakob Scheuchzer early in the eighteenth century. Then Swiss-born Jean-Jacques Rousseau, the apostle of noble savagery, disseminated these ideas to a broad audience.

From 1702 onward, Scheuchzer traveled regularly through the Alps with his students. He used mathematical and physical instruments to assemble data about the exotic environment of the upland world. After personally trudging over virtually all the known Swiss Alpine passes, he published his *Itinera Alpina* in 1708. A half century later, Rousseau praised the natural beauty of the upper slopes of the Alps in his epistolary novel *Julie, ou la nouvelle Héloïse* in 1761. In one passage he describes the emotional impact of the peaks: "It seems as if, being lifted above all human society, we had left every low terrestrial sentiment behind: and that as we approach the aethereal regions, the soul imbibes something of their eternal purity. Imagine to yourself all these united impressions; the amazing variety, grandeur and beauty, of a thousand astonishing sights; the pleasure of seeing only totally new things, strange birds, odd and unknown plants, to observe what is in some sense another nature, and finding yourself in a new world . . . one isolated in the higher spheres of the earth. In short, there is a kind of supernatural beauty in these mountainous prospects which charms both the senses and the minds into a forgetfulness of oneself and of everything in the world."

The book was a best seller and prompted a whole herd of the literate and leisured to pilgrimage to the Alps. The impact was so intoxicating that Leslie Stephen would assert: "If Rousseau were tried for the crime of setting up mountains as objects of human worship, he would be convicted by an impartial jury."

Scheuchzer and Rousseau catalyzed a development that spoke to a class but was as yet unable to motivate widespread support from the masses. A lengthy period of development was needed before ordinary people could set aside fear of the mountains and reconceptualize notions of nature. Venturing into the peaks remained an elitist pursuit at the same time as praise and poetry spread. But even among the privileged there remained dissent. As late as 1760, Gottlieb Sigmund Gruner described the mountains as "terrible," and in 1770 Johann Caspar Füssli (in his *Description of the States and Terrain of the Swiss Confederation*) observed that Engelberg had "dreadful" mountains and "no fields to gladden the eye."

By the late eighteenth century, young aristocrats, especially from England, completed their educations by taking a journey through Europe, usually in the company of their teachers. Though Switzerland was mostly just a land to pass through on the way to

Italy or some other culturally significant provenience, it often awed in ways not described in the itinerary. (The words *tourism* and *tourist* were probably derived from *tour* or *grand tour* in this period.) Among these grand tourers were Johann Wolfgang von Goethe, Heinrich von Kleist, Carl Maria von Weber, and Felix Mendelssohn. Affluent Swiss families also sent their sons on similar educational trips—mainly through their own country, of course. They were often accompanied by clergymen, some of whom wrote accounts of these journeys. One of the best-known narratives was penned by the vicar Johann Rudolf Schintz, describing his travels in the summer of 1773 with seven young people from Zurich and two servants.

Early travel guides played a key role in developing tourism here. In 1789, William Coxe wrote one of the first systematic travel guides to Switzerland (*Travels in Switzerland,* in three volumes). This was followed in 1793 by *Instructions on Traveling through Switzerland in the Most Useful and Enjoyable Manner* by Germany's Johann Gottfried Ebel. It long remained the most comprehensive travel guide and laid the foundations for other works throughout the nineteenth century. In the first part of his book, Ebel lists everything of importance to know when preparing for a journey to Switzerland; in the second, he gives specific descriptions of travel routes with notes on the means of transport (by carriage, by boat, or on foot), also providing information on the structure and condition of roads and paths. By way of introduction, he comments: "It can reliably be said that there is no country, no part of our earth, which would be so curious and interesting in as many respects as Switzerland. Everything that is great, sublime, extraordinary, and astounding, everything that is terrible and dreadful, all that is defiant, dark, and melancholic, everything that is romantic, gentle, charming, cheerful, tranquil, refreshing, and idyllic in the whole wide world of nature, seems to have been united here in a small space in order to make this country into the garden of Europe, a place of pilgrimage for all devotees of nature where they should reap reward and satisfaction for their pure sacrifice in the fullest and sheerest measure."

By 1800, scientific reasons were no longer needed to justify a journey; people were now visiting the mountains for pleasure and for broadening personal horizons. The eighteenth-century fear of the mysterious high mountains now gave way to Romantic swooning, to the joy of viewing nature's horrible power. Now a new travel paradigm was dawning: the content of the journey became more important than its destination. Even women were getting into the act. An English journalist in 1801 nicely summed up the trend: "These places have recently acquired a new degree of interest— the geologue, the mineralist, and mere amateur, repair thither with avidity; and even women are amply indemnified for the fatigue of the journey by the pleasure arising from the view of objects entirely new to them."

Scientists had been energetically interrogating the mountains for their disciplines, but then climbing became a pursuit for its own sake. The Jungfrau was climbed in 1811, the Finsteraarhorn in the Bernese Oberland in 1812, and the most dramatic peak in the known world, the Matterhorn, in 1865. The years from 1854 to 1865 became known as the "Golden Years of Alpinism."

Mountaineers, most of them British, most of them wealthy members of the upper professional classes, academics, or even aristocrats, vied to be the first to conquer Alpine peaks. In response to the foundation of the British Alpine Club in 1857, the Swiss Alpine Club was established in 1863, and before long there were similar clubs throughout Europe.

A storm gathers in the Alps.   Photo courtesy of John Canning

One of the collateral developments of this newfound activity was the advent of the Alpine guide. With few exceptions, the visiting mountaineers ventured into the high mountain ranges accompanied by "pointers-out of paths," many of whom were former farmers, herders, hunters, and smugglers who had taken to this new profession and its enticing economics.

The shores of Lake Geneva, the central Bernese Oberland, and Inner Switzerland, including Lucerne and the now-renowned peaks of Pilatus and Rigi, developed into must-see regions during this period. In 1823, the steamer *Guillaume Tell* was launched on Lake Geneva, inaugurating the age of boat travel for tourists on

European lakes. Lake Lucerne saw its first steamer in 1837. Within fifty years, steamer services had been introduced on all the major Swiss lakes.

Festivals prompted a set of cultural tourists to Inner Switzerland and beyond. The first Swiss Music Festival was held on the slopes of Rigi in 1808, overlooking Lake Lucerne. Festivals featuring wrestlers, stone throwers, marksmen, alphorn players, and singers in an intact rural mountain setting dovetailed with the ideas and feelings of the Romantic era, feelings and ideas that were gripping much of Europe. The festival fever continues today, with some gala every week of the year. There's even a comedy festival in Lucerne, which some in Europe find a funny concept in and of itself.

Literature began to find potent settings in Switzerland in the early nineteenth century. Schiller's play *William Tell* (published in 1804) is set around Lake Lucerne. In 1808, Madame de Staël wrote descriptions of the festivals at Unspunnen and in the countryside. Lord Byron stayed by Lake Geneva in 1816, and accompanied by friends he traveled through much of the country, including the Bernese Oberland. His poems "The Prisoner of Chillon" and "Childe Harold's Pilgrimage" are set on Lake Geneva, and his tragedy "Manfred" takes place primarily in the Bernese Oberland.

Another stream began to merge with these cultural rivers to expand awareness of Switzerland as a place to see. A new form of art found fashion: large-scale landscapes. In 1792, the first panorama of the world was showcased in London, complete with idealized mountains and beautiful views of Swiss-like settings. In 1814, manufacturers at Rixheim near Mulhouse in the Alsace began to produce wallpaper for the parlors of Europe's upper classes featuring peaks, glaciers, and idyllic pastoral scenes of charming cabins and flocks grazing on Alpine meadows.

The incipient flow of foreign visitors prompted the development of a hotel industry. In the late eighteenth century, vicarages, provincial governors' castles, and private country seats were used as accommodations befitting the status of the increasingly sophisticated tourists, while the first pensions came into being shortly after 1800. Here in Lucerne, 1833 marked the start of construction on the lakeside promenade (the Quaianlage), where several illustrious hotels were built in succession: the Schweizerhof in 1845, the Grand National in 1871, and the Palace in 1906. New spa resorts with railway access found fashion around Lake Lucerne: on the Rigi, above Brunnen, on the Seelisberg, and on the Bürgenstock. Lucerne became a watering hole for the elite of Europe, drawing Queen Victoria in 1868 and Emperor Wilhelm II in 1893.

The first mountain inns appeared after 1815 just as paths to the mountain peaks were being developed. The first inn on Rigi Kulm opened in 1816, followed by a second hotel in 1856 and the large Hotel Schreiber in 1875, after the opening of the Rigibahn, Europe's oldest rack railway. In the Bernese Oberland, the first mountaintop inn was opened on the Faulhorn in 1823 as the highest hostelry in Europe at that time. It was soon followed by the inns on the Wengenalp and the Kleine Scheidegg, where I spent several weeks covering John Harlin III's Eiger attempt. In the same period, tourists first ventured into the previously shunned valleys, including Zermatt in 1839.

Napoleon I crossed the Great St. Bernard Pass, unsteadily, on a mule in 1800. Though he may have been disappointed with what he found, his wife, Josephine, imported a Swiss farmer and his wife, plus seven cows and a bull, to live in a mock-Alpine chalet on the outskirts of Paris. Development of pass crossings started in the Valais (not yet part of Switzerland) when Napoleon went on to build Europe's first high Alpine road over the Simplon a few years later. Immediately after

the Congress of Vienna, with its realignment of the European powers, the canton of the Grisons built a network of commercial roads,
and the Romantic poets came calling. In 1816, Byron, Shelley, and
Shelley's soon-to-be wife, Mary Wollstonecraft Godwin, made a trip
to Geneva that ended up influencing the world. The two men applied
all their skills to poems in honor of the Alps. Percy Shelley wrote in a
letter: "I never knew—I never imagined what mountains were before.
The immensity of these aerial summits excited, when they suddenly
burst upon the sight, a sentiment of ecstatic wonder, not unallied to
madness." And Mary found an infatuation with ice that would produce the story of Frankenstein. "The mighty Alps, whose white and
shining pyramids and domes towered above all, as belonging to another earth, the habitations of another race of beings," the gothic author
wrote about the alien aspects of the mountains about her.

chapter six

CARRIED AND COOKED

Sublime places gently move us to acknowledge limitations that we might otherwise encounter with anxiety or anger in the ordinary flow of events. It is not just nature that defies us. Human life is as overwhelming. But it is the vast spaces of nature that perhaps provide us with the finest, the most respectful reminder of all that exceeds us. If we spend time in them, they may help us to accept more graciously the great, unfathomable events that molest our lives and will inevitably return us to dust.

—Alain de Botton, 2002

The mid–nineteenth century ushered in a shift from luxury tourism to a more available type. In 1855, Thomas Cook— the Richard Branson of his day—brought a tour group from England to the Continent for the first time, paving the way for cross sections of society to experience what had long been the province of the privileged.

Born in 1808, Thomas Cook was the son of a Derbyshire farm laborer. As a preteen, he left school to become a gardener's boy, a wood turner, and then a printer before creating a new industry he called "excursionism." The driving force of his obsession lay in his Baptist Christianity. Just out of his teens, he became a village missionary, and by his thirties he was active in the temperance movement. His business in 1841 was the printing of temperance tracts. Setting out to walk to town in June of that year, he had a vision: "A thought flashed through my brain—what a glorious thing it would be if the newly developed powers of railways and locomotives could be made subservient to the promotion of temperance!" he wrote. Travel to uplifting places, he posited, was a potent alternative to mere exhortations on the evils of drink. His first tour to the Alps, from June 26 through July 15, 1863, took a party of sixty-two to Geneva and the surrounding mountains, and it spawned the Anglicization of the Alps in Switzerland. Of the influence of one of his excursions, Cook wrote that it "provides food for the mind; it contributes to the strength and enjoyment of the intellect; it helps pull men out of the mire and pollution of old corrupt customs; it promotes a feeling of universal brotherhood; it accelerates the march of peace and virtue, and love; it also contributes to the health of the body, by a relaxation from the toil and the invigoration of the physical powers." One of his early customers for a trip to Switzerland met him during the journey and called him "a saint!" By the

1880s, Thomas Cook & Son of Ludgate Circus, London, was far and away the largest travel agency in the world.

It was as if the Swiss Alps made possible the obsolescence of the old ideas of rank and inherited aristocracy. Social pretensions were subsumed in the new democratic tourism. Numbers grew through the rest of the century, to the point that the French author Alphonse Daudet wrote in 1888 that Switzerland was a huge *kursaal* (public hall) with opening hours from June until September. The ubiquitous impulse to leave the beaten track had been tapped and its fulfillment made available.

The Belle Epoque ushered in the birth of advertising for tourism: railways and hotels began using large posters to draw attention to themselves about 1870 (at the same time as the rapid development of photography and spread of the railways). Early posters mostly used a number of graphic elements as "pictorial broadsheets" to advertise the resort, the hotel, or the railway. Toward the turn of the century, a naturalistic style of illustration developed which was to make Swiss poster art famous throughout the world.

With the emergence of small-photo printing technology about 1875, picture postcards popped onto the scene, marking the beginnings of viral marketing and user-generated content. In 1899, a British newspaper reported: "The travelling Teuton seems to regard it as his solemn duty to send a postcard off from each stop on his travels, as if he were on a paper-chase."

The sale of souvenirs also became established as part of tourism during the Belle Epoque. In the early nineteenth century, large items such as landscape wallpaper, pictures, or even whole houses were being offered for wealthy tourists to take home with them. The appearance of large masses of tourists led to the invention of the small "takeaway" souvenir, and kitsch was born. Landscape pictures, wood carvings, and pottery became especially popular. Some painters earned their livings in the late nineteenth century as landscape painters in hotels and on promenades at tourist resorts. One of the most famous figures in Inner Switzerland at this time was Josef Zelger (1812–1885), whose paintings of mountains were much in demand after Queen Victoria of England visited his studio in 1868.

Winter sport, in which the English played a major part, had its origin in the Grisons, though it's reported that the appearance of the first skiers in 1859 had the locals shaking their heads in amusement. Things got serious fast: St. Moritz played host to its first winter guests in the mid-1860s. In 1872, on the suggestion of bladers from Vienna, St. Moritz held its first ice-skating competition. It was not until 1888 that the Hotel Baer in Grindelwald became the first establishment in the Bernese Oberland to open during the winter, although an English book titled *Two Seasons in Switzerland* was already promoting winter holidays in the Alpine country by 1895. The first cable railways specifically built for winter sports (on the Allmendhubel and to Chantarella) opened in the winter of 1912 at Mürren and St. Moritz.

Skiing grew up to be a glamour child in the Engadine by the start of the 1880s. Following a winter expedition over the Pragel Pass in Glarus in 1893, the first ski club in Switzerland was founded. The first Swiss ski jumps were attempted as long ago as 1895 in St. Moritz. The first ski races, in the form of distance skiing and jumping competitions, were staged in Bern and Glarus in 1902, and there was even a downhill event from Gurten to Wabern in Bern. The Swiss Ski Federation was established in Olten in 1904. The following year, skiers met in Glarus for Switzerland's first major official ski races, with a long-distance event over the Pragel Pass, a jumping event (the winning jump was fifty-five feet), and a separate ladies' race. Competitive Nordic skiing also made its breakthrough the same year.

In 1882, the first European Ice-Skating Championships were staged at St. Moritz. New ice sports were invented, such as "skijoring," in which skiers are pulled over ice by horses. In 1884, the first bobsleigh race was staged on the road from St. Moritz to Celerina after an English winter visitor invented this new piece of sports equipment by joining two skeletons together. The first curling match on the European mainland was held at St. Moritz in 1880. The first ice-hockey game in Switzerland took place in 1888 in the Upper Engadine. Ice tourism was quickly becoming an economic linchpin for the Swiss Alps.

Tourism to Switzerland reached an apex prior to the First World War, with more than a million visitors a year. In those halcyon days, Europeans traveled from country to country without passports and without changing money. In Lucerne in 1910, more than 192,000 guests registered during the tourist season of May to October in the 111 hotels and pensions offering 8,500 beds. With the advent of war, guests left for the perceived safety of their own homelands; visitors stayed away in droves. The prewar visitation level has never again been achieved. (Last year there were fifty-two hotels in Lucerne offering 5,012 beds.)

The entire infrastructure lay fallow for a long period. Some hotels and railways never recovered from the shock—for example, Switzerland's first aerial cableway from Grindelwald toward the Wetterhorn, which had opened in 1908. There was a massive drop in the number of hotels on the slopes below Rigi Kulm. Most mountain railways experienced a severe crisis lasting well into the 1920s, and there was talk in some places of demolishing the facilities. The tide started to turn only in the midtwenties, when the flow of tourists began to resume due to the improved economic situation.

In the 1920s, winter sports slowly began to develop into popular sporting disciplines when downhill ski events were also included in the winter sporting repertoire. One particular incentive for this change was the second Winter Olympics, held at St. Moritz in 1928. As a consequence, the group of winter sports locations expanded to include all of the Swiss Alps. Finally, in December 1934, the world's first ski lift opened at the practice area of the Davos Ski School. The doors of Alpine skiing were flung wide open.

Summer tourism began to recover slowly after the First World War. Although the 1920s brought several setbacks, tourists started to arrive in greater numbers, allowing further investments in the tourism infrastructure. In 1921 the curtain was raised on the automobile era for mass tourism on mountain roads when the postal bus lines over the Grimsel and Furka passes opened.

For Lucerne, the recovery started in earnest during and after World War II, when the lakeside city became a popular R & R destination for soldiers on furlough. My father, who served in France, may have been one: he fell in love with a Frenchwoman and swept her away to a mountainside retreat, though he is gone now so I will never know for sure exactly where they went. If he did find romance in Lucerne, he was not alone. The neutrality of the waterfront retreat in the middle of the dogfights of empires implanted Lucerne in the American mind as a piece of paradise. It has remained a favorite ever since. There were more than a million hotel nights in 2007, with about 180,000 American visitors (second only to Germans), and tourist income for the city exceeded 715 million Swiss francs. (Switzerland is not part of the Eurozone.) For the whole of Switzerland, there were 1.6 million overnights from the United States in 2007. In 1878, the *Grand Dictionnaire universel du XIXe siècle* described a tourist as "someone who travels out of thirst for knowledge, as a pastime, and because he or she enjoys it." The description did not address The Sublime, the draw to the flame of mountains, but whatever the ingredients, they hold sway today and fuel an industry with the deepest roots in nature on earth.

Finally, over a glass of Williams schnapps, I ask Mark how he sees the future of tourism here. "The future will be exactly like the past, only more expensive," he says with a grin.

That night is a restless one, perhaps from jet lag, but also from turning thoughts. Then I hear the sounds of a storm drumming up. I get up and pull back the curtain to see jagged flashes across the sky, as though a distant war is going on atop Pilatus. I fall back to bed, my mind short-circuited with itself.

TO TELL THE TRUTH

J'aime mieux un russeau qui sur la molle arène
Dans un pré plein de fleurs lentement se promène,
Qu'un torrent débordé qui, d'un cours orageux,
Roule, plein de gravier, sur un terrain fangeux.

—Nicolas Boileau-Despréaux, "L'Art Poétique," 1674

Switzerland is anything but neutral when it comes to landscapes, and a boat trip around the glacier-fed Lake Lucerne is all the proof needed. I catch a ferryboat called the *Uri*, one of five restored paddle steamers built between 1901 and 1929—though with true Swiss eco-sensibility, coal has been replaced by cleaner-burning oil. The vessel is part of a boat-train system called The William Tell Express, which is of course anything but express as the ferry plies the pearlescent waters of the starfish-shaped lake, the body of water with Europe's most extensive inland navigation system.

It is a clear day, and there seems an unbroken wholeness in the flowing movement of our prow. We sail from shore to shore, stopping at every town of any size. Every village seems to have a hotel named Beau Rivage, or "beautiful shore." Each is aptly named. Every town has a white church with a steeple topped by a golden ball. Water streams into valleys direct from melting rivers of snow, creating gorges, waterfalls, and cuts harrowed into the bedrock. On some cliff walls, layers of limestone are folded like blankets. Meadows appear as carefully manicured as golf greens. There are red-soil orchards everywhere, but today the most profitable crop is tourism.

Taking a break from the scenery, I step into the wood-paneled lounge. There, I meet Martina Kälin, a local historian, who volunteers to be my guide as we churn the deep waters. Martina is from nearby Altdorf, most famous perhaps for its monument to William Tell. She studied history and medieval archaeology at the University of Zurich and specializes in the Lucerne region.

Once out into the main part of the lake, we're surrounded by mountain scenery that overspills its boundaries. Martina points out the cable car from Weggis to Mount Rigi scything through the trees.

Farther along, she points at the oldest rack railway in Europe scrabbling up the slopes to the hook-shouldered summit from a station beside the pier at Vitznau.

We make a stop at the storybook village of Brunnen and buy some ultracreamy ice cream. Martina says the town of Schwyz, just inland from Brunnen, is the source of the name Switzerland (*Schweiz* in German).

On the Brunnen jetty, turning my gaze from the village to the lake, I stand like a stopped clock. My eyes traverse along the most striking demesne. To the south are the snowy peaks around the Gotthard; directly across are the misty cliffs of Seelisberg, and to the east the dots of Lucerne. This is a place that has attracted the high and mighty. Martina tells me the mad King Ludwig II of Bavaria took a real shine to Brunnen. During a stay in 1865, he reputedly ordered his boatmen to row him out at midnight into the middle of the lake with a team of alphorn blowers to spend the small hours reveling in the mournful, ethereal sound of the alphorn echoing back and forth, thanks to the sonic architecture of the surrounding mountains. Winston Churchill spent his honeymoon in Brunnen. In 1998, Hillary Clinton came here after attending the World Economic Summit in Davos. And now us.

Almost opposite Brunnen, the boat calls at the tiny landing stage of Treib, with its adjacent chevron-shuttered chalet and dark wood station for the funicular that disappears into the trees on its way to Seelisberg. Turning south through the narrows around the headland on which Treib is situated, the boat enters the Urnersee, or Lake of Uri, the eastern leg of Lake Lucerne.

Above a rock on the west shore stands an obelisk in memory of the German poet and dramatist Friedrich von Schiller, whose play about William Tell did so much to develop nineteenth-century tourism in the area. When I ask the historian Martina about the history of William Tell, she gives me a saucy smile and corrects me: the topic is not "history" but rather "legend."

"It is not the reality that is important; it is the idea. This is the heart of Switzerland. But it's more than a geographical center. It is an ideological center. This place makes Swiss proud. My two-and-a-half-year-old son, Thomas, loves coming here."

William Tell stands alongside such fabled characters as Robin Hood, El Cid, and Ivanhoe as a symbol of freedom from political oppression. It hardly matters whether Tell existed or not. Many Swiss claim he did, despite the absence of any real evidence, though the legend is very precise: it was on November 18, 1307, in Altdorf, above Lake Uri, that Tell refused to bow to a symbol of Austrian authority and had to shoot an apple off his son's head in order to save them both. Even the place where he is supposed to have leapt to freedom from the boat in which he was being taken to prison is commemorated by a chapel close to the pier near Sisikon.

I ask Martina to share the "legend," and she delights in the telling:

By lore, William Tell was an unlikely hero. When he and his small son, Walter, walked from Buerglen into Altdorf one day, they passed by a pole with a hat on top in the main square. They did not realize that Hermann Gessler, Austria's blowhard bailiff in charge of the region, demanded that people bow to his hat, which he hung on a pole in the marketplace of Altdorf. Tell refused the subservient act.

Gessler took Tell's lack of obsequiousness personally and offered a choice: either the father would be executed on the spot, or he could try to shoot an apple off his son's head with his crossbow. Tell was an able archer, so he drew his bow, then neatly split the apple with his arrow.

Annoyed, Gessler mocked him: why did he carry a second arrow when one would have sufficed? Tell replied that if the first arrow had harmed his son, he would have aimed the second one at Gessler, adding, "I would not have missed thy heart."

The defiant words are actually those of Friedrich von Schiller, and without him this might have been just another heroic account soaked in local myth, or the upshot of the narcissism of small differences. But Schiller's play *William Tell* was a resounding success, and the tale went around the world.

Because the Swiss officially declared their freedom on January 1, 1308, Schiller, an outspoken lover of Helvetic liberty, called his play "A New Year's Gift to the World."

Yet Schiller never set foot in Switzerland. He heard the tale in Weimar from his friend and colleague Johann Wolfgang von Goethe, who had visited Tellskapelle, part of the Tell trail. Like Goethe, Schiller thrilled to the story, though he had to ask his publisher for a map of Lake Lucerne and environs.

Guglielmo Tell, the Italian opera by Gioacchino Rossini based on the play, was first performed in 1829. The music is exceedingly familiar to me and many Americans of my generation, as the overture provided the theme for *The Lone Ranger* on radio and TV. To a new generation, it is a too-popular cell-phone ring tone and the music behind a fashionable YouTube video in which "The William Tell Mom" (comedian Anita Renfroe) spouts everything a mother says in a day, condensed into two minutes and fifty-five seconds! Unmoored from the myths then and now, I can't help but hum the galloping melody as we ride these legendary waters.

Martina continues with the story. Tell's deeds did not end with the apple. The enraged Gessler ordered the archer arrested and imprisoned for life in the dungeon of Gessler's castle at Kuessnacht. But the boat carrying the prisoner found itself engulfed in a storm on Lake Lucerne, and the frightened boatmen released Tell (who, providentially, was also an expert pilot) to steer them to shore. Once there, he leapt to safety on a rock—called today Tellsplatte. We sail right by this legendary, ledgelike crag, almost within jumping range. The story continues that Tell, after reaching shore, pushed the boat back into the raging water and escaped through the forest. It was only a matter of time until he intercepted Gessler in a gully and dispatched the tyrant with that extra arrow to his heart. "This is Tell's shaft," Gessler wheezed with his last breath. Tell died later during a fitting act: rescuing a drowning child.

Martina reminds me that if the tale seems a bit of a stretch, not to mind. The end of Gessler, however he was dispatched, was the first step to throwing out the Hapsburgs, the overlords from the north—and it was the beginning of Swiss freedom. A bronze statue of Tell and his son dominates the town square in Altdorf, Martina's home, and the crossbow is the proud trademark of Switzerland. For much of the world, William Tell is an allegory for outstanding marksmanship—in my own fumy youth, I invoked his name when aiming at the bull's-eye in summer-camp archery class—but here he is the magical symbol of liberation.

Today, detailed images of Tell—a man for whom there is no confirmed record of a sighting—are rendered on stamps, on coins, on chocolate, as statues, on restaurants, on boats, on trains, even on the bottle of beer I'm swigging.

We next paddle across the lake to the Rütli Meadow, which also has countrywide resonance and controversy. It is regarded by most as the cradle of Swiss democracy, the founding site of the Swiss Confederation, though some say this too is a myth.

The story goes that at this sloping meadow on August 1, 1291, a sort of Three Musketeers pledge took place when peasants from the adjoining forest cantons of Schwyz, Uri, and Unterwalden affirmed the "Everlasting League," swearing never again to be ruled by a foreign power, crafting the Swiss equivalent of America's Declaration of Independence. In 1940, when Switzerland was surrounded by countries either controlled or occupied by Axis powers and a German invasion was feared, the Swiss army commander in chief summoned his entire officer corps to the meadow to reaffirm their loyalty and commitment to the Swiss Confederation and Swiss neutrality. Even though it can be reached only by boat or a long hike, the meadow remains one of the most symbolic settings in the country, a place that evokes to most Swiss a sense of righteous self-assurance. Whether the story is myth or reality it took guts and imagination to toss out the overlords, and it required robust fellowship to create a new nation out of a parade of isolated Alpine valleys. Today, some down-to-earth spirit of jollity lingers in this place still.

As Martina leads me along a leafy path, we pass blankets of soft grass, a sprinkling of wildflowers that madden the jealous blue sky, stands of straight pines, and three stone benches, monuments to the founding event that supposedly established the world's oldest democracy. "Why can't we all get a lawn?" I quip to Martina, who turns a small, accommodating smile. The meadow doesn't look as though it has changed much over the centuries. Martina tells me that King Ludwig II of Bavaria visited his protégé, Wagner, in Lucerne and tried to buy the Rütli as the site for the composer's new opera house, but the Swiss refused to sell their most hallowed spot. More recently there was an attempt by developers to build a hotel, but local schoolchildren, including Martina's own son, collected money to preserve the site, and it now officially belongs to the children of Switzerland.

chapter eight

THE GEOMETRY OF TURMOIL

You don't need a weatherman to know which way the wind blows.

—Robert Zimmerman, 1965

The next day, the air is crisp and the light buttery and wistful when I meet with Evelyne Mock from Switzerland Tourism in New York. She has just arrived in Lucerne from a seventieth-birthday visit to her father, who lives in Felben near Frauenfeld, about an hour east of Zurich. As I explain the reasons for poking around Switzerland, she lights up with her own version of a sublime personality. "You have to meet one of the *Wetterschmoeckers*!"

"The what?"

"The 'weather sniffers'! They live up a remote valley, but they know nature in a sublime way."

Evelyne offers to be my knight-errant on this quest and drives me up the steep, forested, U-shaped Muotatal Valley, past the ghosts of long-vanished glaciers, to find one of these prophets, or *Meteorologischer Verein,* as they call themselves. We make our way through the cherry orchards of Schwyz, past pastures that ring with the carillon of cowbells as the bovine musicians crop the grass and mill. Then we turn up a lime-stone canyon, as sharp as a Swiss knife. Lord Byron described the walls of a gorge as being made of "rocks that shock, yet please the soul," and that is as true here as at any sight he saw. We steer up alongside a clear creek to a husky camp and restaurant. There inside, enjoying a hot toddy, is Peter Suter, eighty years young and one of six surviving weather sniffers, the sages who know the weather by knowing nature.

Peter takes me for a short walk at the edge of the largest subalpine spruce forest in Europe, where he walks every day. His weathered features, cut by the wind, seem an essay in freedom. In each patient measure of his speech there is the sound of shrewdness born of experience. He explains that his art is one of knowing how to understand the language and grammar of the birds, the perfume of the plants, the majuscules of the forests, and the diagrams of the

The author with Peter Suter, the weather sniffer. Peter's art is reading the idioms of the environment to detect tendencies in the weather. He has been studying these idioms his whole life, and twice a year he predicts the weather for the coming seasons. He claims a success rate of 70 to 80 percent.

Photo courtesy of Small World Productions

clouds—the songs that creeks make, the colors that certain flowers turn if rain is nigh, the patterns of scurrying ants if clouds are coming in. He and his colleagues have been studying the idioms of the environment their whole lives. They gather twice a year to collectively predict the weather for the coming seasons, very much a living version of *The Old Farmer's Almanac*. They claim a success rate of 70 to 80 percent. There is even a fan club for the weather sniffers, with some eighteen hundred members.

We sit on a log, and I ask whether the weather has gotten warmer in recent years. He rolls his pigeon shoulders and crinkles the corners of his eyes as he gazes up valley and says yes—and evidence is clear to all who see the retreating glaciers and the higher snow lines. But, he adds, there was a similar pattern some seventy years ago here. He says he thinks all the fuss about man-made carbon emissions affecting the weather is just that, fuss—that it's all just part of a great natural cycle, and that the glaciers will come back, though we won't likely be around to witness it.

Perhaps he's right. Or perhaps his perspective is skewed, isolated as he is in this hermetic valley. He says he worked briefly down in the flats as a farmer but didn't like it and found himself ill. He couldn't wait to get back to his high and healthy valley, his mountainside, where he stays in motion, maintaining an impressive level of fitness. He's been a weather sniffer since 1947 and walks every day to decipher the signs, reading the alphabet of nature. He walked seven hours yesterday. And he knows the signs of nature that surround him here. I ask if the rest of us should learn to heed these signs.

Yes, especially the young, he says; they are losing their connection with nature. He says they walk through the mountains with their eyes closed. He learned from his mother, who was exceptionally good at predicting snowfall from the songs of birds (though no woman has yet been an official weather sniffer). But while he has seven kids and sixteen grandkids, none has taken the mantle. "If mountain climbers understood the weather signs of nature, there would be 50 percent fewer fatalities," he says.

As I'm leaving, I ask if he might offer a weather prediction for tomorrow. He says he usually doesn't do short-term analysis; he's a value investor. If the gentians bloom twice, for instance, it will be a late spring. He hands me a piece of paper that outlines in slightly fractured English his prognostications, which say that the snow will come late this winter and that there will be warmer than usual weather. The note ends with this summary: "The months May and August will have on most beautiful day in the summer. The autumn with Septembers beautiful harvesting and moving weather." But I chide him a bit about a shorter-term view, and he at last tells me that he carried a stick from a pine tree on his walk earlier, and that as he held it out like a divining rod, it dipped, meaning bad weather is on the way. It will snow tomorrow, he says with eyes as charitable as an eagle's. I look up beyond his plaid shirt to the cloudless sky, and then back to his piercing blue eyes and give him a skeptical wince. There is, of course, the theory that one cannot see things until there is some rough knowledge of what they are. The Maori, it is said, did not see the tall ships from England anchoring off their secluded New Zealand coasts, as they had no concept of what the vessels might be. Mountains to early travelers may have caused that effect. And I certainly see no evidence of a storm. But with a twist of a smile on his face, Peter Suter turns away and pads into the deep, fragrant woods like a cat heading for his final mousing.

A FARE TO REMEMBER

It goes directly to the heart of one of our most powerful yearnings: the craving to find in nature a consolation for our mortality.

—Simon Schama, 1995

Switzerland's origins are defined by its contours, its upended landscapes. It has maintained its ecological integrity through the ages as few other nations have. The League for the Preservation of Swiss Scenery was founded in 1905 as one of the first conservation organizations in Europe. Even today, Switzerland is carving out models for the world to notice and perhaps emulate.

One of these models is the UNESCO Biosphere Entlebuch, a short drive to the southeast of Lucerne. It is an essay in balance, protecting not only the natural assets but also the rich culture in something called "value-creation chains." The idea is for the people who live in the biosphere to craft ways to live that benefit the environment, the economy, and society; no extractive businesses here. Eight municipalities—almost 1 percent of the land mass of Switzerland, encompassing some seventeen thousand residents—elected to accept this innovative status. It recognizes people as part of the ecosystem, not some foreign species that has to be kept out by fences, as so many reserves around the world do, often to their own detriment. Many parks in Africa were gazetted within tribal lands to protect wildlife at the expense of people. The vision was to preserve in aspic the lands of the great beasts of the continent, while indigenous peoples were forcibly moved beyond arbitrary borders and suffered for the translocation. Because they were disenfranchised from their land, they have no interest in its success as a park. Too often, this dynamic has bred uncontrolled illegal activities in the parks, poaching being among the most dramatic and injurious.

UNESCO (the United Nations Educational, Scientific and Cultural Organization) initiated the Man and the Biosphere (MAB) Program in 1970. The goal is to involve intergovernmental and interdisciplinary science to address such key questions as:

How do we safeguard and maintain the diversity of plants and animals and keep the ecology in a healthy equilibrium?

How do we balance this against the material needs and aspirations of a world population that continues to grow?

And how do we link these together for the common good?

The Entlebuch Biosphere Reserve is in a sense an experimental laboratory that attempts to balance the relationship between humans and the biosphere. It seeks to provide ways for people to benefit from the ample lap of nature without damaging it—and perhaps even bettering it. The reserve covers some thirty-nine thousand hectares and includes peat bogs, alluvial and riverine forests, and several impressive caves. The inhabitants aim at promoting regional products, cultivating natural resources (grass, wood, and organic goods), and developing ecotourism.

Theo Schnider, the director of the Entlebuch Biosphere, sees some sort of sublimity in this concept when he says, "We need to accept that neither nature nor we humans can ever be perfect—we must learn to embrace imperfection."

It is a terribly scenic drive into Entlebuch, winding down narrow roads past moors, snowcapped mountains, and choirs of stream and stone. It all works up a hunger, this consumption of the landscape, so I pull into an eatery called the Rössli Inn, in the picturesque village of Escholzmatt in Emmental.

Inside the almost century-old inn, I meet Stefan Wiesner, the alchemist chef of the Emmental. He constitutes living proof that man can preserve and valorize nature and still make a delicious living.

There are a lot of organic chefs in Switzerland, but perhaps none more than Stefan Wiesner; he may be the most organic chef in the world. Dressed in his signature black outfit—a T-shirt, designer glasses, and a beret with an eye of Buddha staring outward—he gives me a tour

The author enjoying Stefan Wiesner's ultraorganic hay soup at Rössli Inn. Hay is the base, but it is also flavored with forty-nine different herbs gathered around the farming community of Escholzmatt.   Photo courtesy of Small World Productions

of his kitchen and points out some of his ingredients: ants, coal, stones, snow, hay, silver, gold, moss, ferns, peat, alpine roses, tree bark, and whiskey. He gathers everything himself and, as he says, leaves no stone unturned as he roots around the biosphere. His seems a demonic menu intelligence that lies somewhere between perversity and fire.

His ultraorganic recipes are featured in his cookbook, *Gold, Wood, Stone,* prominently on display. It won the Golden Laurel Leaf from the Historia Gastronomica Helvetica in 2004 and a "special prize for originality" from the German Gastronomic Academy in Frankfurt, Germany. But rather than buy the tome (it is in Swiss German), I ask Stefan if he'll give me the scoop himself.

Stefan looks half like a whiskey priest and half like a pastry chef as he puffs his chest, pushing with it the hanging pendant made by Moroccan nomads. He proclaims he now has seventeen Gault Millau points (of a possible twenty) and is a member of the Guild of Established Cooks. The Rössli is listed in the Passeport Bleu guide and has been awarded the Gourmet Bib honor in the Michelin Guide.

In his broken English, he talks enthusiastically about his close ties with nature, his rambles through the forests in search of ingredients, and his friendships with local organic farmers, hunters, carpenters, and coal miners, all of whom live and work in the Entlebuch Biosphere.

But I am picking up only table scraps of Stefan's story, as his English gets worse as he gets more excited. I ask him to slow down. Instead, he fetches a copy of an interview he did for a Swiss Broadcasting Corp. Web site that was translated into English, and stabs the words with his finger.

The interview describes how Stefan took over Gasthof Rössli from his parents in 1989 and spent years devising ways of integrating nature more closely with his cooking. His father taught him how to make sausages, and he began to combine the meat with gold and then chocolate.

Then he came up with the idea of stone soup. "This was the first dish that involved going out and finding the ingredients in the great outdoors," he told the Web site. In the kitchen, the stones are boiled in a bouillon made with filleted trout and cream and left to stand overnight. Then the stones are removed, collected moss is added, and the liquid is boiled for another two hours before the final addition—a decadent little splash of Champagne.

"How do you know the components of your menus aren't toxic?" I ask over the iron ticking of a kettle on the boil in the kitchen.

With the silencing hand of assertion he points to a passage in his interview in which he says he instinctively chooses the correct natural ingredients—but just to be on the safe side he takes his harvest to his chemist friend Markus Zehnder for a second opinion. So far, nobody's keeled over.

"What's for lunch?" I ask, and he suggests we go make some hay. I watch as his team of alchemists ladles up a creamy soup which uses hay as its base and is flavored with forty-nine different herbs he's gathered around the farming community of Escholzmatt. He places a bowl in the middle of a nest of hay and serves it with some hay schnapps. I sample a few sips of this novel culinary potage, smack my lips, and utter, in a knowing misuse of the word, that it is sublime— better than a roll in the hay. It makes you want to yodel. I make an oath to return to try his gold-laced risotto, or the bone-marrow ravioli, or the sauerkraut ice cream. Or maybe not.

MAGNIFICENT RUDENESS

Downward, my Muse, direct thy steepy flight,
Where smiling shades and beauteous realms invite;

. . . .

Through dark retreats pursue the winding ore,
Search Nature's depths, and view her boundless store;
The secret cause in tuneful measures sing,
How metals first are fram'd, and whence they spring.

—Thomas Yalden, 1701

A s I continue to drive through the biosphere, across soupy moorlands, past ice-dipped peaks, by fields nodding with gray and tan cows, and through a scattering of farmhouses where wood smoke boils and pours into the sky—man and nature do seem to coexist here in some sort of happy state—I take a turn and find myself lost at a dead end. A van pulls up, and through the driver's window a pair of peridot eyes stares out to me. The door swings open, and out folds the driver. He is Heinrich Hofstetter, a thin-shanked fellow as white as tallow, a retiree who had been a forest ranger here for thirty-five years. He also served at the first president of the biosphere and knows the region like few others. There is a familiar smell to him, like sun on dusty stone.

As I describe my search for The Sublime, he lights up and says he knows a sublime site I have to see. He asks me to follow him up a snowy dirt road to a karst hilltop. We wind and rewind up and up to a plateau with a modest house. Out comes Anita Schnider, mother of four and a local guide, who offers to show us the little-known Schrattenfluh Cave on the slopes of Alp Silwängen.

She lights two propane lamps, hands us headlamps but no helmets, and, looking like a wayward member of the Village People, she leads us out to a patch of snow-dusted earth distinguished by what looks like a black submarine hatch. She unlocks the danger valve, turns the latch, and opens the lid, which creaks like the door to a haunted vault. She quickly turns and lowers herself to an iron ladder, then worms her way out of sight, beckoning us to follow. "Cave bears used to live here," she cites as an enticement. "They've found bones from the end of the last ice age, about twenty thousand years ago."

It occurs to me as I am inching down this ladder into the darkness of this cool grot that the definition of *adventure* has widened and stretched over the years so much that it is but a relic of its former self. Once, adventure evoked expeditions taken by the Alpine mytho-poetics, such as Edward Whymper, Heinrich Harrer, Fred Nicole, Oliver Perry-Smith, even John Harlin II, and, perhaps most notably, Edmund Hillary, who climbed in the Swiss Alps prior to his first ascent of Mount Everest (he climbed five Swiss peaks, each higher than ten thousand feet, in five days in 1949). Now, it is employed to describe countless climate-controlled rides in theme parks or an evening at an ethnic restaurant. Adventure these days is more often than not wrinkle-free, bleached clean of any speck of risk, nothing more than an inconvenience wrongly considered.

But this excursion is adventure in the oldest sense, and Anita's glee, even though she's been down here more than three hundred times, is palpable. This is her contribution to adventure: her Entlebuch ecotour. Once at the bottom of this helical pit, she leads us through a limestone and karst passageway on a journey to the center of the earth, or at least toward Interlocken, surrounded by the fantastic fall-out of hypogene forces: speleothems, dripstones, sensuous flowstones, esophagus-like tunnels, clear pools with tiny blind fish, and the carrot-shaped stalactites and stalagmites (memory rule: stalactites hang tightly from the ceiling; stalagmites might someday reach the ceiling) that grow a centimeter every thousand years. She paints her flashlight along the walls and points out "moon milk," a silky covering of calcium carbonate that has leached from the surface, supposedly what the dragons fed the poor cooper in the grotto on Pilatus. And then Anita's voice goes high with excitement as she sweeps her light over a wall of fossils from a sea that lapped here tens of millions of years ago.

Though this is one of the oldest caves in Switzerland, says Anita, it was discovered just thirty-seven years ago. Making our way down this passage seems like horizontal rock climbing. No place for claustrophobes, this is. The cave is a constant fifty-two degrees year-round, but I'm sweating up a storm maneuvering through the underground alleys, wedging around boulders, sliding down muddy chutes. This seems one of the "tongueless caverns of the craggy hills," that Percy Shelley extolled in *Prometheus Unbound*.

There are moments of respite and fairy-tale beauty, though. The flowstones look like melting cake icing, the helecites like soda straws, the cave corals like popcorn, the draperies like strips of bacon, and the aragonite crystals like frostwork or frozen flowers. The long-winged bat of my imagination soars here. The inspiration for the pods in the *Alien* movie series certainly came from here. "An uncouth place / Where hags and goblins might retire a space," wrote the poet William Browne of such a mountain cave in 1613. And there are all sorts of formations that belong in an erotic boutique.

At the end of the main passage, where the cave squeezes into a wormhole down which none of us wants to continue, Anita gathers us around her and says: "Please turn off your headlights, and we'll have a look into the darkness."

There is a specially constructed booth in a lab at Harvard that is designed to be the most silent place on earth, so acoustically muffled that the occupant is often spooked by the sound of his own blood circulating. At this moment I swear I hear my blood screaming. It is a heady, disorienting sensation, a bit frightening, and something that may border on The Sublime. In his *Philosophical Enquiry,* Edmund Burke argued that "darkness is more productive of sublime ideas than light," and it's easy to imagine why as the perfection of darkness envelopes.

But after a moment or two, with a click Anita's flashlight shines its beam onto the wall like a police helicopter, and, like the opposing sentiments of poets, there is a converse feeling. "Light, the bright effluence of Deity, is sublime," declared James Thomson in 1874. Which is it? I wonder as we follow the beam, inching toward the exit,

The author dropping into the Schrattenfluh Cave on the slopes of Alp Silwängen in the Entlebuch Biosphere Reserve. In his Philosophical Enquiry, *Edmund Burke argued that "darkness is more productive of sublime ideas than light."*   Photo courtesy of Small World Productions

and squeezing up through the entrance tunnel like toothpaste from the tube. Into the bright sunshine we spill, and where once we were white, we now are brown. As we squint into the sun, another of Burke's statements rears: "But such a light as that of the sun, immediately exerted on the eye, as it overpowers the sense, is a very great idea. . . . Extreme light, by overcoming the organs of sight, obliterates all objects, so as in its effect exactly to resemble darkness."

Not far to the south is the Upper Reichenbach Falls, at 295 feet one of the highest in the Alps. It was here that one of the great murders of literature took place. If experiencing The Sublime is when thought trembles on the edge of extinction, yet without crossing that line, then writing about a murder in the Alps must qualify. Arthur Conan Doyle came to Switzerland when his wife, Louise, was diagnosed with late-stage tuberculosis in 1895. He took up skiing, writing that the thrill was "getting as near flying as any earth-bound man can." And he traveled to the Bernese Oberland, where he witnessed the powerful falls and found his setting to kill off Sherlock Holmes and the archcriminal Professor Moriarty.

"The Adventure of the Final Problem" begins when Holmes arrives at Dr. Watson's one evening in a somewhat agitated state and with abraded knuckles. He has apparently escaped three murder attempts just that day. Holmes has been tracking Moriarty and his agents for months and is on the brink of delivering them to justice. Moriarty is the nexus of a secret criminal force, and Holmes will consider it the crowning achievement of his career if only he can defeat Moriarty.

But Holmes needs to escape, and so he and Watson head to Switzerland, where they stay at the village of Meiringen, near the Reichenbach Falls. They take a walk to this natural wonder. While they are admiring the hydraulics, a boy appears and hands Watson a note that says there is a sick Englishwoman back at the hotel who wants an English doctor. Holmes realizes at once it is a hoax, although he does not say so. Watson goes to see about the patient, leaving Holmes alone.

When Watson reaches the Englischer Hof, the innkeeper has no idea about any sick Englishwoman. Realizing he's been tricked, Watson rushes back to the Reichenbach Falls but finds no one there, although he does see two sets of footprints going out onto the muddy, dead-end path with none coming back. There is also a note from Holmes explaining that he knew the report Watson had been given was a hoax and that he is about to fight Moriarty, who has graciously given him enough time to pen this last letter. Watson sees, toward the end of the path, signs that a violent struggle has taken place. It is all too clear that Holmes and Moriarty have both died, having fallen to their deaths down the gorge while locked in mortal combat—and that Conan Doyle achieved his own agreeable kind of horror.

chapter eleven

RAPTUROUS TERROR

See how sublime th' uplifted mountains rise,
And with their pointed Heads invade the Skies.
The hollow Vales their smiling Pride unfold,
What rich abundance do their bosoms hold.

—Richard Blackmore, 1712

Before leaving the Biosphere Reserve, we make a last stop at the farm of Franz Schnider, current proprietor of the first farm in the area to offer organic goods. His sixty-acre plot has been farmed for seven generations. For many years, I had a Bernese mountain dog named Bali, and we ran many miles together, camped and hiked and explored for more than a dozen years. She's gone now, but Franz has a white-chested Bernese named Bäri that is just like Bali, and the beautifully coated dog bounds to greet me outside the store with an enthusiasm that mirrors how my own would greet me after I returned from some overly long overseas trip. I scratch the pup's neck and make a chuffing sound, which always had a pacifying effect on Bali. Bäri snorts in agreement, but then breaks free and feints his path with deft leaps to the left and right like a rat-spooked horse, and I can't resist running around the parking lot for a few minutes with a kindred spirit.

Once I make it inside Franz's Alpenblick restaurant and store, Franz, his eyes as soggy as a sheepdog's, shows off rows of strawberry and blueberry wines, liquors and jams, herbal teas picked from the reserve, local cheese, and bottles of massage lotion made from marmot oil, all from his farm. We generously sample Franz's wares and then step outside to a dark sky and falling snow, flakes twisting in lazy helices to the ground, the kind of weather the Romantic poets called sublime. Peter Suter, the weather sniffer, was right. We race to the car and, with windshield wipers slapping, take the dark band of a road back to Lucerne, where the air is furious with snow.

That night, I dine with Evelyne at the Restaurant Pavillon in the Hotel Schweizerhof. She, with her becoming directness, says she is the one to help guide this search for The Sublime in her country, and I am inclined not to doubt her. We share a bottle of Pinot Noir, and then a second, which seems to pour into the bottle of my soul. Sublime. Say it fast, as the wine taster did swishing around the pinot noir, and there's music playing, a melisma of verse. Say it soft, as a poet might, gazing at an alp—*sublimmmmme*—and it's almost like praying. Outside are the evening couches of the sun, but here we sit and sip toward the light of understanding, or so we think under our vinous breath.

I have now seen the Alps in several of their facets, but it's time to cock my leg on one. So, with Evelyne at the wheel, we head toward the east of Switzerland, to the original sybaritic winter feast of St. Moritz. "It's *sooper*," Evelyne says. "Especially the skiing." Despite having lived and worked in New York for years, she still sports a Swiss German accent with consonants so ripe they linger in the air like little zeppelins.

Along the way, Evelyne fills me with all sorts of meaningful trivia, such as the facts that Switzerland has three hundred types of cheese, four hundred of sausage, and fifty of grapes, along with the smallest vineyard in the world, consisting of three vines and sponsored by His Holiness the Dalai Lama. It is dedicated to the memory of Farinet, the Valaisian counterfeiter and Robin Hood of the Alps who died in 1880. Stones from all over the world surround the vineyard, and a block of marble—the rock of freedom—shows the distance to iconic places on the planet: the Pyramids of Giza, Mount Sinai, Mecca, the Statue of Liberty, and Ayers Rock.

Evelyne continues, sharing that the Swiss eat 12.5 kilograms of chocolate a year. Velcro was invented here, as well as contact lenses, the electric stove, and, apologizes to Al Gore, the Internet as we know it when physicist Tim Berners-Lee created the first browser-editor in 1990. Then she turns to gossip and airs some dirty laundry, such as the tidbit that Brad Pitt wears no underwear other than the Swiss-made Zimmerli. "How do you know that?" I ask, and she responds with a cheese-knife curl of a smile. The day is bright, and I roll down the

Even the cows are pleased here . . . for the scenery and serenity, they produce better milk and cheese than the rest of the world.   Photo courtesy of John Canning

window, poke my elbow into the scenery, and lean out to inhale lung-fuls of Alpine air. The sun glinting on a patch of snow speaks more eloquently than the whole history of Europe, and I realize that this moment is the only past I will ever know.

We pass barns elevated on staddle stones (to deter rodents) and a lowing herd of smooth, brown cows winding slowly over the lea. There are paddocks of grazing sheep and rolls of hay bundled in white, protective plastic, looking like stacks of giant marshmallows. We stop at the Moevenpick Marche, an autobahn emporium in the eastern canton of the Grisons, at the Rhine Valley region that Switzerland Tourism recently dubbed "Heidiland." Near here, the holy Swiss story of Heidi was penned by Johanna Spyri in 1880–81. Spyri spent most of her life in Zurich, where she suffered from depression, but when she vacationed in Maienfeld and took in its painfully picturesque landscape, she felt she had found a cure. She credited the bracing tension of the scenery as being the inspiration for Heidi, which I have never read, but I remember the 1937 Shirley Temple movie version as a valentine to a simpler, more pristine world than ever existed. It harks to the kind of romantic notions about the inhabitants of the Swiss mountains that in part fueled the pilgrimages of the eighteenth-century poets, artists, and eccentrics. They had been inspired by Rousseau's "noble savage" and believed that archetype was manifesting itself among the farmers and herders of Switzerland, an idealized place of health, tranquility, and freedom. (Not all subscribed to the romantic notions. According to one 1889 guidebook: "The people in these exquisite vallies [sic] are without exception the most hideous creatures you can conceive. . . . The women are fearful." Life in the mountains may have seemed idyllic to visiting poets, but because there was little iodine in the Alpine diets, it is true that cretinism and goiters were endemic and life was often grisly and bad-looking.)

Heroes created in Switzerland are most often treated sparingly and magisterially, as with John Harlin II, who has a few hard-to-find plaques near the Eiger. But not Heidi. Everything in this valley is themed after Heidi: stores, huts, paths, a clock tower, a museum, designer water, waitresses in dirndls—even the women out front with penciled eyebrows and high heels are jokingly called Heidihos. The buffet is a smorgasbord of all Swiss foods. I choose *rösti,* the crispy potato cake, and a Rivella, the Swiss carbonated drink produced from whey, and afterward have to take a leak. There in the bathroom is a shining example of Swiss technology and ingenuity. I take aim, and at first impact, an LCD panel on top of the toilet lights up, advertising a service to check on prostate problems. Urol marketing, perhaps.

chapter twelve

DIVINE AND CONQUER

You may tell them that Mountains grow out of the Earth like Fuzz-balls, or that there are Monsters under ground that throw up Mountains as Moles do Mole-hills; they will scarce raise one objection against your doctrine; or if you would appear more Learned, tell them that the Earth is a great Animal, and these are Wens that grow upon its body. This would pass current for Philosophy; so much is the World drown'd in stupidity and sensual pleasures, and so little inquisitive into the works of God and Nature.

—Thomas Burnet, 1681

A little later down the mythic road, we stop in Chur, capital of the Grisons canton and the oldest town in Switzerland, settled by Celts some five thousand years ago. (The name is derived from the Celtic *kora* or *koria* [tribe, clan]). After their conquest of Rhaetia (an ancient Alpine district), the Romans in 15 BC named it Curia Rhaetorum. In AD 284, Chur became the provincial capital. In 450, a recently Christianized Chur became the residence of a bishop. In the twelfth century, the bishops of Chur were granted the status of princes of the Holy Roman Empire, but the Reformation deprived them of their secular authority. When the canton of the Grisons was established in 1803, Chur became its administrative capital.

Chur is at the natural junction of several of the most important routes from Italy over the Alpine passes and as a result incorporates both Italian and Rhaetian influences. It may have been on the route that the Carthaginian general Hannibal Barca took when he drove his elephants over the Alps some 2,200 years ago during his campaign to Italy, but that story, like so much of the misty past here, may well be more myth than record. The Plessur River, a tributary of the Rhine, flows through the middle of Chur. Everything about it looks and feels lapped by the past, except for the McDonald's shoved into the center of town. There are other incongruities. We stop for a drink at Chur's most famous drooling hole, an exercise in some sort of sublimity, the Giger Bar. H. R. Giger's singular brand of bizarre, otherworldly art became best known when he designed the creature and much of the set design in the 1979 film *Alien*.

What a contrast, walking from the wholesome Swiss exterior into the cavernous, skeletal structure covered by double arches of vertebrae that crisscross the vaulted ceiling of an ancient castle. It's like being swallowed by a dinosaur or some unimaginable beast. I wonder if Giger has visited the caves of Entlebuch, which features formations similar to what is on display here.

I sit in one of the exoskeleton chairs, a rotating vessel of dread, and order what I think is probably the most fitting, and sublime, drink for this dark saloon, the drink the Swiss invented, often called "madness in a bottle"—an absinthe. But the Giger Bar doesn't carry it.

So I settle for schnapps, so strong it is viscous, like something from the gas pump. It spurs memories of a couple of years ago, when I was in Grindelwald at the Eiger Hotel, with its incongruous Mongolian barbecue. The Eiger's bar also featured one hundred different schnapps, including one I couldn't resist: *Cannabis sativa*–based, which I think I enjoyed, though I really can't remember.

As we continue to wind up the rutless road it is impossible not to notice the prosperity. As a country with practically no natural resources and restricted agricultural land, Switzerland has always been forced to trade in order to survive. Living off the land has never been easy, and at many times over the centuries has been so precarious that people either starved or were forced to move away to seek better conditions elsewhere. Switzerland has gone from being the poorest country in Europe at the end of the nineteenth century to being one of the richest countries in the world per capita. How did the Swiss do it? How did they overcome—even harness—the great barriers to growth presented by their mountains? The key was, I believe, tourism.

It is in profound exhibit here that it is not faith that moves mountains; it is tectonics. The Alps vaulted into existence a hundred million years ago as a result of the collision of two of the plates that form the earth's crust. Lubrication was key. The plates glided on salt, deposited after ancient seas dried out during the Triassic period. This was the oil that smoothed the passage of the two colliding landmasses, facilitating mountain building that thrust hundreds of miles of rock thousands of

*The northern side of the frozen Lake of St. Moritz is capped with a little laager of tents.
Three feet of ice on the Lake of St. Moritz supports the weight of golf tournaments (using
red balls), horse races, polo and cricket matches, the mad sport of skijoring (in which skiers are hitched to riderless horses), and cook-offs inside the cartilage-colored tents.*
Photo courtesy of Small World Productions

feet toward the heavens. Through time and the ordnances of nature—
rain, snow, hail, frost—these mountains were gradually worn down
to little more than low hills. Then, about a quarter of a million years
ago, further movement of the tectonic plates and profound glaciations
produced something approaching the Alps as they are today—a great
crescent that runs eight hundred miles end to end, with its jagged heart
in Switzerland. It's what the Romantics called "the architecture of the
infinite." Gazing at these shambolic peaks that march into perpetuity,
I find I want to do a little jig, a dance, but then, as Thelonious Monk
might have said, dancing about architecture is like writing about music.

"Mountains are the beginning and end of all natural scenery,"
wrote John Ruskin in his 1856 musing "Of Mountain Beauty." Ruskin
was a fugitive to rustic simplicity from the horrors of the industrial

revolution, a seeker of a moral corrective to the ills of court and city. He visited the Alps first in 1832, when he was thirteen, and continued to do so for the rest of his life. One of his core beliefs was that humankind had deviated from its natural state. In his view, the Alps "formed a background not merely to one particular set of experiences but to all worthwhile existence." When he had to return to the flatlands, he felt "a kind of sickness and pain."

He also believed mountains actually do march. Ruskin spent years pacing the paths of the Alps, sketching, painting, observing, meditating. He concluded that the vigorous originality of mountain ridges is an illusion. Examined with due diligence and patient eyes, mountains reveal their fundamental form of organization to be the curve, and not the angle as might be concluded by superficial observation. Mountains are inherently curved, and mountain ranges are shaped around waves: "the silent wave of the blue mountain."

For Ruskin, this perpetual motion was what made mountains the beginning and end of all natural scenery: "Those desolate and threatening ranges of dark mountain which, in nearly all ages of the world, men have looked upon with aversion or terror and shrunk back from as if they were haunted by perpetual images of death are, in reality, sources of life and happiness far fuller and more beneficent than all the bright fruitfulness of the plain."

Ruskin was right about the movement. Sir Charles Lyell's principles of geology and Charles Darwin's theory of evolution supplied the force required to accelerate from rest the massively inert Victorian worldview of antediluvian stasis and immutable species. We know now that everything moves—continents, planets, mountains—in ways both relativistic and contingent.

As the late-afternoon light sluices the surrounding snow pink, we cross the Julier Pass, the watershed between the rivers Rhine and Danube. As at all watersheds, I try to find some meaning in the divide, but each time I fall short in apotheosis and surrender to feelings less than fear or joy. I have never found on summits or basins the kind of rapture that assumes a sort of mystical disembodiment. Thoreau in his journals often found a natural fact to be transcendent in its very factness.

We then helix down a road so epigrammatic as to crawl into itself, and whorl into the valley called Engadine (which means "garden of the inn"). We trundle by the Swiss National Park, the little republic's largest nature reserve (some sixty-five square miles) and its only national park. That may suggest something about the mountain state's ingrained conservation ethos—that it doesn't need to go out of its way to designate wilderness protection because most of it already is protected. But this is a place set aside for wildlife and true, unmediated land. The Swiss are famous for rules, and here the rules are perhaps stricter than at any other park in Europe, maybe the world. The park is closed to humans for a good chunk of the year; when people may enter, they may not leave the road, make a fire, disturb the animals or plants, or even camp. Dogs are not allowed, not even on a leash. Like Swiss technology, this seems to work: the bearded vulture, which had died out in the Alps around the end of the nineteenth century, was reintroduced here in 1991 and now thrives. Another success was the reintroduction of the mountain ibex in 1906, smuggled over the mountains from Italy after the Italian king, Vittorio Emanuele II, categorically refused to sell any to Switzerland and banned their export. Other animals were subsequently acquired, also illegally. A century later, some fourteen thousand are living in the Swiss Alps. And a brown bear was sighted three years ago, the first in more than a hundred years (the last recorded bear was shot in Switzerland in 1904), and then two more last year.

THE RELIGION OF GLAM

*This Engadin is the most beautiful abode in the world.
I do not easily speak of happiness, but I almost believe
I am happy here.*

—Thomas Mann, 1912

The late-day sun showers bright as we ease into the Upper Engadine Valley (one of the many mottoes is "322 sunny days a year"—the mountains shield the area from the moist air that flows from Italy). As we motor along at six thousand feet, we pass a couple of young girls sauntering through the snow in voluminous fur coats astride two dressage horses. We are on the outskirts of the "top of the world," that pleasure playground known as St. Moritz, the glam destination of distractions and temptations. St. Moritz was named after a Roman Christian soldier who was martyred here when he refused to reconvert to the religion of the Caesars. That searing rebel spirit survives today.

We drive by the local airport, where some nineteen thousand jets, most private, land each year. This is the landing strip for many of the billionaires who attend the annual World Economic Summit in nearby Davos. We edge around the northern side of the frozen Lake of St. Moritz, which is capped with a little laager of glossy white tents that look alarmingly like the Denver International Airport. Three feet of ice on the lake supports the weight of golf tournaments (using red balls), horse races, polo and cricket matches, the mad sport of skijoring (skiers hitched by what look like flags to riderless thoroughbred horses), and competitions among chefs cooking up storms inside the cartilage-colored tents. It's like an Alpine Burning Man for the upscale set.

We pull into the Kempinski Grand Hotel des Bains, a five-star, nineteenth-century lodging palace (built in 1864), next to the cable car to the sprawling ski area, Corviglia. The German poet Rainer Maria Rilke, the Austrian conductor Herbert von Karajan, and the German philologist Friedrich Nietzsche all stayed here seeking their own inner landscapes. I meet Judith Haid, a young marketing manager with large, mountain-spring eyes, who offers to guide me to the

"Ultimate Source." That can mean many things to many people, but to someone who has been in tourism for a long career, it here means the font from which gushed a tourism industry. Downstairs, near the entrance to the spa, a tiny spring trickles from a granite wall into a round metal basin, and adjacent are several cups. This is the Mauritius spring, discovered by passing Celts some three thousand years ago and now legendary for its restorative powers. The poster girl may be Judith, who says she drinks from the spring every day. The Mauritius may also lay claim to being the birth of balneology, the study of bathing and mineral springs.

By the Middle Ages, the infirm, the elderly, and the jaded made summer pilgrimages here to "take the waters." In 1519, Pope Leo X promised full absolution for every visitor of the Christian faith who came to the spa of St. Moritz. In 1553, the famed Swiss doctor, astrologer, and occultist Paracelsus von Hohenheim visited this mineral spring and wrote that it was perhaps the most healing natural spring in all of Europe. That opened the floodgates. Health tourism took off, and St. Moritz became a destination. By the eighteenth century, it became necessary to book accommodations a year in advance.

Balneologists say it's not just the waters that produce beneficial effects; it's also the integration of beautiful surroundings, the providing of a peaceful setting that allows insight and introspection, the breathing of clean air, the drinking of natural mineral water, and the eating of sensible food. Leslie Stephen gave his take in 1871, saying these Alps were "places where we may escape from ourselves and from our neighbors. There we can breathe air that has not passed through a million pairs of lungs; and drink water in which the acutest philosophers cannot discover the germs of indescribable disease. There the blessed fields are in no danger of being 'huzzed and mazed with the devil's own team.' "

In the spirit of the place, I take one of the cups, hold it under the fountain, and take a sip. The water is sour and iron-rich, with what may be a slight bloom of rust, and it reminds me of summer camp, with hormones clacking, drinking from the hand-powered water pump. That water tasted just like this, and was and is a congenial kind of torment.

So it was the water that brought tourists in the warm seasons, but how did St. Moritz become the winter playground it is today? I head up the hill to find out.

Inside the Hotel Pilatus-Kulm, where some suites rent for $5,000 a night, is a partial answer. There in the lobby, past milling guests dripping with sable, lynx, chinchilla, mink, fox, and raccoon (the town is a walking PETA anti-campaign), is a portrait of founder Johannes Badrutt, the man sometimes credited with "inventing" winter tourism. In 1856, he acquired the summer guesthouse Pension Faller, built in the seventeenth century by the Flugi family. He renovated it and renamed it the Engadine Kulm. Like all, he used to shutter his pension with the first snowfall. But then, in September 1864, he made a bet with four British guests that if they stayed the winter and didn't enjoy the experience, then he would refund their money, and pay their transportation home. The weather, he promised, would be better than foggy London's; guests would be able to sit outside in their shirtsleeves in December. It was a strategy that paid off. "Twice in January we dined on the terrace and on other days had picnics in our sledges. . . . I was far stronger at the end of the winter than at its commencement," reads one entry in the hotel's guest book. The guests stayed until Easter. And they returned the following season with friends. Badrutt thereafter opened his hotel regularly for a three-month winter season. Patrons in ever-larger numbers came to enjoy the snow and the nascent sport of skiing. John's Ruskin's influential

The frozen surface of the Lake of St. Moritz   Photo courtesy of Sara Givens

sentiments didn't hurt. He wrote: "I have made up my mind that the finest things one can see in summer are nothing compared to the winter scenery among the Alps." And Leslie Stephen added to the seasonal chorus: "Winter is when the whole region becomes part of the dreamland. . . . The very daylight has an unreal glow. . . . The pulse of the mountains is beating low. . . . The peaks are in a state of suspended animation. . . . They are spell-bound, dreaming of dim abysses of past time or of the summer that is more real to them than life. They are in a trance like that of the Ancient Mariner, when he heard strange spirit voices conversing overhead in mysterious murmurs."

Lost to the swirling flakes of history are the true origins of skiing. Those lengths of ancient, hewn timber pulled out of bogs in Scandinavia and China? Maybe miners working at high altitude invented skiing to get around snow-covered slopes; perhaps postmen determined to get the mail through the mountains invented it too.

If there is no universally recognized site of the birth of skiing, Switzerland has the best claim for having nurtured it to popularity. This was, after all, the country that held the first official downhill and slalom races, and by pioneering Alpine tourism it gave access to mountains where visitors from abroad could indulge in what was commonly known in the late nineteenth century as "ski-running." An early proponent was Sir Arthur Conan Doyle, who predicted: "This is not appreciated yet, but I am convinced the time will come when hundreds of Englishmen will come to Switzerland for the skiing season between March and April."

Wherever you go in St. Moritz, you see the stylized posters of old showing off the glamour of early skiing. However, Switzerland's heritage doesn't always serve the country well. Switzerland's long winter-sport history makes its resorts seem fusty and backward-looking. Among European ski destinations, however, Switzerland breaks the most new ice.

A few years ago, St. Moritz announced imaginative, large-scale applications of "green" technology to produce energy, heating, and cooling. This is from the place where the Range Rover and the Audi Quattro were also introduced. But this new initiative has something to do with survival. There's no business like snow business here, and if the snow and glaciers continue to deliquesce—and they have to a notable degree in recent years—then the valley will be robbed of consequence, and St. Moritz, synonym for excess with a side of skiing, could become a ghost town.

So St. Moritz is going green in a big way. One project was the installation of 180 solar panels alongside the Corviglia funicular, now providing one-sixth of the power for the train. There are wind turbines, microdams, and retrofits for super insulation. Another high-profile initiative is a circular geothermal pumping system that provides 80 percent of the heat for the Badrutt's Palace Hotel (yes, the hotel was created by Johannes Badrutt's family) and reduces yearly carbon dioxide emissions by twelve hundred tons, or 75 percent. It draws warmth from beneath the surface of the Lake of St. Moritz, and then, after a journey through the hotel and a school, the water drops back into the lake cooler than before, allowing it to freeze over earlier in the season, which is good for tourism. I decide to visit the five-star hotel and cross a lobby where furs are draped over laps like pets and the diamonds are as big as the Ritz. This is a hotel where the barman and concierge are reputed to be millionaires because of the huge tips. I take a tour of the pumping plant in the basement. No photos, please, says the PR manager in clipped English. It is all pipes and chipped paint, wizard-behind-the-screen stuff, not for public consumption. But it is the concept, not the decor, that is impressive.

Heat-pump technology is not easy to grasp. But the gist of it is this: Wherever the temperature is higher than −273ºC—absolute zero—there is some heat, which can be utilized. This heat is extracted by coils set beneath the earth or in large bodies of water, and the heat pump concentrates it so that a lot of "only slightly warm" becomes a small quantity of "hot." What is so neat about the St. Moritz installation is that its coil lies in Lake of St. Moritz, and as it extracts warmth from the lake to heat the hotel (and the Grevas schoolhouse nearby), it cools the lake. That means the resort's famous events on the lake's frozen surface stand a better chance of taking place, and "the trout are happy," says the PR director. This sort of technique has been used before, notably in the United States to "precool" water stored for snowmaking. Installing a coil in a lake is also much cheaper than digging it into the ground.

In the bowels of Badrutt's Palace Hotel is a circular geothermal pumping system that provides 80 percent of the heat for the guest rooms and reduces yearly carbon dioxide emissions by twelve hundred tons, or 75 percent.   Photo courtesy of Laura Hubber

As we stand on the balcony of Badrutt's Palace, overlooking the warm schoolhouse, a paraglider—perhaps the ultimate energy-efficient traveler—crosses our field of vision, wheeling on his wing points, and makes a smooth landing on the frozen lake, which winks like a shield in the sun.

It is high season, and there are no rooms in town (and I couldn't afford most anyway; I sometimes feel like a marauder in the forest of the affluent night), so I end up in a village up-valley: Silvaplana, on a shallow lake of the same name that is a haven for cross-country skiers and snowshoers and in summer, as the wind now attests, a popular haunt for kiteboarders and windsurfers (the first windsurf world cup was held here in 1994). The few skiers we pass have their heads tamped down into their bodies against the whipping winds.

This is also near Friedrich Nietzsche's summer getaway from 1879 through 1888, where he wrote *Thus Spoke Zarathustra* and created the expression "metaphysical landscape." He described the Upper Engadine as "transparent, glowering in all colors, all contrasts, enclosing in itself all middles between ice and the south."

It was Nietzsche who succinctly summed up early Romantic articulations of a key element of The Sublime with his phrase "what doesn't kill me makes me stronger." Writing from the Alps to his father in 1863, John Ruskin gave it a more thoughtful rendering: "That question of the moral effect of danger is a very curious one, but this I know and find, practically, that if you come to a dangerous place, and turn back from it, though it may have been perfectly right and wise to do so, still your character has suffered some slight deterioration; you are to that extent weaker, more lifeless, more effeminate, more liable to passion and error in future; whereas if you go through with the danger, though it may have been apparently rash and foolish to encounter it, you come out of the encounter a stronger and better man, fitter for every sort of work and trial, and nothing but danger produces this effect."

ABSINTHE MAKES THE HEART GROW STRONGER

It is a pinnacle of beatitude, bordering upon horror, deformity, madness! An eminence from whence the mind, that dares to look farther, is lost! It seems to stand, or rather to waver, between certainty and uncertainty, between security and destruction! It is the point of terror, of undetermined fear, of undetermined power!

—Frances Reynolds, 1785

n Silvaplana I find a room in a sweet boutique called the Hotel Chesa Surlej, and the owner invites me to his adjacent restaurant for a drink. He serves kirsch in long glasses, and I of course ask about absinthe. Not here, he says. Where? I query, and he says he knows of just one place that serves the devil's brew, the Kronenhof in the Upper Engandine village of Pontresina. So, with Evelyne guiding the way, we head over for an after-dinner drink.

I expect some sort of opium den–type place down a back alley with straw on the floor, but we pull up to a grand, horseshoe-shaped, white-facade palace. Past the iron gates and the circular driveway, we spill into an elegant interior of Corinthian columns, vaulted and frescoed ceilings, and neobaroque accessories such as gilt, baby-pink cherubs, tempting nymphs, dark pine, restored murals, nineteenth-century parquet floors, and leggy, fur-lined guests. No fleece here, at least of the wearable kind. We're led to a highly polished wood door, which could be the upright portal to The Sublime. This door opens to the Kronenhof Bar. I take a seat and order the wicked drink. I'm going green at last.

Absinthe, also known as La Fée Verte ("The Green Fairy"), is the drink that fueled (and some say ruined) a brilliant generation of writers and painters in the late nineteenth century. It was believed to be hallucinogenic, toxic. It could drive you crazy. It could make you blind. It could make you see ordinary objects in a whole new way. When a Swiss man murdered his pregnant wife and two children in 1905, absinthe was found to be the precipitating culprit, and a sort of *Reefer Madness* mentality set in. The Swiss banned the drink in 1910 as a danger to public morals and national survival. In 1912, the *Titanic* sank and the U.S. Food and Drug Administration banned the importation of absinthe.

Absinthe fueled (and some say ruined) a brilliant generation of writers and painters in the late 19th century.   Photo courtesy of Small World Productions

But it turns out the drink was never as harmful as calumny and legend insisted, and so the Swiss ban was repealed in 2005. The United States followed suit shortly thereafter.

What is this drink of mythic unreason? *Absinthe* is the French word for "wormwood" (*Artemisia absinthium*), a shrub in the daisy family that grows wild throughout Switzerland and has real medicinal properties. The leaves and wooded stems of the plant produce a bitter substance used to cure intestinal worms, aid in childbirth, and even induce love.

Absinthe the drink was created—or perhaps developed and first marketed successfully—in Switzerland in the early nineteenth century. Swiss-exported absinthe was particularly popular in New Orleans. In 1878, eight million liters of absinthe were imported into the United States.

Traditionally it contained grande wormwood, green anise, and differing combinations of other herbs, especially "little" or "Roman" wormwood (*Artemisia pontica*), sweet fennel, and hyssop. Thujone, a toxic chemical found in wormwood, was said to be responsible for absinthe's reputed mind-altering effects. (Recent scientific studies show that it isn't; it's just the high alcoholic content that can make you crazy.)

The barkeep produces a bottle of Kübler Absinthe from Val-de-Travers near the French border, where the stuff was invented. The bottle says it was made in an alembic still, following original techniques, using only natural plants rather than extracts or oils, and was finished at 53 percent alcohol. The server taps the bottle like a magician touching a top hat and says, "This is the real thing."

In a grand arc, he pours a long shot into a glass before me and begins the ritual. He places a silver, perforated spoon across the rim and on top positions a cube of white sugar. Then he pours more of the high-octane alcohol over the cube and takes a match to it, which caramelizes the sugar and makes little blue-flaming drops fall into the glass. My instinct is to lean back, as though it's gonna blow. Then he "louches" the drink with cold water, and the gemlike liquid in the bottom of the glass clouds like a crystal ball. After a few seconds, the opalescent swirl assumes strange shapes—like a genie in a bottle or a miniature green tornado—which twist and dance in the neck of the glass. I pick up the sea-foam green concoction and take a sniff. It is sagey, bright, with a hint of anise. Then I bring the brew to my lips, and sip. It is rich, somewhat bitter, but fresh, like drinking a malt whiskey made from wildflower. Now that I know the drink doesn't possess the dangerous properties with which it was once associated, it seems it is absinthe without malice.

THE WIZARDS OF ZUOZ

No one can live in such peace as here.

—Hermann Hesse, 1912

My hungover head rings in the day next. At breakfast, over a third cup of coffee, Evelyne offers to show me a variation on the romantic notions I've been pursuing.

"You have to hear Romansh," she insists. It is Switzerland's fourth official language: the Latin-based gypsy mishmash spoken by just thirty-five thousand people in a country of seven and a half million. It was declared a national language in 1938 to thwart Mussolini, who argued that Romansh was Italian and thus its region was suitable for annexation. Today, with as much as 20 percent of Switzerland's population foreign-born, there are more speakers of Arabic than of Romansh.

Like a captain in a storm, Evelyne wrestles the wheel as we head down the brown and yellowed-brick road to Zuoz, a little village at the far end of the Lower Engadine, a last refuge of Romansh. The air seems to crackle in Zuoz. We pass a statue of a boy in the midst of cracking a bullwhip, and then hear what sounds like a pistol shot. Then a car backfires, or so it sounds. Then there is a repeat of the first sharp snap, and another. We round the corner, past a stone public fountain, and park by a piazza where a dozen whippersnappers are doing just that. They are schoolboys practicing for Chalandamarz (from the Latin *Calendae Martii,* first day of March), a Romansh rite-of-passage festival where boys scare away winter demons and girls in traditional costumes and paper flowers dance, serenade, and romance.

The plaited bullwhips are about twelve feet long. Using the entire body for power, the boys swing their whips above their heads, then crack them just above the cobbles. Though the whips were used for ages to move cattle, now they feature in folk festivals, and the boys are prepping for the one upcoming.

The streets in Zuoz are narrow and cobblestoned, the houses big and old, cream-colored and stuccoed, with wide, gabled roofs and foundations of stone. The arches and corners are decorated with frescoes called *sgraffiti,* geometrical signs and abstract drawings of antique origin and now indecipherable. The windows are deep-set and tiny (to prevent heat loss), and the painted oak doors are wide and big with two gatelike openings, one for the cows and carriages, the other for the owners. These sixteenth-century homes doubled as byres and stables in a climate and terrain that were and are extreme. Outside are long, wooden seats called "lying benches" where the old folks would sit and tell their stories. Once upon a time, one popular story goes, when the village was about to be invaded by a frustrated Emperor Maximilian, the inhabitants hid their possessions in their cellars, set fire to their houses, and took to the woods. When the emperor's army arrived, it found the ashes of the village. The soldiers not only had nothing to plunder, but they also had no food or shelter. They retreated from the village and left it to resume its independent and placid life.

We walk up a steep hill to a frozen rink. There I meet Katia Staub, a kindergarten teacher who also coaches ice-skating. One of Katia's jobs is to teach her students the Rhaeto-Romance dialect, a language that some believe is dying and may disappear in a generation. She proudly skates her charges in a circle around me and has them sing a couple of songs in the linguistic leftover. Most struggle with the lyrics. But one of the little girls, Romina, is five years old and fluent in Romansh. She greets me beneath her silver helmet, sprouting bunny ears, with "Allegra" ("Hi"), and then croons a solo ditty about the animals who seek shelter when the snow falls. I feel I am witnessing the last breath of a culture, one that thrived in the era of the natural sublime—but that concept too, the Romantic sense of The Sublime, has also faded, and it too may vanish into the mountains from whence it was born.

TOO HIGH FOR EARTH, TOO LOW FOR HEAVEN

The scenery everywhere was most exquisite, but of the great pass I shall say nothing—it was like standing in the presence of God when He is terrible. The tears overflowed my eyes. I think I never saw the sublime before.

—Elizabeth Barrett Browning, 1851

he next morning, I awake to what seems a sonic boom and look out the window, past a tracery of icicles, up the steep mountain to the array of avalanche fences. I know the sound. It's a sound I have carried around like a hot rock ever since my trek to Annapurna. It is the bellow of an avalanche not far away. There are some ten thousand avalanches a year in Switzerland, and more than 50 percent of the population lives in avalanche terrain. By some accounts, about two hundred people are killed in the whole of the Alps each season. In 1618, a giant avalanche rolled off Mount Conto onto Pleurs, the "Town of Tears," in the middle of the night. It was so sudden, complete, and overwhelming that not only did every soul perish, but also no trace of the village or of any of the inhabitants was ever discovered. A British writer, David Bogue, traveling through Switzerland in 1846, tapped The Sublime when walking here and wrote: "It is a solemn thing, to stand upon the tomb of twenty-five hundred beings, all sepulchered alive. No efforts have ever discovered a trace of the inhabitants—not a bone, not a vestige."

A key element to The Sublime is proximity to or consideration of oblivion, and the avalanche, viewed from a distance, became the spiritual totem. But propinquity to The Sublime does not ensure survival. In 1806, the Swiss village of Goldau was eradicated when an entire mountainside collapsed onto it. According to records, vast chunks of rock bounced like cannonballs through the valley to land in Lake Lowertz, five miles distant, where they created a wave seventy feet high. When the dust settled, Goldau was covered by a field of rubble measuring five miles long and three miles wide, dotted with hillocks of rock several hundred feet high, beneath which lay the remains of three hundred houses and four hundred fifty people. In 1818, a glacial avalanche fell and rewrote a river in Bagnes into a

The Waldhaus am See, a hotel that sits at the end of the Lake Lucerne like a keepsake fallen from some absent-minded visitor's pocket.

Photo courtesy of Walker Bangs

lake. When the ensuing dam broke, five hundred thirty thousand cubic feet of water (the Colorado River through the Grand Canyon in spate runs less than fifty thousand cubic feet per second) plunged into the valley, destroying four hundred homes and killing thirty-four people. Nothing can withstand a major avalanche, and there exists even today little knowledge of predicting when and where an event will occur. "A stone, or even a hasty expression, rashly dropped, would probably start an avalanche," wrote Leslie Stephen in 1871. Settlements that have been safe for centuries can be smothered in an instant. The sheer displacement of air that an avalanche causes can empty lungs. Its softly pulverizing arrival can turn humans to jelly, bags of skin that contain flesh and small pieces of bone. Several of my friends and acquaintances have died in avalanches, yet it remains true that the sound or sight of one is thrilling, a delightful horror, until the moment the white wave rolls over. Then it is just deadly.

John Forbes, Queen Victoria's personal doctor, articulated these feelings while visiting the Alps in 1848 and witnessing an avalanche from a safe distance: "It is like that [state] which accompanies and follows the triumphant close of some elaborate and difficult air by an accomplished singer at the opera. . . . It would hardly have astonished me if, on the present occasion, the spectators . . . , after their pause of fearful delight, had clapped their hands in ecstasy and ended with 'Bravo!' "

In the summer of 1688, a young English future playwright, John Dennis, crossed the Alps to Italy and wrote to a friend back home of the harrowing experience: "We walk'd upon the very brink, in a literal sense, of Destruction; one Stumble, and both Life and Carcass had been at once destroy'd. The sense of all this produc'd different motions in me, viz., a delightful Horrour, a terrible Joy, and at the same time, that I was infinitely pleas'd, I trembled. . . . Take the Cause and the Effects together and you have the Sublime."

On a walk before breakfast, I pass a poster of Sophia Loren, in a fashionable fur hat, looking down the valley from a mountaintop. The Sublime has always evoked the grand, the perilous, the irregular, and the breathtaking, and St. Moritz has always attracted personalities of that stripe, and lust. Alfred Hitchcock, Brigitte Bardot, Charlie Chaplin, Errol Flynn, Aristotle Onassis, Audrey Hepburn, Elizabeth Taylor, Ernest Hemingway (who got married here), the Kennedys, George Clooney, all found the frisson of fierce pleasure here in the echo of its incessant avalanches.

Just on the lip of the frozen Lake of St. Moritz, I take a bowl of muesli at the Hotel Bellaval in a room with a haberdashery of hanging horns: deer, chamois, and the ribbed rams' horns of mountain goats, which spiral up and out of their skulls like ammonites. Then I wander over the graceful masonry of an old bridge and up a small hill to find a trio of men in deer-hunter hats and red jackets blowing twelve-foot-long alphorns in front of the Waldhaus am See, a hotel that sits at the end of the lake like a keepsake fallen from some absentminded visitor's pocket. About half of the windows are open with guests leaning

122

Richard Wagner used the alphorn in the score for Tristan and Isolde, *which premiered in 1865. After the first performance he said: "The works I conceived in that serene and glorious Switzerland, with my eyes on the beautiful gold-crowned mountains, are masterpieces, and nowhere else could I have conceived them."*

Photo courtesy of Small World Productions

out to hear. After a couple of melancholy songs, I meet the players who make up the Alphorn Ensemble Engiadina St. Moritz, including Dr. Hans Peter Danuser, the retiring tourism director of the world's most famous winter address, St. Moritz. Hans Peter has been playing his alphorn for twenty-five years, including countless gigs at conventions, confabs, and fairs overseas. "I wouldn't leave home without it!" he declares, but that raises the question of how to travel with such a long instrument. He proceeds to show me that the pine-wood and bamboo horns are made in detachable segments. And he gives me a history of the horn.

In 1555, Zurich naturalist Conrad Gesner described a sort of *litum alpinum* horn, eleven feet long, formed of two long, rounded, hollowed-out pieces of wood tied one to the other with a length of wicker. The instrument was used to herd livestock and to communicate from one valley to another. With the wind behind the player, its sound could carry up to six miles.

In 1805, the first alphorn competition took place at the Unspunnen shepherds' festival with just two contestants facing each other, a sort of dueling banjos with alphorns. In 1826, a dairy farmer, Niklaus von Mülinen, from Bern instructed the composer Ferdinand Fürchtegott how to make alphorns, and music began to be crafted for the instrument. Richard Wagner used the alphorn in the score for *Tristan and Isolde,* which premiered in 1865. After the first performance he said: "The works I conceived in that serene and glorious Switzerland, with my eyes on the beautiful gold-crowned mountains, are masterpieces, and nowhere else could I have conceived them."

But somehow the instrument fell out of favor, and by the turn of the century it had almost disappeared. During the founding of the Federal Yodeler Society in May 1910, only one alphorn was present. But, like rock stars in *Behind the Music,* it came back, partly because of the belief that the sound is pleasing to cows and that those who hear it produce better milk and cheese. Today there are some four thousand instrumentalists, and the cows seem pretty pleased.

DELECTABLE HORROR

I meet, I find the Beautiful—but I give, contribute, or rather attribute the Sublime. No object of Sense is sublime in itself; but only so far as I make it a symbol of some idea. The circle is a beautiful figure in itself; it becomes sublime, when I contemplate eternity under that figure. The Beautiful is the perfection, the Sublime the suspension, of the comparing Power. Nothing not shapely . . . can be called beautiful; nothing that has a shape can be sublime except by metaphore.

—Samuel Taylor Coleridge, 1820

Hans Peter is as sunny as the St. Moritz logo, supposedly the oldest trademark in tourism, and for good reason. In 1986, he was behind the strategy to register the slogan "Top of the World" and the name *St. Moritz* as brands, and now some fifteen categories of merchandise in fifty countries pay a licensing fee for the privilege of using those terms. He also helped design the St. Moritz Clean Energy Tour, a themed walk that shows off several pioneering projects, including a dairy that turns waste into power. The Lataria Engiadinsia in Bever no longer hauls its annual four thousand tons of waste in special trucks across the Alps to a disposal site. Rather it transfers the waste to a nearby water treatment plant, where it is converted into about two hundred eighty thousand kilowatts of electricity a year. There's even a certified carbon-offset cheese produced in the dairy, now sold in shops throughout the country, a partially guiltless purchasing statement, like tap water in a restaurant. Here the heightened awareness of the effects of global warming—Lake Silvaplana didn't freeze in a recent season—is motivating all sorts of clean, green enterprises exploiting renewable resources, from water to geothermal to solar to wind and even biogas from restaurants and gardens. This is the twenty-first century version of the Everlasting League.

I notice that Hans Peter has a splint and Band-Aid on his thumb, and inquire. "Ahh; a snowboarding accident," he says with a grin. An evangelist for the activities of St. Moritz, he practices what he preaches, it seems. He even shaves with water from "Pure Power St. Moritz," clean energy that's branded and exported to Germany and Italy. He says the water makes shavers sexier.

"It all started with a friend of mine, a real solar power fundamentalist, who convinced me that we could use our Alpine notoriety as a platform for renewable energy. But then we had to convince our

Dr. Hans Peter Danuser and author Richard Bangs in St. Moritz. Hans Peter broke his thumb snowboarding. Photo courtesy of Sara Givens

politicians, who first round voted us down fourteen to three. But then we started to collect monies for the conversion privately, with corporate sponsorships, local godfathers, and some famous guests. With funding in place we took it back to our local parliament, and it passed unanimously."

In the middle of his sermon, Hans Peter is drowned out by church bells. So we wait for the rings to cease, and he continues.

"Now St. Moritz has become an expert in all things ecological, which seems a little bit of a joke because of our reputation as a hedonistic resort. But we who live here believe that every individual, every resort, village, and city, should do whatever possible on behalf of the planet, and if we all do so, things will improve."

"OK, then, just how is energy produced here?" I ask, wondering if I can scratch this sheen.

"Well, we have a lot of solar, wind, and thermal power. The farmers convert the rubbish from the hotels into biogas, and via biogas they produce ecological power. But it's also about wise consumption. And we have a fabulous public travel system. It's all electrified. And there's another system called mobility car sharing. It's an association with over seventy thousand members with a fleet of a few thousand red cars parked at the railway stations, including hybrids. I'm driving a Lexus because it's a hybrid.

"Mayors and students come from all over the world to study our grid. But we need to improve, especially when it comes to insulation of buildings. There is lots of potential to do better."

"What would you do better?" I can't help but feel I'm being greenwashed by a public-relations master, but I am in some way enjoying the bath.

"Tougher laws that require better insulation for new or renovated buildings. The biggest loss of energy is from the lousy kinds of buildings we produce.

"Switzerland is a small country with a big population. Tourism is one of the leading industries. The most important attraction to tourists is our nature—pure water, scenery, landscape, climate, clear air, and the sun. You can drink straight from the rivers and lakes here. It's my full conviction that we really have to be careful with these main offerings and to protect them.

"A project like the heating system of Badrutt's Palace shows that even companies that cater to the exclusive and pleasure-seekers can contribute to a cleaner environment. And it's good for business. Guests see the hotel cares. And everyone these days, even very rich people, is concerned about what's going on with the climate. The WWF [World Wildlife Fund] was founded by billionaires. So these people can be very sensible.

"We produce here in the Engadine much more electricity than we can use. But we also import a lot of oil, which is a pity. More and more we take heat from the earth, which is also new for this altitude. Because up until now people thought it wouldn't make sense. But with such high oil prices, we found if we use energy from the earth plus solar power for hot water, it not only is better for the ecology, but also for the economics. We have now some big houses that produce more energy than they need, even in winter, and they give to neighbor houses. Technology nowadays is unbelievable.

"When St. Moritz does something, it becomes trendy and sexy. Now other holiday resorts have started similar programs. If all resorts follow this strategy, I think it can improve the situation in the mountains quite essentially. It's like with our gourmet festival or polo on ice. St. Moritz has always been copied, and this time we are being copied for a good purpose."

chapter eighteen

SHIVERING
PLEASURE

*There are certain scenes that would awe an atheist into
belief, without the help of other argument.*

—Thomas Gray, 1739

From this vantage at the edge of the lake a glinting dome overlooks the water. It appears to be a mausoleum for some noble, but it is rather a museum, built in 1908 and dedicated to fin de siècle painter Giovanni Segantini. I make my way to the stone building and climb a set of steep stairs to the reception desk. There I meet curator Verena Lawrence-Staub, who offers to show me about.

Verena tells me Segantini spent the last five years of his life in the Engadine, painting in a small hut up a nearby peak, an eremite with a model. He was born in 1858 in Arco, a town in the Trentino-Alto Adige region of Italy on the northern shore of Lake Garda, in the shadow of the Alps. He ran away from home at age seven, became a shepherd in the mountains, and taught himself to draw. He attended the Milanese art academy Brera, and lived and worked for most of his life in Brianza. In 1886 he moved to Switzerland with his wife and four children. He died unexpectedly of peritonitis while working in his hut on the Shafberg Mountain above Pontresina. He was forty-one.

Verena leads me through the museum and explains how the pictures on display bear witness to the evolution of the artist's style in the course of his career. In his early works, the influence of traditional Lombardian painting is apparent, she says. Moving to the limpid air of the Alps inspired him to produce luminous paintings that reek of allegory. She says he was heavily influenced by the great landscape painter William Turner during this phase, filling his canvases with precipitous scenery and disrupted horizons to unbalance viewers and pull them into the vertiginous world of the Alps. He used oil for these landscapes, paint made from minerals, and pressed the earth into service to express itself.

We step to a room that features paintings of Barbara Uffer, or "Baba," his nanny, muse, and model. There she is as a girl drinking

The view from atop Muottas Muragl to the snow-glinted mountains, and the dots of the Engadine lakes, looking like giant footprints. John Ruskin, in the fourth volume of Modern Painters, *wrote: "There are yet visible the tracks of ancient glaciers. . . . The footmark, so to speak, of a glacier is just as easily recognizable as the tracks of a horse that had passed along a soft road which yet retained the prints of its shoes."*

Photo courtesy of Sara Givens

at the fountain, and again knitting in a summer meadow, and again as a shepherdess in a scoop of radiant Alpine light. Then there is one of her on a balcony at twilight, another in which she's sleeping in a shady garden, then one of her harvesting hay, and one with her dressed as a maid looking at one of Segantini's paintings by the light of a lantern. They all have a weirdly narcotic quality, as though the artist were painting a dream. Baba was in the mountain hideaway where he was working on the completion of the middle section of a triptych when he passed.

Verena then ushers me up a final set of stairs and into the round room, where on display is that large-scale Alpine triptych, *Life, Nature, Death*—paintings that almost pain with symbolism. Segantini had planned to hang his Engadine panorama at the 1900 Paris World Exhibition and had designed a rotunda pavilion, which is the model for this building. He had hoped to present a universal truth by portraying the eternal cycle of human existence, from birth to death to regeneration, and its inextricable relationship with nature. He called it a "premonition of light, which integrates everything and forms the eternal harmony of the Alpine world." But higher-than-expected costs and his untimely death left the dream undone.

Out of curiosity, I take the steep cogwheel tram up the Muottas Muragl to a viewing platform at eight thousand feet, where Segantini's isolated hut can be seen on a graceful whaleback of snow the next ridge over. Also, as I look up the valley, there is the resplendent scene he was painting when he died: the En River winding to the Danube River, the snow-glinted mountains, and the dots of the Engadine lakes, looking like giant footprints. John Ruskin, in the fourth volume of *Modern Painters,* wrote: "There are yet visible the tracks of ancient glaciers. . . . The footmark, so to speak, of a glacier is just as easily recognizable as the tracks of a horse that had passed along a soft road which yet retained the prints of its shoes."

The white realm between here and the hut is voluptuous and sensuously curved, beckoning with millions of scintillas, and I find resistance impossible. So, into the trackless snow I head. So often in my life I have plunged down unknown rivers and pottered into landscapes inflammatory to the imagination, and at some level I believe the impulse is universal—the desire to find a new way of being, an experience unpredictable, immediate, and authentic. One of my favorite films is Michelangelo Antonioni's *The Passenger,* in which Jack

...ompleted in 1912, the line to the Jungfraujoch bores through three ...ountains, including the Eiger (shown here in the background).

Photo courtesy of John Canning

There are two thousand lakes in Switzerland, including Interlocken in the Bernese Oberland.

Photo courtesy of John Canni

*e Glacier Express, billed as the world's slowest express train, takes
l day to hustle the 180 miles from St. Moritz to Zermatt.*

Kleine Scheidegg, at the base of the Eiger: it was here that John Harlin II's fatal fall down the North Face was followed through a telescope.

e curling thirty feet below the surface inside the Guggi Glacier

From atop Mount Pilatus one can see seventy-three Alpine summits and six lakes. Looking across a sea of clouds is the view of the marching mountains of the Bernese Oberland: the Eiger to the left, the Mönch in the middle, and the Jungfrau on the right.

Photo courtesy of Sara Given

The Limmat River rises in Zürich at the north end of Lake Zürich and flows to the Danube. Like many Swiss rivers, it is intensively used to produce hydroelectric power: along its twenty-mile course, its fall is used by no fewer than ten hydroelectric power stations.

Photo courtesy of Walker Bangs

Because the mind is both attracted and repelled by a sublime object, Immanuel Kant identified The Sublime as a "negative pleasure," or one that is paradoxical. His versions of The Sublime include a violen storm, a rampaging avalanche—any powerfully frightening natural force, or set of forces, all of which are abundant in Switzerland.

Photo courtesy of Walker Ban

Nicholson plays a disillusioned journalist who decides to abandon his past and assume the role of a dead stranger. The tale is a journey though landscapes of identity and mystery, shimmering with danger and uncertainty. And it occurs to me that any trek into the mountains is a similar chance for reinvention, for becoming someone different, perhaps someone better; a chance to explore the inaccessible landscapes and unmapped countries within us.

I take a few gingerly steps into the spotless white blanket. No trace exists of anyone ever having been here before me, but now I violate the perfection with crisp prints, like cookie cutouts. The surface of the snow is frozen into a crust. For the first few yards it holds my weight, but then as I move into deeper stuff my boots crunch through into the soft, stuffed interior. At first the footprints reach to the top of my boots, but as I wade farther the snow climbs higher up me—to my calves, then knees, then thighs. It becomes clear I can't proceed without snowshoes or skis or magic carpet, so I abandon this quest and turn back, following my own suture back to the restaurant, where I plop in for a cup of hot chocolate and a view of the peaks swathed in alpenglow. The sky appears underlit by pink lights of considerable wattage; the mountains seem painted in cochineal. In an earlier age this show was thought to be the reflection of sunlight off a trove of bright treasure beneath the ice; others thought it to be fire lapping against the undersurface of the earth. Now it is a delicious lagniappe to a cup of cocoa.

In the pure morning light I head up into Dorf, the glitzier part of town, and walk down Via Serlas, by ski shops, pâtisseries, and the churches of luxury peddling Chanel, Gucci, Bulgari, Armani, Versace, Cartier, and Louis Vuitton. I pass De Nicola, furrier to the stars, and furry shoppers in horse-drawn carriages, and meet a very down-to-earth, six-foot-tall local mountain guide, mother, and aqua-jogging instructor, Christine Salis. She takes me to a favorite haunt, Hauser Restaurant, which specializes in kangaroo (through some logic that makes sense here) and has a well-known pâtisserie attached where more than sixty types of chocolate are made and sold (to which I fail fabulously in resisting). And she offers to show me her version of St. Moritz.

First she ushers me to the site of the original blade runners, the Cresta Run. The St. Moritz Tobogganing Club was founded in 1887 by a group of English sledding buffs who plotted a splendidly dangerous course from St. Moritz down to the ancient village of Cresta (later absorbed by the present town of Celerina). After the club iced down the course and introduced steel-bladed sleds, the sport sped up dramatically. Before the advent of cars and airplanes, Cresta riders were the fastest men on earth. Sledding the Cresta is, in essence, an unprotected and unsteerable version of riding a bobsled down an ice canal. Dozens of speed-dreamers have broken femurs, tibias, ribs, ankles, pelvises, and necks over the past century; at least four have died.

The Cresta Run is not a permanent structure. Every winter it is built from snow and watered until it becomes an icy snake. The vertical drop from top to bottom is 514 feet, the equivalent of a fifty-story building, while the 3,977-foot-long course has a 13 percent average gradient. Speeds of up to ninety miles an hour have been clocked at the finish line. Christine also shows me the nearby Olympia Bob Run, started in the winter of 1896, by the English, of course, and now the only remaining natural-ice bobsled run in the vertical world. I've made a few bobsled runs at Lake Placid in upstate New York, and they were terrifying as we rocketed along a course while sitting up. Cresta riders are prone, and fly out all the time. Anyone can try the Cresta run for a fee of 600 Swiss francs (about $580), and I'm interested, but then Christine tempts me with another proposition: skiing.

She takes me up the Signal cable car, up to the mesmerism of the high slopes, where the snow and the sky merge into a single blinding mass. The view up here of mountains to infinity once again erodes the Renaissance worldview of man as the measure of all things. We can't conquer these forces or even understand their grammar, but we can blitz down them on skis.

Skiing may be incidental to St. Moritz (some estimates peg 60 percent of the visitors as poseurs), but it shouldn't be. The sky is flawless, like a cupola of glass. Lift lines are almost nonexistent. In the cable car is a striking, haute couture–clad woman carrying what looks a new pair of skis but no boots. We make multiple runs down pistes groomed to corduroy perfection, down such runs as Murezzan, Signal, Paradiso, Fis. Half a century ago, these were the natural conditions each winter, but recently there have been some lean snow seasons, so now some three hundred snowmaking machines guarantee what used to be the norm. Today, though, exquisite flowers of snow are falling on these slopes.

When, late in the day, clouds snatch the sun, my hands turn cold. I stop for a moment and thrust my hands into my armpits, then rub them noisily together before heading back down, trying now to ski faster, as if to outrun the biting weather. But the slope I am attempting has turned to ice, and as I scorch down one densely varnished pitch, I cross my skis in a tight turn and almost capsize. For many years in a youth intoxicated with dauntlessness, I understood that everybody has got to die but believed that an exception would be made in my case. No longer. As I reel toward the edge, I glimpse my own mortality, but in the work of a moment of sublimity, I pull back and head safely down the hill.

FONDUE MEMORIES

The sublime forms a fashion that has persisted uninterrupt-
edly into our own time from the beginnings of modernity. . . .
It has always been a fashion because it has always concerned
a break within or from aesthetics. . . . It has been a kind of
defiance with which aesthetics provokes itself—"enough
beauty already, we must be sublime!"

—Jean-Luc Nancy, 1993

That night, the last in St. Moritz, we head to Chesa Chantarella, a former bathhouse converted into a swishy chalet and restaurant high up on the Salastrains Plateau of Corviglia Mountain. Chalets were originally temporary stone shelters where farmers camped while watching their herds graze on the higher slopes in summer. Like *sublime,* they have assumed quite a different interpretation for today's traveler, and a night's stay at a chalet in St. Moritz now costs the equivalent of some herder's yearly salary. As we drive up the mountain, the sky is clear, and the tilted snowfields on the upper slopes flash the moonlight like signaling mirrors. The Chesa Chantarella has the deliciously sublime tagline "where angels meet devils." In front of a snapping wood fire and above the pearl-string lights of St. Moritz, we splurge on cheese fondue with cherry spirits. We take turns spearing bread cubes and potatoes with long forks and dipping them into a communal pot of hot liquid cheese oozing with white wine and kirsch. When I was in college in the seventies, fondue found favor—pot parties of a different sort—but then it faded like bell-bottoms and paisley prints. But in Switzerland it is the national dish and never lost its cool. Centuries ago in the Alpine valleys, fresh food was difficult to come by in the winter months. Cheese and bread were made locally in the summer and fall with hopes they would last through the winter. As the cold months wore on, both became dry and hard, the stale bread so wooden it literally had to be chopped with an ax. Swiss cow herders found that if the cheese were heated with wine over a fire, it softened, and sopping crusty bread with the concoction made the combination edible, even tasty. As the snow blew outside, it became desirable to huddle around the fire and a large earthenware cooking pot of molten cheese. The dish made its way from the fields to the tables of Swiss aristocracy by way of kitchen

On the Glacier Express, the slowest express train in the world
  Photo courtesy of Sara Givens

servants, who prepared the simple dish with the nobles' finer-quality cheeses and wines and served it in their houses with fresh assortments of crusty breads. And so now it is a fine-dining experience imbued with rarefied Alpine cachet in the finest restaurants of St. Moritz.

The Chesa Chantarella offers its guests an unusual taxi back to town: a guided toboggan run under the stars. Robert Louis Stevenson, who in 1887 came to the area to attempt to cure his consumption, discovered the small-scale sleigh, the *schlitten,* used by the locals as a means of transport. He wrote: "Perhaps the true way to toboggan is . . . at night. . . . You push off; the toboggan fetches way; she begins to feel the hill, to glide, to swim, to gallop. In a breath you are out from under the pine trees, and a whole heavenful of stars reels and flashes overhead. Then comes a vicious effort; for by this time your wooden steed is speeding like the wind, and you are spinning round a corner, and the whole glittering valley and all the lights in all the great hotels lie for a moment at your feet; and the next you are racing once more in the shadow of the night, with close-shut teeth and beating heart. . . . This, in an atmosphere tingling with forty degrees of frost, in a night made luminous with stars and snow, and girt with strange white mountains, teaches the pulse an unaccustomed tune and adds a new excitement to the life of man upon his planet."

The morning next, I meet up with my thirteen-year-son, Walker, who is on school break and who has been nuts about trains his whole life. We board the Glacier Express, billed as the slowest express train in the world, and ride across the great weal of the Alps. Railways are the thumping arteries of Switzerland; there are some three thousand miles of track. But perhaps nothing rides a more spectacular route than this run. The sleek red train takes all day to hustle the 180 miles from St. Moritz to Zermatt, "the bouquet at the end," according to Peidr Härtli, a representative for the line, who sees us off. He says a quarter million folks a year take this transalpine jaunt.

There is no "*allllll* aboard." The Swiss are too subtle for that. Instead, promptly at 9:08 a.m., the doors shoosh closed with perfect synchronicity, and the train glides from the station.

As evident with first boarding, this is not your usual commuter train. It is more like a cruise ship on steel wheels. Our club seats are roomy and cushy, and on either side and above are picture-perfect, triple-glass, wraparound windows. Unlike a cruise ship, which typically travels at night so customers can spend days exploring ports of call, here the transport moves only in daylight so riders can soak in the scenery.

There is something primally attractive about trains and their tracks. They sweep away the hindrances of geography and open the acreage of the mind. They make us indivisible from the landscapes we traverse. They are moving arenas of intense experience, places to become temporarily disconcerted or presented with the illusion of menace, all with a comfortable seat and a nicely structured glass of Valais wine.

The route misses no excuse to shoot through a tunnel, negotiating ninety-one in all. It crosses 291 bridges and wanders through several screens of illusion, making many detours off the path of reason. We roller-coaster through terrain that is a triumph of the senses over rationale, riding what writer John McPhee calls "precision instruments that in other countries are known as trains."

We slide down the shadowed floor of the gorge of the River En, cross the ice channel of the Cresta Run, and move into the wide valley dominated by the white knives of the Bernina Mountains. To the south of Celerina we glide by the fourteenth-century, Romanesque Church of San Gian (St. John the Baptist), then through Samedan, main town of the Upper Engadine. Then we turn north and climb the Val Bever, escorted by larches and Alpine fields smoothed with snow. We spiral up to the three-and-a-half-mile-long Albula Tunnel, highest in the Alps, another splendid Swiss engineering attempt to bend nature—one that saw sixteen men die in the thrust and bore through the rock. We then sweep down the other side over eight viaducts, a carousel ride of rolling stock, often teetering on the edge of nothingness. As we gaze over these cliffs into the irrevocable, life's choices are never more clearly defined.

The line between Preda and Bergun is a technical piece of wizardry, with coils and crisscrosses and horseshoe-loop tunnels, all trying to tame the steep gradient. Through the window I see a massive onion dome, a watchtower from the seventeenth century. We pass thick pine forests and a long, gushing waterfall that evokes a heightened awareness of the mere fact of being present. We are gulped by

On the Glacier Express, riders are irresistibly drawn to the unbelievable forces and caprices of natural design on display outside the windows.

Photo courtesy of Walker Bangs

another spiral tunnel only to shoot from the other side onto a curving, arched masonry bridge, the sweep of the six slender stone pillars of the Landwasser Viaduct. As I look down to the river cascading below, it feels as though the viaduct is swaying liquidly back and forth, liable to pitch us to a watery death. It for a moment deceives the mind into imagining its own annihilation, which is reason enough to take this train. I want to steal the fleetingness of this feeling and put it in a bottle.

We pass the Via Mala (Evil Way), the fifteenth-century road that traverses a tight and dismal gash in the great stone book, "the most sublime and tremendous defile in Switzerland," according to John Murray's 1829 *Handbook for Travellers in Switzerland and the Alps of Savoy and Piedmont.* The sun doesn't shine on its floor, delivering a mood gloomy and claustrophobic. It was painted several times by William Turner and sketched by Goethe in 1788. For its era, this was the shortest, fastest, and most dangerous route across the Alps, and it made those who entered shiver. The Via Mala owes its eldritch, ominous atmosphere to the geology. As the mountains here were uplifted again and again, the Hinterrhein River acted as a circular saw cutting through the schist.

The gorge maintained its vertiginous integrity as the embracing Alps were delivered into the jaws of erosion.

I take a moment to try to read a copy of Murray, but my eyes won't let me. In an admixture of pleasure and revulsion they are drawn to the unbelievable forces and caprices of natural design on display outside the panoramic windows. "I must have torrents, rocks, pines, dead forest, mountains, rugged paths to go up and down, precipices beside to frighten me," wrote Jean-Jacques Rousseau in 1775, though he could have been writing about today's Glacier Express, "for the odd thing about my liking of precipitous places is that they make me giddy, and I enjoy this giddiness greatly, provided that I am safely placed."

In the Christian Middle Ages, philosophers articulated not only that man was deficient and flawed by the original sin that drove him from paradise, but also that all nature is damaged and suffers from imperfection and decomposition that began in the beginning. Mountains in particular are rebukes, visible reminders of the wrath of God. The late scholar Louis Ginzberg's *Legends of the Jews* recounts the story that among the punishments inflicted after Adam and Eve were evicted from paradise was that the world "was to be divided into valleys and mountains . . . and finally she shall, one day, 'wax old like a garment.' "

According to Middle Ages thinking, only through the act of Christ's redemptive work could man and nature be liberated from these defects and reattain their original state of integrity. Theologians called this structural defect of nature *natura lapsa* and considered earthquakes and landslides as repair workshops for nature's dents. And that gave the early railroad evangelists an excuse for scarring the mountains with tracks and tunnels: they were out to improve *natura lapsa*.

chapter twenty

FRIGHTFUL TOO FAR

To the geological enquirer, every mountain chain offers striking monuments of the great alternations that the globe has undergone. The most sublime speculations are awakened, the present is disregarded, past ages crowd upon the fancy, and the mind is lost in admiration of the designs of that great power who has established order which at first view appears as confusion.

—Humphry Davy, 1805

We breeze into the Bronze Age village of Tiefencastel, then onward through forests of spruce to cross the Solis Bridge over the Schynschucht Gorge, which the Albula River squeezes through in a torrent of white water. The sides of this gap are incised laterally with dozens of muscular rills left over from the glacial retreat after the Pleistocene Ice Age. There are ribbons of creamy-looking rocks called mylonites, the paste that results when rock grinds against rock in tectonic torture. Looking down the gorge at some points evokes a dizzy, heady feeling, one that Percy Shelley boasted of: "Danger which sports upon the brink of precipices has been my playmate." Dropping from Thusis, we veer north and spool through a landscape that wears the contours of a fairy tale: Burgenland, "land of castles," where every hilltop is festooned with ruined forts and citadels guarding the valley of the Lower Rhine. In *Peri Hupsos,* Longinus remarked that men do not admire "the little streams, transparent though they be, and useful too, but Nile, or Tiber or Rhine." And such is in evidence here. The castles are not on creeks, but boldly looking over the roiling Rhine.

We then purl into Chur, the main city of the Land of the Three Bunds (Graubünden, also known as the Grisons). Looking out the window in the station, Walker tugs at my sleeve and points to a green-snouted brute of a train engine on the next set of tracks. "That's a Crocodile," I'm proud to convey in one of those delightful but diminishing opportunities for parental information-passing when the audience is your own teen.

I take a drawl of Passugger mineral water, which comes from the spring in Chur. The Swiss believe in eating and drinking locally produced products, so finding bottled water from a South Pacific Island or a brand that requires that a tree be planted to offset the carbon spent in its transportation is not easy. We drop into the Flims Gorge. Its chalky cliffs shelve into the Rhine River, which has gathered urgency in this confinement, churning enticingly to a rafting enthusiast such as I in its race to the North Sea. When Wordsworth looked into a similar stream in 1850, he wrote: "If a traveler be among the Alps, let him surrender up his mind to the fury of the gigantic torrents, and take delight in the contemplation of their almost irresistible violence."

Evelyne says this section is called the "Swiss Grand Canyon," and though, having worked for several seasons as a guide in the Grand Canyon of the Colorado River, I wince whenever others evoke the name for their own, I admit to catching myself speaking in hushed tones. We pass the debris of an enormous landslide, one that late in the last ice age dammed the river and turned this canyon into a giant lake. It brings home once again how fleeting and ultimately futile any work of man is against nature.

By the time lunch is announced, our solarium on wheels is describing a serpentine route eastward. There are no curtains on these carriage windows, and it's difficult to imagine that in an earlier era there were, and that they were closed. With the river panorama unfolding on one side, a mountain vista on the other, straight ahead is a glass of Malanser Blauburgunder and a Valais pork steak covered with baked tomatoes and cheese, fattening us for the killer views. The last time I had lunch on a train I had been in Ethiopia and had purchased a papaya, some pumpkin seeds, and a Coke through the window from a street vendor.

As we exit the nine-mile-long gorge, the sides peel back to bright meadows that spool away to distant white peaks, fortified churches, and fifteenth-century houses. Beyond Ilanz, the countryside becomes pastoral, the route gentle and sinuous. There is a rhythm and elegance here that is almost musical. We enter the frame of the peaks of Signina and glide into a forest of alders, stitching up the Greina Pass. Here, as we curve around the mountains, there is a moment, maybe induced by the wine I am sipping, where the mountains seem to stir. For an instant I imagine the mountain shucking off its snow, as if taking off a coat, and challenging this train to a battle for the territory of The Sublime.

Then in Disentis we change locomotives, to the MGB (Matterhorn-Gottard-Bahn) "mountain climber," and with a clang we move to rack-and-pinion mode for the big climb. (A toothed bar placed centrally between the rails is engaged by a pinion on the undercarriage of the train.) We twist up out of the valley of the Vorderrhein, where the eighteenth-century Disentian monk Placidus a Spescha would regularly climb to the summit of one of the nearby mountains and sleep, wrapped in cowl and habit, to spend the night closer to God. At a relatively level stretch, our waitress, Neusa Peixoto, who was born in Angola, demonstrates her skill at "fountain splashing"—pouring clear grappa from a bottle held several feet above her head, down like a thin waterfall to the peculiar angle-stemmed glass. Near the source of the Rhine, we pass through a sheer-walled canyon of snow stitched up high with steel nets and grids, attempts to break the violent power of avalanches and rockfalls. It takes the help of a cogwheel to make the Oberalp Pass, at 6,670 feet the highest point on the journey, desolate above the tree line. To the west we see the summits of the Gotthard Massif, including Piz Badus, whose melting snow is the source of the River Rhine. The dualism of The Sublime is in these summit sights, as they seem both dominantly desirable and terrible. I can quite imagine the joy of reaching one of these crests, but know also how cold and fearful that would be. It is very good to be in this heated car and to gaze out the tall windows and dream.

We curl around Lake Oberalp, and as I watch out the window a glimpse of the landscape looks like a white jacket unzipped by the train tracks. We cross into Canton Uri and then through a long gallery tunnel built to protect the line from avalanches. Then, with the soft creaking and jangling of the engine switching back to gear operation, as though at the top of a roller-coaster loop, we all take a breath before unscrambling the mountain, making a series of elbow bends that allow off-and-on views to the north of the bizarrely formed pinnacles of Rienzenstock. Then we swoop down into the wide trough of the Urseren valley, where we screech to a stop at the junction at Andermatt, at the bottom of the Gotthard Pass connecting to northern Italy. It was this traverse that dazzled Charles Dickens, who had been authoring bleak accounts of the underbelly of soot-filled London. Upon his return from Switzerland in 1845, he wrote, "The whole descent between Andermatt and Altdorf . . . is the highest sublimation of all you can imagine in the way of Swiss scenery. O God! What a beautiful country it is!"

Andermatt was and is one of the grand historic crossroads on the north-south trade route across the Alps. As part of Switzerland's continued drive to transfer movement from road to rail, another epic tunnel is being bored, the Gotthard Base Tunnel, to be the longest in the world, connecting to Milan, cutting road travel time from Zurich to Milan by an hour and emissions per traveler by a not-insignificant amount.

Here, at the great entrepôt of Andermatt, we exit the Glacier Express and decide to take a detour to the Bernese Oberland, where I spent some time a few years back with John Harlin III when he was making his attempt to climb the Eiger.

WE ARE BUT DUST POSTPONED

Reason now gazes above the realm of the dark but warm feelings as the Alpine peaks do above the clouds. They behold the sun more clearly and distinctly, but they are cold and unfruitful.

—G. C. Lichtenberg, 1765

We arrive at Lauterbrunnen in the shank of the afternoon, when the slender Staubbach waterfall, plunging a sheer 984 feet, is backlit, the sunbow's rays arching in the slanted light. This is the fall that inspired Johann Wolfgang von Goethe's poem *Gesang der Geister über den Wassern* (*Song of the Spirits above the Waters*). Lord Byron compared this cascade to the "tail of the pale horse ridden by Death in the Apocalypse." The glacially carved Lauterbrunnen Valley also provided the pictorial model for J. R. R. Tolkien's sketches and watercolors of the fictitious valley of Rivendell and the name of the Bruinen River (*Bruinen* meaning "Loudwater"), which flowed through it. The official tourist brochure for the region calls this the "Valley of Waterfalls," claiming seventy-two, and espouses the poetry it has inspired. It reminds me of what I call an Outward Bound backdrop. For a spell in 2001–02, I served as president of Outward Bound. One of its practices was to encourage participants while out in the wilds to make journal entries, which were shared with others around the campfire and even back home. I had the privilege of reading many of these diary musings, and there was a common theme of inspiration found in mountaintops, sunsets, and waterfalls. At the end of my tenure, I realized that perhaps no organization in history could claim to have provoked so much bad poetry as Outward Bound.

We switch to a small, cogwheel voiture that pushes an open baggage carriage, and we toil up through tunnels and past snow-bowed trees to the nearly car-free hamlet of Wengen. (No roads lead to the town, just the mountain railway.) Walker and I check in to the elephantine Hotel Regina, a short graft up the hill from the station and adjacent to a busy ski path. Proprietors Guido and Ariane Meyer show me about the six-story Victorian, built in 1894, which in areas

evokes the hotel in the film version of *The Shining*. I half expect a
boy to career around the hallway corner on a tricycle. Guido says his
father was the manager when he and his brother were kids, and they
used to run about the hallways and break things. Finally, he bought
the place.

I ask Guido why Wengen, and by extension so much of Switzerland, seems so pristine after all these decades of tourism.

"It's because Switzerland is small; because Wengen is small,
only eight hundred people year-round. And we stay put. In America,
families move every two years. In Switzerland, it's every two generations. Here, some families go back eight hundred years. If I go for
a walk, I know every person in the valley, most by name, so if you
know folks by name you are more careful what you are doing. You
can't just go around dumping and throwing things around because
people will point a finger at you. All people who live up here are
aware. If somebody makes a fire and burns his leaves, it will not take
five minutes until somebody will knock on his door and say, 'You're
not allowed to do that. Will you please stop?' So people act differently here than elsewhere.

"And we are all concerned about preserving our clean environment. Even my son and daughter are into it. When they brush their
teeth, they turn off the water, while older people might not do that.
And if you ask them why, they say, 'We must take care of the water!' "

And so, knowing that the pipes are old and that running water
can be heard throughout the building, I decide to skip the shower this
night.

The best part of the Regina is the view: from my balcony I
can scan the Lauterbrunnen Valley and the Jungfrau. It's easy to
imagine how early travelers from England, used to the flat light
of the lowlands, were swept away with these high vistas. The

visionary amplitudes of altitude must have felt like approximations of divine sight.

This window scene is likely similar to what Lord Byron gazed upon when he wrote several verses of his epic *Manfred*, in which his hero wants to throw himself from the cliffs of the Jungfrau. I can almost understand the draw to the mountain and why it evokes dangerous behavior. But I hear a peal of laughter close to me and look down from the sill to a gleeful group of ice-skaters on a rink, skiers whooshing by, and a Swiss flag, with its distinctive white cross against a red background on a square cloth, flapping on a steeple. Evelyne likes to say the Swiss flag is the only one with a plus sign, and for valid reasons. The flag inherited its shape from the cantonal flags, which were also square. The only other square flag in the world is that of the Vatican, which was probably adopted from that of the Pope's Swiss Guard. When Switzerland joined the United Nations in 2002, protocol officials faced a sticky situation: UN rules say all flags flying at headquarters must be oblong. Fortunately, this was overridden by another rule to the effect that a new flag may be hoisted as long as its total area does not exceed that of the regular flags.

While we are taking lunch at Jack's Brasserie, the baronial dining room, with chandeliers as big as icebergs, in clunks Sammy Salm, head of tourism for the Jungfrau region. He's wearing heavy plastic ski boots, having just schussed down the mountain on his afternoon off. I worked with Sammy a couple of years ago during John Harlin's Eiger climb and am glad to see his wide grin and his perfect Justin Timberlake stubble, which seems to have its own greens keeper. He grew up in the shadow of the Eiger, learned to ski as a young boy, took a detour to Copper Mountain in Colorado for a brief period, but realized he loved the Alps best and moved back to become a full-time evangelist and practitioner. We step outside to a little loggia above a ski run and beneath the blushing Jungfrau to catch up.

As we look around at the various ski lifts and the traces of skiers and snowboarders all over the basin, Sammy reminds me that it wasn't that long ago that the Swiss considered the upper realms of these mountains damned, the dwellings of the devil. Glaciers were snakes of ice, agents of unquiet spirits, and priests were routinely summoned to keep them at bay. Besides harboring the dragons who occupied the upper realms, the Alps were steep, cold, nasty, frightening, and dangerous. It wasn't until the English showed up and started to pay locals to guide them upward that the Swiss found the splendor in tourism and then became tourists themselves in their own domain. Sammy says that most of the skiers on this hill today are Swiss and that they are as filled with deeply charged emotion and suspense about the scenery as any visitor. It does seem the definition of breathtaking. He shares the fact that the Arctic scenes in *The Golden Compass* were filmed here, and I remember thinking that those scenes were more remarkable than all the others that had over-the-top special effects. No FX needed here.

In 1850, Sammy would not have had a job like this. There was no tourism, and the dirt-poor population depended on a precarious Alpine agricultural existence below the snow line. The region was not within easy reach of main Alpine trading routes, so there was little hope for development. The only tourists were some two thousand cows. When the train arrived in 1894, things changed almost overnight. Within a few years there were more tourist beds than today. (That has to do partly with the fact that there were no in-room bathrooms, just common water closets shared by a whole floor, and visitors didn't take many baths back then. The bedrooms were generally smaller, and thus more were squeezed into each hotel.) Over

Sammy Salm, head of tourism for the Jungfrau region, with the author in the car-free resort of Wengen   Photo courtesy of Sara Givens

time, the village earned a reputation, and several notables came for inspiration, such as Tchaikovsky, Wagner, Schiller, and Goethe. It found favor among a set of Americans when six thousand were interned here during World War II. Now, 95 percent of the area's income is from tourism, and many of the residents are far better off than their foreign guests.

Grindelwald, where Sammy is based, is also the place where what is commonly called the Golden Age of Mountaineering began, with Alfred Wills's ascent of the "peak of tempests," the 12,143-foot spire of the Wetterhorn, in 1854. He was a barrister, the man who presided as judge over the final trial of Oscar Wilde, and while on honeymoon he decided to give the peak a go. After a twenty-two-hour ascent along crenellated ridges, one just four inches wide, he and his guides made the summit and planted a couple of flags (one made of a sheet of iron) that the residents of Grindelwald could see. Wills described the scenery as "of indescribable sublimity." Others had climbed the Alps before Wills and had even summited the Wetterhorn, but Wills was a gifted writer as well. Of one moment on the climb, when his team was faced with a sheer drop of nine thousand feet, he wrote: "I am not ashamed to own that I experienced, as this sublime and wonderful prospect burst upon my view, a profound and almost irrepressible emotion—an emotion which, if I may judge by the low ejaculations of surprise, followed by a long pause of breathless silence, as each in turn stepped into the opening, was felt by others as well as myself. Balmat [his guide] told me repeatedly, afterwards, that it was the most awful and startling moment he had known in the course of his long mountain experience."

Wills was perhaps the first to advocate to a wide audience mountaineering as a pursuit worthwhile in and of itself, and his words influenced a generation of Brits to follow in his footsteps and feelings.

Sammy goes on to tell me how things have changed in his lifetime, about how winters now come later and summers are hotter, and how the famous glacier in Grindelwald—the one to which Thomas Cook's clients first disported, the men in dark tweed, the women in voluminous black dresses, all with fanged alpenstocks—used to be a twenty-minute walk from the village. Now it is a ninety-minute trek, so much has it retreated. But, he adds, the Swiss are doing much to reverse the trend, including driving less, using less heating oil, even covering some of their glaciers in blankets to slow the melting. Switzerland is waging a quiet war for the custody of its future, and perhaps the world's. Sammy is a hopeful foot soldier, and his ordnance is a pair of skis. He clicks back into them, turns around, and barrels down the hill.

chapter twenty-two

SHAKEN AND STIRRED

You only live twice: Once when you're born, once when you look death in the face.

—Ian Fleming, 1964

As the next day forms, I awake to a crump and then a distant rumble, probably the musketry of an avalanche. Byron said he heard avalanches falling "every five minutes" in Wengen, but that was before avalanche fences and global warming. I pull back the curtains and see scarves of cirrus rolling across the valley, outriggers of a storm. Byron described a similar scene: "From whence we stood, on the Wengen Alp the clouds rose from the opposite valley, curling up perpendicular precipices like the foam of the ocean of hell, during a spring tide—it was white and sulphury, and immeasurably deep in appearance."

After breakfast we step outside to a day pivoted from clouds to clear sky—there is an incorrigible plurality of weather here—and make our way to Stechelberg, at the plinth of the Jungfrau mountain. Among a cattle herd of skiers, we crowd into the tram to make the vertiginous ride up the Schilthorn. "Men are not made to be crowded together in anthills," Rousseau said in arguing for the liberty of mountaintops. If he could but see this paradox now. Four cable cars, the longest aerial cableway in the Alps, are needed to climb to Piz Gloria, the mountaintop "allergy research center" featured in perhaps the worst James Bond film in the series, *On Her Majesty's Secret Service*. Along the way we fly over a number of recent avalanche slides and the cracks of those upcoming. As recently as February 6, 2003, two major avalanches fell all the way into Stechelberg, and though nobody was harmed, several families were trapped in their homes for days. This is also the slope where "Bond girl" Contessa Teresa Draco di Vincenzo, played by the Sublime Diana Rigg, outskis an avalanche and the bad guys. And this is also a mecca for BASE jumpers, with a host of thousand-foot-high cliffs. Until a recent fatal accident, it was also a bungee-jumping site.

On the tram to the Schilthorn. Four cable cars, the longest aerial cable way in the Alps, are needed to climb to Piz Gloria, the mountaintop "allergy research center" featured in the James Bond film On Her Majesty's Secret Service.   Photo courtesy of Small World Productions

It's a Xanax ride as I look out the floor-to-ceiling front windows—and one in which it is easy to imagine one's demise. If something goes wrong here, as has occasionally happened on cable cars throughout the world, there is no option. Gravity doesn't ever forget itself or temporarily go off duty. But that feeling eases away as we approach the building that looks like a parasol on a White Russian.

We dock and unload to Ernst Stavro Blofeld's villainous lair on the Schilthorn. George Lazenby starred in his one and only turn as 007 in the 1969 United Artists film, and it was all downhill from there. We climb to the summit house above the revolving restaurant at the Touristorama and watch a free fifteen-minute video (who would ever pay?) about the making of the Bond film, complete

On the ride to the Schilthorn it's easy to imagine one's own demise. If something goes wrong here, as has occasionally happened on cable cars throughout the world, there is no option. Gravity doesn't ever forget itself or temporarily go off duty.
Photo courtesy of Small World Productions

with cheesy clips, finishing with a model of the building being blown to bits.

The proprietors milk the Bond association every which way. Vodka martinis—shaken, not stirred—can be tasted at the James Bond Bar. There is a James Bond Champagne breakfast. We stop at the retro revolving restaurant, order a lunch of James Bond spaghetti, and watch as some two hundred peaks of the Bernese Alps scroll by in the hour-long revolution. With two solar-powered platforms spinning at just over 9,750 feet, it is among the highest rotating restaurants in the world. Then we move outside onto Blofeld's helicopter pad—the open-air terrace, bloodstains long gone, now alight with corvine birds sporting red legs and glossy black plumage. Standing on this aerie, in the thin, transparent air, we can practically touch the Eiger, Mönch, and Jungfrau. Beyond, we can see all the way to Mont Blanc and the Black Forest, and just below we see the slope down which Bond chased Blofeld in a bobsled and where the archvillain broke his neck and plotted the revenge that would kill Bond's new bride, Teresa di Vincenzo.

After a panoptic look around, we ride back down the mountain and exit midway at the clinging-by-its-eyebrows town of Mürren. Here I meet Irene Thali, a 27-year-old marketing representative for the Schilthorn Cableway, who tells me she was born in the Alps, grew up here, and started her career as a guide here. A couple of years ago she was offered a high-paying job in the city as a sales rep for a big pharmaceutical company. She took the job for the money, but after a few months realized the mountains were more important than money to her, and so she quit and came back. She says she knew she had made the right decision when a couple of weeks ago she escorted an American travel agent to this loft, and as he looked around he started to cry with joy. "That emotional currency is worth more than any paycheck," she says with a smile.

We stroll the narrow terrace of the eight-hundred-year-old village, traffic-free but crowded with skiers, choughs, and views, including one of the terribly delightful troika of the Eiger, Mönch, and Jungfrau. Mürren may be the birthplace of the "ski turn" and slalom skiing. In 1910, when the train went into service, Sir Henry Lunn, owner of the Palace Hotel here, opened his doors for the winter season. He had noticed that "midwinter in the high Alps is an earthly paradise—the gloom and fog and damp are left in the valley below, while up in the eternal snows the sun is often too hot to bear, and the sparkling atmosphere is more of a tonic than the finest Champagne." Lunn tried to promote the new sport of alpine skiing. But the breakneck topography didn't lend itself to little straight schusses. Sir Henry's

It used to take weeks to climb the North Face of the Eiger. But in 2008, Ueli Steck of Switzerland set a new speed record, climbing the Heckmair Route, first ascended in July 1938 by Heinrich Harrer, Anderl Heckmair, Fritz Kasparek, and Wiggerl Vörg, in two hours, forty-seven minutes, and thirty-three seconds.

Photo courtesy of Didrik Johnck

son, Sir Arnold Lunn, is credited then as being the first to perfect the downhill turn and the inventor of the art of the slalom. In the 1920s, the sport of skiing mostly involved ski jumping and the Scandinavian technique of cross-country. When in 1931 Arnold organized the British Ski Championship on the Scheidegg, consisting of downhill and style competitions, he was severely criticized. His new method of skiing was described as "only for those who were too scared to jump or too weak to cross-country." We know the end of this story.

It was here too that railway tycoon Adolf Guyer-Zeller took a holiday in 1893 and while hiking the steep slopes found inspiration for his greatest work: a train that would corkscrew through three mountains of the Bernese Oberland. We make our way down the sheer slopes and over to the ultimate iron horse traverse.

We depart from Wengen and curl our way first to Kleine Scheidegg, where we disgorge to a giant tepee near the base of the Eiger, where all visitors crane their necks upward, imagining the summit and the view, the inverted gravity of desire. I spent many long days here during John Harlin III's attempt to climb the North Face. The face looks different now. A few weeks after John's climb, a big chunk of the Eiger wall collapsed, cracking apart as rock expanded with the warmer weather that has plagued the Alps, and a hunk of iconic Switzerland is now gone. The erosion seems to be accelerating, but then so is the quest for the simple geometry of The Sublime. When Queen Victoria ascended the throne, it took thirty-six days to travel to the Swiss Alps and back. When Thomas Cook launched his excursion train, it took two weeks. Now one can have breakfast in London, fly to Zurich for midmorning tea, helicopter to the Eiger for lunch, and be back in London for dinner.

It used to take weeks to climb the North Face of the Eiger. But in 2008, Ueli Steck from Switzerland set a speed record, climbing the Heckmair Route, first ascended in July 1938 by Heinrich Harrer, Anderl Heckmair, Fritz Kasparek and Wiggerl Vörg, in two hours, forty-seven minutes, and thirty-three seconds, beating his own record of the year before. If the pursuit of The Sublime continues to accelerate at this pace, we will, at some point, swallow our own tails, or quantum-leap into the future.

We continue up the rack railway for about a mile to the Eiger Glacier Station, where climbers disembark to hike to the base of the North Face and begin their ascent. The view straight up is so disorienting that for a second I feel myself falling upward, and I must bring my eyes back to my lap to regain equilibrium. Then into the darkness we plunge, and for the next four miles the train bores into the mountains, a barmy conceit for any route if ever there was such. In the late nineteenth century, entrepreneurs and engineers began proposing different ways of taking tourists up to the Jungfrau— including one that entailed shooting travelers up a dead-straight tunnel in vehicles propelled by compressed air. It was Guyer-Zeller, a textile and railroad magnate, who hit on the winning formula of riddling through the Eiger, Mönch, and Jungfrau mountains with six miles of twisting track; and it was Guyer-Zeller who wrested into being the technology, persuaded the Swiss Parliament to grant him the concession (he pledged 100,000 Swiss francs to equip a meteorological station at the top), and managed to raise the necessary funds. But Guyer-Zeller didn't live to see the fulfillment of his fancy. The first section opened in 1898; six months later he died of a heart attack at age fifty-nine. His sons continued the work but met with a number of disasters, including fatal accidents and an explosion of thirty tons of dynamite in 1908 that echoed as far away as Germany. The line to the Jungfraujoch was completed in 1912, nine years later than planned and 500 million Swiss francs over budget.

It seems an effort that would be impossible today, if just for the environmental considerations. But it exists, and is a wooziness-inducing ride, Space Mountain as the real deal.

Out the open windows, the view switches from ragged rock to backlit displays of luxury watches, perfumes, and cell phones as we slow to the first stop inside the mountain, the Eigerwand (North

Wall) Station, at about 9,400 feet. We are granted a five-minute break to step through a cold, dripping passage to peek out the huge observation window that looks down to the Grindelwald Valley and Kleine Scheidegg, and beyond Interlocken to Lake Thun. The window was punched through the mountain as a hole through which to eject rock while the tunnel was being blasted. It became an escape route for climbers (and was featured in Clint Eastwood's film *The Eiger Sanction*) and still is the departure route for rescue missions. We used it extensively during the IMAX shoot for John Harlin III's attempt a couple of years back. Looking down this sheer wall, even protected by thick glass, evokes a fizzy, nauseated, faintly erotic feeling of terror.

The heavy machinery of ascent then continues and stops again at the Eismeer (Sea of Ice) Station, at 10,368 feet, which allows a stratospheric view down the glacier of the same name, so white it flashes with magnesium intensity. Through the glass it looks like a photograph, frozen forever, but it is always moving, one way or the other, a piece of geography in a permanent state of flux.

Beyond loom the alarm-sounding peaks of the Schreckhorn, Lauteraarhorn, and Fiescherhorn. The brochure calls this a view of "eternal ice and rock," but, knowing what we do about natural erosion, tectonic-plate movements, and climate change, this must be a case of Swiss optimism.

chapter twenty-three

ROCK
AND AWE

*The immensity of these precipitous mountains, with their
starry pyramids of snow, excluded the sun, which overtopped
not, even in its meridian, their overhanging rocks. . . .
No spectator could have refused to believe that some spirit
of great intelligence and power had hallowed these wild and
beautiful solitudes to a deep and solemn mystery. . . .
To live, to breathe, to move, was itself a sensation of
immeasurable transport.*

—Percy Shelley, 1814

We continue the thirty-minute wind and exit at the Jungfraujoch, at 11,333 feet billed as "The Top of Europe," into a mad, Buck Rogers version of a space-age domed building called The Sphinx.

We first step through a blue revolving door into the Eispalast, The Ice Palace, for a tour inside the belly of the beast of a glacier. We're thirty feet below the surface, and our breath plumes in the cold air as we slip and glide through a vault of blue ice, a rendered version of Kal-El's Fortress of Solitude, but prettified with whimsical ice sculptures of eagles, fish, penguins, and polar bears. We stoop under arches, slide through halls, and mince down labyrinthine, cavernlike passageways. Then our guide, René Krebs, takes us on a little detour, up a staircase to an ice grotto with a curling court and an ice bar, complete with frosted glasses, chilled Swiss wine, even an icy bottle of Jim Beam.

René tells us that ninety years ago, two mountain guides from Grindelwald and Wengen began to hack a hall inside the Guggi glacier, using ice picks and saws in the dark. When done, they charged a single Swiss franc to tourists. It took off and became an attraction. Now the tools are powered, and teams of professionals keep the carvings fresh for the many globe-trotters who pass through. The greatest enemy these days is the heat brought into the Ice Palace by the visitors. The body heat of each guest generates the energy equivalent of a 100-watt lightbulb, and more than three quarters of a million bodies a year tromp through. Three years ago, an air-conditioning system was installed in the Ice Palace to attempt to keep the room temperature at an even twenty-eight degrees Fahrenheit, but even that may not be enough. René says they just had to carve a new entrance because the old one was flooded by melting ice. "If we didn't use air-conditioning, we would have a swimming pool, not an ice palace," René reports.

Glaciers, of course, were among the bizarre phenomena that first caught the attention of British travelers. In 1673, a Mr. Muraltus penned a letter that was published by the Royal Society of London praising the "Icy and Chyrstallin Mountains of Helvetia." The report carried one of the first illustrations of the Lower Grindelwald glacier and this description: "The Mountain it self . . . is very high, and extends it self every year more and more over the neighboring meadows, by increments that make a great noise of cracking. There are great holes and caverns, which are made when the Ice bursts; which happens at all times, but especially in the Dog-days. Hunters do there hang up their game they take during the great heat, to make it keep sweet by that means. . . . When the Sun shineth, there is seen such a variety of colors as in a Prism." Glacier-going was born.

Outside, on the viewing platform, the air smells cleaner and colder, oxygen-flavored. It's good to be out of the inside of the glacier, which was after a time a bit claustrophobic. Joseph Addison suggested why we inherently like platforms over grottoes: "The mind of man naturally hates every thing that looks like a restraint upon it. . . . A spacious horizon is an image of liberty."

We look down the Great Aletsch Glacier. At 45 square miles in surface and 13.6 miles long and shrinking, it is still the longest ice stream in the Alps and the main feeder to the Upper Rhône. Looking down the long tongue, I can see crevasses big enough to swallow the Glacier Express. Beneath us, a helicopter, appearing no larger than a mosquito, buzzes over the ice, shooting a bottled-water commercial. Two men roped together are traversing the upper glacier, looking like ants ascending a bathtub. I can see the cross-sections of the glacier, and even though I suffer from acritochromacy, I am struck by the multicolored strata of ice, white near the surface, passing through shades of cobalt, ultramarine, even hints of green.

The Great Aletsch Glacier is 45 square miles in surface, and 13.6 miles long and shrinking.
Yet it is still the longest ice stream in the Alps, and the main feeder to the Upper Rhône.
Photo courtesy of Didrik Johnck

Evelyne says she took a hike down the Aletsch Glacier just last year and points to the Concordia overnight hut built in the nineteenth century for such excursions. I see a dot hanging from a rocky outcrop high above the glacier. It was constructed at the glacier's seam, but reaching it now requires a steep climb up steps along the granite face. The cold fact is that the Aletsch Glacier receded by more than three hundred feet from 2005 to 2006 and at this rate could be gone by the year 2100. Global warming, Evelyne says, is the culprit. Two years after climbing Pilatus, Conrad Gesner wrote that the Alps "are the Theatre of the Lord, displaying monuments of past ages, such as precipices, rocks, peaks and chasms and never-melting glaciers."

The author with Professor Erwin Flückiger on top of the Jungfraujoch, the highest permanently manned weather station in Europe.
Photo courtesy of Small World Productions

Gesner was wrong on at least one count.

On August 18, 2007, photographer Spencer Tunick, in collaboration with Greenpeace, used 600 naked volunteers in a "living sculpture" on the Aletsch Glacier, a photo shoot meant to draw attention to the shrinking of glaciers. In the course of the twentieth century, more than a quarter of the area of Switzerland's permanent ice disappeared. Stunts such as this can be effective, but all it takes is to travel here and pore down this slope to know the folly of dying ice and feel the vital reasons for preservation.

We grab a lunch at the Crystal Restaurant—if there is a restaurant with "atmosphere," it is this—and I swill a Rugenbräu

Lager Hell. Somehow that seems the right beverage this high up. Then we take an elevator so slow I suspect someone is pulling the cables hand over hand to the satellitic rooftop, just beneath the shiny astronomical cupola and overlooking the watershed of the Bernese Oberland. Here I meet Professor Erwin Flückiger, who wears a hat to suit his name, a red-and-black-checkered felt hunter's cap. Dr. Flückiger is a professor of physics at the University of Bern and the director of the High Altitude Research Station here. It's the highest permanently manned weather station in Europe. He tells me the primary focus these days is on environmental sciences and climate change, the latter of which is in graphic evidence here. Yet too all around us are remnants of radical climate change that occurred well before human influence, such as the North Face of the Eiger, cleaved by a glacier in the last ice age. How can we be sure this current trend isn't just part of a natural cycle? I ask the professor.

"It is difficult to disentangle. Of course we have natural changes, but we have experts who say that now the man-made contribution is significant and what we are experiencing now is both natural change but also man-made." He pauses for a moment to polish his glasses. I wonder whether it is a gesture of metaphor for those of us who live in the lowlands.

I ask what is unique about this research station, and he says that its location, above all the dust of the plains, allows purer measuring and study. "We are sticking our nose in the clean air."

I then question the professor about the fact that he sits above the largest glacier in Europe, the best seat in the house, yet also is witness to the shriveling of the Aletsch, a giant slab of bacon in a frying pan. He affirms that the Swiss are doing what they can, that it's a small country, and that the Swiss love nature. In some areas glaciers have been wrapped in plastic, "but that doesn't resolve the problem," he is quick to add. And the Swiss are perhaps more aware than most in the world of the consequences of global climate change, as they see the evidence first. Therefore, they are adapting to alternative energy sources and changing behavior on levels governmental, corporate, and individual. It is his job to measure the changes and report them, and his hope is that as goes Switzerland, so goes the rest of the world.

We unwind through the mountains, shedding altitude, and disembark back at Kleine Scheidegg, where we must wait for the next train to Wengen or take an alternative means of transport. Long before skiing, the first form of outdoor winter entertainment here was joyriding downhill on homemade toboggans borrowed from villagers. Now we rent some lightweight plastic toboggans and in the rich, liquid light of the late afternoon start gliding down a twisting, two-mile track. These baby-blue vehicles are barely more than tea trays with skids and certainly harder to master: Feet are the only brakes, and the approved method of steering is to swing your body outward on the bends. As we push off, we are suddenly slaves to acceleration. I try to slow down first by planting my boots flat on the path, but that doesn't do the trick, so I end up digging in heels. Evelyne, of course, is a natural and peels around corners like a Formula 1 driver; the curves rhyme with her smile. My aptitude is considerably less. I crash and burn and repeatedly have to hop off and pull through flat sections. But there are some thrills in this endeavor, including a bone-shakingly fast section that ends in a sharp left-hander under a railway bridge. Where the original Romantic notions of The Sublime relied on some sort of catharsis (the climactic mixing of terror with delight while witnessing overpowering landscapes), the new, accelerated Sublime seems to have cheapened such hard-earned emotion into a near-pornographic mountebank. We are crazed and cheered by shuddering down mountains that have no worked claim on our feelings—but they are damn fun!

NOT UNALLIED TO MADNESS

These sublime and magnificent scenes afforded me the greatest consolation that I was capable of receiving. They elevated me from all littleness of feeling; and although they did not remove my grief, they subdued and tranquilized it.

—Victor Frankenstein, in Mary Shelley's *Frankenstein; or, The Modern Prometheus,* 1818

That evening, across the snowy linen of the dinner table, I speak with Laura Hubber, a reporter for the BBC World Service, who is doing a story on the history of environmentalism in Switzerland. When I comment that in my own quest for the connection between The Sublime and today's ecotourism movement I have found quite a bit of physical and historical support, but few living experts, she shares that she knows the person I need to see: Dr. Angela Esterhammer, a professor of Romantic literature who teaches in the English department at the University of Zurich. I unfold my map and see I am not that far from Zurich, only a couple of hours' drive, so I decide that before heading back to the Glacier Express, I'll see if I might visit Dr. Esterhammer.

It's a weekend when I arrive at the university, but Dr. Esterhammer agrees to meet me in her book-lined office. After pleasantries, we sit down to a talk.

RB: *Who were the Romantics who came to Switzerland?*

AE: William Wordsworth, for one, who came in 1790 when he was a university student. He came on a walking tour with a friend that culminated in crossing the Simplon Pass on foot into Italy. That was a very memorable experience for him, which he later reflected on and wrote about in his long poem *The Prelude*. In 1816, Lord Byron exiled himself from England and went abroad. He spent the first few months in Switzerland before going on to Italy.

Then there was Percy Shelley and his partner, Mary Godwin, who later became Mary Shelley. They eloped to Switzerland in 1814 and could only afford to stay for a couple of months, but in 1816 they followed Lord Byron back here, and all of them spent a notoriously rainy but very eventful summer on the shores of Lake Geneva.

Dr. Angela Esterhammer, a professor of Romantic literature who teaches in the English department at the University of Zurich, in her well-stocked library office.
Photo courtesy of Small World Productions

RB: *And that's when she wrote* Frankenstein.

AE: Yes. It was such a rainy summer, first of all. The strange weather conditions had been brought about by a volcano erupting in Indonesia and had an aftereffect the next year on the climate all over Europe. That made the weather so bad it affected the subjects that Mary Shelley, Lord Byron, and Percy Shelley chose to write about. It also probably caused them to write more, because they had to spend so much time indoors because of the rain.

[This was the summer of 1816. The previous year, Mount Tambora on the island of Sumbawa in the Malay Archipelago erupted, killing at least seventy-one thousand people. The pall of dust and cinders carried to Europe on trade winds caused severe climate anomalies, and 1816 became known as "The Year without a Summer." Global cooling saw temperatures drop by up to two degrees centigrade. Crops failed, livestock died, and people froze to death. The weather prompted the worst famine of the nineteenth century, and some of the best writing.]

RB: *The Romantic poets who came here are credited with articulating this new concept of the natural sublime. So what is the natural sublime?*

AE: The sublime itself is a concept that goes back to antiquity. But it came into vogue again in the eighteenth century. It had been a concept that was associated more with language and rhetoric. But in the eighteenth century, writers began to associate it with the experience of landscape. The main idea of the sublime is that it's an experience that produces pleasure, but what they called in the eighteenth century a negative pleasure. The most important writers on the sublime as far as the Romantics are concerned are Edmund Burke in the mid–eighteenth century and Immanuel Kant in his *Critique of Judgment* in 1790. Both Burke and Kant distinguished between things that were beautiful and things that were sublime; both the beautiful and the sublime produce pleasure, but in the case of the sublime, it's this negative pleasure that's always connected with fear or awe or horror or danger. The idea with the sublime is that it's something that's just too large for the mind to comprehend, for human senses to measure or calculate. So when you're confronted with the sublime, whether in landscape or art, it overwhelms the mind. The senses just have to give up, admit defeat. But then, at least according to Kant, another part of the mind sets in, what Kant called a suprasensible faculty, the faculty of reason. And reason is able to step in and restore some kind of balance. That allows the whole experience to be one of greater pleasure, even though it also involved horror and fear.

RB: *Kant was a philosopher. It took the poets and the painters to really make this notion profound and also accepted to a lot of people.*

AE: Yes, in some ways they were the mediators between German philosophy and the British reading public. The poets and painters were also the people who put this experience of the sublime in a form that would reach ordinary readers or viewers in a way people could relate to.

RB: *Blake and Shelley were very popular in England, and they influenced people to actually come and see what they wrote about in Switzerland.*

AE: Yes. Byron was above all the international star in the early nineteenth century. He was a famous, sensational, and, in fact, controversial personality who caused a sensation anywhere he traveled. He was probably most influential in terms of getting people to read poetry about the Alps. Shelley also was popular, more in the mid- and later nineteenth century. We haven't talked about Wordsworth, who, with his famous passages on the Alps, especially the Simplon Pass, certainly had an impact.

Interestingly, with Wordsworth it was a delayed impact, because he had the experience in 1790, but his major poem, which contains this experience in poetic form, wasn't published until 1850. So his experience in the Alps had an impact on a much later generation of readers.

RB: *Didn't Byron write much of* Manfred *while in Wengen?*

AE: Correct. *Manfred* is a dramatic poem that's set in the Alps, and I think the setting is crucial to the experience of confronting death, the supernatural, and confronting the depths of one's own personality.

RB: *There are certain terms, such as the "aesthetics of the infinite" that are often applied to The Sublime. How does that reconcile in your research?*

AE: "The aesthetics of the infinite" could be one phrase to use for the sublime because the idea of the sublime—certainly in the eighteenth century, in Romanticism—is this idea of the infinite, of infinitude, of something that can't be measured and that was beyond the possibility or potential of human sensory perception and understanding.

RB: *Some will say that this gave a renewed faith, to some people, in a higher power. At the time, London was going through a transition, the industrial revolution had kicked in, it was a big, smoggy city—people came out here and saw the "architecture of divinity," and it gave them new faith.*

AE: Yes, certainly the experience of the sublime in itself is a theoretical concept and also the experience of this awesome nature; those were both religious and spiritual experiences to a large extent. Additionally, in connection with the idea of the urban versus the rural, another important aspect here is the material conditions of the people, travelers, in the early nineteenth century. There is certainly in the sublime mental, religious, spiritual dimensions. There's also the more material reality that the period around 1800 was a very turbulent period in Europe. Britain and France were at war for almost twenty years, with very few periods in that time when it was safe to travel to the Continent. This affected the development of tourism as well; there was a short window in 1802 during the Peace of Amiens when British people could travel with more safety to the Continent. Then there was the period after the Battle of Waterloo in 1815 when Continental travel really became possible again for British tourists on a large scale. After 1815, the floodgates were opened. The timing of that is very interesting because that's also when Byron and Percy and Mary Shelley came to the Continent. But the connection between the poetry that they were then writing, which had an influence on the British public, and the new potential to travel to Switzerland or Italy—that had not been there for the decades before—that conjunction, I believe, is very important.

RB: *There was also the transition from the Grand Tour, which was something for the elite, to mass tourism, initiated in the middle nineteenth century by Thomas Cook. He was an advocate of temperance, and this was one of his techniques to move people to a religious point of view.*

AE: Yes, although that's a bit beyond my period.

RB: *From the period of Byron and Shelley to this new consciousness that tourism is a good thing, people came here for the delights and the feelings that became a tourism industry here in Switzerland. It actually changed dramatically everything about Switzerland, because before that it was a very poor area; people who worked in the mountains were farmers or shepherds, and they barely survived. Then they got caught up in the whole tourism thing and recognized that their greatest asset was nature. They became among the original eco-stewards.*

AE: There is a scholarly study of tourism in the nineteenth century and in other periods. People are studying the connection between English Romantic literature and also Victorian literature and the development of tourism in the nineteenth century. Interestingly, the British Romantic poets, writers thought for generations to be somewhat abstracted from everyday life and writing very idealistic literature, were in fact travelers and tourists themselves. They were sometimes surprisingly aware of their role in the tourist industry. Either in their own travels or in the impact they might have on people who read their work. Wordsworth, for instance, wrote great poetry about the Alps; he also wrote a publication called *A Guide to the Lakes,* which was an actual tourist guide to his home country, the Lake District in northern England.

RB: *He was trying to stop a railroad from going through.*

AE: Yes, and he was trying to both promote and control tourism in that area. It's a rather ambiguous publication, really, which is aware of how the natural beauty of the area might be disturbed or even destroyed by the wrong kind of tourism. On the other hand, he also wants to make the area, the nature that he loves, accessible to tourists of the kind who will appreciate it. Something similar was going on with other writers, especially of the next generation, who came to Switzerland and wrote about Switzerland. Percy Shelley, for instance. When we think of Shelley's poetry about the Alpine landscape, the first poem that comes to mind is "Mont Blanc." It's a very philosophical, really a very difficult poem, but he first published it in a small book called *A History of a Six Weeks' Tour*, which he wrote together with Mary Shelley and which was a travel journal. There are very interesting connections between publications that we would call travel journals or even travel guides and some of the most philosophical or intellectual poetry that was written about these landscapes.

RB: *Do you think the natural Sublime, as you know it, could have existed without the Alps?*

AE: I think the Alps had a lot to do with reinvigorating the discourse of the sublime in the eighteenth century in the first place. You mentioned earlier the Grand Tour. In the eighteenth century, English gentlemen were in the habit of completing their education by going on a tour over the Alps to Italy. Actually, the goal of the tour was usually Italy: the cities, the classical ruins, and the artworks. But there were the Alps, in the way. So the idea developed that this experience, the dangers of crossing the Alps, the majesty, the awe of Alpine landscape was a distinct aesthetic experience in its own right. I think that had a lot to do with reigniting the theorizing about the sublime.

RB: *Today, people seem to use The Sublime in quite a different way. People will pick up a piece of chocolate and say that it's sublime. Or sip a glass of Champagne and call it sublime. It seems it's been diluted or trivialized. Do you agree?*

AE: That's probably true, and you've probably been talking to more people about the sublime than I have lately. But that's probably a common principle or pattern, that terms that at one point have a quite specific meaning get watered down, used more generally. Although, even in the Romantic period, that was the case. The poet Samuel Taylor Coleridge—not one of the Romantic poets who visited the Alps, although he did write some poetry about very specific Alpine landscapes even though he had never seen them himself—but Coleridge, with his awareness of landscape, got quite upset when a woman in his hearing referred to a waterfall as "pretty." He thought the waterfall should be spoken of as sublime or majestic or impressive, but not as pretty.

RB: *Blake would talk about The Sublime in a fashion that you could really only feel alive if you were confronted with horror. That's the ultimate sensation. You also said he never really liked nature, but he still expressed this notion.*

AE: Blake is a very different case, for many reasons. He never saw the Alps; he never traveled outside of England. He had a very different attitude toward nature than his contemporaries Wordsworth or Coleridge. He also didn't have much of a sense of German philosophy. Blake's notion of the sublime comes from different sources: from his religious background, from the language of the Bible, and from his training in art. The idea, though, that one can't experience the sublime or feel really alive without an experience of danger or horror is intrinsic to the eighteenth century and the Romantic sublime in any case. It's just a matter of where you go and find your danger or horror. For Blake, there was enough of this kind of sensation in the mind itself. And in art. For other poets of his generation, and the next two generations after that, they perhaps sought this experience in different places, including Alpine landscapes.

RB: *How do the Romantic poets differentiate beauty from The Sublime?*

AE: Both of these experiences resulted in pleasure, whether they were experiencing landscape, art, or literature. However, beauty would give pleasure without disturbance. The sublime experience, which Kant thought would result in even greater pleasure in the end than the pleasure that was connected with the beautiful, always included an element of disturbance, awe, horror, risk, danger, or alienation before you achieve that pleasure.

RB: *Philip de Loutherbourg's famous painting* An Avalanche in the Alps, *which is sometimes called the epitome of The Sublime in oil, showcases the deadly power of nature. How do people reconcile the near-death experience of an avalanche with the uplifting feelings of The Sublime?*

AE: That's a complex question. On the one hand, the people who lived most closely with the dangers and risks of avalanches, Alpine climate, and mountain landscapes—say, the peasants and innkeepers—would not have gone about their daily lives feeling uplifted. Kant tells the story of a very intelligent but down-to-earth Savoyard peasant who called anyone who claimed to love the snowy mountains a fool. We need to distinguish between the everyday risk of avalanche and danger and the experience of English travelers, poets, painters, who certainly did feel uplifted by experiencing the Alpine landscape. But they weren't necessarily going out and putting themselves in dangerous situations. With the possible exception of William Turner, who was, as a matter of fact, famous for seeking out dangerous atmospheric conditions as preparation for doing his paintings of the Alps.

An important thing about the sublime experience is that there's a balance between the need for danger as a part of the experience and the need to have enough of a distance from immediate danger to be able to reflect on the experience. So, the sublime experience is not just from the acute danger of avalanches, much less feeling any joy from the destruction an avalanche can cause; rather, from the knowledge that nature is so powerful and human beings, by contrast, are so weak. Being able to step back and reflect on that danger. Kant would say, from this compensating feeling, that there is something in the mind, a sense of reason, that can bring back balance and a certain type of pleasure.

RB: *An appreciation. So this is something that's innate in human beings, to seek this sort of feeling. Would you say that the experiences that are offered in the Alps today would be a simulation of The Sublime? Say, tobogganing, skiing, roller coasters? The sorts of things that give you that duality of terror but pleasure at the same time?*

AE: Interesting, comparing the modern experiences of extreme sports or adventure travel to the Romantic experience of the sublime. It's a very interesting comparison that you would know more about than I do. I tend to think that the Romantic experience was more distanced; that is, the Romantic sublime is very largely an intellectual experience. You might call it adventure tourism of the mind. Although this aspect of danger or risk is a part of the mental experience, I don't think that Romantic poets or the tourists who immediately followed them had either the resources or the inclination to deliberately seek out acute danger or risk. They were looking for a more contemplative experience. Often an immediate experience, such as Percy Shelley's when he stood at the foot of Mont Blanc in the ravine of Arve and conceived his poem "Mont Blanc" while gazing up at the magnitude of the mountain. The immensity of nature is there, but it's more contemplative and less participatory than what we tend to have today.

RB: *I recall one of the Romantic poets was going over a pass in the Alps and slipped and almost fell, and wrote about it in one of the poems.*

AE: That sounds somewhat like Wordsworth's experience of the Simplon Pass, although it would be very interesting if that's what you're thinking of because that's not quite the experience that Wordsworth describes. In fact, the fall he describes is a very different kind of fall. The point of Wordsworth's experience, as it eventually developed—after he did the actual hike with a friend in 1790 and then reflected on that experience many years afterward—the experience is first of all one of disappointment. He and his friend actually got lost during the hike, and while they thought they were still going upward and had hopes that pointed to the clouds, they were told, when they asked the way, that the pass was already behind them. They were on their way downward, "and we had crossed the Alps," as Wordsworth wrote.

There's a certain disappointment and a "fall" there. The interesting thing for the experience of the sublime is that when Wordsworth reflected on that whole experience, he eventually wrote the account in such a way so that something comes in to compensate for this acute disappointment of feeling that they missed something about the landscape. What compensates is imagination. A much more spiritual feeling about nature.

RB: *On the original Grand Tour, as they crossed the Alps—which was an impediment—they kept the curtains closed. There were ogres and dragons and ugly sights. The Alps were warts on the skin of the earth, boils on its* *face. They upset the natural spirit level of the mind. When did they open up the curtains?*

AE: I wish I knew the answer to that, but I don't have a very specific time frame. Some people would have opened up the curtains earlier than others, and those are the people who started thinking, again, about the sublime in the eighteenth century, who started to revive and retheorize this ancient idea. Another aspect of this whole development is what was going on in Europe at the time. Mainly, the French Revolution, beginning in 1789, and followed by revolutionary wars, the Napoleonic wars. I referred to all of that earlier as an impediment that kept a lot of British would-be tourists out of the Continent because it was simply too difficult or risky or expensive to travel. But in some cases, that excitement is also what drew some people to the Continent. Wordsworth, for instance, came in 1790 as a university student. The reason he decided to undertake this walking tour in Switzerland rather than in the Lake District or somewhere else in England was certainly to see the Alps, but also because he was so fired up about what was going on in France. France and the Continent were an immensely stimulating environment for a university student with radical ideas. The experience of the Alps, for Wordsworth certainly, in a different way for the next generation, for the Shelleys, was tied up with the political and cultural context. The experience of the Swiss landscape, the lifestyle of the Swiss peasantry, affected some of the Romantic poets greatly. They appreciated both the lifestyle and the landscape as an expression of liberty, independence, autonomy, self-reliance.

RB: *Wasn't Rousseau and his noble savage part of this?*

AE: Very much so. We've been talking about how the Romantic poets and their poetry and novels about the Swiss landscape influenced later readers, but Wordsworth, the Shelleys, Byron, they came here in the first place because they had been reading Rousseau and were so influenced by what they had been reading.

RB: *The locals who lived at the foothills of the Alps thought nothing good about where they lived. They would have preferred to have moved if they could have. Yet, in the wake of the Romantics and their influence on the rest of the world that prompted tourists to come here, their whole mind-set changed as well. And that continues today. Can you speak about that at all?*

AE: No, unfortunately I can't. But I could perhaps add more of the reverse, the other aspect of that, how British travelers, particularly the Romantic poets, regarded the inhabitants of Switzerland. I think it is closely connected with the poet's experience of the landscape. On the one hand they were coming and seeing the majesty and awe of the mountains, and this generated a somewhat aesthetic and spiritual feeling of the sublime. But it was also connected with the revolutionary excitement of what was happening during that era. In fact, some scholars have talked about the revolutionary sublime, political excitement as another aspect of the sublime. But somewhere in between was also the Romantic poets' response to ordinary people who lived in Switzerland, who they saw, sometimes even in a clichéd way, as a kind of embodiment of a simple, free, proud life. Wordsworth, for instance, in writing about his experience in hiking across the Simplon Pass, of course talks about mountains and cliffs and waterfalls and forests, but he also writes in the very same passage about the sense of genuine brotherhood and universal reason that is embodied for him by the Swiss peasantry living in the mountains. Or Byron, in *Manfred,* has a character, a chamois hunter, who is a native of the Bernese Alps. And the character Manfred thinks of this peasant as an embodiment of, again, brotherhood, human kindness; he calls him "patient, pious, proud, and free."

RB: *Yet the reality is that many of the peasants had goiter, and they were not that healthy. It was a romanticized version of what was really going on.*

AE: It was quite literally a Romanticized version. And has a lot to do, again, with the idea of seeing what you expect to see.

RB: *So, an agreeable kind of horror. Is that how you would describe The Sublime?*

AE: That's Joseph Addison's phrase, isn't it?

RB: *Yes, in an essay he wrote for* The Spectator.

AE: Yes, if I were talking about the eighteenth century and the Romantic sublime. An agreeable kind of horror. Yes, in eighteenth-century language—that might not be exactly the diction that we would use today, but certainly gets at the idea. It's this distinctive combination of horror and aversion with pleasure and delight.

RB: *You've made an academic career out of studying the Romantics. When you travel to the Alps, do you feel what they felt?*

AE: Yes, in some ways I do feel what they felt. It's an effect of both my interests and profession, that when I go walking in the woods here near Zurich, lines from Wordsworth's *Prelude* come into my mind. And I think a lot of our modern perceptions were shaped by the Romantic period. By what people experienced and wrote about, more or less two hundred years ago. Many things have changed, certainly patterns of tourism. One thing that has changed drastically is the expectations that people have of the Alps. You would know more than I do what expectations people have now, but certainly when the English Romantic poets and ordinary tourists of the period traveled to Switzerland, they came with very strong expectations of what they were going to see. They would have been surprised not to see or experience, or even feel, those things. There were quite distinct itineraries they would have had in mind. Quite specific views that they expected to see. And perhaps most interesting, the feelings they were expected to have in contemplating those views were largely shaped in advance. To a large extent, nineteenth-century tourists saw what they were expecting to see. You'll have to tell me if that is similar to twenty-first-century adventure travel.

RB: *That's a very rich subject: if it's not what the brochure offers, some people are disappointed. But there are others who find delight and meaning in the unexpected. An adventure for some is a well-planned trip gone wrong. Maybe that's the modern Sublime.*

AE: Perhaps. Possibly that's the new "agreeable kind of horror."

And she laughs.

chapter twenty-five

UNFATHERED IMAGINATIONS

What enjoyment is to be compared to an early walk over these great glaciers of the Alps, amid the deep silence of Nature, surrounded by some of her sublimest objects, the morning air infusing vigour and elasticity into every nerve and muscle, the eye unwearied, the skin cool, and the whole frame tingling with joyous anticipation of the adventures that the day may bring forth?

—John Ball, 1864

Heading back to Andermatt and the Glacier Express, we once more coil through landscapes of the vast and circle back to the technology designed to investigate suppositions of The Sublime. So much has changed in our thinking since the Romantics first articulated the value of the vast. The difference between the scale of an Alp and the events of thoughts is so much greater. Our technical language for the huge has increased as we discover language for enormous events—a light-year, a terabyte, a megaton—and huge numbers such as a googol (one followed by one hundred zeros) and a googolplex (one followed by a googol of zeroes), the latter bigger than the estimated number of atoms in the universe. The size of the universe is estimated in the region of ten yottameters, where a yottameter is a distance so big that light would require 100 million years to travel it. The truly untouched Sublime resides somewhere beyond the heliopause.

But what hasn't changed is how The Sublime can move us—how these numbers, concepts, and landscapes can evoke a kind of turbulent pleasure, somewhere between fright and admiration, and prompt us to explore, both inwardly and in the physical spaces. The spaces, seemingly infinite, stir up so much more than mere language. Horace-Bénédict de Saussure wrote: "What language can reproduce the sensations and paint the ideas with which these great spectacles fill the soul of the philosopher who is on top of a peak?" The prize for broaching the Alps is both far sight and insight.

We follow the course of the Furkareuss River and beyond Realp cross through a section so exposed to avalanches that for years it had a temporary bridge that was dismantled every October and reassembled in May. Then we disappear into the Furka Base Tunnel. At Oberwald, daylight once again streams, and Walker blinks at the bubbling stream that spills down from the once-mighty Rhône Glacier. From their inauguration in 1931 until 1982, the cross-country trains ground their way past the Rhône Glacier on the ascent to the Furka summit. Now, with the tunnel, the Glacier Express sees no great glaciers on its course.

We have entered the Rhône basin and the Canton Valais, bordering Italy and France. The canton has ten of Switzerland's highest mountains, the country's driest climate, and the most sunshine. It also boasts Europe's largest underground lake, highest vineyard, and highest cogwheel railway, and the world's tallest concrete dam, an arching piece of man-made sublimity.

We tool by the small town of Niederwald, most noted as the birthplace of César Ritz, a dairyman who went on to found the eponymous hotel in Paris and the lofty hotel chain that articulates The Sublime in its cavernous architecture.

We glide into the first village on the Rhône, Brig, an old trading center at the end of the Simplon Pass from Italy. It was crossing this pass in the summer of 1672 that awoke a feeling in philosopher and churchman Thomas Burnet, one that was against the grain of the age that found the Alps hostile and repulsive. After the crossing, he wrote, "There is something august and stately in the Air of these things, that inspires the mind with great thoughts and passions . . . As all things have that are too big for our comprehension, they fill and overbear the mind with their Excess, and cast it into a pleasing kind of stupor and imagination."

In 1681, Burnet published *The Sacred Theory of the Earth,* in which he explained why mountains were not mentioned in Genesis—it was simply that the original state of the earth was what he called a "Mundane Egg," crafted by The Great Sculptor. After creation, the world was smooth and spherical, without mountains or valleys or caverns. Its flawless surface, though, hid the "Yolk," the inner cavity filled with fire beneath a water-filled abyss upon which the crust of the earth floated. It was Noah's great flood, rebuke for man's sins, that created a storm of rock and crashing hydraulics, and when the waters receded there was left "a World lying in Rubbish." Mountains were the detritus. God had "dissolv'd the frame of the old World, and made us a new one out of its ruins, which we now inhabit."

Brig today remains the portal to Burnet's feelings and to the final leg of this train trip to the zenith of mountain towns, Zermatt, and to what John Ruskin called "the most noble cliff in Europe."

We climb through the Vispa Valley, settled since the Iron Age, and crawl beneath the steep, terraced vineyards that are perhaps the highest in Europe, and then the gears latch onto the cog rail and pull us into the Matter Valley and the uncongenial Kipfen Gorge. Here, we are swallowed up by time. Twenty thousand years ago, during the Upper Pleistocene, the iron road we are traveling would have been submerged beneath millions of tons of ice. Just the thought of this deep time is both exquisite and horrifying. To know that these inexpressibly old and rigid rocks are defenseless against the grinding of time is to acknowledge that we, of the human flesh, are horrendously brittle and brief.

The train sashays rhythmically past St. Niklaus, a village where many Matterhorn guides were born and many were buried after accidents. Just before Randa, we veer around a gigantic cone of rubble, the remnants of the May 1991 landslide that poured across the valley, burying twenty-four buildings, seven horses, and more than twenty sheep, and temporarily blocked all motorized transport. In 1819, some one hundred twenty houses were smashed by an avalanche that hit Randa, though nobody was killed as the residents were in Zermatt helping with Christmas celebrations. The valley now widens, the Matter Vispa roars and foams between banks of green, over shimmering chunks of slate, and we roll by a giant parking lot in Täsch—the end of the paved road.

Then we are in the Zermatt station, as busy as Grand Central, clanging with ski boots and climbing gear.

THE PRATOBORNUM ULTIMATUM

There is assuredly morality in the oxygen of the mountains, as there is immorality in the miasma of a marsh, and a higher power than mere brute force lies latent in Alpine mutton. We are recognizing more and more the influence of physical elements in the conduct of life, for when the blood flows in a purer current the heart is capable of a higher glow. Spirit and matter are interfused; the Alps improve us totally, and we return from their precipices wiser as well as stronger men.

—John Tyndall, 1860

We take a hummer to the hotel—not what you think, but rather a toylike electric taxi cart that hums along the cobblestone streets to the Hotel Metropol, a dark-wood, chalet-style lodge with absurdly picturesque views of "that mountain" from the geranium-boxed balconies.

Zermatt is an old, old village. The town was first mentioned in documents under its Latin name, Pratobornum, in 1235. Some of the houses go back five hundred years. The Matterhorn, which towers above the place, goes back forever. The very top of it is a piece of Africa, thrust northward over Europe in the slow, inexorable tectonic crash. The historian Mott Greene described the Alpine strata before their elevation as a richly patterned tablecloth on a polished table. "If you should place your hand flat on the table and push forward, the cloth will begin to rise into folds. Push more and the folds will flop over (forward) and the rearmost fold will progressively override those before it, producing a stack of folds." Adding erosion and earthquakes to the equation, he continues: "Take a pair of scissors and cut away at the stack from various angles, removing whole sections of the pile of folds. Having done so, push the pile again so that segments become jumbled against each other." And voila, the Matterhorn and its surrounding peaks.

The long ribbon of a village, more of a small town, is strung out along the valley floor on either side of the rushing, glacial-melt Matter Vispa River, a tributary of the Rhône. The river spins simply, but it is a simplicity that lies not before complexity, but rather on the far side of it, spilling from the massif that is tortured geology in action. The Matterhorn is a strangely mesmerizing presence, with a ridge so sharp it seems to cut the sunlight in two. I gasp each time we round a corner and my eyes find purchase on a new dimension.

chapter twenty-six

The mighty Matterhorn   Photo courtesy of Sara Givens

Back in 1820, Zermatt had about twelve visitors. Now it accommodates up to fourteen thousand a night in 116 hotels and eighteen hundred holiday apartments. It has a look of familiarity about it, and it's not just the iconic mountain, the most photographed in the world. The feature-length animated films I grew up with, such as *Snow White and the Seven Dwarfs* and *Pinocchio,* were set in an Alpine world of neat cottages, narrow, twisting, cobbled streets, mysterious forests, and towering cliffs. That was because Walt Disney hired Swiss children's-book illustrators to design the look of his movies. And when he built the Matterhorn ride in 1959 at Disneyland in Anaheim, California, he tapped a new kind of simulated Sublime: rides that evoked the surrendering to forces outside individual control, forces that could destroy if one were not safely attached to tracks. (And over the years enough roller coasters have fatally derailed to keep an element of tension alive.) And even if chocolate is not really Sublime in any Romantic sense of the word, the triangular wedges of Toblerone are modeled after the Matterhorn. In a Zelig-like piece of history, the creators, Theodor Tobler and Emil Baumann, registered their brand in 1909 at the Federal Institute for Intellectual Property in Bern when Albert Einstein was a patent clerk there.

In Zermatt, I meet up with Amadé Perrig, a former mountain guide born in the shadow of the Matterhorn (he thinks he has summited about twenty times) and now living in a home where he can see the bony peak from his breakfast table. It's a great way to start each day, he professes. A past president of Zermatt Tourism, he is no less the evangelist in retirement. If anything distinguishes Amadé, it is his happiness; he has a tremendous, bursting, elemental, infectious, glorious vitality about him, like some bright, burly diesel express pounding across Switzerland.

In the 2008 book *The Geography of Bliss,* Eric Weiner tells of visiting a Dutch professor who has created the World Database of Happiness, in which ninety-five countries are ranked by "Happy Life Years." Switzerland comes in at the top of the list, and Amadé seems the poster child.

In researching his book, Weiner traveled to Switzerland and met a man named Deiter, who explained why the Swiss are so happy. "It's simple," said Deiter. "Nature. We Swiss have a very deep connection to Nature." A few days ago, Hans Peter Danuser in St. Moritz had told me: "The Swiss don't have the temperament of Italians and are not as good lovers as the French, but we are solid, pragmatic people with a good, close connection with nature, and that makes us happy."

Amadé is the embodiment, a man who has spent more than a fair share of time in the mountains and possesses a sort of hypoxic euphoria; he always seems on the verge of breaking out into a yodel. "You cannot do something else when you climb in the mountains," he tells me.

Amadé offers to guide me up to the great Gornergrat Massif on the eponymous train, opened in 1898, which transports some three million folks a year up Europe's highest cogwheel track, a path to the citadel of sublimity. And so we grind our way upward, an invitation into space, along with mountain bikers, birders, snowboarders, and hikers with collapsible Leki poles, up beyond the sweet-smelling arolla pines and larch, by Egyptian-like blocks that glaciers have bulldozed down this slope. The waterfalls are bold and theatrical. The Scottish author Hugh Blair asked in 1783: "What are the scenes of nature that elevate the mind in the highest degree, and produce the sublime sensation? Not the gay landscape, the flowery field, or the flourishing city; but the hoary mountain . . . and the torrent falling over the rock."

Upward we snake on a seam of iron clamped between the peaks, coiling beneath cirques and bergschrunds and through long, wooden avalanche tunnels to the station that offers some of the best non-Disneyesque views of the giant dragon tooth that rises to rip the sky, the limestone and serpentine mass called Matterhorn.

Once on top, we disembark to a hundred-year-old station built in English castle style and a platform where the eye can traverse twenty-nine of the thirty-four highest Swiss mountains, each rising more than twelve thousand feet. There is no other public observation platform in Europe revealing such a roll call of tall peaks, but the grand redoubt of the Matterhorn always dominates. There flies a long bunting of cloud at its crest, snow being blown by the high winds. John Tyndall, an enthusiastic Alpine Club member, wrote of this scene in 1860: "The summit seemed to smoke sometimes like a burning mountain; for immediately after its generation, the fog was drawn away in

Richard and Walker Bangs at the Matterhorn. Today about thirty-five hundred people a year attempt the Matterhorn; about 50 percent make it.   Photo courtesy of Walker Bangs

long filaments by the wind. As the sun sank lower the ruddiness of his light augmented, until these filaments resembled streamers of flame."

The flame of risk was irresistible to Tyndall. That summer, he and a friend, Vaughan Hawkins, decided to attempt to climb the Matterhorn along with Oberland guide Johann Bennen, the "Garibaldi of mountaineering." They were unsuccessful. And before the retreat, both Tyndall and Vaughan were nearly done in by a boulder the Matterhorn hurled down at them. Vaughan wrote of the experience: "These stones and ice have no mercy in them, no sympathy with human adventure; they submit passively to what man can do; but let him go a step too far, let heart or hand fail, mist gather or sun go down, and they will exact the penalty to the uttermost. The feeling of the 'sublime' in such cases depends very much, I think, on a certain balance between the forces of nature and man's ability to cope with them: if they are too strong for him, what was sublime becomes only terrible."

LOCUS OF THE INACCESSIBLE

chapter twenty-seven

What gives value to travel is fear.

—Albert Camus, 1935

We hike a little farther up the hill to the highest hotel in the Swiss Alps, the 3100 Kulmhotel Gornergrat, built in 1907 as a hospice with an observatory, perched at the eponymous 3,100 meters (10,170 feet), right opposite the monolithic pyramid of the Matterhorn. None of its twenty-five rooms has a number. Rather, each is named after one of the mountain peaks that can be seen from the rooms' windows. I ask the keeper for a key so I can take a peek at one of these rooms with a view, and he walks me up the stairs, swings open a door, and there out the window is the framed Matterhorn, the tip unfurling its white flag of cloud. It's like looking at the full moon when it seems all its contours and seams are in full view. Squinting, I can almost make out the imagined pitch in Gustave Doré's rendition of the Matterhorn tragedy of July 14, 1865, in which four of Edward Whymper's companions fell four thousand feet to their deaths.

In 1860, Whymper, a wood engraver and painter, was commissioned by William Longman to illustrate *Peaks, Passes and Glaciers,* a precursor to the annual publication the *Alpine Journal,* the chronicle of the London-based Alpine Club. He visited Zermatt on the job, returned the following year to make more illustrations, and while there made the first British ascent of a near-thirteen-thousand-foot peak. His success prompted him to turn his attention to the Matterhorn, one of the few major peaks as yet unclimbed, which he described as a sugar loaf whose head needed knocking off. His first attempt failed, and he was a bit embittered when he wrote: "There seemed to be a cordon drawn around it, up to which one might go, but no farther. Within that invisible line gins and effreets were supposed to exist— the Wandering Jew and the spirits of the damned. The superstitious natives . . . spoke of a ruined city on its summit wherein the spirits dwelt; and if you laughed, they gravely shook their heads; told you to look yourself to see the castles and walls, and warned you against rash approach, lest the infuriated demons from their impregnable heights might hurl down vengeance for one's derision."

Now obsessed, Whymper made seven more unsuccessful attempts for the stony apex from Italy during the next four years. On his fourth try, he found himself alone when he climbed to retrieve his homemade tent and wrote of the feeling: "The earth seemed to become less earthly and almost sublime; the world seemed dead, and I its sole inhabitant."

Like most British mountaineers, Whymper employed local guides to boost his chances of getting to the top. Many of his initial attempts were made with Italian guide Jean-Antoine Carrel, but when Whymper returned in 1865 to make another bid for the peak, Carrel said he was unavailable. A fervent patriot, he was, in fact, planning his own expedition in the hope of claiming the summit for Italy.

Whymper decided to climb the mountain from the Swiss side. Traveling to Zermatt, he assembled an expedition team comprising local guides Peter Taugwalder and his son Peter Jr., Chamonix guide Michael Croz, experienced climbers Lord Francis Douglas and the Reverend Charles Hudson, and a novice mountaineer named Douglas Hadow.

Setting off at dawn, the party made good progress and soon reached thirteen thousand feet. As the escarpment steepened, however, Hadow needed assistance from the elder Taugwalder. Croz, Whymper, and Hudson took the lead, spurred on by the thought that Carrel's Italian team could already be ahead of them on the other side of the mountain. Eventually, Croz and Whymper rushed ahead of the others to the summit. Whymper was triumphant, writing: "At 1:40 pm, the world was at our feet and the Matterhorn was conquered! Hurrah! Not a footstep could be seen." They later saw the Italian team far below.

The cold fact is that the Aletsch Glacier receded by more than three hundred feet between 2005 and 2006, and at this rate could be gone by the year 2100. Global warming is the culprit.   Photo courtesy of Small World Productions

Their elation was short-lived. On the most treacherous part of the descent, with all the climbers roped together, Hadow slipped. He knocked Croz from his feet and pulled Hudson and Douglas along behind him. As Whymper and the Taugwalders braced themselves to take the strain on the rope, it snapped. The three watched helplessly as Croz, Hadow, Hudson, and Douglas slid and jolted down the steep escarpment and over the edge of a precipice that dropped some four thousand feet toward the Matterhorn glacier below.

When a rescue team reached the glacier, it found a trio of naked and mutilated corpses. The men's clothes had been ripped from them during the fall. Croz, the Swiss guide, had lost half his skull, and the rosary he wore was embedded so deeply into the flesh of his jaw it had to be cut out using a penknife. Of Douglas, the lord, nothing was to be found except a boot, a belt, a pair of gloves, and a coat sleeve.

A few hours later, as Edward Whymper was cautiously lowering himself down the Matterhorn, he saw (or so he later claimed) three crosses floating in the filmy air, one higher than the other two. It may have been the birth of mountain madness, invention, or guilt. Or it might have been, as British author Robert MacFarlane suggests, the Spectre of the Brocken, a mountain phenomenon I once sought by climbing Adam's Peak in Sri Lanka, where it often occurs. Also called the Brocken Bow, named for a mist-cloaked peak in Germany, it manifests itself as the magnified shadow of an observer cast upon the upper surfaces of clouds opposite the sun. It was observed and described by Johann Silberschlag in 1780 as a circumstance that appears when the sun shines from behind a climber who is looking down from a ridge or peak into mist. The light projects the climber's shadow through the mist, and the heads of figures are often surrounded by glowing, halolike rings. It is a relatively rare occurrence, hard to schedule, and when I made my climb in Sri Lanka to seek it, I found only dense, white fog.

The news of the fatalities on Whymper's expedition spread fast, made headlines across Europe, and had an effect opposite what was anticipated. The *Edinburgh Review* asked: "Has a man a right to expose his life, and the lives of others, for an object of no earthly value, either to himself or his fellow creatures? If life is lost in the adventure, how little does the moral guilt differ from that of suicide or murder?"

The queen condemned the climb, as did many others of power and influence. Charles Dickens reproached the Alpine Club as the "society for the scaling of such heights as the Schreckhorn, the Eiger, and the Matterhorn (which) contributed about as much to the advancement of science as would a club of young gentlemen who should undertake to bestride all the weathercocks of all the cathedral spires of the United Kingdom." Newspapers of the day were almost hysterical at the thought of a lord falling off a cliff and denounced mountaineering as "a depraved taste." The *Times* asked, "Why is the best blood of England to waste itself in scaling hitherto inaccessible peaks, in staining the eternal snows and reaching the unfathomable abyss never to return? . . . Well, this is magnificent. But is it life? Is it duty? Is it common sense? Is it allowable? Is it not wrong?" John Ruskin railed against the members of the Alpine Club: "You have despised nature; that is to say, all the deep and sacred sensations of natural scenery. . . . You have made racecourses of the cathedrals of the earth. . . . The Alps themselves, which your own poets used to love so reverently, you look upon as soaped poles in bear gardens, which you set yourselves to climb, and slide down again with shrieks of delight."

But instead of keeping people away, the news fired a grim fascination and opened the floodgates: all of a sudden, everyone wanted to climb the sublime Alps in their own imaginings, especially the Matterhorn, and tourism to Zermatt took off. And it wasn't just the gawkers who came to see the cenotaph. Many made their way up the high flanks and up other peaks throughout the Alps in a newly minted fetishization. Many were not qualified; some were unlucky. To date, at least five hundred people have died attempting to climb the Euclidean scapes of the Matterhorn, and thousands more have met their makers scrambling throughout the Alps. Today about thirty-five hundred people a year attempt to climb the Matterhorn; about 50 percent make it. Leslie Stephen summed it up nicely when reviewing Whymper's book *Scrambles amongst the Alps in the Years 1860–69*: "No advertisement of Alpine adventure is so attractive as a clear demonstration that it is totally unjustifiable."

. . . TO THE RIDICULOUS

I met dozens of people, imaginative and unimaginative, cultivated and uncultivated, who had come from far countries and roamed through the Swiss Alps year after year—they could not explain why. They had come first, they said, out of idle curiosity, because everybody talked about it; they had come since because they could not help it, and they should keep on coming, while they lived, for the same reason; they had tried to break their chains and stay away, but it was futile; now, they had no desire to break them. Others came nearer formulating what they felt; they said they could find perfect rest and peace nowhere else when they were troubled; all frets and worries and chafings sank to sleep in the presence of the benignant serenity of the Alps; the Great Spirit of the Mountain breathed his own peace upon their hurt minds and sore hearts, and healed them; they could not think base thoughts or do mean and sordid things here, before the visible throne of God.

—Mark Twain, 1880

There is an astronomical observatory at Gornergrat with a viewing platform that thrusts out over the cavorting vastness of the Gorner Glacier, second longest in Switzerland. Just to the east are the Schwarze and Breithorn glaciers, separated by a ridge whose curve imitates the contours of a felucca sail on the Nile. Several other peaks, ridges, and mighty rivers of ice are in view, an alporama that makes one want to take flight, like the scores of jet-black carrion crows kekking about, cawing "quark, quark" at the vantages only they enjoy. Nonetheless, at ten thousand feet, facing the mettle of the Alps, this is indeed an attractive paraphrase of the experience of extreme mountaineering. The close encounter can be imagined without the hardship or authentic danger.

In the preface of his 1863 *Handbook* for Switzerland, Karl Baedeker wrote, "The Glacier is the most striking feature of the Alpine world, a stupendous mass of the purest azure ice. No aspect of Switzerland is so strikingly and at the same time so strangely beautiful." He went on to quote Horace-Bénédict de Saussure's imagery as well: "The glacier looks like a sea which has become suddenly frozen, not in the moment of a tempest, but at that instant when the wind has subsided, and the waves, although very high, have become blunted and rounded."

Mark Twain hiked to this vantage above the Gorner Glacier with his family in 1878 and considered the path of least resistance to get down: "I resolved to take passage for Zermatt on the great Gorner Glacier."

He continued: "I marched the Expedition down the steep and tedious mule-path and took up as good a position as I could upon the middle of the glacier—because Baedeker said the middle part travels the fastest. As a measure of economy, however, I put some of the heavier baggage on the shoreward parts, to go as slow freight. I waited and waited but the glacier did not move. Night was coming on, the darkness began to gather—still we did not budge. It occurred to me then, that there might be a time-table in Baedeker; it would be well to find out the hours of starting. . . . I soon found a sentence which threw a dazzling light upon the matter. It said, 'The Gorner Glacier travels at an average rate of a little less than an inch a day.' I have seldom felt so outraged. I have seldom had my confidence so wantonly betrayed. I made a small calculation: One inch a day, say thirty feet a year; estimated distance to Zermatt, three and one-eighteenth miles. Time required to go by glacier, a little over five hundred years! . . . The passenger part of this glacier—the central part—the lightning-express part, so to speak—was not due in Zermatt till the summer of 2378, and . . . the baggage, coming on the slow edge, would not arrive until some generations later. . . . As a means of passenger transportation, I consider the glacier a failure."

Today Mark Twain would be doubly flummoxed, as the glacier is going the other way, galloping back (because of melting) at a rate faster than it used to advance. Here the diaspora is ice.

Standing here, there is a raw, immediate sort of happiness that seems directly related to the elevation and the surroundings. I scan the illustrious causeway of ice, which pours just below the Monte Rosa Massif. Winston Churchill also stood here and was so inspired he took off to climb the 15,203-foot peak spanning the Swiss–Italian border. Despite suffering from mountain sickness and sunburn, which stripped the skin from his face, he reached the summit in his only melee with a mountain.

The convex surface of the Gorner Glacier looks hard, silvered, pitted like old metal, and it is pocked with stones fallen from the cliffs above. At its mouth, the surface is a curdled gray, and the smoothness of the upper ice is ruptured into crevasses and blocks.

Lake Riffelsee. In 1849 John Forbes described his rush of emotions upon climbing the adjacent Riffelhorn: "We seemed to feel as if there could be no other mental mood but that of an exquisite yet cheerful serenity. . . . At the same time, so rapid was the alternation from mood to mood . . . [that] the utter silence, and the absence of every indication of life and living things . . . would excite a tone of mind entirely different—solemn, awful, melancholy." Photo courtesy of Small World Productions

Then there is what looks like a bathtub ring, a stain where the glacier used to be. Like almost all the glaciers in the Alps, it has been in rapid retreat, and it is a cause célèbre in the debate over global warming. So many past poets praised the "eternal snows" of the Alps, never imagining the choice of phrase could be corrupted. Amadé points to the edge of the stain, where the ice was when he first climbed here. But Amadé is not one to dwell on the unseemly. He surveys the scene and then turns to me with a beam and asks if I know how many languages are spoken in Switzerland. I answer: "Four. German, French, Italian, and Romansh."

"Wrong," he says with a grin. "Those are the official languages. There is another language, a mountain language: the language of yodeling." And he raises his head and starts yodel-lay-he-hooing in the direction of Monte Rosa. The sound beats a path across the valley and echoes back.

"Before there were telephones, this is how we communicated across the valley," he explains after a couple of hearty calls. "Sometimes, though, the yodeling caused avalanches. That's why we also call it 'the language of the sublime.' " Amadé widely smiles, completely dispossessed of any of the watery melancholy of an Alpine Byronic hero.

Amid a murder of crows (always wanted to use that phrase) I meet Jan Dekker, a tourist from Holland, one of the flattest countries on earth. He tells me he comes here every year for the views, the air, and the severe and brooding mountain weather, which he says is "sublime."

On the ride down, we step off at the Rotenboden station for a hike to a tarn in a glacial cirque, Lake Riffelsee, with the rock peak of the Riffelhorn forming a shoulder on one frame, the lake mirroring a perfect rendition of the east face of the Matterhorn in its cool waters. As I approach, the sun projects a golden island of light down onto the water. I pause at the little, lapping seam of water and rock. I can feel the cold pulsing off it, as if it were marble. Beneath the surface scuttle schools of small fish; boys along the flowered edges ply their fishing poles. It is a scene that dislodges the pins holding together the tissues of emotional restraint, and I shudder.

These feelings are not new, of course. They come layered with the perceptions of those before me. In his 1849 book, *A Physician's Holiday,* John Forbes described his rush of emotions upon climbing the Riffelhorn and witnessing the "awful circle of Titanic Sphynxes" that surrounded his climbing party. "We seemed to feel as if there could be no other mental mood but that of an exquisite yet cheerful serenity. . . . At the same time, so rapid was the alternation from mood to mood—the immeasurable vastness of the scene . . . [that] the utter silence, and the absence of every indication of life and living things . . . would excite a tone of mind entirely different—solemn, awful, melancholy." But that a book is little more than an abbreviation for experience is never more evident than here.

Then a cloud moves in, filtering the flimsy sunlight. We look skyward, as the cloud seems to slowly explode out of itself, and soon it starts to rain. Fat raindrops splash on the shore and pluck the lake up into a field of fleurs-de-lis. The flourish of the Matterhorn is shattered into a million pieces, and we head back to the train.

INASSIMILABLE HUGENESS

The passion caused by the great and sublime in nature . . . is Astonishment; and astonishment is that state of the soul, in which all motions are suspended, with some degree of horror. In this case the mind is so entirely filled with its object, that it cannot entertain any other, nor by consequence reason on that object which employs it.

—Edmund Burke, 1757

We make the electric glide down to Zermatt, where the sun is still in spate, and we grab a taxi back to the Metropol. Here, though, a taxi is quite a different animal from the rides in Los Angeles or other major cities. No cars are allowed, so the cab is a jangling, horse-drawn affair, not too different from the vehicles employed by the first tourists here. I end up in a ride-share with Daniel Luggen, the current director of the Zermatt Tourism Office, who tells me first-time visitors often confuse the bijou village with something out of Disneyland, when in fact the Disney connection happened the other way around. As we clop along the promenade, he tells me that Zermatt has always been eco-friendly since its human origins some ten thousand years ago. There has never been the noise and air pollution that daunt most hemmed-in burgs, and the city fathers have always managed growth with an eye to authenticity. There are strict style and size restrictions: no Japanese pagoda, New Mexican pink adobe, German Bauhaus, Parisian rococo, or American Craftsman looks here, but lots of sharp-angled roofs and wooden flower boxes.

After the novel cab ride, Amadé shuffles me into one of his favorite haunts, the Arvenstube in the Hotel Pollux. Over a glass of Walliser Bier and a plate of raclette (I've already added fifty cholesterol points on this trip; that may be the most agreeable horror around), he tells me his theory of the evolution of eco in Zermatt. He says that Whymper's well-reported accident put Zermatt on the map, and suddenly tourists wanted to come and see "the killer mountain," just as the 1996 fatalities on Everest spurred record numbers of climbers in the years following. At first, visitors came by carriage, but in 1891 entrepreneurs built a tram from Visp. Proper roads in Switzerland started to stretch at the beginning of the twentieth century to various mountain villages to encourage more tourism, and there

The name Saint Bernard *originates from the traveler's hospice on the often treacherous and terrifying Great St. Bernard Pass from Italy.* Photo courtesy of Walker Bangs

were preparations to pave to Zermatt, but World War I put a halt to the plans. Zermatt remained car-free, not so much by design, but because it already had transportation access, and other places found higher priority. In the winter of 1927, a rail line was opened from Visp up to St. Niklaus, and fifty sleighs were employed to take tourists to snowbound Zermatt. Then, in 1972, a road was built to nearby Täsch, with intentions to extend it to Zermatt. But guests and locals rebelled, saying they liked the quiet and the crispy, clean air. So Zermatt refused the road, and now the lack of one is a point of distinction and attraction. Zermatt is the largest member of the Association of Car-Free Swiss Resorts, whose chiming slogan is "a holiday for you and your car or holidays for your car too."

We take a stroll up the narrow main street of Zermatt, and Walker pulls at my sleeve as we pass two bulky Saint Bernard dogs, who gaze back with polished black eyes but with no barrels of brandy around their necks. The name *Saint Bernard* originates from the traveler's hospice on the often treacherous and terrifying Great St. Bernard Pass from Italy, which in turn was named for Bernard of Menthon, the tenth-century monk who established the station. First reports of the dogs' presence at the pass date to the seventeenth century, and they remained loyal companions to the monks who lived there. These boys are big; the heaviest and largest dog in known history was a Saint Bernard named Benedictine, which weighed 336 pounds.

Then we pass the red-shuttered Hotel Monte Rosa, built on the foundations of the Lauber Inn, which in 1839 became the first hotel in the village, with three bedrooms, lighting by candle, and loos in the back. In 1855, Alexander Seiler recrafted the Lauber into the Hotel Monte Rosa. It became the summer home of the British Alpine Club (even though, or perhaps because, it has no view of the Matterhorn) and the place for climbers of all nations to congregate and plan their expeditions, and then afterward celebrate or drown their sorrows. Edward Whymper slept here and departed for his infamous Matterhorn climb from here. There is a plaque of his stern face on the street, and the hotel restaurant is named Whymperstube. Walker refuses to go beyond the front door because of the many smokers inside, but I venture in just to touch the storied past. I rub my hands across the bar and filch a potato chip, imagining the dramas that played out in the atmosphere of this room.

The hotel is named for the nearby mount, which Leonardo da Vinci may have climbed in the fifteenth century. He penned this about the peak and its atmosphere: "No mountain has its base at so great a height as this, which lifts itself above almost all the clouds; and snow seldom falls there, but only hail in the summer when the clouds are highest. And this hail lies there, so that if it were not for the absorption of the rising and falling clouds, which does not happen more than twice in an age, an enormous mass of ice would be piled up there by the layers of hail; and in the middle of July I found it very considerable, and I saw the sky above me was quite dark; and the sun as it fell on the mountain was far brighter here than in the plains below, because a smaller extent of atmosphere lay between the summit of the mountain and the sun."

A little farther up the road we turn into the Matterhorn Museum and inspect the thin, frayed rope that sent the four climbers to their deaths, along with a letter that Whymper wrote following the tragedy: "For five years I have dreamt of the Matterhorn; I have spent much labour and time upon it—and I have done it. And now the very name is hateful to me. I am tempted to curse the hour I first saw it; congratulations on its achievement are bitterness and ashes and that which I hoped would yield pleasure produces alone the severest pain, it is a sermon I can never forget."

Yet time has a way of polishing the edges of rock and tragedy, and Whymper later fountained: "The time may come when the Matterhorn shall have passed away, and nothing, save a heap of shapeless fragments, will mark the spot where the great mountain stood. . . . That time is far distant; and, ages hence, generations unborn will gaze upon its awful precipices, and wonder at its unique form. However exalted may be their ideas, and however exaggerated their expectations, none will come to return disappointed!"

I also head over to Zermatt's neo-Gothic English Church and see the graves of Whymper's Matterhorn climbing cohorts Croz and Hadow, now buried next to one another, tethered forever by dirt. There are many graves of climbers here, the young and the bold through the ages, including one New Yorker who was just seventeen years old. They all were drawn to the flame of The Sublime, but through bad luck or recklessness they went too far—though for perhaps a moment when they touched the void, they felt the transcendence that is unavailable to those who wrap themselves in walls and never venture to high and open places. The Alps remain a dangerous domain, and that is the everlasting attraction.

The unpleasant reminders of quests gone bad bring me back to a recent outing of my own. Ten years after my aborted trek into the Annapurna Sanctuary, I returned to the mountain, but on a different route, to a different vantage. I was with Ed Viesturs, who was attempting to be the first American to climb all fourteen of the world's eight-thousand-meter peaks. Annapurna was to be his last in the series, even though it had beaten him back twice before because of unsafe avalanche conditions. I trekked as far as base camp on the north side, and between tea and talks with Ed I visited another team, a group of Italians with the same goal as Ed's. One of the Italian climbers, Christian Kuntner, invited me to his tent to share a huge nimbus of bread, some olives, pepperoni sausage, cheese, a flagon of wine, and stories of adventure. Christian was a quiet and unassuming adventurer, the son of a park ranger who grew up in the Alps. He told me about a bike trip he had made along the Silk Route and another from the tip of North America to the foot of South America, which hit a low point when his bike was stolen at a public campground in Alaska. The experience had soured him on the luck factor in adventure. Climbing, though, was his deepest passion, and he had made it to the summits of thirteen of the eight-thousand-meter peaks, all without bottled oxygen. As with Ed, this was to be his last.

A week later, Ed and his climbing partner, Veikka Gustafsson of Finland, stepped atop the blazing white coronet of Annapurna and completed his quest. But then a few days later, Christian Kuntner, on the same route as Ed to the summit, was hit by an avalanche, and died.

chapter thirty

STORMING A MYTH

All hail, Sublimity! Thou lofty one,
For thou dost walk upon the blast, and gird
Thy majesty with terrors, and thy throne
Is on the whirlwind, and thy voice is heard
In thunders and in shakings: thy delight
Is in the secret wood, the blasted heath,
The ruin'd fortress, and the dizzy height,
The grave, the ghastly charnel-house of death,
In vaults, in cloisters, and in gloomy piles,
Long corridors and towers and solitary aisles!

—Alfred, Lord Tennyson, 1827

f the world seems increasingly in flux, a moving target quicker than our notions of it, Switzerland may be the exception that proves the rule. It might be argued that Switzerland was the original inspiration for today's ecotourism sensibility, a green pedigree promoted as a core ethos in places from Costa Rica to Botswana (Costa Rica has oft been called "the Switzerland of Central America," but more for its political neutrality than for any eco-comparisons). Long before any other country, Switzerland was practicing the tenets of environmental sustainability and low-impact travel. The Romantic poets inaugurated an era of eco-travel in Switzerland because they were great apostles of open eyes and preservation of the sights that inspired them. And that legacy continues today in a land of clean hydropower (60 percent of the nation's power comes from water), with an ethos of recycling and alternative energy. Unlike much of the world, Switzerland has not been bulldozed for speed. Instead it features low-impact transportation from trains to Smart cars (which can be rented at some train stations) and trotinettes, the microscooters employed in car-free villages and cities alike. And more people walk here than in any other First World country. As Sammy Salm told me, "Eighty percent of the Swiss can get their groceries by walking, so we don't need to use the car to get our daily bread."

Even the airline I flew, Swiss International, is a member of myclimate, a Swiss nonprofit foundation that funds climate-protection projects in India and elsewhere around the world. Characteristically, the Swiss are thinking globally, knowing the interconnectedness of all things matters, and as a result, money from Swiss International passengers goes to reducing emissions in Karnataka, India, through the production of electricity from agricultural waste instead of coal and diesel.

Switzerland describes a through-line unmatched around the world, as validated by the Environmental Performance Index released in 2008 at the World Economic Summit in Davos. The Yale Center for Environmental Law and Policy together with the Center for International Earth Science Information Network at Columbia University released their scorecard that ranked 149 countries based on twenty-five indicators of pollution control and natural resource management. The United States came in thirty-ninth, behind many developing nations. The top choice—the most environmentally conscientious country in the world—was Switzerland.

When I recently visited Brigitta Schoch Dettweiler, the consul general of Switzerland in Los Angeles, she rattled off some of the reasons Switzerland ranks so high:

- *Since 1987, Switzerland has eliminated 99 percent of all ozone-depleting substances contained in foam, refrigerants, and insulating material.*
- *The Swiss tie with Sweden and Japan for first in overall recycling volume.*
- *The Swiss have the highest consumption of organic foods of any country in Europe, according to the International Federation of Organic Agriculture Movements.*
- *Switzerland is firmly on track to meet its Kyoto Protocol commitments for reductions in the production of carbon dioxide gas. To help get there, a carbon dioxide tax on imported fuel oil and gas was initiated this year.*

Here, beneath the weight of psychic coordinates that is the Matterhorn, I once more grapple with the encoding of The Sublime, what some Romantics in the artificial logic of oxymoron called "the enthusiastic terror." The chaotic and charismatic landscape, thrillingly beset with hazards and asperities, is one of incomprehensible power—power that moves mountains and ideas. Longinus asserted, "The sublime leads the listeners not to persuasion, but to ecstasy." It's a sense of enormity, an exhilarating cocktail of dread and bliss. Why

Rush hour in the Swiss Alps   Photo courtesy of Didrik Johnck

is this important? Because we are naturally drawn to these powerful feelings—they make us feel most alive—and without the Alps, without the vitalizing gifts of grand nature, without Switzerland, these feelings dull and perhaps cease. In a worst-case scenario, we give up—on ourselves and our planet. When we raft the Grand Canyon, ski the Sierras, sail the Galapagos, take a walking safari or trek in the Himalayas, we are heir to a dynasty of feelings that began in Switzerland. We can trace a line from today's ecotourism movement, a continuum of whole cantons of adventures, back to the original quest for The

Sublime that found its vindicating quiddity here. From these artists-travelers emerged an impulse to preserve the mountain environments for their mystery, their power and resonance—as hunting grounds for poetic imaginations. If necessity is the mother of invention, and The Sublime excites the passions of self-preservation, then it may be immoderately important to keep that quest alive today.

For so much of human history we've lived to dominate the natural world, always taking, rarely giving back, believing the earth a machine that would never break. We were victims of the shears that cut man from nature and nature from man. But it was here in Switzerland that one of the most profound revolutions in thought occurred; the transition from loathing of grand nature to its celebration. The qualities for which mountains were once reviled—steepness, elevation, desolation, danger—became among their most radiant attributes. Once the rubbish of the world, they became stones of inspiration. Conrad Gesner, who was so far ahead of his moment as to be a time jumper, declared in 1541: "The consciousness is in some vague way impressed by the stupendous heights and is drawn to the contemplation of the Great Architect. Men of dull mind admire nothing, sleep at home, never go out into the Theater of the World, hide in corners like dormice, through the winter, never recognize that the human race was sent out into the world in order that through its marvels it should learn to recognize some higher Power." Whatever one's personal belief system, the Alps can provide vital perspective and bearings, can feed the springs of reverence and affection, can quicken our sense of wonder, provoke the imaginings of eternity and infinity, and inspire us to great deeds of preservation. As Wordsworth said, they rouse an impulse "to think, to hope, to worship, and to feel." More than any landscape, the Alps of Switzerland validate our brief trek in time and keep the wolf of insignificance from our door.

FOOLS ON THE HILL

Leave paths that common sense, custom, or the average mountain sheep would point out . . . and go in some other direction where the chances appear to be in favor of breaking your neck.

—Albert Frederick Mummery, 1879

The following day, Walker challenges me to one of his games. Starting at the Hotel Bijou on the upper east side of Zermatt, he picks a point across the Matter Vispa River that is seemingly a thousand feet up the steep slope. The game is to see who can reach the designated point first without veering from a straight line. It is a modern version of the *direttissima,* the climbing technique that became fashionable in the Alps in the mid–twentieth century and which John Harlin II had hoped to achieve on the Eiger before his fatal fall. Now, "line orienteering," as some call it, is practiced competitively in all manner of landscapes—finding a clean route from A to B that irons out all the curves.

Walker describes the terrain in video game terms: "We have to descend the Horrifying Hill, cross the Raging River, and climb the Madness Mountain." So, the challenge accepted, we make our way through a muddy corridor by a pen with two dark pigs rooting about, then at the high bank, crisp with frost, we slide down the icy grade to a broad ski path, then attempt to rock-hop across the Vispa (in my haste I slip and drop one of my legs to knee depth into the water), and then we begin the scuttle upward. We have to claw up grassy tufts, using marmot holes as toeholds. We thrash through thornbushes and snarl up snow patches and over craggy black and gray rocks that spall with touch. My foot loses purchase on one face, and I flatten against it, sticking like a cat, and catch my breath for a few minutes. Walker seems unfazed, but at six foot two, his legs are longer, and he practically fizzes with youthful energy.

Just short of our artificial goal, we pull ourselves over an outcropping and into a raving wind. It penetrates my coat and whistles through my ribs. It is difficult to say where the cold air does not come from. I hug the stem of a small larch and stamp my feet to keep warm. Much of the view is veiled by the dramatic obscurity of the low, unfettered clouds, like a scene in a William Turner painting, but we can look down to barns and dappled sheds and weather-beaten chalets with dark roofs of slate arranged in geometric patterns, blue smoke lazily lifting from the chimneys. The winds are bringing us a mixed draft of aroma, perfumed messages from both the village and the mountains. But as we round a boulder seeking refuge, there, up valley, is the gleaming silver blade of the Matterhorn, which had been absent for most of this scramble. We are both stunned into silence with the view and stand on a point of stillness. Suddenly, we hear a crack and a rush, and turn our heads to see a puff on the middle high slopes of the Matterhorn. From a safe distance, we watch as an avalanche rolls down the mountain.

You, ye Mountains,
Why are ye beautiful? I cannot love ye.

. . . .

I feel the impulse—yet I do not plunge;
I see the peril—yet do not recede;
And my brain reels—and yet my foot is firm.
There is a power upon me which withholds,
And makes it my fatality to live.

—Lord Byron, 1817

224

RICHARD BANGS'

Adventures

WITH PURPOSE

AS SEEN
NATIONALLY
ON PUBLIC
TELEVISION!

DISPATCHES FROM
THE FRONT LINES
OF EARTH

To discover more about the adventures of Richard Bangs, read on. "Up the Wall of Death" is excerpted from Bangs's recent book *Adventures with Purpose,* from Menasha Ridge Press.

Richard Bangs' *Adventures with Purpose* Dispatches from the Front Lines of Earth

Running wild rivers such as the crocodile-infested Tekaze in Ethiopia, Richard Bangs lived for the adrenaline, for the rush of reveling in the misery of hardship and sidestepping death around every bend. Bangs's classic, *The Lost River,* which recounts first descents in Ethiopia and demands a single-session chair-gripping read, epitomizes the rough-and-ready formative years of Bangs as the explorer's explorer. As Bangs and his compadres survived river after river, a new purpose presented itself, though. Now an eminent and respected conservationist, Web pioneer, ambassador, and explorer, Bangs still travels to exotic and difficult environments, but with a new purpose:

"Over the decades, I have witnessed many special places preserved and lost, and the critical vector in their survival or demise was more often than not the number of visitors who trekked the landscape or floated the river and were touched deeply by their unique beauty and spirit. When such a space became threatened, there was a constituency for whom the place was personal, a collective force ready to lend energy, monies, and time to preservation."

The result of Bangs's philanthropy is now the preservation and promotion of threatened peoples, places, habitats, and animals. *Richard Bangs' Adventures with Purpose* follows Richard from Bosnia to Libya, Panama to the American West, Rwanda to Thailand, all in a search to make sense of disappearing cultures and rivers, to save them by bringing them to life.

In typical Bangs narrative, *Adventures with Purpose* plows to the heart of the matter, painting peoples and places as he weaves among them, creating landscapes that tell their own story.

To order, visit **www.menasharidge.com**.

UP THE WALL OF DEATH

Another soul sent to Valhalla
Another murder for the Wall
On the Eigerwand in winter
Is the hardest climb of all.

"The John Harlin Song,"
—Tom Patey in *One Man's Mountains*

One rope length from The White Spider, the last great defiance on the mountain wall that is one of the world's deadliest, the seven-millimeter fixed line broke. John Harlin II, the first American to climb the legendary North Face of the Eiger in the Swiss Alps four years earlier, fell four thousand feet into the void.

A short time later, his nine-year-old son, Johnny Harlin III, heard the news from his sobbing mother. It was news he couldn't fathom. His father was among the world's greatest climbers, a pioneer of straight-up routes, a man almost mythopoetically at home in the vertical world.

That was forty years ago.

Now John Harlin III, a half-year shy of his fiftieth birthday, has returned to attempt to climb the hard, black limestone wall that killed his father, and he has brought his own nine-year-old, Siena, who will wait with her mother at the Bellevue des Alpes Hotel at the base of the spear-shaped mount. There is here in the air that indefinable smell of tension that precedes a storm. Even the mountain seems to have cried with this concept as just days ago it filled the Lutschine River in a hundred-year flood that tore away chalets and barns. Tears streak faces, including my own, as the deed is discussed.

I've spent the last few days with John Harlin, Siena, and his wife, Adele Hammond, and his two climbing partners for the attempt, German climbing stars Robert "Dr. Eiger" and Daniela Jasper. John and the Jaspers have spent most of their spare time training on the Leen Cliffs of Interlaken and at climbing gyms. They've also spent time with a crew from MacGillivray Freeman films, producers of *Everest* and *Mystery of the Nile,* who are here to document the climb for an IMAX movie, and the media elements, including my own presence, have added an extra degree of anxiety to what was for years thought to be a very private enterprise. But John agreed to the coverage, believing the results would honor and capture his dad's "love of the Eiger, of Switzerland, of life."

But much of the time here is spent in retrospection. The pater's shadow looms throughout the region, from maps that show the eponymous John Harlin Direct route to the old-time guides who have vivid remembrances of the American rock star, such as seventy-one-year-old Ueli Sommer, who was serving on the local mountain rescue team when the accident occurred, but didn't become involved because after a fall of such height, "there was not much left to rescue."

I'd heard stories of John Harlin II from fellow adventurers over the years, including Royal Robbins, who had a falling-out with Harlin while blazing a direct route up the West Face of the Dru in the Alps in the mid-1960s. And I'd read James Ramsey Ullman's hagiography, in which without a wink he says, "In a still earlier time, one feels sure, John Harlin would have been literally a knight. . . . A few centuries later he might well have been a conquistador or privateer." Most climbers of the day were in awe of John Harlin II. One rope mate called him the man who "flamed up a mountain." Others called him "The Hardman," in both the flattering and deprecatory sense. His onetime student Larry Ware described him as having "a godlike physique" and "a vision and power that emanated from within," but added that his bulldozer personality turned some off, and several who had climbed with him refused to attend his funeral. But this is a time to hear the stories straight from the son.

By the mid-1960s, John Harlin had been a fighter pilot, a dress designer, a football star, a schoolteacher, an artist, and a groundbreaking rock climber. He loved intrigue and Ian Fleming, and fancied himself cloaked in mystery and adventure, sometimes alluding to an undocumented incident in Rome that involved a casualty, perhaps a sanction. John Harlin III told me that Clint Eastwood's character in the film *The Eiger Sanction* (based on the book by Trevanian), Jonathan Hemlock, a lover of art and an accomplished climber, was in part based on his dad.

In 1965, John Harlin was running his own International School of Modern Mountaineering in Leysin, Switzerland, and had been on the Eiger a dozen times, but had summited just once, up the classic route. He had become an enthusiastic proponent of the pure ascent, a plumb line from bottom to top, routes that ironed out the curves, crooks, and zags of traditional ascents on the big walls of the Alps. It was here he conceived of a first ascent of a clean line straight up the Eiger North Face, one that unbent the bows of the 1938 route that saw the first summiteers, including Heinrich Harrer, who later went on to live and write *Seven Years in Tibet*. It was, by some reckonings, the last great alpine enigma to be deciphered, a wall greater and harder than anything on Everest.

It was also here that the younger John Harlin felt the force of his father on his own life. He was aware of his father's reputation for toughness and enterprise, for being a superman of the rock. And he suffered his father's dissatisfaction with his own comparative lack of hardness. When young John fell in a ski race, the father was distressed and made it known. When young John was bested by a school bully, the father was furious. Young John dreaded his father's judgments and was ashamed he didn't measure up.

By mid-February of 1966, John Harlin II had gathered a crack team of English-speaking climbers, including American Layton Kor, the Scot Dougal Haston, and Britain's Chris Bonington, and all were readying for the attempt at the base of the mountain when Harlin dislocated his shoulder while skiing. The doctor forbade Harlin to climb for at least a fortnight, so he retreated home to Leysin, about two-

and-a-half hours from the Eiger, where he hung about with his family and friends while recovering.

But then word came that a German team of eight was heading up the North Face of the Eiger in a *direttissima* attempt. It was now a race, and Harlin and team headed out. At first there was hostility. The Germans pelted Bonington with snowballs as he tried to take photos, but when a blizzard forced a retreat, a mutual respect took over, and as the teams started up again they now shared fixed ropes and coffee.

After several weeks of fixing ropes and bivouacking in precarious snow caves, the two teams were positioned for a final push to the summit, though John Harlin, believing his team the more experienced, felt confident the trophy was his. Harlin and Dougal Haston were checking gear at Death Bivouac, where the North Face froze its first two victims in 1935, when Harlin heard by radio that a German climber was above him on a small snowfield called The Fly. With the news, Harlin felt his Anglo-American prize slipping away. He decided to rush upward to try to catch the German team so at least there could be a shared victory.

Just short of the upper ice field called The White Spider there was a hundred-foot free-hanging drop from a planed wedge of rock. Dougal Haston went first, and with some difficulty he made it in about twenty minutes to the top of the pitch, where one of the Germans was also perched. Haston called down to Harlin to clip in and start jumaring up the rope.

A half hour passed, then an hour. Then thirty minutes more. Another of the Germans arrived on the platform on his way down to fetch a load, and Haston asked him to check on John Harlin. The German rappelled over the lip, but then returned a few minutes later with the news. The fixed Perlon rope had broken near the top, and

John Harlin II was gone. From a telescope at Kleine Scheidegg, journalist Peter Gillman had watched the four-thousand-foot fall.

Life magazine eulogized John Harlin II with a double-truck spread titled, "I'd have thought the Eiger would break before John did," a quote from John's climbing partner and friend Bev Clark.

Although five days later Dougal Haston with four Germans completed the climb and named the route The John Harlin Direct, some in the family remained bitter. Sometime after the climb, Dougal shared with Marilyn Harlin, wife of John II, mother of John III, that he had noticed the thousand-pound test rope was frayed as he made the last pitch before the break. He never called down to that effect, and with his admission a finger of blame was set.

Now John Harlin III is here at Kleine Scheidegg preparing to meet the ogre that has haunted him for forty years. He is taking time off from his job as editor of the *American Alpine Journal,* the prestigious annual where his father published accounts of his climbing exploits. The living John has had moments of doubt many times thinking of this endeavor, which he describes as a pilgrimage. The North Face has been called the *Mordwand* ("Murder Wall") and The Wall of Death, with some sixty fatalities to date, and John openly admits his fear and wonders about the probity of risk.

The weather is not good. It has been too warm, melting the high ice fields, sending frozen daggers and rock down the face like rain. But climbing this countenance is something John desperately wants to do, hopes to do this season, to make a long-sought father–son connection, to bring some sort of closure, some healing to a family wound. "My father would be proud and pleased with this," he substantiates. But he also admits his motivations are hard to understand. "If I think about it rationally, I probably shouldn't be doing this. Yet, I've always felt that there was no climb I had to do except the Eiger."

Through a telescope he examines the concave architecture and the road he intends to make, a route he has never tried but knows like his own neighborhood. "A vertical chess game," he calls it. Then he sets out to practice and to wait as a cloud pillows in from the southeast.

An enormous eddy of warm air has slipped into the Jungfrau. The bane of climbers on the Eiger, a *foehn* is coming in. Like a chinook, it is a coil of air that thaws ice and snow and triggers avalanches. Worse, directly after a *foehn* there is often a big chill that varnishes rock walls with a thin sheen of ice that neither ice ax nor piton can grip. That thin ice layer is called *verglas. Verglas,* John Harlin repeats in almost a mantralike way, is not something he wants to face on the Eiger.

And so he waits.

As we're gathered in the Victorian salon of the not-overstated-in-name Bellevue des Alpes Hotel, we take turns making introductions. We go through the film crew, the supporting climbers, the Yahoo team, then John Harlin III, and finally his wife, Adele, who midway through describing a new school for her nine-year-old daughter, Siena, cracks her voice and struggles to hold back the tears. While not all in the room know the grim history of the North Face of the Eiger, everyone knows how risky this concept is and how terribly wrong things could go.

By the mid-1930s, every major face in the Alps had been climbed, save one. After years of consideration and covetousness, Munich-based Max Sedlmayer and Karl Mehringer made the first incursion onto the high North Face in 1935. But a storm drove in, trapping them halfway up the mountain's thirteen-thousand-foot summit, and they froze to death at a spot known since as Death Bivouac.

A year later, Germans Edi Rainer, Willy Angerer, Andreas Hinterstoisser, and Toni Kurz were killed retreating from the mountain in brutal weather after a rock-fall mishap. Within earshot of the tourist railway tunnel window a third of the way up—where the caretaker had already begun to brew tea for the climbers—all except Kurz fell to their deaths. Kurz hung on for a night and a day, one arm frostbitten and useless, while local guides tried to rescue him.

Somehow he found the strength to clamber back up to Angerer's body, where he cut a length of rope, unraveled its three strands, and tied them together to make a line long enough to rappel down to his rescuers. As Kurz dangled beneath an overhang, so close the guides could almost touch the soles of his boots, a knot jammed. He yelled down, *"Ich kann nicht mehr"* ("I'm finished") and then slumped over, dead.

Finally, in 1938, the year Germany annexed Austria into the Reich, Austrians Heinrich Harrer and Fritz Kasparek, along with Germans Anderl Heckmair and Ludwig Vorg, cracked the code and made the first successful ascent. But the accomplishment stirred its own storm after a photograph was published of the four climbers flanking Adolf Hitler at Breslau, inciting accusations that the climb was a Nazi propaganda effort, something denied to his last day by the last surviving member, Heinrich Harrer, who died in January 2006 at ninety-three after living out his final days in his native Austria.

Today the route that Harrer and companions blazed is known as the Classic Route, following the lines of weakness up the face, and it is the one John Harlin III hopes to attempt in a few days time, if weather permits. Twenty-five years ago John had wanted to retrace The John Harlin Direct, but something happened to change his will.

If the child is the father of the man, the six-year-old Johnny's genetic predisposition inspired his dad, as that year saw both the son's first multipitch climb in the Calanques of southern France and the father's ascent of the Eiger North Face, the first Anglophone to do so. John Harlin III continued to climb after his father's fall. At thirteen he climbed Mount Chamberlin, highest peak in Alaska's Brooks Range. In college in California, he became president of the mountaineering club, as his father had been two decades before at Stanford, and his dorm room was decorated with posters of Himalayan peaks he hoped to climb. By his early twenties, he was an extreme skier and accomplished climber and began to contemplate a path that would connect him to the climbs his dad had done. Then in 1979 he set out to Mount Robson in the Canadian Rockies with a climbing partner, Chuck Hospedales. After climbing its Wishbone Arête, they were descending in the late afternoon beneath a huge couloir, a hanging wall of ice, without being roped up. John led, and after negotiating over a knob and down a ten-foot section of vertical rock, he looked up to coach his less-experienced cohort. There was an unnaturally long pause as John waited, and so he yelled up, "Can't you feel the handhold?"

"I can't," Chuck muttered back. And he peeled off the mountain. John lunged, and felt the fabric of Chuck's jacket, but found no grip. Helplessly, John listened to a death scream and watched the sparks of Chuck's crampons as they repeatedly struck the rock through the five-hundred-foot fall.

John scrambled down in the darkness to the hut, where he wrote in the logbook: "This mountain game isn't worth it."

The next morning, he reached the police station, and a helicopter was dispatched for the body. John couldn't bring himself to call Chuck's folks, but he did call his mom, who was overwrought with the news. John realized then how awful it would be for his mom should he die in a climbing accident, and at that moment he vowed to quit alpinism, "for my mom's sake." What he once felt was the finest expression of self-validation and freedom he now saw as a photographic negative: everything white was black.

Sitting in front of the gleaming wilderness of the North Face of the Eiger, John touches a deep spring of memory; his disinheriting countenance breaks, and he cries. Then for a moment the alpine world seems to balance on a point of silence.

John then gathers himself and looks to the middle distance. "I don't know why we deliberately put ourselves in harm's way. But some things are part of you that you can't leave behind."

John took a twelve-year interregnum from radical alpine climbing, but in its place he mastered extreme skiing, making descents of Orizaba and Popocatépetl in Mexico, the first three-pin descent of Peru's Huascarán, and the first ski descent of Bolivia's Cunantincato, and performing other ski heroics in the Rockies and Alps.

But John likes to say, "The most important characteristic for an alpinist is a short memory. You forget the suffering and try again." And so in 1991 he was back, making an ascent of the Matterhorn and then other peaks throughout the Alps.

In 1999, John brought Adele and Siena, then three years old, to Leysin, where they planted flowers on his father's grave. He decided then to attempt the Eiger, but when he put his girls on the train he found himself in a spate of tears wandering about the station. "What's wrong?" he asked himself. He felt as if he were saying good-bye. And he imagined how awful it would be for his daughter to grow up without a dad.

But the Eiger was in poor condition that season, and the climb, with some relief, was aborted.

John went on to pioneer a new route up Mont Blanc, and made hard climbs in Austria, Germany, Italy, and throughout Europe. He even made an attempt on a virgin peak in Tibet. But always the dark wall of the Eiger dropped stones into the pool of his life, rippling interminably.

If for a time his spirit was skyjacked, it has now come home. And here, amid the clank of climbing gear, John Harlin III is hoping he can join the one club that has nagged him throughout his life, chalk off the one item on his life list, and reach the peerage that would make his father proud.

Like a massive muddy wave frozen in the midst of a squall, the Eiger seems about to crash down upon on us at its base. But then clouds mushroom in; it begins to snow, and the face is veiled. The storm is upon us, and the climb hangs.

Mountaineers are dragon seekers, bent on improbable deeds. But peel back the large codes, chip the granite faces, and you find souls chock-full of qualms and romantic terrors. Although John Harlin has been waiting his whole life for this moment, he is waiting still until conditions are just right. There is a constant tension here between the cult of daring and obligation to family; between the blistering attraction to the flame of risk, and the want for well-being and safety. "Safety is most important," Greg MacGillivray, the IMAX film producer, asserts, sharing that his partner died in a helicopter crash years ago while making a film. "The number one killer in the mountains is impatience," adds Pasquale Scaturro, the renowned expedition leader who has witnessed a share of field fatalities and who is here as the character George Kennedy played in *The Eiger Sanction,* the veteran in charge of mountain logistics and operations.

For these and other reasons, John Harlin III reached out to professional climbers Robert and Daniela Jasper to be his partners on this jagged grail. Although he has never climbed with either, John met Robert three years ago at a conference in southern France and learned of his passion for the Eiger. Known locally as Dr. Eiger, Robert has made twelve ascents up the North Face, all different routes. I watch Robert train on nearby rock, and he moves like liquid mercury pouring upward. I've never seen anything like it. John, who hasn't climbed since March, seems clunky and unsure by comparison; he doesn't dance the rock, he fights it, which is how his dad's climbing style was once described. By all other standards, though, John is indeed an exceptional athlete, and his forty-nine-year-old body is buff like a bullock's.

Robert Jasper, thirty-seven, who sports shaggy, rock-star hair and the conspiratorial grin of one who lives his passion, started climbing as a small boy up pine trees in the Black Forest. By age ten, he was scaling significant rock faces with his dad. At seventeen, he first climbed the Eiger. Now he lives in a chalet in Speiz, near Interlaken, not far from the Eiger, so he can be close to the peak he so loves. "He shares the same spirit for the Eiger as my dad," John offers. "That's why I want to climb this mountain with him."

Many issues evoke unease as the climb looms, but none more than safety. "Speed is safety," John intones several times. Daniela Jasper, thirty-four, is also part of the climb. She too is a world-class climber, with several first ascents to her name, but she is also a new mother, with a two-and-a-half-year-old boy, Stefan, and a baby girl, Amelie, just fourteen months into the world. "I climb laundry mountains these days. The Eiger will be a vacation from raising my kids," she says, cascading in laughter, belying a deep concern that others share. Earlier this week, she awoke in the middle of the night hearing her daughter cry, and as she tended her baby she cried out loud, "I can't do the Eiger." But she and Robert are partners, and he says, "The climb is a big adventure for our relationship."

In addition, Daniela must deal with the Alison Hargreaves syndrome. When ten years ago a sudden storm plucked the thirty-three-year-old Scottish mountaineering superstar off the south face of K2, leaving her two children, ages four and six, motherless, there was an international frenzy of censure, an outcry that mothers of young children should not climb dangerous mountains (Hargreaves first suffered criticism after climbing the Eiger six months pregnant). Now Daniela deflects her paradigmatic decision to climb by questioning why the same fury doesn't swirl around fathers who indulge in extreme adventures. Rob Hall of the 1996 Everest disaster famously left behind an unborn son, yet was never demonized as Hargreaves was. "What's the difference?" Daniela asks.

Families in all permutations are concerned with this climb. John's mother, Marilyn, would not come to Switzerland "for all the tea in China," according to Adele, John's wife. Adele also remarks that it is very important to Siena that her dad remain a part of her life, and that Siena was crying in bed the other night, "worried about what she would do if her daddy died." And Adele, who lost a sister some years ago, declares she is a terrible base-camp wife. "It's very difficult for me. I don't like to wait and watch," sentiments shared by John's mother forty years ago when she chose to sit out the block-buster climb in their chalet rather than be in the audience of the Eiger's vertical stage.

But Adele, who met John at seventeen, has perspective that tends to the sanguine as well. "If John didn't do this climb in his lifetime he would think something was missing." Just as he has supported her extended equestrian expeditions to South America, she supports John in this quest unequivocally. And she sees that there is worth beyond the personal, that success will bring inspiration to many, that it will stand as a triumphal symbol of "every person's internal struggle to face demons" and the courage to overcome "challenges that seem insurmountable," no matter the terrain.

Although risk cannot be blocked, it can be managed, and John, who has no intention of letting his daughter grow up without a dad, as he did, is taking every step to ensure the dangers and pitfalls of this rotting limestone balk are considered and allayed.

"I love being with someone who is willing to be out there on the edge," Adele says, dabbing watery eyes with a tissue. "But even more, I appreciate being with someone who cares even more about coming back."

In the wake of the storm, the sun briefly peeks through the clouds, shimmering as though dipped in a bowl of crystal. And there suddenly is the cenotaph to John Harlin II, the giant monument wall of the Eiger. Of all the celebrated climbers who have been on this famous face—Krakauer, Messner, Hargreaves, Terray, Bonatti, Buhl, Clint Eastwood—nobody is more associated with it than John Harlin II.

Word comes down that a fixed rope set by the support team a few days ago near Death Bivouac is now cut in two from a rockfall. Even with rope thicker and stronger than what was used in 1966, the objective dangers loom, and the randomness of rock still rules. The climb again is postponed.

While we sit with John Harlin in the still Billiard Room of the Bellevue des Alpes, he gets a call on his cell phone. It is Robert Jasper calling to announce that the climb will start tomorrow. The weather is provisionally merciful, cold enough to slow down the ice falls for the next couple of days, and yet clear. In three days, another front is predicted to roll in.

John hangs up and looks sheepishly toward me. "Oh, my. I have butterflies in my stomach."

If since 1979 John has lived with approach avoidance to the ogre on his back, he can no longer. After a couple of minutes' reflection, he offers: "In the words of Ed Hillary, 'I hope we knock this bastard off.' "

There is a good distraction, though, in Larry Ware, a friend and protégé of John's father, who has made the trek up from Leysin, where he teaches comparative literature at the same American college where John Harlin II once taught. John has brought a scrapbook of articles about Harlin II, and together they pore over the memories, laughing at the media circus that covered the 1966 climb and the escapades of climbers they know and knew, comparing the gear in faded newsprint photographs with that of today. Looking at a picture of the double boots John had designed expressly for the Eiger, John the son quips, "I couldn't walk in my father's boots; they're too long for me."

Then Larry, with beer mug in hand, does a lively, broguish reading of "The John Harlin Song," a sniggering poem to those who overworshipped the legend of the brightly hued American climber.

Larry also describes the similarities and differences between father and son. He says that where the father was aggressive and argumentative, the son is soft-spoken with little hubris in his pennant. They both clearly had love affairs with the mountains and found joy in being a part of nature, wanting to be accepted by nature. John the father had a dream to parachute his family into the wilds of New Guinea and start a colony. John Harlin III has taken his family to Mexico to live for months at a time. But the dissimilarity enjoyed the most here becomes clear when we all gaze at a photograph of John Harlin II taken during a climb in the year of his death. He looks north-weathered and hoary, old beyond his years. At forty-nine, John Harlin III looks younger than his dad did when he was thirty, and that gives the son a jiff of delight.

But then the mood turns a bit somber as Larry remembers that he was at this hotel during the last climb of John Harlin, and even spoke to him on the radio when John was at Death Bivouac. It was one of John's last communications. Now when I ask Larry what he thinks about John Harlin III making this attempt, he stops and seems to fight back memories. "I'm worried," he states, and then moves on to another yarn of flummery on the rocks.

At 7:15 this next morning, John and his family pick at the same hotel breakfast buffet that has been the fare for the last couple of weeks, a syrupless, Alpine-style repast of dry cereal and bread, jam, cheese, lunch meat and canned fruit, and orange juice. Siena gripes while John takes some bread, makes a couple of simple sandwiches for the climb, and stuffs them in his pack. At 7:45, John starts out the hotel door when Siena asks him to stop and stoop. He accommodates, and she stuffs a piece of paper in his pack, secret messages from his girls.

At the Kleine Scheidegg train station, the Jaspers and John Harlin III shoulder their kits, banked with the currency of climbing: carabiners, pitons, ice axes, and crampons, with which they hope to purchase this mountain. They step onto the cogwheel train that takes a half million tourists a year through a tunnel that bores through the bowels of the Eiger to "The Top of Europe," an emporium of restaurants and views. The climbing team, though, gets off at the first stop, a seasonal hostel in a meadow of gentians and purple saxifrage just between the Eiger glacier and the beginnings of the mountain wall. There, John gives Adele a kiss and Siena a tight hug, and he and the Jaspers begin hiking down a scree path toward the radiant point where they will unleash themselves from the surly bonds of the horizontal world.

Less than an hour later they pull on their harnesses and don their helmets (rigged with tiny high-definition video cameras). Robert is brimming with his usual brio and bliss; Daniela giggles nervously, and she looks tired, having barely slept the night before. John makes his awkward grin and shakes my hand, then points to the sky. With the foreshortening that happens at the base of mountains, The White Spider looks to be a few pitches away, when in fact it is a vertical mile straight up. I dodge a few rocks that come tumbling down the slope. The constant skin shedding of this pocked and icy face is perhaps the most dangerous aspect of the Eiger. In the Eastwood film, a main character is hit by a falling rock and dies on the mountain; in an elliptical narrative fit for the movies, a cameraman shooting *The Eiger Sanction* was hit by a falling rock and died. As I turn to head back down to the hotel and to our Brunton telescope, I notice the crushed plastic lining of a climbing helmet in a rockfall ten feet away. I resist the urge to pull away the rock to see if anything is beneath.

The next hours are ones of waiting and watching. Alternately, Adele, Siena, and others in the support crew peer through the telescope and see three tiny ants crawling up a refrigerator door. I take a turn and make out John in his yellow jacket bringing up the rear. It was here at Kleine Scheidegg in 1966 that journalist Peter Gillman was watching through a scope when he followed a red-jacketed falling star down the face . . . the body of John Harlin II. "It was stretched out and was turning over slowly, gently, with awful finality," he wrote of the scene.

As John climbs he tries to tune into the mountain, to adopt a climber's mind-set. He doesn't want to think about family or friends, or things precious, or Eiger lore; he wants to leave the rest of the world behind and concentrate on the task at hand. He wants to shut out emotion and fear. He wants to be a hard man.

But despite his vows, he thinks about his father. When he passes a set of rusty pitons, he wonders if his dad had placed any of them. And he thinks that his eyes must be seeing the same views his dad saw; that the tinkling cowbells from below must be among the same sounds heard. And he feels some sort of connection through the rock.

Under a bright sky, at 2:44 p.m., John and the Jaspers reach the Japanese Bivouac, a tapering, shoulder-width ledge beneath an overhang that is the ultimate room with a view, except for the poor taste in wall decorations, a scrawl of graffiti left by residents prior. Their check-in time, though, is superb, as the sun is just striking the top of the Eiger (this will precipitate the day's foremost cascade of rock and ice falls). Slowly, carefully they prepare their vertical camp, in which they sling themselves to the wall, and slip into sleeping bags. John discovers he forgot to pack eating utensils and so must sup with his knife, a minor piece of metal cruelty compared to when his father forgot to sharpen his crampons for the Eiger forty years ago.

By 4:00 p.m., a giant cloud has wrapped itself around the Eiger North Face and plunged temperatures to below freezing. At 4:30, John radios his family. "Could you ask the sun to move around a little further please? Could you apply some heat to make the clouds dissipate?"

"How are you?" Adele asks.

"It's been a good day so far. But this is the easy part of the mountain. Hard part is tomorrow," he reports. Then Siena takes the walkie-talkie: "Did you get the note I put in your backpack?"

There is a long and uncomfortable silence on the deck of the hotel. Then the radio crackles: "I just found the note! It says, 'Dear Daddy. We're all thinking of you as you go up the mountain. Who knows, we might have something different for breakfast when you get back. Love, love, love, love, love, Siena.' "

Then John reads the words from Adele: "Dearest John: Embrace this experience. Think one step at a time and remember that we all are with you at all times. I love you, Adele."

Adele takes the radio: "Can you carry that extra bit of weight all the way up?"

"I would carry nothing else but this if I had to." He seems to twinkle through the radio.

Forty years ago, Marilyn Harlin, wife of John Harlin II, sent a letter to her husband, who was camped at Death Bivouac, readying for his final, historic push to the summit. It said: "Don't play with the gods up there. We give you all our support through this last stretch. And much much much love."

John Harlin III signs off, as the Jaspers want to call their kids and there is much prep to do before nightfall. Daniela is thinking of leaving the climb at an exit point farther up the wall, as her back is hurting, and she yearns to return to her children. This is the first night away from her children since Stefan was born more than two and a half years ago. But she will decide tomorrow. After tea and hot noodles, they will all try to sleep early, as tomorrow is a very big day, and there is a German team close on their heels. It is not a competition as it was in 1966, but there are eerily reminiscent dynamics. If the German team catches up, it will crowd the mountain, rendering extra danger. So John Harlin III wants to move quickly and stay ahead of an unexpected coefficient on this irresoluble limestone brick, until now a mislaid cornerstone to his life.

Although the Eiger has an aura of the absolute, it seems to bend this next morning as John and the Jaspers cruise upward, making better time than expected. Behind is not just one German team, but now a second, a guide-client combination. For weeks, potential climbers have been waiting for the right conditions, and now the mountain is crowded.

John and the Jaspers make the Hinterstoisser Traverse along a fixed horizontal rope. They hack up The Ice Hose. Then into The Ramp. Up they inch, Robert and John alternating the lead. Early that afternoon, the German guide–client team, which began the ascent by climbing out one of the train windows, passes John and the Jaspers and knocks off ice chunks as it picks its way upstairs. Ping, ping, ping goes the volley. "Leave a little ice for us," John yells upward.

John reaches Death Bivouac, where his father spent his final week, read his final letters from his family, and made his last radio call; and then farther up he sees the overhang, off and above to the right, where the skinny, colored rope that held his father failed. John the son doesn't stop to dwell. Emotional distance he wants. But then he wonders why there are no ghosts on this mountain. Old large houses have ghosts, and so many souls have been taken here. Yet he has never heard of a spirit on the Eiger. Nonetheless, something here delineates the ephemerides of his father's spirit, and it imbues a state of grace as upward John glides.

A bit farther up, they reach the snow-covered Brittle Ledges, narrower than the shelf they enjoyed the night before, but a port in the storm. It won't accommodate three full climbers, so Robert volunteers to be the one who will sleep with his legs dangling over the edge. As they settle in, the second German team passes them, which gives pause as with two teams above, progress will no doubt be slowed.

The next morning, they are up early, but progress is at a crawl. They find themselves stuck below the German teams, waiting for the Germans to reach points where their jetsam won't crash directly down on John's team. The sky has darkened, and a storm may be rolling in. The support team watches through the telescope, and several professional Swiss guides announce that John and the Jaspers are woefully behind schedule; that they won't make the summit today, and may find themselves enveloped in a storm. There is talk of rescue by roping down from the summit or by helicopter.

But slowly they grind on. They edge across The Traverse of the Gods, where John can look straight down four thousand feet to the spot where his father's body hit the ground. Daniela hates this traverse, with its severe exposure. She began as a sport climber and never really took to the dizzying challenge of crossing walls that overhang infinity. Soon, though, they are on The White Spider, and then shimmying up the start of the Exit Cracks. Then one of the Germans above accidentally dislodges a football-sized rock that whizzes down a safe distance past John, flies out into space, then hits the middle of the White Spider and plunges between the two members of yet another German team on the mountain, just missing the tethering rope.

Back at the base, there is much jockeying for a spy through the one telescope at hand, and Adele snatches a moment only to watch as John's crampon slips and he makes a short fall, arrested by his rope. Her heart skips a beat. Behind her Siena scrambles up a sharp hill like a chamois, stopping at its crest, where she stares at the wall. John recovers and continues to climb, while Adele retreats to a section of the hotel without windows facing south.

By midafternoon, the climbing team seems to smell the barn and begins moving faster, and with confidence. John is leading the final pitch, and as they reach the Summit Icefield they bathe in sunshine for the first time on the climb. A wave of relief seems to wash over Adele and all at the base. The shadow of the Eiger seems to have lifted. But it's not over until it's over, of course, and a number of climbers have fallen off the knife-edge west ridge after touching the sky. So Adele, Siena, friends, and filmmakers grab the train to the Jungfraujoch and then start hiking across the snowfield toward the Monch Hut, a little shy of 12,000 feet, which John and the Jaspers hope to reach by nightfall.

There is a climbing occurrence related to post-traumatic stress syndrome, in which after a major, death-defying ascent, a bout of depression sets in, sometimes permanently, sometimes fatally. It is a sort of "what's next?" condition, as after months, perhaps years of dreaming, scheming, and preparing there seems little to fill the space that was so intensely a supreme ambition now achieved. Several Himalayan veterans have returned to low ground and turned to alcohol, drugs, and a stasis state of rueful reminiscences, unable to find a new passion or purpose. At least one Everest summiteer committed suicide. As we make the steps upward in the thin air, I ask Adele if this might be an aftereffect of John's reaching his lifetime goal.

"No!" she asserts. "The opposite. The Eiger has been a large and scary monster in his closet. He'll be liberated when this is done. He'll have a whole new lease, a new beginning."

And as she describes predictions of her husband's future, the radio sputters.

It is 4:03 p.m. It is John Harlin III standing on his dream.

"I'm on the summit, sweetheart."

"How is it?" Adele pipes back.

"Oh, just wonderful."

They talk lovingly in sound bites for a couple of minutes, and Siena has a turn, and then the radios go off, as the batteries need to be preserved in case of emergency. It is still a four-hour traverse down a flank of the mountain over to the Monch Hut in fading light. Daniela, who is near utter exhaustion and misses her children terribly, chooses not to make the trek and calls for a helicopter, which plucks her off the summit and deposits her in a field in Grindelwald, where she has to hitchhike to her car. John and Robert Jasper have that option as well, as the summit success belongs to all. But John and Robert choose to make their way down by foot to the hut, as "the top is only halfway," John likes to say. For Robert Jasper too there is special meaning in this climb. It was twenty years ago this month, at age seventeen, he made his first attempt up the Eiger, one in which he turned back. Now he wants a full rendering for his anniversary, one that includes clambering down to the first outpost of civilization.

As we trudge up the final steps to the Monch Hut, Adele grins. "I guess John's got to hold off on his AARP membership for another year."

John and Robert traverse the blade of the summit, the most spectacular place John has ever seen. Then they work down the East Ridge, making four rappels, crossing a saddle, and fudging around a steep ice field. And then they start across the last glacier. It is getting dark, so when they come to a crevasse they decide to traverse a snow bridge rather than take the time to skirt the blue fissure. Robert crosses first with no problem. But as John is halfway across, the bridge begins to crumble, and John begins to slide into the void. He falls and swims against the tide, finding enough purchase to crawl back to the arch of the disintegrating bridge and scramble across to safety. Most climbing accidents happen on the way down, when fatigue trumps judgment. John sometimes cites the maxim of Ed Viesturs, the only American to have climbed all fourteen of the world's eight-thousand-meter peaks: "Getting to the top is optional; getting back down is mandatory."

Just as the last licks of light are painting the surrounding peaks in alpenglow, John and Robert rise over a ridge and make the last few steps toward the Monch Hut. Adele and Siena run to them and first hug Robert, in the lead, then sprint to John. They embrace and swirl and fall into the snow in a giddy pile of euphoria.

When later John makes his way over to the others who have come to celebrate this moment, I lean to his ear and say, "John, you're a hard man."

He grins back. "Oh, I don't know about that."

Once inside the sanctity of the hut, John unwraps a moist towelette and wipes his face and hands. "I wash my hands of the Eiger," he pronounces with the gesture.

Minutes later, John Harlin III is walking down the snow path toward the Jungfraujoch, his family in hand, as the moon-washed Eiger fades away behind him.

ACKNOWLEDGMENTS

First of all, an entire range of thanks to Evelyne Mock, who showed the way too many times to count and was the superstar and shining light throughout. Her enthusiasm, creativity, and depth of knowledge are unparalleled, and whatever success this project enjoys is due in no small part to Evelyne. And to Alex Hermann, who had the vision and the daring to support this project from its inception; Urs Eberhard, a fellow board member and inspiration; and Fausto Zaina and Maja Gartmann, my Swiss friends and neighbors.

I want to thank my friend John Harlin III, a true student and teacher of the Swiss Alps.

And the Glacier Express; the Gornergrat Bahn; Swiss International Air Lines and the cities of Zermatt, Lucerne, and St. Moritz; the William Tell Express; the Glacier Garden in Lucerne; the Swiss Museum of Transport and the Bourbaki Panorama in Lucerne; the Jungfrau Railways; the Pilatus Railway; the Schilthorn Cableway; and Muottas Muragl.

I want to thank the Hotel Schweizerhof Luzern, the Hotel Regina in Wengen, the Hotel Chesa Surlej in Silvaplana, the Hotel Bellaval in St. Moritz, the Hotel Metropol and the Hotel Bijou in Zermatt, the Hotel Adler in Zurich, the Hotel Allegra at the Zurich Airport, the Restaurant Taube, Jack's Brasserie, the Chesa Chantarella (with the finest fondue in the world), the Alpenblick Restaurant, the Arvenstube in Zermatt, and the Kronenhof Bar at the Grand Hotel Kronenhof Pontresina, which is absinthe no liqueur.

And of course, the ever-resourceful Jacqueline Pash from SWISS.

In Lucerne and surroundings, Marcel Perren, Mark Meier, Sibylle Gerardi, Mrs. Evelyne Bueler, Patrick J. O. Hauser, the remarkable "weather sniffer" Peter Suter, Heinrich Hofstetter, Anita and Pius Schnider, Franz Schnider, Stefan Wiesner, Peter Wick, Colette Richter, Marina Hubeli, and Martina Kälin.

In the Engadine, the inimitable Dr. Hans Peter Danuser, Ruedi Birchler, Fabrizion D'Aloisio, Priska Zahner, Verena Lawrence-Staub of the Segantini Museum, the gifted skier and guide Christine Salis, J. & H. Frey, Barbara Studer of the Grand Hotel Kronenhof Pontresina and Kulm Hotel St. Moritz, Susi Cheshire of Badrutt's Palace, Judith Haid of the Kempinski, and Katia Staub, and in Chur, Peider Härtli for the Rhaetian Railway.

In the Jungfrau, Sammy Salm, Professor Erwin Flückiger, Joan and Martin Fischer, Irene Thali, René Krebs, Marina Tonn, Stefanie Tischhauser, Guido and Ariane Meyer, and Daniela Fuchs.

In Zermatt, the indefatigable Amadé Perrig, Daniel Luggen, Claudia Staber, and Franziska and Gabriel Taugwalder-Krähenmann.

In Zurich, the thoroughly impressive professor, Dr. Angela Esterhammer.

And I want to thank Carey Peterson, who helped with research and transcribing. She is the scaffolding of my books. And my friend from Bosnia, Suzanne Arbanas, who was on-site and helped in ways that can be appreciated only by new parents. Also my friend the great Swiss guide Anna Bezzola.

I want to give special thanks to Mountain Travel Sobek for its continued vision and keenness for all Swiss adventures, and especially Anne Wood, Nadia LeBon, Kevin Callaghan, and Kim Beck.

And there can be no adventure taken without ExOfficio, the brand of exceptional clothing and gear I have been wearing and punishing to no ill effects for more than twenty years now. I want to especially thank Steve Bendzak, Brady Miller, and Chris Keyes, who have been so key to keeping me in "Clothing for the Adventurous Spirit."

And that goes for my luggage of choice, Eagle Creek, and my tireless footwear from Teva, and my hardy mountain outerwear from Mountain Hardwear and Chris Strasser, and the ever-insightful sunglasses from Brad Abbott at Costa Del Mar.

A big-screen-sized thanks needs to go to the incredible film crew that captured this odyssey for public television and beyond. It includes executive producer John Givens; director-writer Patty Conroy; cinematographer extraordinaire Ian Devier; super adventure videographer Didrik Johnck; grip and production coordinator Sara Givens; genius editor–composer–graphics guy and super hyphenate talent David Ris; American Public Television executives Nelsa Gidney and Chris Funkhouser for believing in, distributing, and promoting *Adventures with Purpose* documentaries to the stations; and of course my compass, producer-writer-director, mastermind, moral supporter, and muse, Laura Hubber.

And I want to thank the team at Menasha Ridge Press, including Howard Cohen, Ritchey Halphen, Molly Merkle, and Tricia Parks, and my wise and talented editor, Russell Helms. My gratitude also to this book's copyeditor and fact-checker, Steve Millburg, and to sharp-eyed proofreader Michael Trotman.

Page references followed by *p* indicate photographs.

Photo courtesy of Walker Bangs

Richard Bangs has often been called the father of modern adventure travel. He has spent 30 years as an explorer and communicator, and along the way he has led first descents of thirty-five rivers around the globe, including the Yangtze in China and the Zambezi in southern Africa.

Bangs has published more than one thousand magazine articles, sixteen books, and a score of documentaries. He also founded Sobek Expeditions, which in the early 1990s merged with Mountain Travel to become Mountain Travel Sobek. His recent book *The Lost River: A Memoir of Life, Death and the Transformation of Wild Water,* won the National Outdoor Book Award in the literature category. He is currently producing and hosting the PBS series *Richard Bangs' Adventures with Purpose,* with companion books from Menasha Ridge Press.

For more information, visit **www.richardbangs.com** or **www .adventureswithpurpose.tv.**

Future Switzerland explorer Jasper Bangs   Photo courtesy of Laura Hubber